BATTLE FRONT: USA vs. MILITIA

Ian Slater

FAWCETT GOLD MEDAL • NEW YORK

By Ian Slater:

FIRESPILL
SEA GOLD
AIR GLOW RED
ORWELL: THE ROAD TO AIRSTRIP ONE
STORM
DEEP CHILL
FORBIDDEN ZONE*
WWIII*
WWIII: RAGE OF BATTLE*
WWIII: WORLD IN FLAMES*
WWIII: ARCTIC FRONT*
WWIII: WARSHOT*
WWIII: ASIAN FRONT*
WWIII: FORCE OF ARMS*
WWIII: SOUTH CHINA SEA*
SHOWDOWN: USA vs. MILITIA*
BATTLE FRONT: USA vs. MILITIA*

*Published by Fawcett Books

A Fawcett Gold Medal Book
Published by The Ballantine Publishing Group
Copyright © 1998 by Bunyip Enterprises, Inc.

http://www.randomhouse.com

ISBN 0-56865-885-0

Manufactured in the United States of America

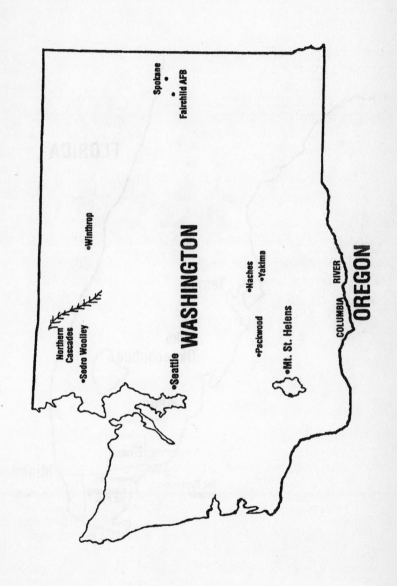

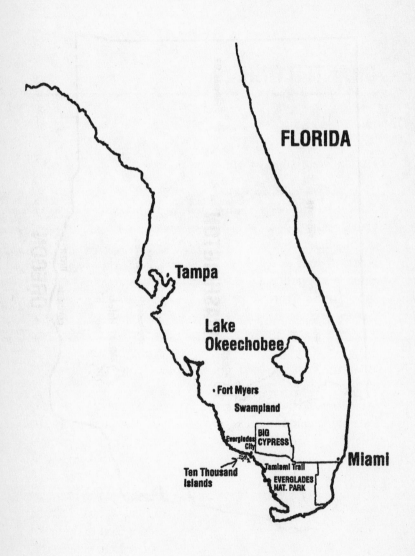

CHAPTER ONE

Florida Everglades

THERE WAS A shot. A hundred yards apart, one chasing the other, two airboats slithered and swerved through the Everglades mangrove islands, the boats' wakes scratching bruised, storm-colored water. The gunshots from the man in the pursuing boat sounded like the sharp cracks of a stock whip. Frightened egrets were startled to the air over the darkening green islands, appearing as flying white clouds above the wide expanse of brown saw grass bending obediently in the wind. In the fleeing boat, Bob Kozan, a young park ranger, was now only fifty yards in front. A long streak of lightning followed by a thunderclap set Kozan's black Labrador retriever, Laddie, to howling. The distance between the two boats narrowed farther as the sky opened up and rain pelted down, churning the swamp water into a steaming caldron in the high humidity. The pursuer slowed the flat-bottomed boat, knowing the fleeing park ranger somewhere ahead would have to slow too if he were to navigate the mangroves through the curtains of rain.

It began because only the rangers and the Miccosukee Indian guides were allowed to use airboats in the national park. Kozan had spotted the unauthorized boat not more than ten minutes before, and, using his loud hailer, had ordered the man to pull over. In response, the man made a sharp U-turn, heading full throttle straight for the ranger, firing a handgun.

There was another thunderclap. In the quiet that followed,

the pursuer, his boat barely moving in the hiss of rain, could faintly hear the sound of Kozan's dog whining.

"Goddammit, Laddie!" Kozan kept his voice as low as possible. "Shut up!"

Suddenly the dog perked up, emitting an impatient whine, his front legs tattooing on the no-slip aluminum strip on the bow in his eagerness to investigate.

"Shut up!" Kozan pleaded. The heavy rain prevented him from seeing more than a foot or two in front of him. He cut his motor, drifting, every sense alert for danger. Why had the man gone ballistic when all he'd been asked to do was stop? Surely there was more to this than bad temper. Either that or his pursuer was just plain crazy.

"Don't go!" Shirley had told him at breakfast. Bob Kozan was a fit man of medium height and build, light brown hair with striking blue eyes. Those eyes, Shirley had once told him, were the first thing she noticed about him. They had been married for six years, and by now he thought he could read her moods. But this morning he had been taken by surprise. She'd never said anything so forcefully. Besides, the Everglades was a new posting and he wanted to make a good impression. For a moment, drinking his coffee, he'd thought she was kidding. Maybe she wanted to make love—a "dawnbreaker" they called it in their more relaxed moments. But when he'd looked up at her—she suddenly seemed much older than twenty-five—he could see she had something else in mind. Clearly, she was frightened.

"What's wrong?" he had asked.

"I had a dream last night that you were dead."

He'd swirled the last of his coffee in his cup, smiling. "Well, I'm not."

"I'm serious, Bobby. I dreamt you were dead in the Everglades. You and another park ranger disappeared, like all those people in that Valujet crash."

"Ah," he'd said dismissively. "You worry too much."

"Is it any wonder, with all this business in the West?"

"Ahhhh," he said again, bending over, pulling on his boot laces, his easy tone underplaying the "business in the West." But he knew that it had been the most violent clash of arms of Americans against Americans since the Civil War. "That's over with now, hon. General Freeman's seen to that." He was referring to the legendary general, Douglas Freeman, formerly commander-in-chief of the federal force. Freeman, now retired, had done battle with the massive uprising of the militias—the Sagebrush Rebellion some were calling it—which, like many militia outbreaks in the West, had started with a clash between locals and the federal government. Much of the land in the western United States was still owned outright and administered by the federal government, a fact little known by Americans in the eastern U.S., where only a tiny percentage of land was government owned. A hunter and survivalist by the name of Ames had killed a wolf up in Washington State's Cascade Mountains. Government agents had moved in to arrest him, the militias came to his aid, and before anyone could stop it, the entire Northwest—already seething with discontent against what they saw as Big Brother government in Washington, D.C.—was literally up in arms.

"Anyhow," Bob Kozan assured Shirley, "it's over with now. National Guard units are mopping up. Besides, that's the Wild West, hon. We're in Florida."

"It's a nationwide problem," she retorted. "There are militias everywhere. If there weren't, do you think the President would be planning to go to Spokane—try to steal the thunder from the militia convention? That Louis Rukeyser on *Wall Street Week* says that if the President can't show he's the boss, foreign investors'll get the jitters, the dollar'll tumble, and then there'll be massive layoffs and—"

"Don't worry so much," Bob cut in, pulling her toward him, holding her tightly, kissing her on the cheek. "You had a bad night, that's all. It was just a dream."

"I hear there are even militias down here in the Everglades," she said, "getting ready for—"

"It's all talk," Bob had told her, releasing her and slapping his thigh. "Laddie, come." The black Labrador bounded in from the yard, scratching frantically on the screen door, eager to hit the road. Bob smiled back at her. "See you tonight."

"Where'll you be?" she called after him as the screen door banged shut.

"The islands." He meant the Ten Thousand Islands. He might as well have said he was going to Siberia, the area was so vast. There were channels, mangroves, and, inland to the east, saw grass as far as the eye could see. You could lose a city in there. He remembered how the Valujet had disappeared. The Everglades had sucked it down in seconds.

The storm continued, unabated.

"Where's Kozan?" the ranger superintendent asked. His secretary didn't show any sign of recognition. "You know," he explained, "the new man."

"Oh yes," she said. "Let's see . . ." She peered down through her reading glasses at the sign-out clipboard on the wall. "He's somewhere in Ten Thousand Islands."

"Huh!" the superintendent grunted. "*Somewhere* is right. He call in on the crackler yet?"

She shrugged. "Might have, but with this storm, the cracklers are really *cracklin'*, if you get what I mean." She smiled at her little play on words.

"Geez, Elma," the super said, walking over to the coffeepot, mumbling. "You'll wind up on Letterman. If Kozan does get through, you tell 'im not to panic in this storm. Just tie up on an old bayhead tree and wait 'er out."

"Yes, sir."

"He take that stupid dog with 'im?"

"Laddie," she said. "I don't know for sure."

"Well, if he gets lost, we'll just have to listen for the dog. Never heard such a noisy mutt."

"He's no mutt. Purebred Labrador retriever."

The super picked up the sugar container and let it pour.

" 'Sat a fact?"

"Uh-huh."

* * *

Kozan's pursuer reloaded slowly and spun the chamber. He was in no hurry. He could wait out the storm the same as the ranger. One thing was for sure: if any goddamn government officials came snoopin' around, they were going to find the ranger floating facedown in the Gulf with all the other swamp debris. Son of a bitch had gotten too close.

At last the rain ceased. The militiaman stared through the rising fog. He could hear the dog whining and the sound of a chain just ahead.

"Drop the gun!"

The voice came from behind him, and he swung around, gun in hand. Kozan fired and the militiaman was flung out of the boat. As he hit the water, Kozan's dog strained to free itself from the chain that anchored it to a small mangrove island. With lots of gators around, Kozan knew he'd put Laddie at terrible risk, tied up like that, but it was the only way of suckering his pursuer forward in the fog. Even so, Kozan was almost too late. As he grappled and began hauling the dead man aboard, two gators slid off mangrove roots nearby, Kozan barely able to unchain Laddie in time and get him aboard.

Kozan radioed in on the "crackler," informing the superintendent what had happened. Sometime later, as he came in to tie up the boat, the dead man lying stretched out at an angle to the bow, he was surprised to see that a crowd had gathered around the dock. The onlookers included half a dozen reporters and angry members of the South Florida militia who'd been plugged into the ranger frequency, several of them already promising that there'd be serious repercussions for the "murder" of one of their members.

Even before Kozan stepped ashore, microphones were being thrust in his face, the reporters shouting questions. "Did you fire first?" one of them asked.

"No, he did."

"Did you draw your gun first?" another asked.

"No, I did not."

"Then why d'you think he fired at you?"

"I don't know. All I did was hail him to stop."

"That's all?" a skeptical ABC correspondent asked.

Kozan nodded.

The correspondent clearly didn't believe him, and shared his skepticism with a colleague. "Has to be more to this. Must've seen something or someone he wasn't supposed to."

The next day, after his report to the homicide detectives, Bob Kozan knew he had to go back out into the Everglades. It was like being in a serious auto accident. If you didn't get back behind the wheel immediately, you might never drive again. Refusing to take the rest of the week off, he and Laddie were back at the dock, Bob arguing with the super, who wanted him to go with a partner. Kozan told his boss that traveling on the airboat with his dog was the equivalent of having a human partner. In fact, in many ways Laddie's acute sense of smell and hearing made him a better partner than any human. Out West, Kozan pointed out, General Freeman's elite Special Forces had used dogs to track down Latrell and Hearn, the Nazi, two of the most wanted militiamen in America. Latrell, it was reported in the media, had murdered a black man in Oregon. Hearn had killed a highway patrolman, cutting him in half with a shotgun at point-blank range, and was also a suspect in the murder of several black men. Latrell had managed to elude capture, but the National Guard had taken Hearn from Wentworth to Camp Fairchild, a compound for captured militiamen near Fairchild Air Base outside Spokane.

It was his dog, Kozan pointed out, who had provided the diversion in the fog that he'd needed to trap his pursuer in the mangrove swamp.

"Pursuer, manure!" the super said. "Go with a partner. They started doing that out West in the national parks in 'ninety-five because of these damned militias."

"That's the Wild West," Kozan protested, as he'd told his wife just the day before. "Got a gun nut every five yards. This is Florida."

"Yeah, where they shoot tourists at Miami Airport. Take a partner."

A gator call came in on the crackler then, from a frightened senior, the reptile a reported eighteen-footer. "In my backyard. Better come quickly!"

The super, one hand over the phone, rolled his eyes heavenward at Kozan. "Never seen an eighteen-footer in my life," he said, but he had to send out the ranger whom he'd initially assigned as Kozan's partner. "Looks like you win," he told Kozan. "Though I don't know why in hell you're so keen to go on your lonesome."

Kozan grinned boyishly. "Chief, wasn't one of the reasons you joined the Park Service that you wanted to get away from people?"

"Since when is a partner a crowd?"

"I like to work alone."

"Oh," the super said. "One of those, or are you just trying to impress me with your self-reliance?"

Kozan smiled. "Trying to impress you."

The super sighed heavily. "Off you go, then, but keep in radio contact."

"You got it," Kozan said.

Yes, he admitted to himself as he left the office, he *was* trying to impress the super. Dammit, he was trying to impress everyone with his independence, particularly the locals. Take a few days off to settle his nerves? Not him. He sure as hell didn't want it to get around that he was afraid of going out again, alone. With that kind of reputation, every illegal fisherman and smuggler in the glades would call your bluff. Besides, he loved being alone with only Laddie for company. It was a simple yet profound thing to be alone—not lonely, but alone—and yet it was such a difficult thing to convince other people of. Deep down, Kozan knew people were terrified of being by themselves, particularly in the wild, especially those who, like the overwhelming number of Americans, lived in cities and suburbs. Shirley was an exception. She understood, even if she did worry too much at times.

* * *

The Everglades' watery vastness was like a tonic to him. He never tired of watching the changing hues of blues and greens and the crimson-streaked twilights passing over and through the Ten Thousand Islands.

"What d'you think, Laddie?" he asked as he started up the airboat's fan.

Laddie's moist, black nose was avidly sniffing the fetid odor of the swamp up ahead, the dog eagerly stretching so far over the bow near the grass roll bar that it amazed Kozan he didn't fall in. Kozan eased the boat away from the jetty. The bow lifted slightly as he increased speed, and Laddie moved back toward the front seat well of the boat as the craft slid quickly past tangled growths of Australian pine and the grotesque remains of long-dead trees, the watery world going on forever. Bob glanced at his watch. Ten-thirty. He'd turn back from patrol at about three, and he'd get laid tonight for sure—Shirley so glad to have him back. And another thing, though he sure as hell wasn't going to tell anyone—he'd been shit-scared there for a moment yesterday, unable to see anything in the teeming rain. But after he'd shot the guy, the adrenaline rushing through his veins, he'd been on a high, so horny he figured he'd stay hard all afternoon.

What he hadn't known, couldn't know, was that he would soon become one of the most pivotal men in American history.

The White House

The President of the United States sat in one of the Oval Office's white lounge chairs, ringed by his advisers, who were planning his controversial visit to Spokane while watching last night's tape of *Larry King Live*.

King faced a panel of experts on the militias. "Look, you guys, help me out here. There's the Aryan Nations group, patriots, survivalists, Posse Comitatus—that how you pronounce that? Com-it-*ta*-tus? That's a right to bear arms movement, right? Right. Okay, so what do we have here? I mean can someone give me a figure, and I don't mean out of thin air. I mean based on some kind of research—anything from FBI or FEMA?" He meant the Federal Emergency Management Agency.

"Well, Larry," one of the panel responded. "Hard-core fully armed militiamen, we're talking a hundred eighty to two hundred thousand—"

"Nationwide?"

"Yes, nationwide."

"How many states?"

"Forty, and growing."

"Yes," one of the other pundits added. "And I think we have to remember how Professor McCauley of Bryn Mawr College put it to *Time* magazine." He glanced down at a clipping. " 'If you think these people are crazy, then you have to ask if there is anything the federal government could do that would make you willing to take up arms against it. If you can answer no, then you're entitled to think these people are crazy. But if you say yes, then you'd better hazard a thought that they are human beings just like you.' "

"So you're saying," King responded, "that while there are only a hundred and eighty to two hundred thousand armed militia . . ." He paused. "That sounds a lot to me."

"To me also," one of the experts said. "That's ten divisions in military terms—two armies."

"Yeah, and if I'm hearing you guys right, you're saying that there's more support for the militias than we think."

"Oh yes, there's a lot of racial stuff out there, and if you factor in all those people who are strongly antigovernment so far as taxes, environmental laws, and antiabortion are concerned, and the pro-gun, pro-school-prayer lobby, Second Amendment people, you're looking at five percent of the population."

One of the President's aides was dismissive. "Five percent? That all?"

The chief executive did a little math. "*That's all?* D'you realize how many people that is in this country? Over twelve million. National Rifle Association is three and a half million

alone. That's more than our entire armed forces, for Christ's
sake!"

Another aide, though he thought better of it, was about to in-
form the President that for several militias, the chief executive's very use of the Lord's name in vain a second ago would
automatically condemn him in their eyes as unfit to lead the nation, and justify his removal from office—*forcibly,* if necessary.

CHAPTER TWO

Washington State, Operation Clean Sweep, Morning

"DON YOUR FLAK jackets!" the young lieutenant yelled.

"Don *who?*" a trooper asked.

"Don Rickles," another joked, throwing his flak jacket onto
the floor of the helicopter. The vehicle was vibrating like it had
the DTs, its engine roaring, rotors a blur, blowing swirling snow
about the squad of National Guardsmen about to embark on mission Clean Sweep.

"Don flak jackets!" the lieutenant repeated, but the other
eight troopers, all older than he, ignored the lieutenant, also
dumping their Kevlar jackets on the floor, sitting on them, one
trooper joking with another.

"What did you say?" the lieutenant called out to him.

"I said fuck off!"

"I could put you on a charge!"

"Yeah, yeah," an older trooper said, shouting above the noise.
"Listen, sonny, this is the National Guard, not the fucking Marines. And you weren't born when I was humping in 'Nam. We're
sittin' on our flak jackets 'cause we don't want our balls shot off

if any o' those militiamen gives this bird an AK-47 burst in the belly. So chill out!"

"You're talking to an officer!"

"Yeah, an' if you know what's good for you, Lieutenant, you'll sit on your flak jacket too. C'mon, the sooner we mop up these militia stragglers and take 'em back to Fairchild, the sooner we all get home."

They were National Guardsmen—weekend soldiers, not regular army—but some had been in 'Nam, and they weren't going to put up with young lieutenants who didn't know dick.

A month before, a Washington State militia group on maneuvers, part of the USMC—United States Militia Corps—had gone ape in the Sawtooth Wilderness in the Cascade Mountains and mixed it up with a federal hundred-man Special Forces contingent from the Army, serving under General Freeman. The militia had lost, but with local knowledge of the rugged terrain on their side, had inflicted over fifty percent casualties, dead and wounded, on Freeman's elite federal force. What followed was a massive uprising of militias in the Northwest. Only after thousands of federal troops had been sent in were the militias defeated—at least for the present. Most militias had surrendered after Freeman's forces had trapped and killed General Mant, their leader.

Now, Army helos, with the help of the National Guard's Clean Sweep squads, were rounding up units of still rebellious militia stragglers, to imprison them with the remaining militia rebels from Butcher's Ridge—the site of the furious battle in the Sawtooth Wilderness. All prisoners were being taken to Camp Fairchild in the arid semidesert of eastern Washington.

It was a small enough thing: how the thousands of militiamen marching in Spokane for the funeral of Wilfred Ames were not only keeping in step but were in perfectly straight lines. Watching it on CNN, retired General Douglas Freeman was struck by the precision. These men had come to pay their respects to the militiaman Ames, whose illegal wolf kill had sparked the flashpoint between federals and militia in the Northwest and who had been killed by federals in a close-quarter battle for the Astoria Bridge over the Columbia River between Oregon and Washington. But these weren't anything like the ragtag coalition of dissatisfied citizens Freeman had seen in earlier years in drag-ass formation shuffling sullenly in military fatigues in front of the cameras. They were a highly disciplined body of men, and, he noticed, some women. Apart from West Point, Britain's Sandhurst, and a few military schools like the Citadel, Freeman hadn't seen drill discipline like it. It had come as a complete surprise to the fifty-nine-year-old general as he was channel surfing, a habit that had become more pronounced in his widower's retirement in a life besetting him with boredom, though he still kept himself fit with five to ten miles of fast walking each day.

Not so many years had passed since he'd alienated important people in the Clinton administration by referring to his commander-in-chief as "Draft Dodger Bill." After that, he'd been "eased" into retirement. At first he believed he could begin a second career. There were dozens, no, hundreds, of books he wanted to read on war history alone, on subjects ranging from the fifth century (B.C.) Greek navy to the advanced laser systems of today. The problem was finding people with whom he could discuss what he'd read. Most of his friends were dead, a good many the victims of war, the others having succumbed to the ravages of old age. And those still active in the service were too busy with day-to-day management of the armed services to spend time with him. He still had a few informal "spies" sprinkled throughout the Pentagon, however, who kept him informed of the political squabbles and impending crises within the services.

"By God, look at these militiamen," he said to his sister-in-law as she was dusting in the bedroom. If Freeman's deceased wife, Catherine, hadn't made him promise to visit his sister-in-law Marjorie for a few days now and then, he would never have bothered coming to see her.

"Doesn't mean they're good soldiers, does it?" she opined.

That's right, Freeman thought. Pick an argument, no matter what he said. He could tell her the weather was fine in Florida and she'd tell him of a disturbance moving into the Rockies.

"That's what some of my colleagues used to say—good drill troops don't necessarily make good fighting troops. On the contrary, Marjorie. In my experience, men who drill well together fight well together. They fight as a team. No room for prima donnas!"

"That's rich coming from you." Now she had the damned vacuum cleaner on, its motor sending static lines across the TV and threatening to drown him out.

"What d'you mean?" he called out.

"You love to be in the limelight, Douglas. Anonymity would kill you."

"Generals are supposed to stand out, to lead. That's our job. We're like coaches. Someone has to be in command. A little flamboyance is good for the troops' morale."

She didn't answer. Goddamn it, he knew she'd heard him but wouldn't reply—drove him right up the wall. All right, so he was a prima donna. Troops had called him "George C. Scott," after the actor's portrayal of General George Patton in the 1970 movie. Freeman had the same flair, the same kind of hard-driving obsession with battle, the same thirst for glory. The fact that he bore a passing resemblance to the actor only entrenched the nickname.

Finally, Marjorie finished with her bedroom and began to attack the living room. On the TV, CNN's stunning redhead, Marte Price, known as "Dolly" for her bustline, was interviewing a militiaman in Spokane. He was one of those who had escaped incarceration—but not probation—by having surrendered to the federals. He remained vehemently antigovernment. There were blow-up photos of the Nazi, Hearn, the recently slain militia general, Mant, and Wilfred Ames, the survivalist whose death, along with that of his young wife and his two eleven-year-olds, Rebecca and Luke, had fired up the Sagebrush Rebellion. "What do you believe happened?" Marte Price asked the obstreperous militiaman.

"Murder, plain an' simple," said the militiaman, a "former" member of the militia's Washington State Third Rifle Regiment, which called itself the "Wolverines." "Bill Ames was shot down in cold blood, same as his wife, Laura, and the two young'uns. Same as what happened to Randy Weaver. Same as Waco. And if the federal government thinks it's going to get away with it, it's dead wrong. Federals might think they've beaten us down. We might have been scattered for a while, but come the annual Spokane convention after this funeral, and we'll be back twice as strong." The militiaman, marks on his Army-issue tunic from the recently removed bars of a lieutenant, looked straight into the camera. "We're givin' the federals fair warning. *Back off!*"

Marjorie made a tut-tutting noise. "All those guns!"

Normally Freeman might have agreed with her that citizens shouldn't be forming paramilitary organizations like the "Wolverines," but despite his renowned fair-mindedness, he simply could not bring himself to agree with anything Marjorie said. "They wouldn't have to have all those guns, Marjorie, if the federal government paid more attention to the Constitution and gave more people some elbow room."

"Room for what—to kill one another?"

"To defend themselves. Police have got their hands full on the streets. Remember the L.A. riots? Those Korean shopkeepers with the handguns—they had to rely on their own resources. Not enough cops to go 'round."

"Then you're for the militias. Like that dreadful Hearn man. You think they have the right to shoot policemen?"

"Goddamn it, Marjorie! I've just *defeated* them—before I was put out to pasture. And *no*, no one has the right to shoot policemen, but sometimes—usually when the feds get involved—they go in with overwhelming firepower, frighten the life out of everybody. Nervous people make for nervous trigger fingers. Then before you know it you have a debacle on your hands like at Waco and Ruby Ridge, and pretty soon you have to call in the Army."

"So," Marjorie said, bullying the vacuum cleaner into a tight corner between the TV and bookshelf. "What would you have done at Waco? Given them gifts, maybe?"

"If I'd been at Waco," he said, trying to contain his temper, "I would have surrounded the place and then told Koresh that we were going to move in with tear gas and infantry—maybe with tanks—but I would have shown them the M-1s first and given them all the time they needed to make up their minds. Tell 'em to send out the womenfolk and children if they wanted to do that, and, as much as I distrust the media, I would have had them broadcast my conditions over TV, radio, whatever, so the public would know we were giving them ample time to surrender before we moved in."

"And what if they didn't want to come out?"

"I would have had fire trucks, ambulances, standing by, and I would have ordered in crack troops under cover of tear gas. I would not have used the tanks if there had still been children in there."

"I don't know," Marjorie said. "There are just too many guns."

His pride wouldn't permit him to admit he agreed with her.

CNN's Marte Price cut in with an update of a national park ranger by the name of Robert Kozan in the Everglades who had apparently shot a Florida militiaman dead.

"Goddamn it!" Freeman said. "What are those bastards doing down there?" He paused. "They must be hiding some—"

"I wish you wouldn't use that language," Marjorie cut in.

Straitlaced old biddy, he thought. 'Least it got her off the militia business. In fact, Freeman was on the verge of one of his infrequent black depressions. Trouble brewing and him not in it? If push came to shove between the militias and the government during the annual Spokane militia convention, somebody else would be handling it.

He knew that his habit of speaking his mind was not liked by either Marjorie or the top brass. The Joint Chiefs considered him a loose cannon whose standing order, like that of Patton, to his troops had been Frederick the Great's entreaty: "Audacity, audacity, always audacity!" In war he had his uses. In peace he was a liability, often referred to at the Pentagon, in mock Indian parlance, not as George C. Scott, but as "Mouth Like a River."

CNN had returned from the Florida update to Spokane—with photos of the Nazi Hearn in Camp Fairchild. "What I want to know," Freeman said, "is who's taken over now that their General Mant is dead?" But no one was listening, as Marjorie's vacuum filled the hallway with its disrespectful roar.

CHAPTER THREE

The Everglades

KOZAN'S BOAT WAS skimming along the blue-mirrored surface of the swampland, Laddie's eager nose sticking out like some ancient bowsprit. Kozan was grateful for the breeze created by the airboat as he entered a twenty-foot-wide channel choked with saw grass between growths of melaleuca seedlings.

Laddie began barking and a flock of wood storks took to the air, the black edges of their white wings a blur against a pale, washed-out sky. Kozan spotted a snake slithering over gaseous mud and marsh and saw the flat blue of another, narrower channel racing toward him off to his left. He made a sharp turn.

The three-round burst from the M-16 slammed Kozan back against the fan. Devoid of rudder control, the airboat lurched hard aport, throwing him off. Laddie too was in the water when the second burst came. Where Kozan's chest had been there was now only a fiercely bubbling cavity of blood, Kozan dead after the first burst. One of the shooters, wearing a back-to-front cap and militia fatigues, tossed in a stick of dynamite for good measure. After the explosion they could see a rain of dead fish coming down and hear the splashes of gators hitting the water, hurrying from the fetid mud banks into the bloodied water.

* * *

When Kozan didn't call in, the superintendent gave him another half hour, during which time the super organized a posse and launched a waterborne search party. A Coast Guard helicopter buzzed low over the channels like a huge dragonfly, its shadow flitting quickly along the surface of the water and bent by hammocks. But despite the help of the air search, it was a frustrating venture amid the thousands of small islands, the mangroves shading the near-bank areas, effectively hiding them from the helo pilot and his observer.

The waterborne search party, consisting of six ranger airboats and a small flotilla of a dozen civilian boats, looked impressive from the air. The reality was that once one of the airboats, *Lady Bee,* took the main channel and the rest had spread out over the thousands of acres of swampland, the search party was pitifully inadequate. They found nothing but swarms of insects.

Mosquitoes engulfed the searchers, staying with them like dark halos as the airboats turned about in the twilight, heading home, suspicions of a militia payback growing with the enveloping darkness.

"Militia probably figure they got even now," a searcher named Lou Rheinhardt told the tired and worried superintendent.

"You know anything about them?" the super asked grumpily.

Rheinhardt, tying up his boat, shook his head. "Not much 'cept they're well-armed."

"Hell, I know that, Lou. Everybody—"

"I mean machine guns," Rheinhardt cut in. "M-60s. Grenades. Regular, concussion, and Willy Petes."

"What in hell's that?"

"Willy Petes?" Rheinhardt said. "White phosphorous."

"What in hell they want that for?"

"For when they're attacked!"

"Who by, for Christ's sake? The *Park* Service?"

Rheinhardt, walking forward of his *Lady Bee,* tied a bowline knot and shrugged. "The federals, I guess. FBI, BATF—usual crowd. The Waco boys."

"Hell," the super said, swatting a mosquito, "Waco's gettin' a bit long in the tooth, isn't it? Back in 'ninety-three, for cryin' out loud."

"Maybe, but eighty-two people were killed, 'cludin' women and children. 'Sides, the group—Branch Davidians—weren't doing no harm. Free country—"

The super grabbed Rheinhardt's empty five-gallon gas drum. "Ah, maybe you're right. I don't pay much attention to all that crap on TV. Never get the full story. I've been mentioned coupla times in the local rag—hell, you're lucky if they spell your name right."

"There you go," Rheinhardt said. "Waco could've been a big cover-up."

"Maybe," the super said, more from fatigue than conviction. "I'll come out again tomorrow."

"Appreciate that. Let's hope we find something."

"He might be okay. Radio on the blink, motor trouble, anything."

"Hope you're right, Lou. See you sunup."

"You got it."

"Any luck?" his wife asked.

"No," the super shot back irritably.

"Pardon me for living."

He strode into the bathroom. "Susan, where's that goddamn calamine lotion?"

"Top shelf, I think."

"You *think*! I saw it here the other day, goddamn it! I saw it here. Can't you keep anything straight in this house?"

"Have you taken your blood pressure pills?" she asked.

"I'm not talking about goddamn pills. I'm talking about the goddamn calamine."

"Here, I'll get it. Don't take everything out on me. I didn't shoot Mr. Kozan."

"Who said he's been shot?"

"After that business between him and that poor poacher."

"It wasn't a *poor poacher*. Son of a bitch was a *militiaman*. He shot at my ranger and got what he deserved."

"Here's the calamine—right in front of your eyes."

The super grunted.

After the superintendent had left the *Lady Bee*, Lou Rhein-hardt used his calling card inside the phone booth by the wharf. As he waited, he noticed how vandals had nearly destroyed the booth: perspex was cracked, directory gone, graffiti, the stench of urine. Whoever vandalized it needed a good horse whipping, he thought, like they did to that yahoo American kid in Singapore. And Clinton asked the prime minister not to cane the yahoo, for cryin' out loud.

"Mason," came the voice on the end of the line.

"Hey, Rory—Lou here. We never found young Kozan."

"Aw," Rory Mason said in mock sympathy. "What a pity. Nothing at all?"

"Zilch. Nada."

"Aw, tough shit."

"Super was worried about not findin' anything—you know, a body or somethin'."

"He won't neither."

"You promise?"

"Scout's honor."

"How 'bout the boat?"

"Same thing—bottom of the swamp. Why?"

"Just making sure. I took *Lady Bee* up the main channel from here. Kept the others spreading out. Made it look like we was really looking."

"You want a medal?"

Rheinhardt hung up, dissatisfied. Just what they needed. Work your butt off trying to keep the Florida militia's secret under wraps, and what happens? One of the boys whacks a ranger. Beautiful. Still, in all fairness, maybe the ranger had gotten too close.

CHAPTER FOUR

Washington State

FBI AGENT LINDA Seth and ATF agent Bill Trey flew aboard the government's unmarked Learjet from Seattle over Washington State's Columbia River basin. Halfway between the thirteen-thousand-foot-high Cascade range to the west and Montana's Rockies to the east, they were struck by the dramatic geological change east of the high, craggy Cascades.

Below them lay the huge brown bowl of ancient volcanic ash, and the verdant green farmlands and orchards of the valley. The orchards depended on a vast network of irrigation canals that in turn depended on the snowfields of the Cascades. The snowmelt formed the Yakima River, which flowed through the valley south of the Rattlesnake Hills until it reached the Columbia on the mighty river's journey. It continued westward through Portland, Oregon, down to the Pacific Ocean at Astoria, where the ferocious battle between the federals and militia had been fought over the four-mile-long bridge linking Oregon to Washington State.

While Trey would soon be Spokane-bound to report on the situation there, Linda, posing as a Realtor, would be canvassing the valley out of Yakima for any information concerning the disappearance of two fellow FBI agents who'd been missing since the fighting between the federals and militia. Linda Seth had another unofficial interest in infiltrating the militia. They had killed her younger brother Bryan, a Navy SEAL cut down in the battle for Astoria's bridge.

"As a young Realtor," Bill Trey told her, "you'll be expected to be nosing about for new properties to list, so hopefully no one'll be too suspicious of you moving all around the valley counties."

"I like your confidence, Bill. Hopefully no one'll be *too* suspicious."

Trey shrugged. "What else can I tell you? Rural folk always cast a suspicious eye at newcomers or strangers passing through. It's one of the reasons the militias are so difficult to penetrate. Realtor's about the best cover the Bureau can give you, Lin. And Raemar Realty has been around for years."

"How did Washington get Raemar to accept me as a rookie Realtor?" she asked.

"Apparently, Internal Revenue did an audit of Raemar and found what they call 'certain discrepancies.' "

"So we've blackmailed Raemar Realty to accept me?"

"Not to put too fine a point on it—yes. But I wouldn't worry," Bill Trey assured her. "Raemar, in the person of Randy McAllister, has a lot to lose if it doesn't cooperate."

Linda had a last look at the Raemar Realty file. "McAllister is the only one who knows my real identity?"

"Far as we know," Trey replied. " 'Course he's married, so you have to assume his wife knows."

"Why?"

"Never been married, huh? It's a good idea when you're dealing with married couples to assume one partner tells the other everything."

"Is that how it was with you?" She paused. "Oh, I'm sorry, I—I didn't mean to imply that—"

"It's okay," he said, forcing a smile. "You're right. My wife didn't tell me about the other guy." There was an awkward silence before he added, "I'm just saying Mrs. McAllister may know. He'd *have* to tell her. Otherwise she might suspect him of hiring you just because you're pretty."

Linda blushed. "I have to confess, Bill, I'd feel a heck of a lot better if we were working together on this."

"Well, so would I, but with this tension between the militias and us federals—manpower's stretched to the limit." He paused. "But I know how you feel. I like backup as much as the next agent." He hesitated. "You think our two agents were murdered, right?"

She nodded, reluctantly. She didn't want to admit she was scared.

"First thing that shows up, Linda, you call me in Spokane. I can always come down, give you a hand, put it down in my report as a factor affecting my mission of evaluating the advisability of the President's visiting Spokane."

"I appreciate it, Bill. Thanks."

"Don't mention it."

The pilot told them to buckle up as they began their descent. There was heavy turbulence east of the Cascades.

Yakima

Linda Seth kept her Class A smile for her meeting with McAllister of Raemar Realty. It quickly deserted her. He was a small man, a flashy dresser—in seersucker and gold. His manner went with his suit: lightweight, and about as sincere as a rattler. When he'd been notified that an agent, Seth, would be contacting him, he had automatically thought it would be a man. The appearance of Linda was a pleasant shock. If he had to get out of his IRS difficulties by cooperating with a good-looking brunette, so be it. To underscore his goodwill, McAllister informed Linda, with an all-knowing grin, as they pulled up outside her hotel, that he was willing to give her "a hundred and ten percent," that he was prepared to go "all the way."

"I want to rent a car," she said.

"Now?"

"Right away."

"Hell, you just arrived, Lin. Need to—"

"Linda'll do, thank you." She paused, looking around. "I want you to know that if there's a leak, the slightest hint of one, we'll not only close you down, but we'll hand everything over to the IRS."

McAllister's grin vanished. "Who the hell you think you're talking to? Some poor wetback begging for a green card? Or you figure we're all hayseeds up here?"

"I'm just telling you," she replied.

"I know what you're telling me—that you're a hotshot from Washington, D.C., and I'm just a hick. Listen, Miz Seth, I did two tours in 'Nam. I don't have to take this shit. This country up here feeds you bureaucrats while you decide how we should live."

"You've made your point."

"Good." He gave her the details of various farm locations. "They'll probably pick up on your accent."

"Good," she replied. Was he trying to frighten her?

"I told people around here you were coming, but I didn't know you'd be a woman. All I knew was your cover'd be a Realtor from Washington—movin' out here after a divorce."

The area of the militia she was to investigate lay over fifteen miles northwest of Yakima in an area east of sage-covered camelback hills. Here, fields and orchards grew the crops that made it prosperous, much of its produce—including much old-stand lumber from the West Coast—being shipped to Japan, where a Red Delicious apple from the Yakima Valley fetched ten dollars.

Linda rented a gray '97 Ford Taurus, the most inconspicuous color, and headed out of Yakima, winding down the front windows so the sweet, new-mown grass smell soon filled the car. It was her first assignment in the Northwest, and just because she was at work she saw no reason not to enjoy it. The only thing that bothered her at the moment was that the car's lights went on automatically with the ignition. Driving with lights on day or night might be good safety sense in the normal world, but in her world, announcing your presence too soon could be fatal.

Rainbows were everywhere, arcing above the huge, rotating, sparkling sprinklers, arms held steady by guy wires as they swept over green crops made lustrous by the noonday sun. Her plan, prearranged through McAllister by Washington, D.C., was to drive up and down the valley, talking to farmers about selling their properties. Since the Second World War, agricultural machinery had developed far beyond expectations, and while it made for greater efficiency, it meant fewer hands were needed on the land. This not only affected the number of migrant workers from Mexico but also meant that smaller farmers were retiring, selling out lock, stock, and barrel and moving for retirement to the coast.

Linda didn't know what kind of a Realtor she'd make for McAllister, but it would give her the chance to try to infiltrate the militia. She figured she knew most of the redneck arguments, and so should have little difficulty in penetrating any reticence to open up to a stranger. The agency had asked McAllister to go undercover, but he said he'd rather go to prison than do that. The IRS could ruin him, he said, but he wouldn't do *that*. The community in the valley had treated him well. When a lot of folks were ignoring or spitting on Vietnam vets, the people of Yakima had welcomed him in. Even those who didn't agree with the war had treated him with respect.

Maybe she'd come on too strong, she thought, being used to fighting her way through male bastions like the FBI and ATF. She pictured Trey. He would be in Spokane, checking out the President's prospective route and trying to track down illegal arms sales. He would be in contact with her, the ATF insisting that after Waco there had to be closer liaison between agencies.

The siren startled her, and it shouldn't have. She should have seen the unmarked emerald-green police car, its nose hidden by an escarpment. She immediately pulled over to the side, automatically checking her hair. She watched the tall trooper advancing down the driver's side, his right hand on his holster. He was a handsome man.

"Afternoon, ma'am. You realize you were doing over seventy miles per hour?"

"Yes. I'm sorry, my mind wandered."

"Highway's not a good place for that."

"I agree." Be nice, she told herself.

"Could I see your driver's license please?"

"Certainly. " She didn't show him anything with FBI ID.

"This Washington, D.C., address—still current?"

"Yes. This is a rental car."

He went back to the unmarked police car and she saw him with his head down, no doubt running the license plate number through the computer. She waited, embarrassed. As he walked back, she could hear his footsteps crunching on the gravel. He handed her license back.

"You been in the state long?"

"No. Just arrived."

"Holiday?"

"Business."

"Uh-huh." He paused, getting another good look at her and inside the car. "Enjoy Washington State, but slow down a little."

"Thank you, I will."

As he returned to his car, Linda became conscious of the enormous silence of the countryside, punctured only by the stutter of the huge sprinklers amid the rainbows, her senses made more alert by the absence of any other noise. She had an overwhelming sense of déjà vu. Had her vanished predecessor, Tracy Albright, been here? It gave her the shivers. Linda was a twenty-four-year-old woman who'd lived on a steady diet of facts these past two years—ever since she'd entered the FBI as a college graduate with a major in political science. The FBI had taught her that she could rely only on facts. She told herself to focus on them now.

The first farmer on her list was a Stanley Merk, whose orchard was farther up on the banks of the Naches River. As Linda drove north she fantasized about making love with the speed cop and felt herself becoming moist. She rounded a curve, saw an enormous hill of hay dead ahead being pulled by a tractor. She was tempted to pull out and swing around the tractor, but the road dipped and she didn't have a clear view over the hill that rose to meet her. In the side mirror she could see another vehicle way back, a blob of shimmering green. Everything was so different from Washington, D.C., so vast, so isolated, that she welcomed the other car.

When she saw it was clear up ahead, she pulled out, and as she passed, a farmer and a little girl under a faded canopy waved. Linda gave a *bip* on the horn. They waved again, and for a moment Linda knew that the world—her world—was safe.

The gate to Stanley Merk's bright green apple orchard was plastered with KEEP OUT and TRESPASSERS WILL BE PROSE-CUTED signs. "Ah," Linda told the car, "welcome to the North-west." She got out and went to open the gate but couldn't figure it out. Devoid of normal hinges, it defied logic.

"Drive over it!"

She swung around, the voice coming from her left, at the end of a long line of apple trees. "It's a knock-down spring-up," the man said, emerging from a nearby row. He paused for a moment, pulling a notepad from his shirt pocket and ostentatiously writing down the license of the gray Taurus. "You Miss Seth?"

"Yes."

The man looked in his fifties, but Linda suspected he was younger, his leathery face made older by years in the sun and arid climate of the Yakima Valley.

"Mr. Merk told me to come down, let you through. House is 'bout half a mile. Just follow the tractor trail."

The drive through the orchard, amidst the apple trees, was pleasant, the air clean, fresh. Throughout the rows she saw what looked like large black stovepipes, five to six feet high, resembling the stacks of old-fashioned locomotive engines. Each of the pipes, louvered at the bottom, was anchored to what looked like a huge pot. The rough tractor tracks swung abruptly to the right, out of the trees, and she saw a tall, thin, shabby-looking man in blue overalls standing at the bottom of the front steps of a white bungalow covered in a fine red dust. As she drew closer she saw that he was about sixty, and frowning as if gazing into the sun against his will. His thinning white hair was tousled by a light breeze that rustled through the valley, a little spiral of dust taking off among the apple trees nearby. Turning the motor off, Linda was once again struck by the eerie silence of the valley. She felt as if she was a thousand miles away from the nearest civilization. She flashed a smile and extended her hand. "You must be Mr. Merk."

He extended his hand as if it were more a chore than a willing civility. "You the real estate agent?" His breath reeked of onions and stale tobacco.

"That's right. Mr. McAllister told me you might be interested in—"

"Haven't made up muh mind yet."

"That's what he told me."

"Don't see the point of you comin' all this way, then."

"Oh, it's not far from Yakima."

"I mean from the East." He said "East" as if it was a fatal disease.

"Ah, Professor Higgins," she said, giving him a friendly smile.

Merk thought for a moment. "You mean that joker in *My Fair Lady*?"

"Very good," she said.

"Yeah, we're not all stupid up here, y'know. We see movies. Got telephones too. And the Internet. And those flush toilets."

"Oh, I didn't mean to sound condescending."

He grunted. What the hell did a woman know about real estate? Orchards in particular? "We grow four different types of apples here. Did you know that?"

"Granny Smiths, Winesap, Red and Golden Delicious," she said, having read the file. *That will put him in his place,* she thought.

Merk grunted. "Adds to the value of the land," he said.

"Not necessarily, Mr. Merk. If it's not an orchardist who wants to buy, then she won't care how many types of apples you sell."

"What d'you mean, *she?* You already got a buyer?"

"No, I just said 'she' because it might be that a woman is the buyer."

"Huh, not likely 'round here."

"Really? I thought a woman used to be governor of the state."

"And she made a hash of things. Dixie Lee Ray spent all her time suckin' up to the environmentalist terrorists. Hell, hadn't been for the Hanford reactor out thisaways, wouldn't've been able to make that A-bomb for Nagasaki." He paused. " 'Course, now the Japs come over and outbid Americans. Sending our best A-grade old growth lumber to Japan."

"They buy fruit too, don't they?"

Merk didn't answer. Instead he asserted he wouldn't sell out to anyone who didn't want to grow apples, and he sure as hell wouldn't sell to any "Jap." The Northwest *was* a different America, she thought.

"That might limit the clientele," Linda said. "I thought you were keen to close a deal."

"I am—with Americans."

She was satisfied she'd drawn him out enough. She looked about, as if concerned someone might be listening. "To tell the truth, Mr. Merk, I understand. My grandfather fought against the Japanese—at Buna, in New Guinea. It's just that as a Realtor I have to—well, you know, I'm sure—make allowances. So many government regulations you have to abide by. Otherwise you can have your business license pulled for discrimination."

For the first time in their conversation, Stanley Merk seemed to relax. He pulled out a pipe and, holding it in one hand, began rubbing a swatch of dark navy cut tobacco into fine weed, its aroma like that of sweet figs. "That's the trouble all over—too many regulations strangling this country. Democrats, Republicans—all the same. We had that damned alar business. You know about that?"

She did but she shook her head. He was sounding more and more like militia. "Well, lot o' growers, includin' me, used alar to spray the apples so they wouldn't get too soft. Stayed on the limb too till we were ready to harvest 'em. Damn environmental terrorists started saying alar caused cancer. Well it might if you drink a bucketful for breakfast—"

"Now I recall," Linda cut in.

"Cost me half my crop. Frightened off foreign sales as well, not just domestic. Some of the Jap buyers wouldn't buy a damned thing. Hear tell their enviros are worse'n ours."

Linda watched him stuff the navy cut into the cherrywood bowl pipe, light up, and blow an aromatic cloud of bluish white smoke heavenward. It poured from his mouth and nose as if his head was on fire. She didn't try to get away from it; on the contrary, she was breathing it in. "I love the smell of pipe tobacco," she said. "Reminds me of my father."

"Huh . . ." It was another grunt, but his facial expression was as near to a smile as he'd get. "Well, pretty soon we won't be able to smoke, period, way those damned E.T.'s are going."

Linda guessed Merk meant "environmental terrorists."

"I know," she said wistfully. "Same with firearms. All the do-gooders want to ban everything. Well, no way they're going to get mine. I don't feel safe without it, especially in the city."

Merk looked at her through the billowing smoke as if he was seeing her for the first time. "You want to come in for a drink?"

"Thank you, could I have something nonalcoholic? Have to drive back."

"How 'bout some cold apple cider?"

"Sounds great."

"You betcha!"

There was a small hallway opening out to a living room that had a rifle above the mantelpiece, a clock in its stock, its barrel silvered, and a row of electric bells along the opposite wall.

"Elephant gun," Merk told Linda. "One shot is all you had. Less kick in it than you'd think. Beautiful, isn't it? Take a look at that silver inlay. Now that's craftsmanship, eh?" Merk exhaled heavily and, taking the pipe out of his mouth, shook his head. "Don't make 'em like that now."

"I wonder you're allowed to keep it in the house," she ventured. "I think there are regulations about that."

"Fer sure, 'cept the gun no longer works. Had to have it neutered. Y'see," he continued scornfully, "someone might come in off the highway, take it off the wall, and try to commit suicide with it."

Linda laughed, and wondered when she was going to get the apple cider. "What are the bells for?"

"Uh, oh, that's for when a cold snap hits. When thermometers in the orchard drop to near freezing, the bells tell us. Then we gotta move—fast—light the smudge pots, keep the air warm. You probably saw 'em on the way in."

"Yes, I—"

A worn-looking woman, graying hair, late fifties, appeared with a tray with two glasses on it and two bottles. Wordlessly, she offered it to Linda.

"The wife," Merk said. "May, this is Linda—"

"I heard," she said, wiping her hands on her apron, and disappeared back into the kitchen.

"May don't say much," Merk said.

Linda gave him a smile and poured out the homemade cider. It was cold and delicious.

"You like that?" Merk asked.

"Delicious. You sure it isn't alcoholic?"

"Yes, ma'am. Mine is from the fermented lot. Your bottle is strictly Sunday stock."

"So you brew your own?"

"Yes, ma'am. You want a dozen or so, I can sell 'em to you—wholesale."

"Isn't that against the law?" She laughed easily.

"Yes, ma'am. Here, take a seat."

She looked around the room. There wasn't another gun in sight, but she noticed an umbrella stand—which struck her as odd in such a dry area—made from an elephant's leg.

"So," Merk said, "what kind of sidearm d'you carry, Miss Seth?"

"Nine-millimeter Sig," she answered.

Merk nodded approvingly, striking another match and moving it back and forth over the bowl. He's packed it too tight, she thought, remembering her dad. "It used to be my father's gun. William Seth. He was in the Michigan militia."

The second match over Merk's pipe bowl stopped moving. " 'Sat a fact? He still alive?"

She shook her head.

"I'm sorry," Merk said, his face more relaxed, the sun-riven lines still there but softer now.

"Thank you," she said. "It's been a few years now."

"Still an' all, you must miss 'im."

"Yes." Whenever she thought of her dad, how she loved him, it made her sad and she abruptly changed the subject. "I'm puzzled by your accent. It sounds southern."

Smiling, he jabbed his pipe stem toward her. "You're right one hundred percent. Appalachia. Lots of us Tar Heels moved up here when the mines back home went bad. Been here ever since."

He hadn't said a thing about a militia, and she remembered Bill Trey's advice not to overdo it, to harness her impatience, to give him time.

"I tell you what, Mr. Merk. I've got a couple of buyers lined up who I think are interested in the orchard, not just the acreage, but I think they'll find your asking price too high. You prepared to come down?"

" 'Tween you, me, and the gatepost, Miss Seth—"

"Call me Linda."

"Well, 'tween you and me, Linda, I'm prepared to sell for five thousand less. Next showdown won't wait."

"I'm not sure what you mean."

He stared at her as if she was demented. "Against the federals."

"Oh."

His tone grew irritable. "Hell, everyone can see it. Not just in Washington State. All over." He stopped, biting hard on his pipe before he spoke. " 'Course you wouldn't know, comin' from Washington. They don't know squat 'bout the peripheries." He paused. "You see, there ain't no way the people are gonna let the federals take away their guns. No way. We bought them, we're constitutionally entitled to 'em and guaranteed a 'well-regulated militia.' We've got to be ready. Not just here, understand. Everywhere. Act in unison. Your daddy would've understood. After Butcher's Ridge and Astoria Bridge, the federals think they got us by the . . . think they've whipped us."

"I've heard some people talking about that," said Linda, "but—I mean, when do you think it'll be?"

"Sooner than later," Merk said.

"Uh-huh. Well, look, thank Mrs. Merk for the refreshment, but I'd better be getting back." She put out her hand. "Nice meeting you." She turned toward the kitchen. "And you, Mrs. Merk."

There was no reply.

"May!" Merk called out. "Miss Seth says—"

"I heard."

"Guess she's busy," Merk said awkwardly, walking Linda to the door.

As she got in her car and started up, Stanley Merk came over, knocking ash out from the pipe. "Linda?"

"Yes."

"No Japs, though. I won't sell to Japs. They're like the federals. Federals tried to take over with Waco. Japs try to do it with dollars. I won't sell to Japan."

"I understand, Mr. Merk. We'll keep in touch."

"You betcha."

As she drove down toward the gate past the strange-looking smudge pots and their "chimney stacks," Linda was going back over their conversation. Merk's use of "peripheries" and "in unison" struck her as significant—the kind of words you wouldn't expect from a Tar Heel. They were words that had obviously been given to him by someone else.

She saw the same worker by the gate, waving pleasantly at her, and wondered if he was in cellular contact with the house. He was brushing off some leaves from around the base of one of the many smudge pots. There were so many, she stopped and asked him how they managed to light them all in time, seeing as Merk told her they had to do it fast.

"Flamethrower." He grinned. "On the back of a four-wheel drive. Have all of 'em lit in less than fifteen minutes."

"Uh-huh. *Flamethrower?*"

"No kidding," he said, but he still had the grin.

"Yeah, right," she answered good-naturedly, and waved good-bye. As she drove over the grill, her body shuddering from the impact, she noticed the grass about the gate was much greener than anywhere else, the kind of new growth you see soon after a fire.

Merk drained the last of his cider, burped and went into the kitchen. "What you think?" he asked May.

"A slut."

"Oh, c'mon, May, she—"

"Boobs were sticking out through that sweater. Sells more than land, I'll warrant."

"I didn't notice anything that—"

"Your eyeballs just about fell out." May grabbed the empty cider bottles, rinsed them, put them noisily in a bushel box, and, mimicking him, said, " 'Would you like to come in for a drink?' Little slut."

"Will you drop it? You know what I meant."

May snatched the empty glasses, rinsed them, and put them in the sink. "She's a federal."

Merk was cleaning his pipe, knocking out the spit dottle in his hand, tossing it into the garbage can under the sink. "Don't go all sour on me, May, 'cause she's good-lookin'. Ain't my fault."

"She's a federal, Stanley Merk, an' if you can't see that you're a fool."

Merk blew through the pipe. It sounded clear, so he took another dark slice of navy cut and began kneading it hard in his left hand. What he wanted to do right now was have this Linda Seth up against the packing shed, yank up one of her legs, wrap it around his waist, and give it to her hard. He could still smell her perfume. Big tits or not, he'd have to put his fantasy on hold, least until he'd checked her out. 'Course, maybe May, her breasts like a coupla dried-out old wineskins, was out to lunch on this one. It was just plain old-fashioned jealousy.

CHAPTER FIVE

Florida

THE SUN WASN'T shining in the Sunshine State—at least not along the Gulf up on the Florida panhandle along the strip of salt-white beaches known as the Emerald Coast. The gun metal sky caught the mood of the small funeral cortege that made its way down from Seaside, a little wooden coastal town that had a quaintly surreal air about it. When bathed in sunlight, the town shone in a way that other towns couldn't, its carefully crafted geometric shapes complementing each other, the town itself surrounded on three sides by a vast bushland of pine trees and by the Gulf immediately south of it.

It was where Bob Kozan's parents lived. In happier times, Shirley and Bob had vacationed there. If the authorities had found his remains, Shirley would have agreed, however reluctantly, to bury him in the Everglades, a place that for her, despite all its natural beauty, was now nothing more than the repository of evil. But the ranger superintendent and other searchers had found nothing but a piece of the airboat's blue sponge-rubber seat, caught in a side stream of the glades, bumping idly against a hammock of stunted gumbo trees and cabbage palms. Nor any remains of Laddie. For Shirley's sake, the superintendent had prolonged the search well after there was no hope the gators and crocs had left anything undevoured.

The fact that the airboat was gone as well as the dog pointed to murder. Lou Rheinhardt, owner-skipper of the twenty-foot *Lady Bee*, suggested to the superintendent that they bring in divers. Maybe they could find the dead man's wallet, even if the water did move a half mile a day.

"So?" the super had asked, remembering the hopeless task of the divers who had to dive in the tar-black waters around the Valujet crash in '96. "If we bring in divers, and sharpshooters to protect them from the gators and moccasins, what good is that? He's gone."

Rheinhardt had shrugged. "Thought it might help his missus."

The super shook his head. "You could get the best diver, Jhordan Canfield, down here, but I doubt he'd find anything. And I could lose him. Sharpshooters can only protect what they can see. Besides, I hate to sound like a tight-ass, but it'd cost the taxpayers a bundle. Not worth it."

"I could get my buddy Mason down here. He's a good shot. Might do it for nothing."

"Thanks, Lou, but I think we'll let sleeping dogs lie—I mean, I didn't mean that. I mean what is, *is*. We can't change it now. Best we have the memorial service up near his folks' home at Seaside and leave it at that. If the sheriff down here wants to keep looking, that's his business. We're rangers, not deputies. But I'll tell you this, Lou—if the militia isn't behind this, I'll eat my hat. It's clear as crystal that this is a payback killing for that first son of a bitch who had a run at Kozan."

"Think so?"

"Know so." He paused. "I'll tell you somethin' else—from now on my boys go out in pairs or not at all."

"Good move."

"Yeah." The super slapped his arm, killing a mosquito. He started worrying about catching AIDS. He wiped the blood off his arm with a crumpled Kleenex. "What I can't figure is why in hell they fired on Kozan in the first place. I've been thinking a lot about that. One of those reporters from Atlanta asked if the militia was making hootch in the glades. Maybe Kozan stumbled on a still."

Rheinhardt said he didn't think much of that idea. "Goddamn reporters from the city. Shit, they still think it's the roaring twenties down here—rednecks and hooch."

"Hell," the super said, "nothing wrong with bein' a redneck. My daddy—"

" 'Course there ain't," Rheinhardt cut in. "What I'm saying is that those smartasses from the big smoke think we're nothin' but hillbillies by the sea."

"Well then, why'd they shoot at him?"

"Payback, like you said."

"No, I mean first time around?"

"Damned if I know," Rheinhardt said. "But I'll ask around. If I hear anything, I'll let you know."

"Appreciate it, Lou."

Shirley and her husband's parents moved silently along the beach until the preacher stopped. Without any explanation as to why this particular spot was better than any other, he turned, waited a moment or two, and began the service without a body.

After the service, two men approached her, showed their FBI badges and told her the Bureau wouldn't rest until Bob's killer was found. While they wouldn't bother her right now, they'd call on her later. In the meantime, they said, if she heard anything of importance, she should contact them immediately. One agent, Michael Ma, gave Shirley his card. It showed he was stationed farther along the gray coast, in Panama City.

"It was the militia," she said of her husband's death.

"Do you say that because of the first attempt on your husband's life?" Ma asked.

"Yes."

"We're looking into that, Mrs. Kozan."

She doubted it—not their sincerity, but the practicality of it. What could you find in that evil place, full of alligators and poisonous snakes? Besides, the federal government and all its law enforcement arms were preoccupied with the situation in the Northwest. Right now the militia out there was getting all the attention because there'd been open warfare, and if the President didn't get a handle on it pretty soon, he could say good-bye to reelection. She heard a screech behind her and turned quickly, her heart thumping like a drum. It was a small child coming from

Seaside, running excitedly ahead of his parents, the screeching noise made by his little feet on the dry, white sand. The child's parents were smiling. Shirley Kozan began to cry.

CHAPTER SIX

Near Naches, Washington State

FOUR BLACK-UNIFORMED NAZIS and their passenger were heading west in a Hummer from southern Idaho into Washington State, toward Stanley Merk's orchard. For a long time none of them spoke except for the odd obscenity they spat out at the radio as they listened to the White House press conference. The President was saying that the militias had to be "curbed," that hatred of any ethnic group "will not be tolerated by the government of the United States."

"Jew boys are behind this," one of them said.

A car came into view heading toward them, its lights on high beam. "Dim your lights, you faggot!"

"Uncle Dolf would've fixed all those Jew boys if he'd had time."

"And the faggots as well," the one driving said.

"Right on," said the Nazi who'd broken the silence. "Would've barbecued the lot of 'em. Would've fixed the chinks and the Japs too if he'd had time. Friggin' slant-eyes comin' 'cross here in all their damned Lexuses, driving round like King Muck. Can't stand chinks. Never just talk to one another—always yellin' at two hundred decibels. Don't give a fuck for anyone else. Shoulda locked 'em up with the Japs during the war. Dropped an A-bomb on Beijing."

" 'Course," the passenger corrected them, "the Chinese were fighting the Japs."

"Don't matter. All the same underneath. Think all white men smell like wet dogs. Call us barbarians because we've got hair on our bodies and—"

"Oh yeah?" the man driving cut in. "Then how come all the old chink bastards have white beards?"

This observation struck one of the two Nazis in the back with the force of revelation. "Well, I'll be—never thought of that. Huh—so they don't like *our* beards, but when they grow old they— Bunch of damn hypocrites!"

"You know," the driver said, "in Germany the Führer started with private militias."

"There you go," one of the others put in.

"You remember what they said 'bout the Nazi party?" the driver said.

"What *who* said about them?"

"Know what the *New York Times* said?"

"You gonna tell us or not?"

The Nazi driver gave a short chortle. "Assholes said—" He laughed again. "—after the Munich putsch—you know about that, when the Führer tried to take over in 'twenty-three . . ."

" 'Course we fuckin' know. What'd the *New York Lies* say about the Führer?"

"They said, 'The Munich putsch definitely eliminates Hitler and his National Socialist followers.' Ha!"

"Yeah," said the Nazi sitting next to him in the front seat. "Well, they sure as hell were wrong."

"You betcha. In 'thirty-three he was chancellor of Germany."

"And all those Jew boy industrialists thought they'd use him like a puppet till they wanted to be rid of him."

"The best thing they ever did was put 'im in Landsberg Prison," the driver continued. "He was depressed as hell to start with. You know that?" He paused, then glanced in the rearview mirror at their fellow passenger. "Isn't that right, Mr. Vance?" In the backseat sat a lean man, around five-foot-eight, in his late forties, blue eyes deeply recessed, dark brown hair. They called him "Mister" rather than by his rank because the federals in "Clean Sweep" were still hunting militiamen, particularly their high-ranking officers, running them to ground.

"That's right," Vance said.

"But then," the driver went on, his voice rising with the sound of the Hummer engine negotiating one of the foothills east of Coeur d'Alene, "then he had time to think, to see it all. God's plan starin' 'im in the face. Wrote *Mein Kampf*—the blueprint. Right, Mr. Vance?"

"Correct."

"Money he got from writin', that got him a little hut up in the mountains near Berchtesgaden. Loved the mountains. Right, Mr. Vance?"

Vance didn't answer, his silence emitting a sense of anger at the driver's badgering, sycophantic tone.

It started to snow.

"World's weather's goin' crazy," said Norman, the biggest of the four Nazis. In the darkness, Vance grimaced from an old war wound, the left side of his chest involuntarily going into spasm where he'd taken a hit, or rather, several hits, from a federal's flechette-loaded shotgun. He was lucky to be alive.

The Nazis' Hummer crashed into Stanley Merk's orchard gate beneath a sullen sky. It was halfway to the house before the orchardist's hired hand could reach him by cellular, the Hummer's two rear whip aerials all but lost in the cloud of powdered red dirt as the vehicle skidded to a stop in the twilight. The four Nazis were already out, forming a defensive perimeter, M-16s at the ready. Vance wore civilian clothes, dark blue cotton slacks, a light blue shirt matching his eyes, and a heavy black gabardine raincoat. He stepped out from the Hummer.

"Stanley!" he called out, extending his hand.

"Colonel Vance, sir," Merk said respectfully, immediately adding, " 'Bout time. Was wonderin' when the high and mighty would visit."

"Never fear, Stan. We look after our people." Vance turned

to the four Nazis. "Stan, let me introduce you to my guardian angels. Norman, Andrew, Zane, and Ian."

Merk nodded. "Boys," he said, and the *boys*, all four—he guessed they were in their mid- to late twenties—gave a *Sieg Heil*, hands not up and straight out, but like the Führer used to, arm bent at the elbow, parallel to their body, in what for the uninitiated could be taken as a nonchalant, halfhearted stop signal.

But Merk sensed there was nothing halfhearted about these four blue-eyed Aryans. It was said amongst the First Regiment of the Washington State militia that Norman, Andrew, Zane, and Ian weren't their real names, that the four of them from Hayden Lake, the U.S. Aryan militia HQ in Idaho, had taken names whose first letters together formed the acronym of the National Socialist Party, NAZI. They were the storm troopers assigned to guard Vance, who was officially the ILO—information liaison officer—for NWTO—Northwestern Theater of Operations. Of the four storm troopers, Norm and Ian were both over six feet, Andrew and Zane around five-nine, but all of them wore black SS uniforms, had cropped haircuts, carried Ruger 9mm sidearms and SS death's head daggers, and looked very much alike. The ferocity of their eyes and the determined set of their jaws were the first things Merk noticed about them.

For security reasons, which Vance said he was sure Merk would understand, they had come to the orchard without warning, their purpose to set up an interim HQ for hit and run attacks on federals in central and eastern Washington State.

"Federals think the party's over, Stan," Vance informed Merk easily as they made their way to the house, Vance taking off his coat, but not before he had carefully tucked in both ends of its belt into the side pockets. He hated drag-ass belts, and was as fastidious about his appearance as he was about his battle plans and the lies he told. He was especially careful about the contrived fiction that he was still Colonel Vance, United States Militia Corps, liaison information officer in NWTO—when in fact he'd been secretly promoted to General, C in C NWTO, upon General Mant's death. It meant that while the federals' hound dogs from the FBI, ATF, and the rest were busy looking for a General Nordstrom—who they believed was the supreme commander of the militias, but who didn't exist—Vance could move more freely about the countryside. And, just as important, under cover as liaison information officer, Vance would be confided in by junior officers and men and told things they would not normally feel comfortable talking about to a General Nordstrom or any other militia general.

It was as ILO NWTO, for example, that Vance, while knowing that in SETO—Southeast Theater of Operations—for example, morale was high in units such as Florida's Ten Thousand Islands Second Infantry Regiment, also knew that morale in Washington State was rock bottom. The Northwest militia, as one legendary militia captain, Lucky McBride, had described it, had been given an "unmitigated hiding" meted out by the "son of a bitch genius," federal General Freeman, both at Butcher's Ridge in the Cascade Mountains and around the Columbia River delta on the Washington-Oregon border. Oh, there hadn't been what the tabloids were claiming to be "massive defections." What happened in the wake of the FEDFOR victory was that thousands of militiamen in the Northwest had simply taken off their telltale WW II helmets and battle dress, buried their illegal M-60s and AK-47s, and returned to their farms, merging back into the civilian population, but still burning, indeed more so, with hatred of the federals. What was needed, Vance had come to realize, was something to raise morale before it was dissipated in a slough of despondency about the militia's ability to strike back.

The four Hayden Lake Nazis and Vance were getting an earful on this score from Stan Merk, who said he knew how to deal with federals. Around the time of Butcher's Ridge, he'd "fixed" two of them—woman, name of Albright, and an ATF agent, Gordon—when they'd come nosing around.

"So I see," Vance said. Vance was almost, though not always, as fastidious in his speech as he was in other aspects of his life. A pet peeve of his was the widespread use, or rather, misuse, among militia officers and men of the phrase "You did good," when what was meant was, "You did well." No one else seemed to give a damn, but for Vance it was yet another sign of the "dumbing down of America," the failure of English-speaking Americans to stand on guard for their heritage, to allow what he called "the bastardization of America by the flood of illiterate Third World immigrants, Hispanics, and blacks," a further sign of the "mongrelization of America by nonwhites." He didn't see any enrichment of a melting pot of cultures, but rather a soup of incompatible ingredients.

They walked into the living room, where May, Stan Merk's wife, had put out cold bottles of cider.

"I saw green grass about your gate," Vance said. "Saw it in the headlights—plain as day. Quite obvious there's been a fire—a very intense fire—not long ago."

"So?" Merk said, in what he knew was a weak attempt at nonchalance. "Could've been a dozen different reasons for a fire."

"Uh-huh," Vance said, looking around at the four Nazis. "What would you think, Norman, if you had been federals coming down from Butcher's Ridge and two of your agents told you they were going to visit an orchardist? Then they disappeared."

Norman was looking over at Stan Merk, who passed him another stubby of his illegal homemade cider. The Nazi took a swig before he answered. "Might figure their buddies got hit along the way."

"You might," Merk conceded, but his tone was disbelieving. "On Highway 97 it's over a hundred and twenty miles down here from up around Butcher's Ridge. Anything could've happened along that route."

Andrew burped unapologetically, and Vance said nothing of the Nazi's bad manners. No point in antagonizing people who, whatever their lack of social graces, were prepared to die protecting you. Andrew burped again. "You'd have to be eagle-eyed to pick that stuff up—about the grass."

"That's what I reckon," Zane chimed in. "Like who's gonna be lookin' for that kind of shit?"

"*Investigators,*" Vance said coldly. "People who are trained to see such things." The colonel, having refused any cider, looked around attentively at the four storm troopers as a tutor might study his students. "As far as I know, the SS didn't drink on duty." He paused. "Certainly Hitler didn't." He might as well have slapped them across the face. Suddenly they were very attentive.

CHAPTER SEVEN

Washington State

THE NATIONAL GUARDS' drab, olive-green federal force helos appeared in the sky like so many gnats, the persistent beating of their rotors getting closer as they descended beneath the depressing gray ceiling of stratus cloud over the southern Cascade mountains. Beneath them, scattering like ants in every direction, were the fleeing remnants of a rebel company from WIOC—Washington State, Idaho, Oregon, and northern California—Third Infantry Brigade's Second Battalion. Together with other elements of the decimated Third, they had been engaged in a fighting retreat all the way north from the Washington-Oregon line.

Among the retreating militia was Lieutenant Jeremy Brigham Eleen, a devout twenty-eight-year-old Mormon militiaman and grandson of Korean War Medal of Honor winner Samuel Brigham Eleen. Jeremy's grandfather had been one of the U.S. Marines who, in one of America's darkest hours, fought so tenaciously in the Corps' famed retreat from North Korea's Chosin Reservoir. Lieutenant Jeremy Brigham Eleen had always tried to live up to these standards, as he did now while leading what remained of Second Battalion's Charlie Company toward the relative safety of eastern Washington. Having joined the battle for the Astoria Bridge on the Washington-Oregon border with a full complement of 120 men, they were now down to forty-three. Most had been killed in the initial withdrawal from FED-FOR armored thrusts once the bridge was lost to the federals, and the militia's General Mant killed. Twelve more were killed in the militia armored vehicle retreat north on I-5. The circling federal helicopter gunships, like birds of prey, withheld fire at first for fear that some of the vehicles were carrying and/or being driven by civilian hostages.

Initially, Army Chief of Staff General Walter Shelbourne refused to give his pilots "weapons free" status, and the militia's mobile, if ragged, column had gotten beyond Mount St. Helens National Volcano Monument near the intersection of the north-south I-5 and state highway 12.

The political pressure had mounted in Washington, D.C., as the international audience on CNN viewed the apparent impotence of the most powerful government in the world, unable or unwilling to close on militia rebels. Shelbourne finally caved, citing an earlier case when his subordinate, General Douglas Freeman, then commanding officer of a FEDFOR, had ordered a subordinate of his to fire on civilian hostages if it were necessary to capture a bridge.

The helos then unleashed a terrible fire upon the militia, which killed or wounded another thirty-four men of Charlie Company. Lieutenant Jeremy Brigham Eleen and his forty-three comrades were now still alive only because a banshee-wailing blizzard had swept in from the cold northern Pacific, reducing visibility to zero, blinding the FEDFOR chopper pilots and gunners. It allowed Eleen and what was left of Charlie Company to hightail it east on Highway 12 before the passes were completely cut off.

The deeply religious Eleen believed the storm was sent by God, as surely as God had helped the Marines escape from Chosin Reservoir, as surely as He had parted the waters of the Red Sea for the Israelites to escape the oppression of the Pharaohs. Just as surely as he and his men were fleeing the oppression of Washington, D.C., from whence an army of faceless bureaucrats continued to harass the Mormon state of Utah, telling it how many blacks and other coloreds it should take into its schools and universities in order to get federal funding, and still telling the elders that they could not have more than one wife. What business was it of the government? he wondered. If the wives were happy, what was the problem? Washington, D.C., should keep its nose out of a person's private life. It was Eleen's belief that such persecution had led Brigham Young to flee Washington's oppression, leading his people west on the Oregon Trail to build a great city in the wilderness around the Great Salt Lake.

It stopped snowing and the eight helos came in at two hundred feet in a wide counterclockwise circle. Suddenly, the overcast sky was filled with what seemed confetti as thousands of pamphlets from FEDFOR's Psychological Operations branch fluttered down.

GENERAL MANT IS DEAD
MILITIA FORCES HAVE BEEN DEFEATED
LAY DOWN YOUR ARMS AND THE FEDERAL GOVERNMENT
PROMISES THAT YOU WILL BE TREATED FAIRLY.
GENERAL WALTER SHELBOURNE C IN C U.S. ARMY

"Yeah," Corporal Mulvane said. He crumpled the pamphlet in his fist and threw it to the ground. "Treated fairly! Christ, like shooting everybody up at the fucking junction!"

"There's no need for that," Eleen said quietly. He meant the bad language, particularly using the Lord's name in vain. But he agreed with the corporal. The federals couldn't be trusted. He'd seen civilians shot both at the junction and during the battle for the bridge. But the militia was far from defeated. "Defeat," Eleen said, "is a state of mind."

"Except when you're dead!" Mulvane countered.

"Even then," Eleen said. "In the hereafter, God'll know we fought oppression. Remember, the first American militiamen were branded as traitors by their oppressors but now we know different. History'll vindicate us, you'll see."

"Yeah, well," Mulvane said, "if we sit here much longer we're not gonna see anything. We'll be snowed in. So what are you gonna do, Lieutenant? We gonna show the white flag or not?"

Eleen's response was inaudible, lost to the sound of the choppers. His men, who could detect the sharp, clean smell of impending snow above the wash of gasoline fumes, knew they would once again be blinded by snow. And Eleen knew that, tough as they were, all of them were exhausted, nerve ends raw from the long, painful retreat. "We don't know for sure just how many militia have surrendered in the West, let alone east of the Mississippi. And some of the Florida regiments have—"

"Christ!" Mulvane shouted. "Never mind them. Do *we* throw in the towel or not?"

"I release you all from my command," Eleen said sadly, with a calm that would have surprised most troops in the circumstances. But Jeremy Eleen would not panic. God was by his side.

"But *you're* not going to surrender?" Corporal Mulvane asked exasperatedly.

"I can't. I gave my word to—"

"Well, fuck you, Lieutenant," Mulvane said. "You're the fucking limit, aren't you?" With that, Mulvane, an ex-Marine, raised his SAW and fired a long burst at the nearest helo. "Semper Fidelis!"

It started snowing again, but the choppers weren't leaving. They answered Mulvane's unequivocal defiance in a fusillade of machine-gun fire, the .50 caliber red tracer rounds coming down in what seemed like long, lazy arcs. In fact, the firing was so intense that several of the guns overheated and jammed. Three of the eight choppers flew higher, inclining their nose and switching to their 2.75-inch air-to-ground rockets, which came streaking in at two hundred meters per second. The rockets created a hail of shrapnel so hot that infrared scopes on the helos were temporarily confused as the snow kept coming down around the staggered convoy of militia pickups. The other five choppers withdrew momentarily but then turned about as if still intent on staying around, but away from the militia's small arms fire. Then they disappeared. But Eleen guessed the truth, or at least part of it—that the Blackhawks had disgorged their troops all around him before leaving the area. "We're surrounded," he told the forty-three militiamen.

"So what's new?" Mulvane muttered.

"I figure eight choppers—about a hundred sixty troops in all."

"Piece o' cake," Mulvane said, smelling the hard, cold air of snow. Visibility would soon be zero.

"Then we move through them," Eleen said. "One squad at a time. Single file, alternate fields of fire. Move!"

CHAPTER EIGHT

Near Packwood, Washington State

AT FIRST THE snow had come down in big, sloppy, wet flakes that melted the moment they hit the ground, but soon these big flakes had given way to a downpour of pea-sized dry snow that initially bounced like hail, rapidly covering the ground. By the time Eleen had his five squads in a line of over forty men and they approached the area where he'd estimated the helos had descended for a time before moving off, the snow was over six inches deep. He signaled the column to stop, but visibility was so bad his hand could be seen by only two or three men behind him. By the time his signal had been relayed down the line in zero visibility, the last three squads of twenty-seven men had bunched up, so that instead of five separate squads, there was one long line with only a pace or two at most between each man.

Eleen moved cautiously forward again for about ten paces, gave the stop signal, and went down on one knee, listening for any sound ahead that might have been muffled by the snowfall or by the footfalls of his five squads. There was only silence in the whiteout, broken, albeit softly, by the faint whistling of what he at first thought was the wind drifts scattering before him in ghostly, elongated shrouds of snow, until he realized it was the man directly behind him breathing. The fact that he had mistaken the sound behind him for a noise up ahead in the blizzard told him something he'd suspected but didn't want to admit: he'd suffered a permanent hearing loss. It was the result of the heavy and almost ceaseless FEDFOR shelling as the thousands of militiamen tried desperately to withdraw north from the Columbia River through the marshlands of the Willapa Wildlife Refuge. The federals' 105mm and 155mm howitzer rounds had kept coming overhead with the weird shuffling sound that told you it was too close—before the high explosive tore open the earth in geysers of mud and water, shrapnel whistling chaotically through the salty air. More than half of Charlie Company's original two hundred had been cut down by FEDFOR cannons, and the whistling sound of the man behind him had brought on a flashback, so intense that Eleen almost committed one of what his father used to call the greatest sins. He experienced a surge of temper that almost caused him to tell his fellow militiaman to shut up—to breathe through his mouth if necessary, instead of his big, stupid, hairy nose. Instead, Eleen checked the impulse, got up, and waved his men cautiously forward.

Visibility improved momentarily to about twenty feet or so, and he saw several snowy bumps ahead. He went down flat and could hear the soft *whump!* of the men closest behind him following suit. It could have been boulders blanketed in snow. Or it could be infantry from the helos—camouflaged and waiting.

Eleen waited a few more minutes. He could hear nothing but the wild banshee moaning of the wind. Then, making sure of his bearings, getting up from the kneeling position, his squad and the other four squads that remained of Charlie Company moved forward into the blizzard. They were soon swallowed up by the bad weather. With visibility at zero, the forty-three militiamen of the five squads now formed an almost continuous single-file line, each man no more than a few feet away from his comrade in front. Eleen spotted a grayish blur through the falling snow, then just as quickly it was gone again. A federal helmet perhaps? But wouldn't the federals have donned "whites," the overlays that would blend in with the snow? Eleen's men had improvised, putting their white singlets and T-shirts over their militia's camouflage combat uniforms, some men using the T-shirts to stretch over their WW II helmets. It was a small detail but one that testified to the militia's natural bent for improvisation against a larger and often better equipped force. Eleen knew that the as yet unseen General Nordstrom had paid attention to such detail, eschewing, for example, the regular Army's khaki underwear for white in the Northwest. In the Southeast, however, Nordstrom had ordered all militiamen to wear khaki T-shirts that would blend in well with the Everglades.

The secret project going on in the Ten Thousand Islands was but one of many spawned, indeed made possible, by what in 1996 was identified by *U.S. News & World Report* as the DRMO—Defense Reutilization and Marketing Office—scandals throughout the United States. The job of the DRMOs was to itemize and classify military surplus before it was given away to other government agencies, including museums. Anything left over was supposed to be sold by sealed bid auction to the public, and all weapons and spare parts were to be "demilled"—demilitarized—by chopping them up and/or removing vital working parts. Problem was, if a piece of equipment—say a helicopter fuselage or can opener—was incorrectly coded, it might end up for sale to the public or as a giveaway to museums, who in turn were allowed under federal law to give away what they didn't want in return for civilians' services or other vehicles. But *U.S. News & World Report* discovered that at Robins Air Force Base outside Macon, Georgia, the DRMO "lost track" of over $39 million worth of surplus equipment. They also discovered that a Pentagon investigation had found "three complete TOW antitank missile systems for sale."

In another case, Air Force personnel were told by a civilian, "I don't know why you're so excited . . . Sparks [a buyer] has sixty or seventy of these things." These *things* were Cobra gunship fuselages. It turned out the man was wrong about Sparks. Sparks didn't have sixty or seventy Cobra fuselages. He had eighty-eight. Another buyer in Montana readily told the Pentagon that his chopper was "fully armed. I had rockets on it and machine guns. I was out shooting coyotes with them." In San Antonio thousands of top secret encryption devices and hardcased field computers used for sending coded communications were discovered along with Wang computers with hard drives intact, one intact floppy disk labeled "Top Secret SCI," which meant it contained special intelligence. All this was on the way out of the country, hidden beneath tons of scrap metal. The investigation also uncovered an instance of over $700,000 worth of "tank and howitzer parts" buried in a sea container of automotive parts, and "thirty-seven separate inertial guidance devices for the F-117A Stealth fighter and F-11 bombers" heading for Shanghai.

"God knows," one of General Shelbourne's chief investigators told him, "how much stuff the militias have been able to stockpile by now." He continued quoting the *U.S. News & World Report*: "A hundred and fifty-seven million dollars worth of parts bound for China, Hong Kong, Vietnam, the Philippines, Taiwan and elsewhere. . . . One can only imagine how much state-of-the-art military surplus from the DRMO and in the museums all around the country has been obtained by the militias."

Shelbourne's blood pressure rose to near stroke point when he was told that it had been established that over a half-dozen

DRMO "coders" were in fact militia sympathizers. What they had coded too low as "A"—surplus that could be sold without being demilitarized—was in fact equipment that should have been demilitarized but was sold virtually intact. In several suspected cases it was believed that so-called "sealed" bids by buyers were in fact fixed, and Shelbourne wondered how many had been made by militias. Buyers, the magazine reported, had been tipped off well ahead of the auction date and given a list of other invitees whom they might wish to "contact."

Quite apart from the possibility of intentionally corrupt auctions where the fix was in, the DRMOs were in such a state that a perfectly respectable, law-abiding citizen like retired Navy Captain Mike Norton in Indiana was able to obtain a "fully flyable A-6" Intruder fighter/bomber.

The black smudge reappeared momentarily, perhaps thirty feet away, then just as quickly vanished. "A dog," Mulvane whispered.

"Wolves," Eleen said.

They were both right, not for the obvious reason that a wolf is a type of wild dog, but because the acronym WOLVES was used by the Army's Canine Corps to designate those dogs outfitted with "wireless operational listening and video systems," the small, yarmulkelike box atop the dog's head holding the camera, the listening sensor on a breast plate harness. It meant that the federals now knew precisely where Eleen's force was situated. If there was any doubt about this, it evaporated a minute later as mortar shells came whistling through the whiteout, the crash of their high explosive sending up geysers of dirt-streaked snow, two men killed outright, another three wounded. Eleen had no choice. He had to move. But where to? If he pulled back into the whiteout, the dogs would still be monitoring him. "Take out the dog!" he shouted.

He needn't have bothered. Mulvane, struck by the fact that the dog hadn't hightailed it amid the noise of the mortars exploding, assumed correctly that it was some kind of tracking canine and let fly at the smudge with a three-round burst from his

M-16. The smudge leapt and bucked in the blizzard-strewn air, dead before it hit the stained snow. Naturally, the federals would assume the militiamen would now retreat. With the memory of the Marines' fighting retreat from Chosin Reservoir in mind, Eleen was tempted, but he opted instead for the kind of audacity that had made militiaman Lucky McBride and the federals' General Freeman legends on opposite sides of the war. Eleen decided on a four-pronged attack with his single line of combatants behind him, ordering them to split into four lines of around ten men each, all four prongs advancing, each point man selected from among the most experienced of what was left of Eleen's Charlie Company.

The 81mm mortar rounds kept crashing well behind Eleen's men, the federals' mortar crews obviously not getting feedback from any WOLVES and assuming that the militia would be retreating. Which was precisely why Eleen ordered his men forward instead of back, counting on the element of surprise to bust out of what Eleen was sure was a federal encirclement. Eleen acknowledged to Mulvane that the federal pilots were brave bastards, coming down low to unload troops to surround him. He heard an explosion off to his right, about two o'clock, different from the mortar rounds, then a visceral scream.

"What the—" There was another explosion, ten o'clock, ten feet away, and this time he saw something black and stringy like a wet black mop, the shredded victim's boot spinning off into the blizzard. Its owner's foot, or what was left of it, lay in the snow looking curiously splayed, like a scuba diver's fin that had been axed vertically, shining with smears of blood, arteries, and torn cartilage. The man was writhing in agony, his buddy ripping the hypodermic from his helmet band, tearing the plastic wrap off with his teeth, his fingers frozen as he fumbled for a second or two, intuitively ducking as a mortar round whistled down before injecting the man with the morphine.

Eleen had been caught in a trap, suckered into going forward by the overreach of the federals' mortar crews. What Eleen had thought was the noise of the federals' helos dropping off federal troops to surround him had been the sound of the helos dropping aerial-deliverable "gravel" antipersonnel mines. Snow covered them within minutes of the drop from the fishnet mine slings beneath the helos. The federal troops had then been dropped in a wider circle so the mine field formed a deadly moat of hidden explosives between the encircling federals and the trapped militiamen. All the unseen federals had to do was keep lobbing the mortars in the vicinity of the telltale explosions of the antipersonnel mines.

Within minutes, because of a ham radio operator picking up the federals' interhelo chatter and the radio traffic between the helo commander and Yakima federal HQ for south-central Washington, news of the pending annihilation of Eleen's force was flashed around the world, courtesy of CNN and Murdoch's news channel. Viewers, which included Americans who were politically and philosophically against the militia uprisings, nevertheless had a sneaking sympathy for the underdogs. Eleen's forty or so men were at the moment outgunned, outmanned, and plain outmaneuvered by the federal commander, a Major Irwin of I Corps, First Special Forces Group (Airborne).

Within an hour Irwin and Eleen were names known to millions of viewers around the world. In Las Vegas, odds were six-to-one in favor of the federals. Unless some kind of ad hoc militia relief column could break through the federal ring or somehow surround it, the fate of Eleen and his men seemed sealed, merely a matter of time.

CHAPTER NINE

Near Naches, Washington State

EAST OF NACHES in Merk's house, the Nazis were warming to the orchardist recounting the exploits of Frederick Latrell, who was due to arrive later, and the Nazi skinhead Michael Hearn.

"So these two guys," Norman prompted, "Latrell and Hearn, are drivin' along the I-5 and this uppity nigger comes up."

Vance's attention, by the look of his eyes, was split between listening to the four Nazis and Merk on the periphery of his consciousness and something else that was increasingly demanding his attention.

"So," Andrew pressed. "This nigger's comin' up behind our two boys on the I-5."

"Yes siree," Merk said. "On the Oregon side of the Columbia."

May was watching them from the cool darkness of the veranda while in the background a rerun of *The X-Files* flickered, the TV giving off an aura of eerie blue light. Like Mulder and Scully in the TV show, May knew there was government conspiracy every way you turned.

"Freakin' Indians," Zane said suddenly, "are bad as the niggers. Always complainin'. Ain't got this, ain't got that. 'Course, what's the liberal government do? Suck up to 'em, that's what. Honorin' some damn fool treaties signed a hundred years ago. Say the white man took their land from 'em. Boo hoo! Where you think the fuckin' Indians got their land?" Merk turned to see if May had heard the cursing, holding up a cautionary finger to Zane, who took absolutely no notice, answering his own question. "I'll tell you where they got their land. Took it in battle from some other son of a bitch Indian. That's life, right?" His hands were outstretched in a gesture of earnest inquiry, a cigarette in his left hand, cider in the other. "Am I right?"

"Right," Zane said, peeling the homemade "Best before" label on his cider. "They're all the same. Can't stand 'em or their ugly squaws."

"Ha!" Merk said. "You know what Mikey Hearn said when he and Fred Latrell came by—after the nigger business?" Merk didn't wait for an answer. "Mikey said no way you could make love to them squaws. So damn fat you couldn't find it!"

"Ha!" Norman blurted. "So damn fat you couldn't find it."

"There you go," Zane chimed in. "Fat and drunk. So damn ugly could use 'em as scarecrows. Only trouble is—" He took a drag on the cigarette. "—I feel sorry for the crows."

Andrew thought it was so funny, he spat his gum out. Vance smiled. Part of the colonel's fastidious nature was an unrelenting hatred of Indians, his great-great-grandfather having been one of those killed in the infamous Nez Perce Indian war. He was amused by Merk's easy reference to Latrell as "Fred" and to Hearn as "Mikey." Hearn wasn't the type to be called "Mikey" unless you were really close to him, and from what Vance remembered, no one got close to Hearn. Hearn had started out as just another skinhead Nazi moving around the country like any other hitchhiker. Then he'd been given a lift up from Cannon Beach in Oregon by militiaman Latrell, who'd started talking about Aryans and how the country was going to hell in a handbasket. Vance was sure of one thing: Hearn wasn't called "Mikey" these days. Up in Camp Fairchild the federals called him the "Iceman" because of the murders he had committed, but as far as Vance was concerned, it was a misnomer. "Iceman" implied cold calculation. That was true enough when the mechanics of what Hearn had done were considered, but it was a passionate, burning fire in the young Nazi's blood that had led him to do the things he'd done.

"Anyway," Merk said, "this nigger is tailgatin' Fred and Mikey, so Fred gives him the finger, then this nigger in this beat-up Cutlass starts firing, so Fred says to heck with this, pulls out his handgun from the glove box."

"What kind?" Zane asked.

"Thirty-eight," Merk said irritably.

Vance, fastidious as usual about detail, almost corrected him—it had been a 9mm Browning—but why interrupt the story of a militia legend?

"So anyways," Merk continued, getting into it now, leaning forward in the old overstuffed chaise lounge, "they play cat and mouse, lane to lane. The nigger loses it, fires off a coupla more shots, and pop goes the Cherokee's windshield. Mikey said it looked like a—" He looked around, couldn't see May. "—like a fuckin' spider's web. Couldn't see a goddamn thing, so Fred, one wheel on the hand—"

"Hand on the wheel," Zane said.

"What? That's what I said. Fred's got his hand on the goddamn wheel, reaches into the backseat with his other hand, pulls out his shotgun."

"What kind?" Zane asked.

"I dunno. Twelve gauge—double-barreled."

"A Remington," Vance said, unable to contain himself. "Pump action."

Merk slumped sulkily back in the chair.

"Go on," Vance urged him.

"No," he said, glaring at Vance, then nodding toward Zane. "He knows everything. Let him tell it."

Zane took another swig of cider. "I don't know the fucking story. I just wanted to know what kind of weapons we're talking about here—automatics, semi, what?"

"He gave the *gun*," Norman said, "the *Remington*, to Mikey, and Mikey blew the fucking nigger's head off. That's what I heard."

"Right. That's it," Merk said with an air of allegiance to Norman. "Little black turd's Cutlass crossed the line, slammed into an oncoming bus, flew right off the road into the brush. Fred

Latrell said that's what happens when niggers screw 'round with Aryans."

"Right!" Norman said. "Then they catch Latrell and Mikey after Mikey does the cop that pulls 'em over across the state line and they join Lucky McBride's outfit on top of Butcher's Ridge. Latrell gets wounded by one of these fucking National Guard posses but gets away. Mikey gets taken POW with all the other militia guys who hadn't thrown in the towel. Now they're beating the shit out of him in Fairchild."

Vance was feeling itchy, not all over but here and there, a manifestation of the anxiety he felt at having to listen to a string of inaccuracies. It didn't bother him that he had been one of those wounded who'd had no choice but to surrender and be part of a prisoner exchange, before the amnesty was withdrawn, but he *hated* inaccuracies. The Nazi, Hearn, did *not* shoot the black; it was Latrell, who would be arriving at Merk's later that night, who had fired the shotgun. And it wasn't a bus but a semi that hit the Cutlass. And finally, Latrell hadn't been shot on Butcher's Ridge by National Guardsmen or by any of Freeman's elite Special Forces commandoes. What happened was that, when captured, Hearn had pointed down at one of the unrecognizable militia corpses strewn about the ridge and told Freeman's outfit that it was Latrell, who had later fought on the Washington-Oregon front.

But despite the temptation, Vance resisted the urge to dot the i's and cross the t's, as it were, of Stanley Merk's story, for he had hold of something far more important. No matter what the "facts" about the assassin Latrell and cop-killer Hearn were, they had, like Randy Weaver, Wilfred Ames, McVeigh, and others, become legends to the militia. And sometimes legends, whether in the mountainous Northwest or in Florida swamps, were more important than facts. Legends were especially vital now to rally a host of potential volunteers who, Vance believed, were holding back because it looked to many, particularly in the mainstream media, that the militia, as the New York *Daily News*, reporting to the federals' chief of staff Walter Shelbourne, put it, "had had their ass whipped."

* * *

A half hour later there was a knock on the door. It was Latrell, a tall, lanky individual in his forties, wearing a sheepskin-
lined flier's jacket of World War II vintage, and, now that he
was on the run, sporting a thin, graying mustache the same
color as his hair.

When the Nazis at Merk's house, including the unusually quiet
Latrell, saw the various news reports, they wondered aloud about
the best tactics to employ against the hated federals. Norman
and Ian, the other tall Nazi, favored a spearhead militia attack,
strong, violent, and maintained just long enough to forge a corridor to the west, along Highway 12, through which Eleen's men
could escape through the inner moat of mines and the ring of
federals just beyond the minefield. "Be less federals than you
think," Norman posited. "How many helos did they say? 'Bout
eight, maybe ten. So what've we got—about a hundred feds,
including mortar crews? Bigger their circle, the less minefield
they can cover. And it's in a fucking blizzard. If the militia's
quiet enough, they could slip through a corridor in five, ten
minutes."

"What about the mines?" Andrew asked.

Zane was looking to Norman for an answer. "Listen, we
don't need a fucking freeway here," Norman said. "All you
need is a foot-wide path to walk out."

"Yeah," Zane conceded. "But how do we clear it?"

A smile of admiration was on Vance's lips at Zane's use of
"we," the Nazis immediately assuming they'd be involved in
any rescue attempt. Say what you wanted about the Nazis—
Vance had to admit they were warriors, unafraid to fight the
federals no matter how outnumbered.

"We clear the minefield with snakes," Norman said, looking
over at Vance. "You must have some in your Yakima detachment." A "snake" was a long, coiled rubber-hose-like flexitube
containing explosive charges every meter, which, when fired by
mortar above a minefield, rapidly uncoiled to lie across the minefield like a very long snake. When detonated, the snake's ex-

plosive power created sufficient overpressure to detonate mines along its entire length, creating a safe corridor several feet across through the minefield.

"Yes," Vance answered unhurriedly, his tone lacking the sense of urgency exhibited by the Nazis. "But by the time the Yakima group is alerted and can get through those mountain passes—*if* they can get through in a blizzard—it'll be too late."

Merk, despite not considering himself the equal of Vance when it came to strategy, threw in his lot with the Nazis. "We can alert Yakima easy enough," he said. "Just a phone call away."

"I know that," Vance replied. "The problem is, by the time they get halfway there, it could be all over."

"Well, it will be if we don't do something fast," Norman said, glancing impatiently at the other three Nazis as he spoke, his irritated tone and body language drawing in the support of his comrades, whom he nearly always called *Kamerad*, as if he were German. The question in his Aryan eyes was clear enough: What in hell was wrong with Vance? He was the highest ranking militia officer next to the mysterious Nordstrom, the man Norman and his *Kamerads* spent driving around and guarding twenty-four hours a day. He was the man responsible for everything in the organization, including the forthcoming "unofficial" mass rally of "ex-militias" in Spokane, a direct in-your-face challenge to the federal government. And yet now Vance seemed to be paralyzed by indecision. "I know it's snowing there," Norman told him. "But a relief column from Yakima might make it in time."

"At least," Merk put in censoriously, "we should try to help our boys out."

"And what if our rescue team is cut up?" Vance said. "The federals are hearing this battle courtesy of CNN and Murdoch the same as we are, and they have more resources than we do. Plus they've got airpower."

"Not in the snow they haven't," Merk said. "That grounds pretty much anything they've got."

"Especially," Norman added, "when Eleen's boys are so

close to the federals. Federals drop anything from the air, they're just as likely to hit their own."

"So," Vance said, "I order in a militia company—it's still a static situation. The federals simply move in more troops. This isn't our kind of war, gentlemen. In a mobile war, yes, we'd stand a good chance, but Eleen's trapped. Throwing in more militia is like throwing good money after bad."

"You sayin'," Norman charged, "that your trapped boys aren't good enough to rescue . . . not worth . . ."

"You know precisely what I mean, Norman. Eleen's fighting heroically. They're first-rate troops, top of the line. Fought and outmaneuvered Freeman's mop-up boys all the way up from the Columbia River."

"Then they're worth rescuing," Norman retorted.

"Where's your phone?" Vance asked, his tone one of exasperation.

"Kitchen," Merk said.

"Use your cellular," Zane said.

"In this weather?" Ian said.

Vance shook his head. "Never mind the weather. A land line's more secure. I'll have to go to code anyway, so everyone stay out here in the living room."

"Understood," Norman said, relieved that at last Vance was finally going to do something. Even if Vance was using a number-for-word "one-time" pad, the message shouldn't take him that long.

When Vance walked into the kitchen, May was there pounding dough. "If you'll excuse me," he said. She left grumpily, slapping her hands on her apron, a white cloud of flour rising.

CHAPTER TEN

THE SOUND OF the mortars that threatened to cut Eleen's men to pieces was being picked up by the feds' mikes and being fed into the CNN broadcast. Though viewers around the world could see only CNN reporter Marte Price in her parka veiled by a curtain of snow, they could hear the snow-muffled *crump* of mortar rounds exploding, and short, often frenzied stabs of conversation in the background.

"Marte," said Linden Soles, the CNN anchor's voice from Atlanta, "have you been able to ascertain how many militia are trapped in the area and just how big that area is?"

"Linden, as far as—" At the sound of another salvo of mortar rounds, Marte Price instinctively flinched, then continued. "—as far as I can tell, the helo-borne federal troops still have the militia completely surrounded in a circular area about a half mile in diameter. Weather conditions are appallingly bad—it's well below freezing—but federal forces here under the command of Major Irwin believe this will not further impede operations. We can't say for sure, Linden, but—" Static invaded the screen, and for a moment Marte Price was gone, some viewers erroneously believing that the bursts of static were the noise of machine-gun fire. Only the voice feed came through. "Linden, we can't say for sure because of course we're not privy to Major Irwin's strategy, but it would seem that the federal troops are prepared for a waiting game. Sooner or later the militia's going to run out of ammunition and food. Remember, Linden, this renegade group of militiamen refused to surrender to Freeman's federal forces—" Marte had to glance down at her notes, which were flapping furiously in the blizzard. "This militia force, reportedly led by a Lieutenant Eleen—though that hasn't been confirmed—have traveled all the way from the Columbia River. So they're bound to be exhausted and, one would think, short of supplies."

"Yes," Linden Soles answered, "though of course, Marte, one could assume that the surrounding federal troops in that mountainous area might soon have the same problem of running out of food and ammunition."

"The federals might not have that problem, Linden. The scuttlebutt here is that snow crews are attempting to clear the road to the east so that resupply from Yakima will be possible."

"Uh-huh. Is there *any* chance, Marte, of the militia being resupplied?"

"Well of course, Linden, the militia as a whole have surrendered by order of their General Nordstrom and have supposedly laid down their arms, Eleen's men notwithstanding. Officially, there's nothing the militia as a whole can do to help their comrades, although it's clear that General Nordstrom, whoever and wherever he is, must be under considerable pressure from the militias all around the United States to intervene here to attempt a—" Static invaded the picture, and this time a noise in the background, like linoleum being torn, was indeed machine-gun fire.

Vance gave the Yakima militia a string of numbers which the commander, Douglas Berne, took down, then stroked off after every seventh number. Vance knew that unless Berne had pressed his phone's star symbol and 69, he would not know the number from which the call had been placed.

The FBI, however, *had* pressed star 69 and a few other buttons as well for a number-perfect intercept printout, and notified FBI agent Linda Seth in Yakima and Bill Trey in Spokane to be on standby for a possible visit to the Merk farm, beyond the mountains and the raging blizzard. Within minutes copies of the numerical sequence Vance sent had been faxed to the National Security Agency in Fort Meade, Maryland. In the old days, under Hoover, the FBI would have kept the message strictly for Bureau distribution, but under this President, any bureaucrat guilty of holding on to such information because of interdepartmental jealousy would be severely reprimanded if not canned outright. Still, having a copy of the message at FBI HQ in Washington, NSA in Virginia, or in any other federal agency, didn't mean you knew what the message said, and now a computer analysis was under way. A cipher specialist, or code-breaker, at NSA sat and thought about it for a while. "The message," he told his assistant, "is from suspected militia, right?"

"Right," confirmed Sally Winn, a bright B.A. out of Princeton who'd discovered that a major in English literature wasn't exactly in hot demand in the business world, but who had an affinity for foreign languages, especially Spanish, America's second language. Computers that could do a code search were one way of attacking the message, but English majors had their uses, such as feeding the computers with RELPS, or regional literacy pools. If Sally Winn had the name of any region in the United States or Canada, she could tell you the most commonly read books, for it was almost certain that a number-for-letter code referred to a book, the first three numbers—a combination of any three numerals—being its pagination, the second two numerals indicating the number of a paragraph on the given page, and the last two of the seven numerals indicating the letters of the alphabet. But the key to all this was what book was being referred to by the seven-number groups. In the old days, *Catcher in the Rye* was a favorite among foreign agents because it was so popular and so widely read you could get a copy easily, especially in used book shops, and no one would look twice at anyone reading the Salinger book.

"What d'you think, Sally?"

She had short, blond hair with a pert curl near her left eye, which she brushed away in an unconscious manner, tilting her head forward as she did so, revealing the nape of her neck.

"Militia?" she said, pursing her dark red lips. "In the Northwest I'd say *The Anarchist Cookbook* or the *Poor Man's James Bond*, Volume Two, but general availability is the problem for a militia with members from all over. With that in mind I'd say the Bible was a pretty good bet."

Her boss nodded, adding, "Lot of Hispanics up around Yakima."

"Uh-huh," she said. "But I wouldn't choose a Spanish Bible. Not nearly as widely distributed as English Bibles."

"The Gideon," he proffered. "In every hotel, motel, in the country."

"Sí," she said for a little fun, but her boss didn't even crack a smile. His brother, a member of the 82nd Airborne out of Fort Bragg, had been killed by the militia in the war. He wanted to crack the code as quickly as possible. A lot of people, including his nineteen-year-old son, a chopper pilot at Special Operations at Fort Walton, Florida, expected the militia en masse to start fighting again, all over the contiguous United States and Alaska.

"All right," he told her while watching the computer screen. "Let's do a search. New Testament or Old?"

"Old," she said. "Randy Weaver-type fundamentalists and the militia especially like the Old Testament. Fire and brimstone."

"And Revelations," he said darkly. "Apocalypse."

"That's true," she replied. "Trouble is, the Bible is so obvious, isn't it?"

"Not to today's kids," he said. "They know more about *Star Trek* than Moses."

Sally couldn't tell whether he regretted the fact or not, his facial expression one of utter concentration at the computer screen.

They were correct. The computer's search was remarkably straightforward, its analysis taking less than eleven minutes. Every set of seven numbers was applied to the most common edition of the Gideon Bible, King James version—the militia detested modern Bibles with their heretical "Our Mother/Father who art in Heaven." The number-for-letter code was coming out of Genesis through to Leviticus:

> Attack enemy supply convoy wherever possible. Do not attempt rescue of militia. Nordstrom. Acknowledge.

As Yakima militia commander Douglas Berne decoded the message, both he and the White House—the latter having just received the decode from NSA—were nonplussed. Why bother striking the federal convoy which was now on the way from Yakima to Packwood when at that very moment it was Major Irwin's federal force at Packwood that needed to be attacked if the trapped militiamen had any hope of being extricated?

It seemed as if Nordstrom's militia was cutting off its nose to spite its face, or as presidential aide Delorme put it, was being told to fight "with one hand tied behind its back." Hit the convoy but not the main force?

"It makes no sense," the President argued. "If you're going to break the truce terms anyway, why wouldn't you go all the way?"

"Maybe," put in Army C-in-C Shelbourne, stepping over the President's pet sheepdog to the map stand, "they haven't got the capability." He drew an imaginary line with his finger east of the Columbia River mouth. "Freeman beat the crap out of 'em all along the Columbia front and in the Alvord." The Alvord was a desert of playas, dried-up salt lakes, in the far southeast of Oregon, spread out below the massif that was Steens Mountain. "And," Shelbourne continued in his down-to-earth explanation, "we took hundreds of militia prisoner before they had a chance to run home and hide their fatigues." The general turned to the chief executive. "Mr. President, they're a spent force, which explains this token half-assed directive of Nordstrom's. And of course now we know his instructions to this Yakima group whose leader is, ah . . ."

"Berne," Delorme said. "Douglas Berne."

"Yes," the general continued. "Well, now that we know his

orders, we can alert the convoy. Send out a large mobile force on the supply convoy's flanks."

"It's too late for that," Delorme interjected. "My information is a convoy's already in the mountains and past Tieton Dam. It'll be approaching White Pass by now."

"Then we could airdrop supplies," the President said.

The Air Force chief looked up from the map and peered over his reading glasses. It never ceased to amaze him how little the civilian population, including the President, knew about the Air Force's limited capability in bad weather. They had seen too many movies.

"Mr. President, we can't do a supply drop by pallet or chute drums in a blizzard, particularly not in rugged terrain. This Eleen joker's militia is in such close proximity to our troops that the militia could end up getting half the supplies." He was thinking of the disaster that had befallen the massive drop on Arnheim in 1944 when the Nazis ended up eating chocolate and other stores intended for the Allies.

"It can be done, Mr. President," Shelbourne responded, his optimistic tone concealing any doubt he had.

"But at what cost?" the Air Force C-in-C cut in.

"Our choppers flew in it," Shelbourne reported.

"Your choppers," the Air Force general said, "had no option, besides which, as I understand it, the blizzard wasn't fully upon them until after they dropped this ring of mines. And—"

"Gentlemen," the President interjected. "This isn't the time for any interservice rivalry. We have to focus on the problem at hand. What about all this pinpoint, black light capability I've been told about? The attack on Baghdad, et cetera?"

"Mr. President, that was on a clear night when there was no danger of blue on blue. But in a blizzard with wind gusts up to eighty miles per hour, zero visibility in whiteout conditions, not even the best pilots can manage that."

"I'm not talking about sending in C-17s or Hercules here. Couldn't we use big helos? Chinooks?"

The Air Force chief felt the pressure in the room, all eyes on him. "Sir, you're my commander-in-chief and I'll do whatever you order me to do, but it'd be terribly risky and ..." He paused.

"Go on," urged the President.

"Well, sir, we have the best of it by far. Our men under Major Irwin have the militia outnumbered by more than two to one, and we've got them locked in a pocket with a minefield encircling them. I propose we wait till—" He glanced at his Rolex. "—0600 ... dawn. That'll be in a couple of hours. The militia's not going anywhere with those mines all about them. Come dawn, the blizzard will probably have abated. Could be clear weather. And by then the convoy from Yakima will have reached them with resupply. Nordstrom's coded message notwithstanding, the militia won't have time to assemble a force big enough to stop them, and the mountain logistics works against them."

The President concurred. There was no point sending pilots into a maelstrom of bad weather. He remembered Jimmy Carter and the catastrophic fiasco in the sand blizzard of Iran, choppers colliding, American bodies all over the landing zone. He had no intention of acting too hastily and ending up doing a Carter. Hell, it had cost Carter a second term.

"All right, General. Till dawn."

"Yes, sir."

"But I want them beaten. Decisively." The President told both generals, "I'm determined to go up to Spokane, in the heart of the Northwest's militia. I have to show them and every other American, and our investors abroad, that I, and not the goddamned militias, am running this country. And gentlemen—" His gaze around the room took in everyone from Delorme and Attorney General Helen Wyeth, to the Joint Chiefs of Staff. "—I do not want to go to Spokane with egg on my face. Is that understood?"

The murmurs of assent ranged from a studied acquiescence from the Air Force to a "Yes, sir!" from the Army. The Navy nodded—after all, the Navy was out of it. This had been the first continental conflict on American soil since the Civil War.

"Doesn't mean," the President continued, reaching down and stroking the sheepdog's head, "that we have to be brutal."

"Beg your pardon, sir," General Shelbourne said. "It nearly always is. Brutal, I mean."

The President frowned. "Well, meanwhile I want that convoy from Yaki—" He hesitated.

"Yaki*maw*," Delorme said.

"Yes," the President said. "I want it heavily protected."

"There's not enough time," Delorme said. "Not before dawn."

"We could send Douglas Freeman in," General Shelbourne suggested. "Special Forces. He's had a lot of exp—"

"No, by God!" the President retorted. "Not Freeman. One, putting in someone of that rank would immediately elevate this incident to a national crisis in the news media. And two, the man is a public relations disaster. No wonder they call him Blood and Guts Two. One Patton was enough for this country. No, keep him leashed."

The Air Force looked for ground support, but seeing none, dived in anyway. "Well, sir, I thought it was, *is,* a national crisis."

"Of course it is," the President snapped. "I'm not a *complete* idiot, Charles. I understand perhaps better than anyone in this room how serious it is. Goddammit, if we're seen to buckle under this direct militia challenge, every goddamn militia will feel free to weigh in, and before you know it, the whole country will become embroiled in internecine fighting and civil war. *Again!* But to send in Freeman would signify . . ." He was lost for words.

"Panic," someone said, and immediately wished they hadn't.

"Panic! We're not talking about panic."

"We're going to let Major Irwin handle it," Shelbourne put in.

The President looked up irritably over his bifocals, which made him look sixty-five instead of the fit fifty-five he was. "Yes. Irwin. He's the man on the spot, isn't he? He's got—" He swiveled his chair toward Shelbourne. "How many militia are there, around fifty?"

"Forty something," Shelbourne answered. "At least that's

the information we have—or *had*. Until the militia shot the dog."

"They killed a dog?" the President asked, clearly shocked.

"Yes, sir," Shelbourne said.

The President was shaking his head, and glanced at his own dog lying on the Oval Office's carpet, his shaggy head resting on the Great Seal of the United States. "Callous bastards!"

Shelbourne looked over at the Air Force general, the latter's lower lip thinning in an expression of disbelief at what the President had just said. It was obvious to the Air Force chief, as it was to Shelbourne and one or two other Gulf War veterans in the Oval Office, that the President had never been in combat. First thing you did to any canine sniffing around your position was kill it, as quickly as possible. The unspoken exchange between Shelbourne and the Air Force general gave Shelbourne an idea for a coup in the war of information being waged between this Nordstrom, whoever he was, and Washington— *mano a mano* between the commander-in-chief of the U.S. Militia Corps and the commander-in-chief of all U.S. federal forces.

"Very well," the President answered. "That's all for now. While I'm in Spokane the vice-president will be managing day-to-day affairs." He addressed Shelbourne. "Anything really urgent, General, page me, but I emphasize to all of you, keep as low a profile as possible on this thing." He surveyed everyone in the room. "The lower the better. Among a host of other troubles, the dollar has taken the worst beating so far this century because of the militia rebellion. We are just now winning back investor confidence from abroad, and to reestablish some notion of good order in those rebellious parts of the country, particularly in the Northwest and Southeast, I reiterate, ladies and gentlemen, the whole purpose of the trip to Spokane is to show clearly that we are not afraid of the militia, that we will *not* be intimidated by them. *And* that *we*, ladies and gentlemen, and *not* the militia, are in control."

"Hear, hear!" It was the FBI deputy director, a Harvard man

whose graduate studies at Oxford had left him with British expressions of appreciation. Everyone began clapping. The President smiled for the first time that morning.

As the meeting broke up, Shelbourne motioned over to Delorme.

"Can I help you, General?"

"I think," Shelbourne replied, "that you and I can help everybody. That is, everybody on the federal side."

"How's that?"

"I suggest you put out a press release of the situation vis-à-vis the militia and let it be known—a 'well-placed source' if you like—how the tracking dog our boys used at Packwood was *butchered*. You know how to phrase it better than I. I think it would make for a nice short paragraph or two on the irony."

Delorme got the point. It would enrage every pet owner in the country, draw them to the government side, but the irony eluded him.

"Well," the general explained, "the fact is, the flash point for this whole damn thing was that militia guy, Ames, shooting that wolf—a protected species—up in Alaska. Environmentalists outraged—federal marshals go up to arrest him. A shootout, he kills them, and bam! We're in a war. And then when Freeman's Special Force went up against the militia, they shot one of *his* dogs."

"You think animal lovers will rise up?" Delorme asked half jokingly.

"Try it and see," Shelbourne said. "I think you'll be surprised. And I think you'll agree that we need all the support we can get. Signal and human intelligence, including NSA phone intercepts from all over the country, confirm that the militias have more support than any of us realized. From people fed up with the IRS and government in general, to the drug cartels pouring money into the militias to fight us, there's widespread support for Nordstrom's army. And—" The general and Delorme had begun moving out of the Oval Office, Shelbourne glancing about to make sure he wouldn't be overheard. "—worst of all, SIGINT and HUMINT confirm that ever since the Clinton presidency there has been substantial support for the militias in the armed forces. And I'm not talking here about the skinheads, drug dealers, and malcontents like McVeigh. We're talking whole *units* whose sympathizers are much more in tune with right-wing causes than with the liberal policies of the government. National Guard units are particularly unreliable. They're all local members who reflect community values, and in a lot of places those values are firmly ensconced on the right."

"What kind of strength are we talking here?" Delorme asked.

"In all, divisional strength."

"Jesus!" Delorme was no military expert, but he knew a division was around eighteen thousand men.

"I'm not exaggerating," Shelbourne continued. "And I don't have to tell you how one bad apple in a unit can affect a whole company. Remember all the fragging incidents in 'Nam? You have one back-shooter in your unit, the entire outfit freaks out. One guy who hated officers, hated the draft—murdered three C.O.'s before the CID rooted him out. That whole unit, a battalion, a thousand men, wasn't worth a pinch o' shit until that got straightened out. Hell, we already know there are Nazi cells all over. And you know as well as I do that if one link in the chain of command fails, then the whole chain breaks."

"All right," Delorme said. "I'll make the point about the dog, but I don't think it'll have as much impact as you think."

"Uh-huh," Shelbourne replied. "You ever owned a pet?"

"I'm not an animal lover."

"Then with all due respect, Joe, maybe you shouldn't write the news release."

"I'll do it," Delorme said. "I know the buzz words for the Animal Rights lobby. 'Wanton disregard for animals and their habitat,' et cetera, et cetera."

"There you go," Shelbourne said. "And find out the dog's name. That'll make it more poignant."

They were now standing by Shelbourne's limo beneath the portico, and Delorme asked him, "General, if you'd been in this militia officer's position—Eleen—and you'd seen the dog, what would you have done?"

Shelbourne was taken aback by the naiveté of the question. "Shoot the son of a bitch."

"And you still think it will bring people to our side?"

"Absolutely."

And the general was absolutely right. CNN, starved for details of the blizzard-bound battle near Packwood, went back to Marte Price for an update, but even she, a veteran of the Gulf and other wars, was unable to contribute much. To her chagrin, the Murdoch network scooped her with the name of the dog, "Rusty."

The outrage from the general public was swift and loud. Radio phone-in shows and TV talk shows were bombarded by legions of angry pet owners. Parents all over the country jammed the net and news stations with reports of children being traumatized by the news reports of Rusty, who now presently lay frozen stiff in the cold arctic storm that had swept down through the Cascades. Once the Murdoch network had broken the story, CNN was quick to catch up, with Marte Price having "*bust*ed," as CNN staffers in Atlanta referred to her exploit, her way into an exclusive interview with one of the federal dog handlers, his Malinois tracking dog the same brownish color as Rusty.

What surprised and elated the White House staff was the outburst of antimilitia sentiment from Europe, particularly in England, where dogs and cats, indeed pets of all kinds, were often considered as having privileges accorded not even human family members. British opinion was quick to point out what they called the "striking similarity" between IRA and militia "terrorists," both organizations charged with having "absolutely no regard for innocent bystanders—animal or human." The White House as well as the Prime Minister's office in 10 Downing Street knew the comparison between the Irish Republican Army and the United States Militia Corps to be completely askew, but it was in neither government's interest to correct the comparison. The President was encouraged by a six-point rise—

up from fifty-six percent—in public support for how the federals were handling the Packwood "situation," as the White House press called it.

The President buzzed Delorme from his smaller workroom down from the Oval Office. Delorme walked quickly down the hallway.

"Mr. President?"

"Joe, your release about those bastards killing that dog has worked wonders."

"Thank you, sir."

"Quite frankly, I didn't think you were much of an animal lover."

"I'm not, Mr. President." He flashed a smile, glancing down at the President's pooch sprawled indolently on the carpet. "Benjamin excepted. But I know a lot of people who are."

"Well, good for you. You have any more good ideas like that, you run with 'em."

"I will, sir."

CHAPTER ELEVEN

IT IF HADN'T been for the "sentimental slop," as one CNN producer described the dog story, Eleen would never have thought of a possible way out. By now, fully a quarter of his men had been killed, or wounded so badly they couldn't fight, which left him with thirty-one men at the edge of the minefield. Despite the noise of the battle—easing somewhat because the federals were running out of mortar rounds—Eleen tried to remember all that he'd been told about minefields, especially the lessons taught him by Lucky McBride, the legendary militia-man, a 'Nam and Gulf War veteran who recalled "Stormin' Norman" Schwarzkopf ordering his men in Vietnam to use shaving cream to mark the positions of mines to guide his men out, since they had no other means available. But Schwarzkopf had been on a tropical hillside, not in a mountain region during a blizzard whiteout that lifted enough only now and then to reveal the body of the dead WOLVES dog beyond the snow-crested slit trenches that the trapped militiamen had dug. Some of them had not stopped digging until it was several feet deep, affording them more cover from shrapnel.

"Mortars are easing off," Mulvane said.

"Until they're resupplied," an M-60 gunner remarked.

"Yeah, well," Corporal Mulvane growled, "gives us a chance to dig in until we get relief."

"You sure about that?" the militiaman from the next foxhole asked.

"Don't worry," said Eleen, who had no doubt God was on his side. "General Nordstrom'll send a relief column."

The firing died off. "Sounds like the bastards are running short on ammo as well," Mulvane remarked.

"We should do something," said the man in the foxhole, now invisible because of blinding snow.

"Like what?" retorted Mulvane. "Run through the fucking minefield? You're a bright fucker, Billy."

"That's enough," Eleen said. "We'll have to wait until we're relieved. Dig in, secure our position. They can't see us any more than we can see them. Mulvane, how many claymores have we got left?"

"A grand total of two."

"Well, put them in front of us in case the federals do rush us."

"Rush us?" Mulvane said, his tone angry and impatient. "Come right through the minefield?"

"They laid the mines," Eleen explained, "before the snow covered them up, so they'll probably know a path through it."

"Shit, sir," Mulvane replied, "they didn't have time to mark a minefield. You can't do that with air deliverable—they just tumble down higgledy-piggledy. No mapping those bastards."

Eleen felt stupid. Mulvane was right. The federals' moat of mines, now covered by snow, would have been laid completely at random. But that didn't mean the federals wouldn't attack. Once they got a mine clearer—an M-1 tank, for instance, fitted with a blade or chains—they'd explode a path through and finish off his militiamen. It was simply a matter of time.

"Damn!" Eleen said, shocking Mulvane, who'd never heard the Mormon captain say anything stronger than "Darn!" The truth was, as Mulvane knew, Eleen was tired, and maybe just as scared as the rest of them. They were all veterans, as used to war as possible in a fatal business, but most of them had never been trapped as they were now, encircled by a minefield.

"General Nordstrom'll see us through, right?" Eleen said.

"Yeah," Billy said from his foxhole. Though shivering from cold and fatigue, he continued packing snow hard about the top of his hole. It would soon be icy hard and might just deflect a bullet.

As the snowfall increased, the mortar shelling fell off even more. Whether there was a connection between the two, Eleen didn't know, but he wondered about the dog. Perhaps its camera eye and listening microphone had kept transmitting pictures and sounds even after it was dead. Or perhaps the heavier snowfall was proving too thick a curtain for the federals' electronic gadgetry to work. Perhaps the federals were down to their last three-round pack of 81mm rounds. Whatever the reason, he was happy for the respite, and told his men if the mortar offensive stopped altogether, they might crawl forward and, using their knives, probe for mines.

"That's a long shot," Corporal Mulvane opined.

"I'm open to suggestions," Eleen said, exhibiting the kind of open-mindedness that particularly endeared him to his men. He might be a legendary fighter like Lucky McBride, but he had never affected the pompous, if unspoken, airs that some officers on both sides assumed.

"We could backtrack," Mulvane said.

"Uh-huh," Eleen replied. "Where to?"

Mulvane shrugged.

"We'll hunker down here for a while," Eleen said. "Wait for—" A mortar round exploded. Everyone instinctively ducked—even Eleen, who, despite his militiamen's apparently hopeless position, nevertheless felt that his number had not yet come up. He knew God was by him, that God understood the reasons for the militia's stand against what he considered an oppressive central government whose invasiveness permeated even the sanctity of the family. Washington's dictatorial voice couldn't tell men how they should live.

The snow kept falling, and Jeremy Eleen thought of Christ in the manger and of Ruth—how it had been snowing outside the small church in Olympia—and when a guest at the reception asked impertinently where they would be going for their honeymoon, that Ruth had said they were going up over the Cascades, to ski up at Mount Baker. The guest, looking down at them condescendingly over half glasses perched on his nose, had said, "The Cascade road? In midwinter? That's risky." Ruth had fixed him with a smile and replied, "Life's risky, Mr. Piedmont."

It wasn't until they passed through Winthrop, where, Ruth reminded her new husband, Fenimore Cooper wrote *The Virginian*, that Jeremy realized old Piedmont had a point, the windshield icing up so badly that even with the defroster on high there was only a small, clear semicircle of glass no bigger than six inches in diameter. The remainder of the windshield was a solid layer of ice through which the occasional oncoming headlight glared like a riotous moon, momentarily blinding as snowflakes raced at him like incoming tracers. Back then, ten years ago, when they were so newly married, the whole world buried in snow had looked new, taking on an ethereal aspect. Being alone with the person he loved most, amid the Cascade snowstorm, he was more excited by the prospects of the honeymoon than afraid of the increasing violence of the storm.

"You have chains, Jeremy?" Ruth had asked. Her silhouette, like that of Ingrid Bergman, he thought, was starkly revealed by the glare of headlights. He swerved away from the vehicle and drove into a culvert's thick wall of snow, which collapsed on their vehicle like a ton of powdered sugar, burying them. It had all happened so fast, neither he nor Ruth knew how deeply buried they were. What had struck him then, and now, was how calm Ruth was. Although they'd been going out for over a year at Washington State University, they had never been in a really tense situation.

It had taken them a half hour to dig out, and then he'd moved back and forth, from inside the car to outside, to warm his hands just long enough to affix one, then another chain to each tire. By the time he'd made his fourth attempt to attach the chain to the third tire, Ruth was shivering violently, but when he insisted that she put on his coat, she shook her head adamantly. Besides, he knew she was right. Out there in the all but uninhabited Cascade Mountains, if he froze up and couldn't finish putting on the chains, they'd be in deep trouble.

Now, the mortars were silent, and the only noise he and the militiamen could hear was the ungodly wailing of the blizzard about their ears, the cold so intense Eleen could feel his ears burning, not too far from being frostbitten. All around them nothing but the swirling white maelstrom of the storm. "We'll go in file," he said croakily, his throat dry from fatigue and fear. But he didn't show it—it was his job not to show it. "Me first." He drew the knife from its ankle scabbard and moved forward, probing gently, the handle feeling frozen even through his glove. The temptation was to let the steel blade plunge into the powder snow, but he knew he had to control it. Too much force on the knife would do more than find a mine; it would explode it in his face. Beneath the cotton wool softness of the most recent layer of powder snow, he could feel the blade crunching through earlier, more crystallized snow as if it was passing through coarse sand. There was a whiplike crack in the air. Then nothing. A stray shot? Someone's rifle off safety? It was a little known fact that among raw troops there were often more casualties from accidents than from the enemy. But none of Eleen's men was green, they were as battle hardened as he. He paid the noise no mind. Perhaps it was a federal firing wildly, trying to get the militia to respond, pinpointing their position. Jeremy withdrew the knife from the gravelly snow and, sliding a few inches forward, probed again. His main worry was that soon the snow would become so deep that a blade wouldn't sink far enough to touch any mines. The blade tip struck something hard—he could feel the slight, almost imperceptible jar.

There were times when even he admitted to himself that he wished it were all over—that an explosion would at least finish the unbearable tension.

Years ago, by the time he'd gotten the chain on the last tire, Ruth was in the first stage of hypothermia. An hour later she was dead.

Yakima militiaman Ray Marsden and his son Danny, who'd been in the mountains, hunting, when the blizzard struck, were now lying down behind a hillock of snow after laying a puncture strip across the road east of Packwood. They knew about the predicament of Eleen's militia from shortwave news broadcasts, and they'd wanted to help—by trying to stop the federal supply convoy. Now, they could hear, or rather feel, the deep throbbing of approaching trucks. Given the extraordinary muffling of sound that comes with snow, it meant the vehicles must be no more than a hundred yards off in the whiteout. Then they saw the squarish shape of a Hummer, grader blade attached.

"Goddamn!" Ray Marsden said, the militia having planned and trained for the most obvious contingency—fighting in the warmer warring months. They had, of course, thought of snow as an outside possibility, but nothing as deep as this.

"Maybe the blade'll clear our puncture strip," Danny said.

"C'mon," Ray replied. "Let's get back to the Blazer."

Crouching low, they trudged behind a copse of snow-laden pine to their truck, which Ray flicked into four-wheel mode and drove off from behind the hill down along the snow-clogged road.

"What are we gonna do now?" Danny asked.

"Plan B," his father said. "Roadblock. Cut one of them poplars down by the creek—if we have time. When they hit the puncture strip, they'll probably stop for a few minutes, trying to figure out what to do. Soon as we get down there, start up that saw. I'll cover you from the rise."

Danny said nothing. The determined look of the Hummer back there beyond the hill had suddenly brought home to him that this wasn't some kind of war game he and his friends were used to playing in the foothills.

Had the two Marsdens waited for a few minutes atop the hill, they would have seen just how determined the National Guard convoy was. The driver of the Hummer felt a slight hesitation as his vehicle's grader blade struck the buried puncture strip. He pumped the brakes to signal the ten-ton truck behind him, the first of ten, to stop, then reversed for a few yards. One soldier exited the Hummer and walked forward along the front left tire's tracks to inspect what the hidden obstacle was. Another man, his head sticking through the Hummer's rear hatch, manned the ring-mounted .50 caliber machine gun in order to cover his comrade. The first soldier saw a black steel spike of the puncture strip, the Hummer behind him impatiently sending up a steaming column of exhaust into the frigid air. The soldier, a black man, walked back to the Hummer.

"First sight of the enemy, brothers. Fucking strip. Out with the old entrenching tools."

"Fuck," another said, getting out. "How 'bout you, Weston?" he asked the black man on the machine gun.

"Nah. Got to man the point fifty, man. Standard procedure for possible ambush. Right?"

"Yeah, right," the other soldier said, in good humor while feigning exasperation. "Careful someone don't shoot your fuckin' head off."

"No way, José. Can't see beyond their noses in this weather."

"Fer Christ's sake," the driver said in a strangulated voice, almost a whisper, a Saint Christopher medal suspended from the roof in full shudder from the vibration of the idling Hummer. "Keep your voices down. Move the strip. Let's go!"

It had taken less than five minutes to peel the spiked steel strip out like the backbone of a cooked fish, dumping it unceremoniously to the side of the road. As the first Hummer began to move again, the whole convoy—maintaining radio silence—buzzed with rumor as to what the delay up front had been about. By the time the tenth and last truck in the convoy got the message, three militiamen were said to have been killed.

"Never heard no shot."

"Hand-to-hand."

"Fuck! They all around us?"

"Dunno."

The driver of the last truck slid open the Judas panel and looked back at twenty cold National Guardsmen. "You guys hear that? Bastards are all around us. Look sharp!"

"You look sharp—we can't see a fucking thing back here."

"I mean, be ready."

"Hey, we're ready, Jack! You watch the fucking road. Okay?"

"I *am* watching the fucking road."

"Well that's good, 'cause we don't want you running over no mines. Blow us to fuck!"

"You dork. We safe, man. Front end's gonna get blowed if anyone does."

"Oh, is that right?"

"Yeah, that's right."

"Fuck it is. You ever heard of DEBRE?" He pronounced it *Debris*. "Detonation by remote control."

"Holy shit!" the driver said, instinctively shifting position, lifting himself a little off the seat as if he could somehow will his genitals higher into a safer position.

"He's pullin' yer leg," the other driver said.

"You pullin' my leg, soldier?" the first driver asked.

"Hell, no. Like those little toy cars kids play with. Just push the button, man, and you're with Jesus!"

"Hey," put in another Guardsman, holding an M-16 with an infrared scope attached. "Cut that out."

"What?"

"Taking the Lord's name in vain."

"What are you? All high and mighty? You should be in the militia."

"Yeah, well I agree with them about that."

"Ah, stick it up your ass."

"All right, you two," a sergeant growled. "That's enough. Save your spittle for the militia."

"Hope I never see the fuckers," said the man who'd offended his religious comrade. "Is *fuckers* all right, Mr. Billy Graham? Can I say *fuckers*?"

"That's enough!" the sergeant repeated sharply. "I'm warning you two, if you don't—" They lurched forward as the truck braked hard and started a slow but inexorable slide, its left rear fender slamming into the bank of piled snow at the side of the road. The driver heard a string of obscenities from the back of the truck, then a sharp crack. Somebody shouted, "They're shooting at us!" and there was a commotion as the National Guardsmen scrambled about, trying to take cover beneath the fold-down board seats, the sergeant yelling at them to get out of the truck. There was another crack and they heard glass shattering and the driver screaming he was hit. Panic surged all down the line, from the rear truck in the snowbank to the front vehicle behind the Hummer that had been stopped around the turn by a felled tree across the road. The Hummer's machine gunner swung the .50 from twelve to six o'clock on the right flank, unable to see anyone but squeezing off a couple of bursts in fright.

Two hundred yards away, on a rise ahead and east of the convoy, Danny Marsden, sighting through his rifle's scope, fired again, this time into a truck midway down the line, no more than a blur in the falling snow.

Panic still gripped the convoy, several officers yelling at their men to spread out, others shouting contrary orders, as no one was exactly sure of where the shots were coming from.

"You see a flash?"

"See nothin'."

Another shot.

"Take cover!"

No one needed the order. Everybody was ducking under the trucks, or using the wheels on the western side, the shouted consensus being that the enemy shots were coming from somewhere to the east.

"Get the I.F. on the bastard!"

"I've *got* the fucking I.F.!"

"See anything?"

"Nothin'."

"Well, keep it—"

"Got a hot spot! Range, three o'clock—one-niner-zero."

"Right!" an exuberant lieutenant shouted. "Three o'clock, everyone," and to a sergeant, "Johnson, your squad on the left flank. Marty—right flank. Take 'em!"

"Take 'em, fuck!" one of Johnson's men said. "Take 'em yerself."

"Take 'em," the lieutenant repeated, leading Johnson's squad forward but left of the hot spot. "They move?" he asked the infrared man, shouting into his mike over the noise of the Hummer's .50. "Don't shoot *us*!" he added.

"We won't—"

The lieutenant fell, pistol first, into the snow, cursed and got up, having lost his radio earpiece, which he now fumbled for while at the same time slapping his thigh with the .45, snow falling off it but the barrel still choked with the pinhead-sized balls of powder snow. He looked east again, thought he saw movement, then it was gone. Meanwhile, he tried to keep the right flank patrol in sight, but they had already been swallowed up by the blizzard and he was hesitant to fire at anything lest it be at one of his own.

With the noise of all the firing, especially the .50 putting out long arcs of one-in-four red tracer overhead, it was as difficult for Sergeant Johnson's men on the right flank patrol as it was for the lieutenant to tell whether the militia were still firing.

Then, during a break between the Hummer's .50's bursts, there was a distinct *crack!* The machine gunner's head flew back as if some invisible fist had smashed his face, and he slumped in the hatch, then disappeared noisily from view. Inside the Hummer, a medic reached to cradle the man's head but there was nothing but a lifeless cavity from which a mash of splintered bone and brain poured forth. "Bastards are using dumdums!" the medic shouted.

The infrared scope operator, one of the best of the weekend soldiers, refused to be distracted, keeping the scope fixed on the 190-yard position at about three o'clock. The blur of a heat spot showed above the snow like a watery mirror. "They're still there." The Hummer's .50, its new gunner getting the same information, opened up again. A ball of flame belched skyward from one of the trucks, everyone's eardrums thumped with the sound coming a millisecond after the flash as one of the militia's shots tore through a box of 72mm M-60 ammunition, starting a chain reaction. The ammo truck's gas tank blew, spewing a rain of burning gasoline on trucks on either end of the convoy. Several National Guardsmen dove into the snowbank to save themselves by smothering the flames.

The man holding the I.F. scope heard the commotion. A sliding truck nearly sideswiped him, and he hurried out of the way, taking his eye off the scope. Realigning the scope, he could see the lieutenant leading the squad off to the left. He picked up the heat blotch again and told the lieutenant via radio that the squad must be no more than thirty yards away from the hot spot.

The lieutenant thought he saw something move on the incline up ahead—or maybe it was snow kicked up by shots from the right-hand squad closing. He fired his Colt .45, then dropped it, clasping his face and screaming as he hit the snow. The snow that had been shoved into the gun's barrel when he'd fallen earlier had frozen, and when the bullet struck it, a back blast of cordite seared his face. It completely threw the squad off balance, and thinking the lieutenant had been struck by a militiaman's bullet, they all hit the ground and quickly disappeared in the snow, the only fire directed at the hot spot coming from the right flank squad now opening up with three-round bursts.

When they finally reached the spot, there was no one there—there hadn't been for the last ten minutes. There were only two Grabber D-shaped, seven-hour charcoal-activated hand-warmers of the type used by hunters and skiers to warm appendages. All that remained of Ray Marsden and his son's presence was a patch of black-stained snow where a bullet had penetrated one of the Grabbers.

"Bastards!" the squad's corporal said, his breath frosty in the air. "Flown the fuckin' coop!"

"No sweat," said a tall, black sergeant, motioning toward a snowy rise ahead of them. "Pricks'll be the other side o' that."

"How do you know?" the tail-end Charlie ventured, only now reaching the hot spot.

"Tracks," the black sergeant replied. "All we gotta do is follow 'em."

"Maybe we should head back to the convoy."

The sergeant looked about him at his squad. Every face said, "Go back to the trucks." The sergeant shook his head. "So you want to be sniped at again?" He paused, giving them a moment to take it in. "Better we track 'em down now. We go back to the truck, they can just sneak back, start laying fire on us. You want to do this all again?"

"I say go like fuck in the convoy—get out of the area."

"Have to go mighty fast," another guardsman said, "not to take some hits."

"Exactly," the sergeant agreed. He looked over and saw the lieutenant, the medic wrapping a bandage about his eye. "I'll ask the lieutenant."

The lieutenant told him to take the squad forward. "Keep in radio contact with me. We'll keep going as we started—you, right side of their tracks, my squad on your left, but keep in sight. Our boys are moving a felled tree now. Apparently the road goes into a big right-hand turn up ahead, then crosses a bridge. Meet us on the far side of it. Make sure it isn't booby-trapped."

"Okay," the sergeant said, adding, "You all right, sir?"

"I'll be fine," the lieutenant said, the bandage already blood-ied from a scalp wound over the left eye.

"Look like a pirate," a PFC said. The way the bandage had been wrapped about his head, his hair stood up, and though it would soon be wet with snow, like a mop, the men in both squads were calling him "Kramer" from the *Seinfeld* show. It was the only moment of levity they'd had so far.

"All right," the lieutenant said, looking like hell from cuts and abrasions but adopting their mood. "Then giddyup!"

Both squads, only twenty yards apart in the falling curtain of snow, could hear the muffled sounds of the convoy starting up and the tat-tat-tat of the .50 caliber Browning on the Hummer laying down a V of fire fifty yards ahead. The convoy had moved about a hundred feet past the sidelined tree when the Hum-mer's windshield cracked. The driver's hands were flung away from the steering wheel, blood gushing from his chest. The Hum-mer sped up as his whole body stiffened momentarily as if elec-trocuted, then slumped sideways, falling into the other driver, who was reaching frantically for the wheel. The machine gun-ner above still fired as the vehicle slewed toward the right-hand shoulder. By the time the Hummer was brought to a halt, the co-driver was also dead. The machine gunner, while threading a new belt of .50 rounds, panicked—the gun jammed. A shot ripped through his shoulder, his other hand instinctively reach-ing for the wound as he slid down through the hatch. Falling snow disappeared the moment it touched the warm blood. Everyone was ordered to get out and get down, bodies scram-bling beneath the trucks.

The eye-patched lieutenant had glimpsed a flash—so had the black sergeant and several other National Guardsmen in the right-hand flank. "Must be down by the bridge!" the sergeant said.

"Right, let's go," the lieutenant said into his throat mike. "But careful—don't shoot one another." The lieutenant had a thing about blue on blue, or friendly fire, incidents because he knew that in many an engagement there were more casualties caused by your own than by the enemy. "Remember, you guys," he added, "militias wear surplus World War Two helmets and—"

There was the *crump* of a mortar from the convoy, the muffled hiss of a snow-dirt geyser somewhere ahead, probably near the bridge, though the lieutenant couldn't see it through the blizzard. "Cease firing!" he yelled into the mike, knowing the two squads must be approaching the bridge. "You'll shoot *one another!*"

There was another *crump* and the whistle of shrapnel, both squads going to ground with expletives filling the air, then silence as the convoy's mortar and every other weapon shut down. "We've got his position!" the lieutenant told the convoy's C.O. optimistically. "We'll get him—we've got his tracks!"

"Well, hurry up," the C.O. said. "We've got to reach those boys at Packwood."

It's all right for him, thought the lieutenant. He's probably behind the goddamn Hummer. We've got no protection. "Yes, sir."

Crouching down, convinced the militia sniper or snipers were using thermal scopes and that his squads would soon be in view of the enemy—he guessed there were no more than two—the lieutenant waved his men forward, having stuffed a loosely crumpled Kleenex in his .45 barrel. He had a gut feeling that he would be the first to see them, sobered by the equally strong conviction that they might be first to see him.

They didn't, but by the time the lieutenant had reached the location of the flash, the two militiamen had moved again.

"Cunning bastards," the sergeant said.

"Yeah," the lieutenant agreed, the throbbing pain in his bandaged eye having increased since he'd been hit. "But we still have their tracks. We'll get 'em."

Ray Marsden was trying to bring his breathing under control, the run down to the creek from their last hot spot position having pretty well winded him. Danny was also trying to steady his aim, but it wasn't the run that was making it difficult for him to get a good shot away, it was the fear and excitement.

He had always heard that most men were scared stiff in their baptism of fire, and he was afraid. But, protected by the lip of the creek bank, feeling momentarily safe, he was also exhilarated at having stopped the convoy dead in its tracks—until he saw the shapes of four men emerging from the whiteout off to his right, one of them crouching, carrying what looked like a squad automatic weapon, two others toting M-16 rifles, the fourth—now there were six of them—armed with nothing, it seemed, but handguns. Danny told himself to breathe deeply, exhale—but not totally—hold steady and squeeze, not pull, the trigger. His Sporter kicked, snow was kicked up by the barrel's hot wash, and one of the figures fell. It was the man with the SAW. Suddenly he could see only one of them scurrying over to their felled companion, either to check him out, grab his SAW, or both. Danny fired again and the man crumpled.

"Might be playing possum," Ray cautioned his son. "Hit 'em again!" Danny did and the crumpled shape didn't move. "You got—"

There was a long rattle of fire, and bits of snow were jumping up all along the lip of the creek's bank as if a string of buried firecrackers had been set off. Danny swung his rifle hard left in the direction of the firing but could see nothing. "You see 'em?" he asked his dad.

There was another, shorter burst of fire too high, slapping the air above them, thudding into the opposite bank fifteen yards behind them. "Dad?" Ray Marsden lay inert. Immediately, Danny thought his father was dead, but Ray was still breathing, his face gray, pupils dilated. *"Dad?"* His weapon in one hand, Danny shook his father with the other. He could see Ray trying to move his lips, but no words came, the only sound a godawful groan.

Another long rattle of fire came from the left, and now there was a line of soldiers no more than fifty yards away, the fog having lifted like a curtain. In a panic, Danny fired, and shook his dad violently as if trying to wake him from a deep sleep. Only his father's eyes moved, accompanied by the same groan that frightened Danny as much as the eruption of firing coming toward him. His panic unabated, he tore off his white overlay, and throwing its hood over the end of his Sporter's barrel, raised the rifle, quickly waving it to and fro. Unexpectedly, the line of federals slowed. Despite their blood being up, or because of it, the one-eyed lieutenant had ordered the line—formed by both squads having merged—to ease up. The lieutenant had never been in combat either, but he was a natural leader and instinctively understood that now was the time to calm things down a bit. Besides, the surrender flag could be a trap. "Come forward!" he yelled in the direction of the riverbank. "Hands up. Way up where we can see them!"

Danny, his throat dry as parchment, did as he was told. Two of the National Guardsmen wanted to shoot him on the spot, but "Kramer," the one-eyed lieutenant, ordered everyone to "chill out." Besides, he told them that the two militiamen would likely hang for having committed murder *after* the militia had surrendered.

"Nah," said a black soldier who'd picked up the SAW from his fallen comrade in the other squad. "Some smart-mouthed fuckin' lawyer'll get him off."

"Yeah," another put in. "Maybe the fucker's underage. How old are you, creep?"

Danny tried to speak but nothing came out. He managed some spittle and said uneasily, "Nineteen."

"He's old enough to hang," one of the others said.

"I'm telling you," the black soldier with the SAW said. "Some smart-ass fucking Yid'll get 'im off."

"Hey!" said another soldier, "I'm Jewish, you bastard!"

"You know what I mean—fucking lawyers."

"Well, say fucking lawyers. Got a mind to show you, you bastard!"

"Hey!" It was the one-eyed lieutenant, glaring at both soldiers in turn. "Chill out! Jesus, we're supposed to be fighting the militia, not one another. Next guy who's outta line I'll put on a charge."

"Sir . . . ?" It was a plaintive entreaty from Danny. "Can you help my father?"

"He's dead!" the black man with the SAW said.

"Good riddance, I say," another put in.

"Yeah," someone else agreed.

The lieutenant called for a medic, who walked over the lip of the riverbank and knelt down by Ray Marsden. After a brief wait, one man saying "Fuck this" and sitting down, the lieutenant asked the medic what was wrong with Ray Marsden.

"A stroke, I think," the medic replied. "We'll have to carry him back to the convoy."

"Screw 'im," said the man sitting down. "Let 'im die."

The lieutenant didn't like it—not so much *what* was said, a normal enough reaction from men who'd just seen their buddies killed, but the tone of growing insubordination. He looked down at the man who'd just spoken. "All right, Lawson, *you* and—Riley. Rig a stretcher."

"Oh shit, we—"

"Now!"

Lawson dragged himself insolently to his feet, dusting the snow from his backside.

"Lieutenant Kramer—" Riley began. There was stifled laughter. Lazily, Riley pointed his rifle at Danny. "Why don't we make this prick carry 'im."

"Right on!" the black man with the SAW said.

The lieutenant insisted on Riley and Lawson rigging a stretcher, using their load vests and weapons. As soon as he'd given the order, the lieutenant knew he'd made a mistake, letting his pride overrule a sensible suggestion by Riley, but he had felt that discipline had to be maintained. Otherwise things would get out of hand.

CHAPTER TWELVE

IT WOULD BE said that, having stopped the convoy, Ray Marsden and his son were responsible for what happened at Packwood between Major Irwin's National Guard and the "mined-in" militia under Jeremy Eleen, but this wasn't so. What changed the situation was a flash of brilliance under enormous pressure on the part of Eleen. The fact that the WOLVES dog lay dead not more than fifty yards away told him that beyond the dog's body the ground must be mine-free, otherwise the dog would have set off a mine, which meant that the minefield moat all about his thirty-one men must be no more than fifty yards in depth. If he and his men—though they were without a "snake" of antimine explosives—could somehow clear a path for no more than fifty yards, then they could breach the entire minefield. "Mulvane?"

"Sir?" the corporal answered, the puffs of his breath directed at his right hand, his left encased mittenlike in a sock from one of his dead comrades.

"Collect all grenades from the men. We're going to blast our way through."

"But sir, we don't know how deep the—"

"Yes we do," Eleen cut in, a tone of self-congratulation coming through despite his Mormon belief against vain pride. "It's no more'n fifty yards. Get the men ready to rush it. We won't have much time."

When Mulvane had scrounged up eleven grenades, all that remained of the remnants of the once two-hundred-strong Charlie Company, Eleen told him, "You and Rubinski toss, I'll lead the rush. We'll be right behind you. Pass the word—wounded to the rear."

Now the militiamen who had earlier cursed the blizzard thanked God for it as they saw their chance to break out. When he'd given the order down the line, Mulvane told Eleen that he thought the choppers were still in the area. Parked. Waiting.

"Maybe," Eleen answered, his gut muscle going into spasm from the anxiety he was feeling. His job, he reminded himself, was to stay "calm, cool, and collected," as his father used to say. This was his, Jeremiah's, Chosin Reservoir. He would get his men out, including the wounded, or die in the attempt. And he had to move with lightning speed, or whatever pace he and his exhausted men could muster during this lull in the fighting— before Irwin's men could organize a surprise of their own.

Mulvane and Rubinski had the grenades. Mulvane had six, "Rubin," as he was called, five, in open haversacks that they'd slung over their shoulders like two peasants about to sow seed in a field.

Eleen, his heartbeat palpable against his chest, took his M-16 off safety and nodded to Mulvane. "Go!"

Mulvane took a step forward, threw a grenade into the snow ahead and crouched. The grenade blew with a purplish flash, dirtied snow erupting. Rubinski tossed the next one a bit farther, and Mulvane tossed the next. Seven mines went off, shrapnel whistling. In all it took less than fifty seconds, each rough circle of blown-up snow overlapping, except for one spot about five yards across, leading like some giant's soiled footsteps through the field. "One more to blow," Mulvane said, tossing his grenade to the uncleared spot.

The overpressure caused a chain reaction of other mines detonating, and despite federals firing in the general direction of his men, Eleen got up and led them through the field, each man's weapon pointing to the opposite side of the man in front of him so that both flanks were covered. Four men were down and would never get up, but the remaining twenty-seven were through, returning the federals' fire, though neither side saw the other until over half of Eleen's column were beyond the minefield—or so Eleen thought. He had made a terrible mistake: the dead dog hadn't stopped where he was shot because the ground ahead of him was mined and the area behind him unmined. He had merely sniffed his way there as, like all other canines anywhere in the Canine Corps, he'd been trained to sniff out explosives as well as drugs, and so, guided by the natural smell radar of his nose, the dog had navigated his way *into* the minefield. There was another twenty yards of minefield behind his body. Eleen had led his men into a still active minefield.

There was no time to lose. The federals, though still not visible, were getting closer, from the sound of their firing. Eleen prayed and kept running, but another five men were blown up by mines, there being no time to exactly follow in the footsteps of Eleen, Mulvane, and Rubinski, the latter screaming, his left foot gone, the stump a blackened, angry red. There was mayhem behind him. Eleen suddenly saw the dim shape of a chopper ahead, a startled figure moving in the cockpit. Eleen fired a burst. Perspex split with a resounding crack and the man, probably a pilot, crumpled. Another man suddenly appeared in front of him, hands up, yelling, "Don't shoot!" Then another pilot, having already dropped his sidearm, emerged from the whiteness with the same desperate plea.

"Start the engines!" Eleen shouted. "Start—"

"Yeah, yeah, okay, okay, whatever—"

"Shut up!" yelled Mulvane, who, while Eleen kept his eyes on the two pilots, called out to the remainder of the militia column to board the two Hueys.

A man ran back toward Rubinski and was shot by oncoming federals.

"Don't shoot!" screamed one of the two terrified pilots. "Jesus—don't!" but he couldn't be heard over the sputtering roar of the other helo engine, the rotor a blur in the heavily falling snow.

Rubinski cried out for help as the last of the militia scrambled aboard, Mulvane aiding a couple of wounded men too weak to haul themselves over the fuselage's edge. Rubinski, unheard in the increasing roar of the two helos' rotors, called out again, and Eleen, hearing him, turned to go back. The helo he was in was rising. "Too late," Mulvane called, holding Eleen by the collar as the chopper rose ten feet, then fell with an awful grinding noise as pieces of the rotor, shattered by federal fire, flew off, a piece going through the cowling and into the engine.

"Jesus!" someone shouted, and there was a tremendous jolt. Falling backward, Eleen struck his head against the helo's M-60 machine gun mount so hard that, despite his helmet, he was concussed. As he heaved himself up, he saw the ugly end of an M-16 in his face, its owner warning, "Don't you move, Jack—or you're dead. Understand?" It was a young federal soldier, no more than twenty at most, and he was as frightened as everybody else.

There was an enormous flash of light and the blizzard turned apricot at the ear-thumping explosion of the second helo, brought down onto the minefield by a fusillade of federal small arms fire. There would be much argument among the federals as to who could claim the kill—between those who argued that the helo with fifteen bodies crammed inside was way overloaded, the Huey's normal load being eight, and those who claimed, like the Australian infantry in France that had shot down Von Richthoven in WW I, that it was the accurate small arms fire that had done it.

Whatever the truth—the fuselage was peppered with holes and the chopper was overloaded—there were now only twelve men, three of them wounded, two badly, left out of Eleen's original forty-three. As they were led into captivity, Eleen couldn't bring himself to look at his men, Rubinski least of all. Had Mulvane really pulled him back from returning for Rubinski, he asked himself, or had discretion or cowardice got the better part of valor? Had he merely used Mulvane's tug on his collar as an excuse for not going back? The question haunted him. He could think of nothing else—how he had shamed his father.

He could only imagine what Rubinski was thinking as he

too had been taken prisoner. All Eleen could hope for was that Rubinski would be taken as quickly as possible to the hospital at Yakima, while he and the other eleven men would be taken across the state to the POW camp at Camp Fairchild, a few miles from Fairchild Air Force Base, one of the biggest of the old Strategic Air Command. As they were waiting, stamping their feet for warmth in the bitterly damp cold, Eleen and the other survivors could see the dim shapes of federal soldiers moving through the dead and wounded, and trucks arriving. Mulvane, exhausted and feeling dizzy from lack of food, saw a soldier kneeling with what seemed the barrel of a handgun against Rubinski's throat, Rubinski propping himself up on an elbow. Rubinski's torso was still.

"Jesus! Jesus!" Mulvane shouted, instinctively rising.

"Sit down!" bellowed one of the National Guardsmen, a sergeant, knocking Mulvane down with his rifle.

"Murderers!" Mulvane yelled.

The man kicked him in the gut. "You're the murderers, ass-hole. You get up again, I'll blow your fuckin' head off." Two of Eleen's ragtag eleven restrained Mulvane. "Cool it, man."

"That's right," the sergeant snapped. "Cool it or you're dead."

Jeremy Eleen and his eleven survivors, all that was left of Charlie Company, were taken northeast to Camp Fairchild in one of four trucks transporting other militia POWs rounded up from southern Washington. In all there were over eighty prisoners who had been run to ground and now huddled in the canvas-covered ten-tonners that were protected fore and aft by two twenty-five-ton Bradley Infantry Fighting Vehicles.

After Ruth's death, this was the lowest point of Eleen's life. He had not been able to get *any* of his men out, and now the seed of doubt had been planted by him in his own mind. The last thing he would remember about the battle was the sight of a federal bending over Rubinski; Rubinski, who had called out to him for help. He seemed unsure of anything anymore, most of all himself. That seed of doubt, begun in an instant, would invade him, become an obsession, questioning his very reason for being.

Mulvane, on the other hand, was sure of what he'd do to the next federal he managed to lay his hands on, and, like a prairie wildfire, Mulvane's version of what he'd seen swept through all the POWs in the trucks, and soon swept through the whole camp, his charge: the federals were no better than the Communists, preferring to shoot the wounded rather than bother taking them prisoner. A few militiamen, however, were not filled with thoughts of outrage. They had been in the Tet offensive in 'Nam and knew what had happened to a lot of wounded Viet Cong. War was war.

As the Bradley-led convoy arrived at Camp Fairchild's POW camp, or "cage," as it was already known, Eleen's heart sank. There were ten rows, each with five-hundred-foot-long, thirty-foot-wide prefabricated huts that had been hastily erected and fenced in with high barbed wire, rolls of concertina razor wire, and guard towers, which the federals were euphemistically calling "observation points," at three-hundred-yard intervals along each quarter-mile-long side around the square-mile perimeter. Which meant that each quarter-mile side of the square had three of the "observation points," which the first batch of over five hundred militia POWs promptly dubbed "goon towers" for their striking resemblance to World War II POW camp guard towers.

The Nazi, Hearn, the most infamous prisoner at Camp Fairchild, was kept in a separate concrete blockhouse. It was adjacent but off to the left of the main entrance, where a guard tower looked directly down on it. Though one POW camp looks much like any other, some of the federal authorities, in this case the regular Army's military police assigned to run the camp, were embarrassed by the camp's unintentional resemblance to the German stalags of World War II. In an attempt to offset the likeness, they took every possible opportunity to remind the public, through the media, that their most infamous prisoner was a self-avowed Nazi as well as an accused murderer awaiting trial.

CNN's Marte Price, using all the considerable tight-sweater charm she could muster, had repeatedly tried to get an exclusive interview with Hearn, but had been rebuffed, until now. A sudden influx of prisoners, including Jeremy Eleen and his eleven comrades and scores of other recalcitrant militiamen captured at various places east and west of the Cascades, gave her an idea. Over seventy of the militiamen had been taken prisoner in the Idaho panhandle near the Alberta border, where they had planned to cross into Canada to join Canadian militia units in southern British Columbia and Alberta. These Canadian groups were as vehemently anti-Ottawa as those in the U.S. were anti-Washington, D.C., and, despite some infiltration by the Royal Canadian Mounted Police, had amassed large caches of ammunition, weapons, and food.

Despite finally obtaining permission to interview Hearn, using what she called "the Canadian angle" as a ploy to get into the camp, the camp C.O., Major Freeth, told her he'd give her "twenty minutes maximum!" Price's cameraman was told he could not take any pictures of the camp itself.

"Security concerns," Freeth explained. "You can take your footage inside the blockhouse and only inside." It would be difficult—the only outside light available inside the block was through a high, barred, six-inch-square window in each cell.

"May I ask what these security concerns are?" Marte Price asked.

Major Freeth, a dark, heavily built man with a brushlike mustache and a mid-age gut, was caught off guard. "Ah, the—ah other prisoners might, ah, see possible means of escape."

"You mean they have television?" she asked with exaggerated surprise.

"What? Er, no. Ah—not yet. I mean they might, and in that case they would be, ah, privy to the layout."

"But won't they see the layout anyway when they're outside? Or are you planning a permanent lockdown?"

"Ah—no. They'll—they'll, ah, be free to move about in the facility."

"Then why won't you allow me to shoot some footage of the prison? If they're going to see it any—"

"It's not a prison," Freeth interrupted tendentiously. "It's a holding facility."

"You mean they'll be released soon."

Freeth was sweating and flushed with anger, his lips pressing tightly before he spoke. "No. They won't be released, Ms. Price. They are terrorists who refused to surrender to the federal authorities. That's why they're here. It was their choice, not ours."

"I still don't understand why we can't take pictures of the *facility* if they're not going to see TV anyway. What possible—"

"That's not definite yet. Ah, they may be getting TV. It's still under discussion."

"Who by?"

Bitch, Freeth thought. "By the authorities."

"You?"

"No—ah, my superiors in Washington. Look, you either do the interview in the blockhouse or there'll be no interview. Period."

She spread her hands accommodatingly. "Okay, you win. But can I say they'll be getting TV?"

"You can say it's a *possibility*," Freeth said.

"You'll look a lot better if I can say they will be," she prompted him. "You know the sort of thing—federal authorities show some compassion for the prisoners."

So that's her angle, Freeth thought, and seized the moment. "Yes, you can say that."

She nodded. "I'll make you look good."

In fact she was only half right. The news that the militia POWs might have TV broadcast on CNN by a direct feed to *Headline News* did indeed make Major Freeth and his superiors in Washington look compassionate to many voters—those sympathetic to the militias. But to the rest of the nation it was just another case of their elected officials being soft on riffraff, including Nazi skinheads like the murderer Hearn, who wanted to overthrow the very government that was apparently treating him with kid gloves. The White House, radio, TV station, and newspaper switchboards were jammed with complaints from America's outraged citizens. The White House, via Chief of the Army Walter Shelbourne, abruptly demoted Major Freeth, and transferred him from Camp Fairchild to I Corps Ninth Infantry Regiment, at Fort Lewis, Washington, replacing him with a Major Ernst Schmidt from Colorado's Fort Carson's Fourth Infantry Mechanized Division.

Both men's careers hung in the balance, and each understood the reasons behind their transfer: Freeth was being made the sacrificial lamb, to placate the voters who thought the federal government was being too soft on the recalcitrant militias, while Schmidt saw his appointment as a get tough, no nonsense assignment, both men avowing that as far as treatment of militia POWs was concerned, from now on it was hardball. "No fucking TV," Smith told his subalterns. "No pretty please. If the bastards don't do what they're supposed to, break their balls!" And the federal government, through White House adviser Delorme, announced that for these "hard-core" militia there would be no amnesty, and under the rules governing insurrection, there would be no pardons. No bail. To underscore their determination to prosecute all of the 983 militia at Camp Fairchild, the White House referred the media to the transcript of the blockhouse interview between Marte Price and Hearn.

PRICE: Is it true, Mr. Hearn, that you're an avowed Nazi?
HEARN: That's a stupid f—— question. Of course I am. And proud of it. This country needs to get rid of all the undesirables.
PRICE: Who do you regard as undesirables?
HEARN: Niggers, Jews, Socialists, and freaks.
PRICE: Who do you mean by "freaks"?
HEARN: I mean freaks. Cripples who can't pull their weight. Society freaks.
PRICE: But there are many people who are challenged in some way or other that contribute to society.
HEARN: Challenged? That's liberal bullshit. People who are physically and mentally deformed are a drain on the nation's

resources. We've got too many regular people who need help. There's simply not enough resources to go around. You know that, I know that, so why don't you and all your bleeding heart liberals cut the crap and let this country fulfill its destiny?

PRICE: What destiny is that?

HEARN: To be the world's greatest nation.

PRICE: Aren't we that already?

HEARN: We *were* when we were fighting the Communists. Now look what we've become. The white race—God's *real* chosen people—are being polluted. Official language of California is Spanish—that and black babble Ebonics. Can't understand a thing they say. Look at all the wetbacks coming up here. Not one of them over five-foot-four. Unsanitary.

PRICE: You can't be serious.

HEARN: Don't believe me? Go ask your neighbors. I'm only saying what they think. And in San Francisco you might as well be in Shanghai. In L.A. you've got more Asian trash. Young white people can't get a job. And at the universities what've you got? Gay rights.

PRICE: I thought some Nazis in Hitler's Germany were gay.

HEARN: And what did the Führer do with them?

PRICE: Well—he had a lot of them killed.

HEARN: Right.

PRICE: You don't seriously think—

HEARN: Are you f—— preaching to me or asking questions? I'm not interested in what *you* think.

PRICE: All right. Do you advocate discrimination against—

HEARN: Yes. Do you discriminate between a good wine and a bad one? Between a purebred and a mongrel? Well, do you?

PRICE: I'm doing the interview, Mister—

HEARN: No you're not. You're like all the media. You pretend objectivity—until you don't like what you see. Then you use the media as your pulpit, preaching your liberal politics. You know what everyone thinks. Everyone nods their head when you liberals espouse your tolerance for all kinds of shit, but when you're gone, sister—when you and all your suckerfish leave—everyone closes the door and says no way my kid's going to marry a nigger. We don't want shit-colored grand-children. . . . What's the matter—cat got your tongue?

PRICE: Do—do you honestly believe that most Americans think like you?

HEARN: "No. I don't *believe* it—I *know* it. I talk to Americans, real Americans. All you talk to are liberal lapdogs in New York. Unless we purify this country, we're lost. Militias are the only ones who are willing to do something about it. To go the distance. We need to finish what Germany began.

PRICE: Ethnic cleansing?

HEARN: You're a f—— bore.

The interview ended with an overlay of Major Schmidt ad-dressing the most recent truckloads of militia POWs, telling them that any POW trying to escape would be "dealt with."

Within minutes of the interview ending there was another verbal onslaught via the phones—militiamen and women call-ing in from all around the country, disavowing any connection with Hearn. Every organization, they seemed to be saying, at-tracts some trash like Hearn.

There were other calls, mainly from the South and South-west from public phones, mostly saying that Hearn had simply spoken the truth, which no one else had the guts to do, that he'd merely said what a lot of people think, or, as one caller from the Florida panhandle put it, "what they feel in their heart of hearts. Not all of it maybe, but some of it." A call purported as coming from militia HQ somewhere in the Northwest disavowed every-thing Hearn had said.

No one in Camp Fairchild had seen or heard the interview, for "Commandant" Schmidt, as he was already called, had given strict instructions to his guards that no TVs or radios were al-lowed in the camp.

CHAPTER THIRTEEN

FUELED BY STANLEY Merk's cider, the earlier braggadocio that had marked Merk's living room account of Latrell killing the black man, and Vance's dispatch of militia to attack the convoy bound for Packwood, now gave way to Merk morosely opening another cider and talking tough about a real estate "bimbo" from back East who had come around earlier that day. "Tryin' to interest me in maybe sellin' my land to a bunch of Nips," Merk explained. "I told her no way would I sell to Japs— no-o-o way. This land—" He burped. "—is for Americans. An' I don't mean niggers."

"Niggers aren't Americans," Latrell said, slouched in an overstuffed lounge chair across from Merk.

"What about this bimbo?" Vance inquired.

"She's federal." It was Merk's wife standing in the doorway to the kitchen. "A federal, that's what she is—an' you boys better be careful. We don't want no Waco 'round here, thank you."

Vance's usual calm suddenly gave way to alarm. "That right, Stan? She a federal?"

Merk shrugged and took a swig of cider. "May reckons she is. May's like a hound dog when it comes to sniffin' out federals."

"What'd she say?" Vance pressed.

"Nothin'," May retorted. "She's a charmer an' a liar. Told Stanley some cock an' bull story 'bout her daddy bein' in the Michigan militia."

"We don't know," Merk said. "Coulda been tellin' the truth."

May didn't respond. She returned to the kitchen, thinking it was up to Vance and his tattooed friends to figure it out, if they weren't too bombed on cider.

Vance was staring across at Stan Merk, whose cheeks were flushed with the booze. He looked up at Vance for a moment. Their eyes met. The silence was making Vance's point.

"Maybe," Merk said, "we should find out whether she is or not."

"Makes sense," put in Norman, the oldest of the Nazis.

"If you even think she might be a federal," Vance said, "it's your *duty* to find out."

"Yeah, well," Stan said defensively, relighting his pipe. "I didn't like to bother the boys in Michigan. They're busy gettin'—"

"Never mind about that," Vance told him. "We're all busy. Everybody's busy. Doesn't mean we shouldn't check it out."

In the kitchen, May was doing battle with a bag of potato chips. She poured them into a bowl and brought them in with dip. Merk took one an' his lips puckered. "Holy—these are salt and vinegar!"

"You don't like 'em," May declared, "don't eat 'em." She knew he was procrastinating, trying to get off the subject by wasting time talking about the damn chips.

"I like 'em, but not with dip," he said.

"Dip's fine with me," Vance put in.

All right, May thought, picking up a few empties. She'd tried to be diplomatic and it hadn't worked, so now she was going to say it whether it embarrassed Stanley or not. "Stan hasn't asked Michigan 'cause he doesn't like figuring out the fax. He's not a big reader." Even now she was pulling her punches, trying not to embarrass him too much. She knew that Vance had known Stan for over ten years and hadn't picked it up— didn't know. Men were stupid like that, unobservant—could know one another for half a lifetime and still couldn't tell you what color eyes each of them had.

"You can't read?" the Nazi Andrew blurted, startling everyone.

" 'Course I can read," Stan said quickly, pushing the recliner's handle forward and abruptly sitting up. "Who in hell said I can't read?"

"It's all right," May told him just as quickly, replacing his dead cider with an ice-cold new one. "Nobody said you couldn't read." She knew this would happen. No matter how you tried to ease around it, finally the truth would out. "It's Stanley's arthritis," she said. "Finds it hard to write."

"You can't write!" Andrew said.

As if a duelist had thrown down a gauntlet, Stanley picked it up. "Fer Christ's sake," he shot back, rising from the recliner, " 'course I can write! Goddammit!" He slammed his cider down and stalked off. "I'm goin' to the toilet."

None of the others spoke until they heard him slam the bathroom door.

"I'm sorry, May," Vance said, who then turned to Andrew. "Needn't have been so damn blunt, boy."

"What?" Andrew asked, grinning in a cider high. "What'd I do?"

"Never mind," May cut in. "Damage is done. I just think you oughta check this real estate woman out. Send a fax to Michigan."

Vance nodded, then asked her, "What happens when you *receive* a fax? How's Stan respond?"

"I do it," she said.

Now Vance was staring wide-eyed at her. "You mean you know the code?"

"No," she said. "I just acknowledge receipt. We don't send. Stan tried to teach me the code but he can't get it straight. Anyway, all Stan uses it for is to get weather warning temperatures from other militias. Saves him having to watch the TV weather channel all the time."

They heard the toilet flush, so May spoke quickly to Vance. "Will you do it?"

Vance nodded.

"Do what?" It was Andrew, stuffing himself with chips, as many going in his lap as his mouth.

Stan reentered the room. "S'pose you're right, May. Better get my readin' glasses out. Can't remember where I put 'em."

"Glasses're a pain in the neck," Vance said sympathetically. "I know other friends of mine—always looking for them. Tell you what, Stan, don't worry about the coding for Michigan. I'll look after it."

"Appreciate that," Merk responded awkwardly. He was sweating. "Problem is havin' to be here for the reply an' stuff. Temperatures dropped bad a few nights back and—"

"I understand," Latrell said. "Those bells start ringin', you got to get out there fast to those smudge pots."

Vance looked across at Norman and explained, "If the temperature suddenly plummets and Stan doesn't get to those air heaters, he could lose his entire crop."

Andrew stared drunkenly at Vance. It was impossible to know if he understood or what. " 'S'at right?" he said finally.

"Yes," Vance said. "Frost comes, sounds like a fire hall 'round here. That right, Stanley?"

"That's right."

Andrew, reaching for another cider, told May, "Don't you stay up on 'count of us, May."

"I won't," she said. "See you boys in the mornin'."

Norman and Ian, the two sober Nazis on watch, said good night.

"More chips in the kitchen if you need 'em," May said. She was glad to go—she'd had practically a whole day of paperwork behind her, ordering everything from new sprinklers, extra fuel for the smudge pots, and packing cases for the harvest—if frost didn't beat them. Besides, even though she'd expressed her doubt about the real estate woman, she didn't want to hear what contingency plans the boys might prepare if they found out she was a federal. That way, if it ever came to it—called to court by the federals to fink on the militia—she could honestly put her hand on the holy Bible and swear she'd never heard any talk about planned violence.

She said her prayers to the Almighty, confident that He

understood how the federals were the agents of a nonbelieving world, the Devil's state, and as such must be destroyed. Amen.

Back in the living room, Merk was gazing into an empty bottle as if it were a holy mystery. " 'Course," he said, "maybe we're all wet. Woman mightn't be a federal after all."

"True," Vance said. "But if she is—"

"Yeah. When you gonna send the fax?"

"Tomorrow."

"It's tomorrow already," Merk said, indicating the clock set in the stock of the elephant gun. "Past two."

"Well, I won't code it now."

"You drunk?"

"No, but I'd rather do it when I'm fresh. No mistakes. What she say her father's name was?"

"Walter—William—goddamn, I can't remember."

"Seth," Latrell said. "William Seth."

"Not a common name," Vance observed.

"Not around here," Latrell conceded. "But maybe it is in Michigan."

Latrell was the only one who understood what was going on with Vance. If the militia up around Packwood were defeated by overwhelming federal force, they would instantly become martyrs all the way from Washington in the Northwest to Florida in the Southeast. Cunning bastard, he thought.

By the time dawn stole upon the orchard of the Yakima Valley and the tut-tut-tut of sprinklers began, Stanley Merk, Latrell, and the Nazis, except for the two on guard, were in various stages of hangover, empty cider bottles and a dozen or so empty Bud cans strewn about, the stale smell of beer, cider, and old pipe smoke permeating the small living room. May was already up, banging coffeepot and cast-iron frying pan on the stove, not caring whether it hurt their heads or not, and beating a bowl of pancake mix into subjection. Matter o' fact, she hoped it *would* hurt their heads, wake 'em up.

Ever since his semiretirement at sixty, Stanley had become

lazier and lazier, leaving the day-to-day operation of the orchard up to his foreman and the Mexican illegals he'd hired. It bugged May that he was practically always around the house, phoning his pals in the militia and drinking more cider than was good for him, burping and breakin' wind without so much as an excuse-me. She heard someone moving around, bumping into one of the light stands, and the next moment saw one of the Nazis groaning, walking gingerly down the hall toward the bathroom.

She watched the coffeepot perking, as if willing it to hurry up. She wanted Stanley and his friends out of her domain as soon as possible, especially Zane, the skinhead with a swastika tattoo peeking above his collar. He'd been polite enough and he was an Aryan, she'd give him that, but one thing May couldn't tolerate was people who made themselves look different just to attract attention. Shaving their heads, knees out of their jeans, and *earrings*?

"Coffee's ready!" she hollered into the living room. "Anyone want some?"

"Wha—" Latrell began, eyes suddenly opening, then closing, looking like a stunned mullet, his voice croaky. "I'll have some."

She poured him a mug, then just as threateningly stood over her husband. "Stanley!"

She heard the skinhead throwing up, followed by the roar of the toilet. *"Stanley!"*

"Yeah, what?" He sat up abruptly. "What's wrong?"

"Nothing's wrong. I want you all out. Stinks like a tavern in here."

"I'll have some coffee," Vance said.

The flipping of the pancakes went well, but when the eggs and bacon began sizzling, the aroma invading the living room, Andrew heaved himself out of the deep chair and ran toward the toilet.

"First," May told Vance, "you have to send that fax." In the same off-putting tone, she asked if he wanted breakfast on the TV tray or in the kitchen.

"Kitchen," he told her, his tone uncharacteristically imperious, May's bossy air not appreciated by the colonel. It was times like this that Vance found it difficult to maintain the fiction that he was not head of the militia but merely its liaison officer.

Andrew was returning from the toilet, his cheeks a pale shade of avocado. "I feel a bit better now," he declared.

"You'll be fine," Latrell said. In the background they could hear the measured chatter of the fax in a tiny room that Merk pretentiously called "the study."

CHAPTER FOURTEEN

Camp Fairchild, Washington State

IT WAS SNOWING, and inside one of the POW huts, militia sergeant Lucky McBride, still dressed in the tiger-stripe camouflage fatigues he'd been wearing during the surrender, was trying to relieve the boredom of POW life by giving a lecture on survival in the wild to his twenty-nine fellow prisoners of war. The right side of his floppy hat was still buttoned up from his habit of having carried his AR-15 rifle in a sling, his vest load weighted down with C mags of a hundred rounds, or, more precisely, ninety-nine in the mag, one in the chamber. Except now he had no rifle or ammo. He was one of the over nine hundred militia behind the wire.

"Now listen up," McBride told his "platoon." "Remember, best way to get meat is to trap it. One shot for a deer or a rabbit will get you fresh meat and will also get you killed. Fire one round, you might as well shoot up a flare, tell the federals where you are. Save your ammo for them. Same thing goes for a grenade, flash bang, or Willy Pete, toss one of 'em in a river you get all the stunned fresh fish you need, but you've given away your position." McBride was walking from one side of the room to the other, and it took him a few minutes to realize that almost everyone was watching him cross the room or watching the snow falling rather than listening to what he was saying, so he stopped.

"Now I don't mean the federals'd necessarily be able to pinpoint your position, even though they've got some pretty smart STDs—that's sound tracking devices—but they'd almost certainly know your general location and send helos in." He paused. "Another thing I know, most of you are pretty well bush-trained already, seein' you live in the back country, but it's your responsibility and mine to help the guys here who are in-bush for the first time. Remember, no smoking, no deodorant, nothing that'd make it easier for enemy patrols to pick you up. Got it?"

There were a few nods and grunts. Ex-drill-sergeant McBride roared out, *"Got it?"*

It was as if he'd dropped a grenade. "Got it!" the twenty-nine men answered in unison.

"Now the hard part," McBride said. "If you must chew gum, make sure all the sweet crap is out of it before you move out. You'd be surprised how far out you can smell gum. If you take a crap, dig a hole before and bury it. If you're in bivouac at night an' start to miss your sweetie and go jerk yourself off, bury it too."

"What?" someone asked. "My dick?"

There was a roar of laughter. In the Marine Corps, in which McBride had served, recruits wouldn't have dared such levity, but McBride, for all his hard-driving training, had to remember that try as you might, it was more difficult to keep tight-ass discipline among what were essentially weekend soldiers, and among men who had been thoroughly demoralized by incarceration. But it didn't mean you couldn't keep training them. And he took some comfort from the fact that, in accordance with General Nordstrom's standing order, every militia company of a hundred or so men, like those in the German Wehrmacht during the Second World War, should wherever possible be composed of squads made up of men from the same township or area. Knowing one another made for close-knit bodies of men whose behavior under fire was more reliable because they knew that their village or town would soon know how they had performed. McBride, for example, a 'Nam vet, already knew more than twenty of the twenty-nine men he was instructing, and they knew him. In a tight situation it could mean the difference between victory and defeat. No one wanted to go home tainted "yellow."

"Okay, listen up. Sammy Wong, the brother of Johnny Wong—who's still at large, lucky bastard—knows how to trap game better'n anyone in Yakima Valley. During the Great Depression, Sammy and Johnny's great-grandparents lived off this land and they passed it on to the boys." McBride paused. "How many of you have eaten at old man Wong's restaurant in Yakima?"

A phalanx of hands shot up.

"Okay," McBride said. "How many of you had the chicken?"

Another forest of hands.

"Yeah. How many of you knew it was rattlesnake?"

"Oh shit!" said someone in the hut's second squad. This was followed by laughter from the whole platoon, including Sammy Wong, who sat grinning. When everyone settled down, Sammy told them Sergeant McBride was lying "like a—" Sammy almost used the word "federal," but that was too serious an insult even to joke about.

"Like a sumbitch!" someone from an 81mm mortar squad called out.

"Right," Sammy said. "But I'll tell you one thing—rattlesnake ain't bad. I'll tell you somethin' else 'fore I tell you how to set a trap for small game. I'm quite prepared to eat rattlesnake again if it means the federals are comin' to take away my rights as an American citizen!"

There was an accolade of clapping and hollering. "Go get 'em, Sammy. Skin the bastards!"

"Yeah," another shouted. *"Alive!"*

Sammy, also a Vietnam vet, wasn't naive enough to think there was no anti-Chinese feeling in the militias. But he believed the militia was the place to be when the federal government moved against the Second Amendment, against the right, *his* right, as an American citizen to bear arms, to defend himself. He was certain it would happen. And piss on the federals' drive to have all guns registered. Hell, any fool could see that once the feds knew exactly who had guns, they'd move to confiscate. That's what gun registration was all about.

"First," Sammy Wong told the militia platoon, "you have to stay still, and I mean rock still, and *observe* a water hole. You'll see critters come and go. Second, don't put the trap I'm gonna show you right near the water hole. To begin with, the animal comin' to the water hole's more interested in water than the bait you may have as a lure in the trap. Third, don't put your trap too close to an animal's lair or his water supply because that's where they're most alert to danger. Instead, backtrack 'em either from the watering hole or lair and put your trap well away from each. I like a snare the best 'cause you can get both small *and* large game. You can use wire or string for the trap and attach it to a stump or whatever. It's like a vertical lasso, right? If it's wire you're using, it's easier because you can shape it better."

He made the shape with his fingers and showed them how to make a loop about five inches in diameter set horizontally about three inches above the ground. The loop's two supports were Y-shaped twigs sticking up three inches above the ground, the end of the snare attached to a stake about a foot high. In all, it looked like a figure 6 on its side. "The animal's head goes into the noose or bigger game steps into the loop and is caught. Tighter the animal pulls, the tighter the lasso loop around its leg or the throat. Got it?"

"Got it," answered Bill Franz, a short, thickset logger from the Cascades, adding, "Tell 'em about a spring trap."

"You do it," Sammy replied convivially.

Franz got up, glanced at it still snowing outside, and told them how to rig it so the noose's string or wire could be attached to a small sapling, the latter pulled down, half an arrow-shaped piece of wood hooked to another piece of wood anchored in the ground. "Main thing to remember," Franz said, "is not to leave your scent all over the place. Rig the trap *off* the animal trail and use the same wood. By that I mean don't haul in a piece of pine if the wood you're using for the anchor stake is fir. Animals know their area, that's why you see 'em sniffing the air so much. Remember, game can smell a hell of a lot better than you can, so when you've finished setting the trap, best to scatter campfire ash over the place, particularly where you've had to break wood for the trap, leaving a fresh sap odor. Animals are used to bush-fire ash smell, so that will cover you."

Franz looked at Sammy Wong. "That about do it?"

"Outstanding," Lucky McBride cut in. "Only thing I'd add is—"

"Goons!" came a lookout's voice. "Main gate."

Within seconds the men had broken up, each man, except for a clutch of five or six standing nonchalantly around the stove, returning to his bunk, a few reading, some smoking, others playing cards.

Near Naches

At Stan Merk's orchard, they were waiting for the coded fax reply from the Michigan militia. Merk shook his head in disgust, watching a CNN report of yet another militia-federal confrontation, this time near Everglades City. "Ruby Ridge all over again," Stan growled. "Same tactics. Federals creep up on a guy and—"

They heard the fax machine's chattering stop.

A few seconds later Vance returned with the fax. "It's in plain language," he said, "about our convention in Spokane. They say we should expect at least five thousand militiamen, from as far south as Florida. HQ organizer is worried about not having enough hotel space for us all. Having to set up trailer parks, a tent city maybe."

Latrell drained the last of his coffee. "Never mind the convention. Anything about this Realtor woman?"

"Nope," cut in May, who had gone in to check the fax. "It went through to them all right, though. Machine said it was a clear transmission."

"Ah," Stan said despairingly. "Can't trust damn machines."

"Don't be impatient," May said.

"Huh—thought you wanted us out of here."

"I do—soon as you hear about this Realtor."

"We'll wait," Vance said, sitting quietly, hands in his lap between the huge arms of the lounge chair.

" 'Course," Latrell said, looking across at Vance, "they'd have to check every militia in the state."

"True," Stan said. He called back to his wife. "What is it, May? 'Patience is a virtue, seldom in a woman, never in a man.' "

"That's right," she said. "I'm throwin' the coffee out. Anyone for a refill?"

"Ah, what the hell," Fred Latrell said, holding up his mug. "In for a dime, in for a dollar."

"You got it figured out if you find out there ain't no Seth on the Michigan list?" May asked as she poured.

"You betcha!" Latrell said, shifting his attention to Vance. "That right, Colonel?"

Vance nodded and glanced at his watch. Andrew, the hungover Nazi, looked at both of them, then at Stan, but in his postbooze haze it was still a mystery to him as to what in hell they were talking about. Fred Latrell saw the skinhead's bemused look and asked him to put on one of the Nazis' tapes of Uncle Dolf's speeches—one about the Jews.

"They're all about the Jews," Andrew said.

"Well, put something on."

"I got Goebbels with 'Folk rise up and storm break loose!' When he says that, it sounds 'bout the same in English an' German."

"There you go," Latrell said. "Put it on." As Andrew walked over to the tape deck, May asked him if he had to shave his head every day to look like that.

"No," he answered defensively, wanting to ask her how often she shaved the pits under her arms. She stank like a wrestler too. How in hell could Merk screw her? Maybe he didn't.

Goebbels was starting up. He was good too, though not as good as the Führer. At times it was like listening to hard rock, the actual words drowned in the fury of the speech.

Fred Latrell heard the fax machine. Receiving. "I'll get it," he told Vance, who merely nodded again, still thinking.

The message consisted of a page of groups of seven-digit numbers. It was simple and safe, so long as you used a different book every so often. Latrell was burping as he decoded the message.

"What's it say?" Stan Merk hollered from the living room. Latrell didn't reply. When he finished the decoding, he took it out and showed it to Vance. Stan Merk was annoyed with him. Goddamn it, Latrell could never just tell you anything—had to make a drama of it.

Vance couldn't find his reading glasses and held the fax way out from him, the message too dark, blurred but readable. He read it aloud: " 'No William Seth in Michigan militia.' "

"Christ," Merk said, "that isn't what I asked them. We want to know if there ever *was* a William Seth. Jesus, nothing works and nobody cares. Now we'll have to ask them again." He turned his head, looking into the kitchen. "What you think, May?"

"I say she's a federal."

"Yeah, but if we're gonna frighten her, we'd better make sure."

"I suppose," May said. "Suit yourself."

"I'm not suiting myself," Merk said grumpily. "Doin' it for the militia." Vance was in the room but not of it. He seemed utterly detached until he spoke to Latrell without looking at him. "Stan's right."

Latrell took the sheet from his hand. "I'll send it again."

"Appreciate that, Fred," Vance said, again without looking at Latrell.

"You're welcome," Latrell said, his tone verging on sarcasm, the colonel still preoccupied with his own thoughts.

CHAPTER FIFTEEN

DEEP IN THE Cascade Mountains, battalions of storm clouds gathered, congealing over the mountains in which the recalcitrant Moses Lake chapter of the Washington militia was carrying out maneuvers. There were few vehicles except for the assortment of four-wheel-drive Jeeps and similar conveyances that had transported Sergeant Johnny Wong's platoon deeper into the wooded ravines north of Diablo Dam.

Johnny Wong, on point, was sweating despite the cooler air of the mountains. He could sense danger ahead. Call it what you will, his experience, a natural intuitive sense—perhaps because the crows were cawing out a warning, or was it an unusual smell?—he felt he was leading his nine-man patrol into a trap. He stopped, signaling those behind to do likewise, and froze in position. There was a sudden rush, the branches of a pine tree moving. Behind him, to his left, someone fired an M-60 burst, and all hell broke loose with the sound of other M-16 bursts crashing into the densely forested slope near the ridgeline. Henderson, Wong's opposition in the exercise, and Jurez, his RA-TELO, or radio telephone operator, went into the prone position, the radio's aerial whipping the air and, despite its khaki paint, catching a glint of fading sunlight that betrayed his position to one of the ambuscade's men, who was then able to spray fire in his direction.

"Hold it! Hold it!" It was Wong standing up. There was shouting, a few more bursts from M-16s and a SAW, and then the eerie silence of the mountains. "Who the hell fired that M-60?"

No one answered.

"C'mon, who was the dink who fired first?"

"Guess it was me, Sarge."

"Jeez, Wayne, it was a friggin' deer. You ID'd the whole damn patrol for a deer. By now we'd be caught in overlapping fields of fire. Your job," he bellowed, "is to patrol, to reconnoiter, not to engage unless absolutely necessary. *Do you read me?*"

"Got it, Johnny!"

"All right, but remember, look before you shoot. If that'd been a bunch of federals, we'd all be dead. Now to make sure you remember this screw-up, you'll take over as point." Johnny Wong told himself to chill out. He was lucky to have a platoon after the militia's mass surrender. Their volunteerism was evidence of high morale, and he was grateful for that. "All right, now I want you boys in the patrol"—and they *were* boys—"to break to nine o'clock; that is, sweep left and forward on the flank at the enemy positions. Got it?"

"Got it."

"All right. Now Jimmy," he called to another new militiaman, "if I yell two o'clock, how do you move?"

"Forward, half right."

"Yeah," Johnny said. "East-nor'east, right?"

"Got it."

"Good, let's move out."

By now Johnny Wong's ambush unit had moved farther north and over the ridgeline to come up *behind* the militia's "enemy" position. Johnny smiled to himself. Henderson, the other militia platoon leader, would kick himself if his tail end Charlie didn't see or hear his men coming.

"Beer's on me," Johnny promised, "*if* we whack 'em."

"How 'bout some of Merk's cider?"

"That too," Wong said. Goddammit, he was having the time of his life.

They were unable to find Henderson's patrol, and everyone in the platoon was tired, wet, and hungry. But there was no alcohol for them, and their evening meal, in Johnny's phrase—one he'd picked up from the Aussies he fought next to in 'Nam—was "hard tack": C-rations and cold. With sentries posted, Wong called for two volunteers to do a "blind test." No one volunteered. Johnny Wong designated two men who'd made the mistake of finishing their Spam before anyone else. A poncho was laid on the ground and, using a flashlight, Wong stripped down a Stoner and an M-16 rifle, mixed the parts up, switched off the flashlight, and told the first of the men to reassemble the weapon. It had to be done by *feel*, not sight, the weapon reassembled within four minutes. Both men did it within the allowable time.

"Excellent!" Wong said. At least they knew their weapons. "Before we move out, one point. Some of you have watches with fluorescent faces. Either reverse them on your wrist or, if that's too uncomfortable, fix them to the back of your pack. That way the guy behind you can follow you a bit better."

"What if the enemy's behind?" came a voice from the darkness.

"You're in deep shit. Any other questions?"

"When can we go home?" Wayne asked.

"After you've dug in defensive positions, overlapping fields of fire."

"Thought you said a militia's best to keep on the move—hit and run."

"This is for when there's no place to run." A few good-natured, albeit blasphemous oaths came forth, to the consternation of the few evangelicals in the platoon.

"Enough moaning," Wong said. "Platoons all over the state are practicing the same maneuvers in secret, at night, so you aren't the only ones."

"C'mon," said a young, thin man nicknamed String. "Let's do it."

Soon Wong's platoon was digging in rifle team foxholes and SAW positions on the flanks and others in between with overlapping fields of fire. They could also set up claymore mines but had none this trip, as all claymores, like the small and compact Arpac handheld antitank missiles, had to be strictly accounted for and were kept in hidden ammo dumps throughout the foothills, never more than a quarter mile from a main or arterial road. There'd been a lot of argument about this, a large number of militia members at last year's USMC conference wanting everything they needed right by them, ready to go. But Colonel Vance had nixed the notion, arguing that forcing everyone to rendezvous at one place—the ammo dump—was a way of making sure that everyone worked as a team, at the *same* time.

"Yeah, but what if the federals find one or somebody tells 'em?"

"Anybody tells them," the colonel had told them, "you kill the informer—as an example."

"Yeah, meanwhile you'd have no ammo."

"Yes you would. Your hunting arms and ammo at home. So far, they're exempt from seizure. You could use them in a pinch. And might I remind you, gentlemen, that any militiaman who can't improvise something at home—ever heard of the *Anarchist Cookbook?*—isn't worthy of being called a militiaman." That shut 'em up. The cookbook was second only to the Bible in a militiaman's library. Johnny thought of his older brother, Sammy, now incarcerated in Fairchild, who had taken him through the cookbook page by page. Hell, first thing most of 'em had learned was how to make a pop can grenade. Besides, wasn't it the fact that what defined a militiaman was that he could fight and survive *by himself*? In keeping with this self-reliance, Wong had taught his new recruits not to rely on radio communication, for example, as important as it was, in a battle. For this reason, he'd drilled them in hand signals and alternate ways of communication. He wanted them to be like the American riflemen who defeated the British in *their* revolutionary war, particularly as most of the experienced men in the Moses Lake militia, like his brother, had already been captured.

"Okay." He opened up his left hand and placed it palm against his face. "What's this mean?"

"You're gonna blow your nose."

"What's it mean?"

"Enemy dead ahead."

"You hope 'dead,' " Wong said. "Right. What's this?" He went through several more hand signals, and got the correct answers. Last one he did was to put his right arm across his waist and left arm high at an acute angle to his body. Nobody knew what it meant, neither hand holding a weapon.

"All right," he said, "it means, 'Shall we dance?' "

A shower of snow and other loose projectiles rained down on him as he took cover beneath his field map. At least he could report to militia HQ that morale was high.

That evening, the second decoded fax from Michigan left Vance, Latrell, Merk, and the four Nazis in no doubt.

No William Seth past or present.

"Looks like you were right, May," Latrell said.

May was silent, her restraint appreciated by Stan Merk, who was feeling more than uncomfortable now that what he'd feared most had come to pass. In the boozy haze of last night, talk of dealing with the phony real estate agent with "extreme prejudice" had come more easily. In the light of day it was different. If it had to be done, it had to be done quickly. Vance impressed this upon them. Though he took care not to show it, he was alarmed at the possibility of discovery. If he was to execute his new as yet undisclosed plan, he would have to move north, fast. Stan began talking of ways to really put a scare into her.

"Oh yeah," Latrell said. "How you gonna do that, Stan? Go into Yakima in militia fatigues and jump out at her?"

"You know what I mean," Merk said.

"No, I don't know what you mean," rejoined Latrell, who turned to Norman, by now the Nazis' spokesman. "You know what he means?"

Norman stood up, spooning diced fruit from a can, and shook his head, enjoying Merk's discomfort.

"I *mean*," Merk said defensively, "it has to be thought out carefully."

"You don't want her hurt," Latrell said irritably. "That right?"

Merk was shifting position in his chair, as if unsure of where he wanted his backside to finally rest. Vance sat silently. Latrell went out to the kitchen to pour himself another coffee. May was waiting. She filled it for him. Latrell nodded his thanks, and she looked across the mug at him in a way that told Latrell that she knew what to do. If Stan wasn't up to it, he and the Nazi could do it. And he knew he could count on May in an emergency. She was cut from the same cloth as Randy Weaver's wife, who had gone around armed. If some gun-happy federal, like those who murdered the Florida militiaman, came stomping into the orchard, May'd give 'em a warning—one only— then she'd let fly. She knew better than Stan what was at stake if even one federal—FBI, ATF, whoever—infiltrated. They'd all be sold down the river before they knew it. She handed him a piece of rumpled notepaper the gatekeeper had given her. It was a license number.

"Maybe," May said, offering the open cookie tin to Latrell, "we *should* think about selling this place to the Japs, if they're the ones who want it."

Latrell nodded appreciatively. "So Miz Seth should come out—talk again?"

"Yes," May said. She didn't offer the cookies to Stan, Vance, or any of the Nazis.

"How 'bout that, Stan?" Latrell asked, returning to the living room. "Invite her out."

There was silence, broken only by Latrell asking May, who'd followed him out, what was wrong with Merk.

"He *likes* this one."

"Uh-huh," Latrell acknowledged, and turned back to Merk.

Stan looked up slowly. "You mean I call her here to discuss a price?"

"Yeah," Latrell said. "That'd do."

"Well, we do want a good price," Stan said. "We move to the coast to retire, we're gonna need a lot of cash."

"Exactly," Vance said. Latrell was standing, coffee in hand, munching a chocolate chip cookie.

There was a long, awkward silence. Finally, Stan Merk couldn't bear it. "I suppose I could call 'er."

"Fine," Vance said.

Merk squinted uneasily at the clock inset in the elephant gun's stock. "Gettin' late."

"Aw hell," Latrell said. "She won't mind, will she, May?"

"No," May said. "She'll come."

Stan Merk's fingers, Latrell saw, were tapping the arms of his lounge seat like crazy. "Maybe they got things mixed up in Michigan."

"Like what?" Latrell asked, not bothering to hide his irritation.

"I dunno—like, maybe it wasn't her father's full name. I mean, maybe it was two t's in Seth or—"

Latrell turned abruptly to Norman and the others. "You ready, boys?"

"Ready as we'll ever be," Norman said, rising from his seat.

"For what?" Merk asked.

"For anything," Norman replied, the edge of the tattoo disappearing as he'd stood up. "You just get her out here."

"Right!" Latrell said, and began walking out, speaking to the Merks without turning his head. "Call you folks later. Maybe get that cookie recipe."

Out in the four-wheel-drive Blazer, Latrell gamely, given that he was outnumbered, asked the Nazis if they were serious about being Aryans—not just proud of it. Any fool could and ought to be proud of it—but would they stand up and be counted, or was the "swas-teeka," as Latrell called it, all bullshit?

"We'll stand up and be counted," Norman said.

"All right," Latrell said, starting the motor and pumping a couple of times. "Then buckle up."

As he drove out from the orchard, a row of smudge pots

were caught in the headlights and a tumbleweed was blown into the grille.

CHAPTER SIXTEEN

"CALL FOR YOU," a friendly Randy McAllister told Linda as she walked into the realty office at the end of a long, hard day in the valley. "Old Merk," he added. "Wants you to phone."

She had to think for a moment, she'd seen so many faces in the last forty-eight hours, driving all over the valley, trying to tease out any lead at all about the militias. Everyone had been close-mouthed. What she'd like to do was have all their phones tapped for a day, have the National Security Agency listen in, and she could do it too. Under the new post-Waco antiterrorist legislation, following the Oklahoma bombing, verbal authorization for a wiretap could be made immediately for "due cause"—written authority to be obtained within forty-eight hours to maintain the tap.

For NSA, listening in on half the world already, it'd be no problem. But there were bureaucratic delays in having the tapes transcribed into hard copy, unless she requested a D.I.—a digital immediate. But as in so many other situations, agents like her and Bill Trey had only a finite amount of credit with their agencies insofar as wiretapping was concerned. Using that credit on wild hunches was a sure way to lose your credibility. First she needed some hard copy of her own, some definitive evidence of conspiracy.

At his computer, McAllister was watching her bend at the water cooler, and regretted they'd gotten off to a bad start. He was trying to make up for it. If she was going to be here for a while they might as well be friends. Maybe that was hoping for too much.

As she straightened, she tossed her head back to get her hair out of her eyes and her desk lamplight caught the sheen. Man, he could jump her right there and then. When she looked at the screen, the print was all but washed out from the angle she was standing at. She automatically moved closer to him to block the light, and her perfume, plumeria, washed over him.

"What's N.J.?" she asked, looking at the screen.

His throat felt dry. "It means New Jersey."

"What?" she asked, nonplussed.

McAllister glanced round the office to make sure no one was coming in. "No Japs," he told her. "That's what it means, but if anyone sees it on the screen we just say that it's a listing we also have in our New Jersey office."

"You have a New Jersey office?"

"No."

"You have any other cute little initials I should know about?"

"Don't get sore. It's business."

"It's discrimination."

"Bullshit. I don't mind the Nips."

"Really?"

"Yeah. Quite a few girlfriends of mine were Japanese. They were terrific, if you know what I mean."

"I know perfectly well what you mean and I'm not interested," she said, adding before she could stop, "Did you pay for it?"

"*Ooh,* nasty. I thought you weren't interested."

"I'm not."

"Matter o' fact I did pay for it. I was on leave in Yokohama. Is that all right?"

"You've already told me you were in Vietnam. We know you were a hero."

"Yeah, well," he said, getting up. "Piss on it. I wasn't any hero, but I tell you what, I was up to my ass in leeches and swamps while you types were safe at home on Mommy's titty."

"I never said I was against the war."

"You implied it."

"I did not." She was breathing quickly and it mesmerized him, her anger somehow making her even more desirable. "And," she continued, "I don't need your bad language."

"What bad language?"

"You know."

"Lady, you ain't heard nothin' yet."

"I'll bet." She walked quickly back to her desk, then, embarrassed that she hadn't gotten Merk's phone number, had to return to the computer, got it, tried to compose herself. In truth, she admired the men who had gone to Vietnam when called, more than some presidents she knew. She stabbed the numbers hard on the touch telephone. After three rings Mrs. Merk—Ms. Happy Face—answered.

"Merks!" It sounded like a warning. Old bitch.

"Hello, Mrs. Merk. It's Linda Seth returning your husband's call. Is he there?"

"Don't know where else he'd be. I'll get him."

Linda talked to Stanley Merk, and though he sounded somber, her tone brightened as if she'd won the lottery. "That's great, Mr. Merk, I think you've made the right decision. I know it must have been difficult for you to— Pardon? Yes, I'll drive up now if you like, if you don't mind me coming after dark. It'll take me that long to— Oh no, it's no trouble at all. . . . Yes, yes. 'Bye."

She turned to McAllister. She felt good. Maybe she'd overreacted to him. Anyway, she might need his advice. Her urge was to crow about how she had apparently turned old Merk around. It gave her a real boost to think that she was so good as a Realtor. After retirement from the FBI, "Seth Realty." Why not?

"Well," she said to McAllister with a friendly smile. "You can zap out your N.J. Mr. Merk has thought it over *and* he's decided to sell—to the Japanese if necessary. By which he obviously means if the price is right."

He had to give it to her, McAllister thought. Whatever she'd told the old boy, it was working. "You've done all right," he said, adopting her mood. "Maybe you might want to move here permanently. Set up shop—with me, though, not agin' me. Christ, what am I sayin'? You'd get all the commissions."

They both laughed. What the hell, she thought, life was too short to carry on bickering with one another.

"Want to grab something to eat before you head off?"

"Okay," she said. "We'll go Dutch."

"Whatever. Old Wong's place is—"

"Fine," she said. "Have to be quick, though."

"No problem. Only takes 'em a few minutes to skin a cat."

"Oh lovely," she answered. "How appetizing." Normally it would have been the kind of comment from McAllister that would raise her ire, but she was in too good a mood. Of course, she knew she wouldn't get to keep any of the seven percent on the Merk sale. Either the FBI or the IRS—or both—would look after that, but she figured that Merk was her best bet for probing about the militia.

As they waited for their meal in the booth, McAllister ordered a Tsingtao beer. "Sorry, Linda, I should've asked you first. Too long on my own, I guess."

"No problem," she said easily. "Water'll do me. I'll be driving."

"Oh yeah—right."

"I thought you were married."

"I am, technically."

She wanted to back off, but he'd seen a gap in the wire and was going to take advantage of it. "Melissa and I aren't getting along."

"Uh-huh," she answered as neutrally as possible. She really didn't want to hear about it.

"Yeah," he said, "but we've got no kids so it isn't irreversible. I mean we both go our own separate ways, if you know what I mean?"

What could she say? "Sorry."

"No need. We made a mistake, that's all. Divorce'll probably be through by summer. House stuff and all that crap. I just want out."

"Uh-huh." All right, she knew he was available. Stud service courtesy of Raemar Realty.

He sensed it wasn't working, so shifted to another topic. "You making much headway with your inquiries?"

Linda glanced about nervously. The restaurant wasn't full but there were too many people around. She shrugged nonchalantly. "Well, I'm interested in selling the Merk property." There was silence as Mrs. Wong put down two big steaming noodle bowls on the table. McAllister told Linda he didn't like the idea of her driving up by herself. Maybe he should come along, keep her company.

"Thanks, but no. Merk's a funny old boy. If I bring you up, it could sour the deal. I don't know why. No offense to you." She leaned forward. "You know what I mean. After all, he told you he won't sell to Japanese—might be embarrassing for him."

"He told you the same thing—first time around."

"I know, but I figure, you know, it's easier for a man to change his mind with a woman."

"That's true," McAllister said. "Look at us."

She desperately wanted to get away. "You shouldn't worry about it."

"About what?"

"Me going to see old Merk."

"It could be a setup, couldn't it?"

She shook her head. "No. I thought of that, but it hasn't got the feel. He's money hungry—wants to see how much he can get."

"Or how much you know?"

"Listen, Randy, you're the only one here who knows why I'm here. Merk doesn't."

"So you believe."

"Oh, have you been telling everyone?"

" 'Course not. Haven't told a soul."

Linda recalled her conversation with Bill Trey on the flight up from Washington—telling her how most secrets were shared between man and wife.

"Does your wife know?"

"No."

"Then no one knows." She smiled.

Red lips, he noticed, toying with his food.

"Look," she told him, "I'll find out when I see him. If I think he's got me pinned—" She raised her fork. "—so he's got me pinned. No big deal. There are plenty of other farmers left in this valley I can talk to."

"Yeah, and they all have telephones." He paused. "You make sure you have your cellular."

"Don't worry about it. I'm a big girl now."

She was beautiful just as she was; naked, she'd be . . . "You have my home number?" he asked.

"Yes. Stop worrying, I'll be fine." She leaned forward, unwittingly tightening her bust line, and said quietly, "I carry a gun."

"You know how to use it?"

She sat back and put down the fork. "Are you serious? I was the highest female scorer on the Quantico range."

He liked her like this. "How many women were there?"

"Three." She laughed easily at herself, but McAllister guessed she must've been pretty good to qualify.

CHAPTER SEVENTEEN

The Everglades

SHIRLEY KOZAN WAS lonely, but didn't want to talk to anyone for fear she would start crying again. She could manage, just, providing no one spoke to her about Bob or Laddie. It was the same, she remembered, as years ago when as a teenager she had lost her cocker spaniel, killed in a hit and run. The moment friends, or indeed anyone, had mentioned the spaniel, the dam would burst. Because she and Bob were newcomers to the 'glades, they hadn't had time to make many friends, and for this she was now grateful, for while it was sympathetic company she needed in her loneliness, she didn't want to feel that she had to talk. She felt exhausted all the time, but couldn't sleep. She shuffled about the bungalow, unable to settle on doing anything, losing track of time, trying to lose herself, trying to flee the unbearable agony of having lost the person she had loved more than anyone she'd ever known.

Outside, an old cypress stood white and gnarled with age, Spanish moss hanging from it in a scene primeval, a flock of white egrets passing overhead against a cobalt sky, the sun having broken out of a morning mist rising from the 'glades like steam from fresh manure, the air pungent with rot. She had agreed to Bob's parents' offer of staying with them awhile up at Seaside at a later date. But for the moment she knew, though she didn't feel like it, that if she could muster enough strength to get through the first week by herself, she might be able to survive. To accept their offer straight off might mean that she would become afraid to leave them, and that in time their compassion for her would turn sour.

There was a gentle rapping on the screen door, and she saw the man—Michael something—who'd spoken to her at the memorial service. He showed her the FBI shield again from outside the door. "Michael Ma, Mrs. Kozan, and Agent Riley. Sorry to intrude at a time like this but we'd like to ask you a few questions if we may?" Riley, at six feet about the same size as Ma, nodded, presenting his shield and smiling at her as he followed Ma inside.

"How can *I* help?" she asked, surprised that she could possibly know something that would help them catch her husband's killer—for she was convinced, like most people in the area, that it had been murder. Laddie would have somehow got back otherwise, and she'd flatly rejected the suggestions of some locals that Bob had gotten lost in the myriad of look-alike hammocks, islands, and channels where part of the enormous, slowly moving, seventy-mile-wide river of grass reached the sea. Yes, the Everglades *had* claimed scores of people who'd become lost, panicked, and who, in their haste to get out, had fallen exhausted, or unwittingly gone too close to a gator pool. Taken down in the flash of an eye by one of the reptiles, who moved with a speed that had to be seen to be believed, they'd been gripped in its enormous jaws, the gator gulping, unable to chew, rolling furiously in the water, whipping its head from side to side, the jaws still chomping as the bones broke before the victim drowned.

"We'd like to know, Mrs. Kozan, if your husband had any enemies—anyone."

"Poachers," she said. "People who violated the park rules—illegal fishermen, power boaters. None of them like rangers."

"Ah yes," Ma said. "But they'd hardly want to—I mean—"

"Some of them would," she cut in. "It's redneck country down here. Some of them'd rather shoot and run than talk."

Riley was looking around the small pine-paneled living room, cheap knotty timber, a photo of Kozan and his wife on some beach, but not the detergent whiteness of the Gulf Coast sand, several striped changing booths in the background with a royal palm nearby. Europe, he thought, maybe Cannes or Nice. He turned to Shirley. "Mrs. Kozan, did he ever mention drug smuggling?"

She looked at him blankly; she hadn't really been listening. He asked her again. She forced herself to concentrate. "No. I— Well, he used to say the islands would be ideal for smugglers."

"Drugs?"

"He wasn't specific."

Ma was struck by her use of *specific*. An educated woman. You could live here for ten years and never hear a word like that. "When you say he wasn't specific," he said, "d'you mean he didn't name names, or what?"

"No, not names. He just said the 'glades, where they meet the sea, was a natural hiding place. All the islands."

"But he didn't say what for—I mean heroin, marijuana, what exactly."

"No, nothing in particular."

"Uh-huh," Riley said. "After he shot that militiaman, did he say anything then—about drugs?"

"No."

"How about the militia?" Riley asked. "Did he say anything about them?"

"I don't know. Maybe. He said they were touchy. You know, easily ignited."

"Why? Did he say?"

Shirley felt dizzy and lethargic—the doctor had told her the Valium might do that. Only now was she aware that she hadn't asked them to sit down. "I'm sorry," she said, waving them to a couch.

"It's all right," Ma said, as if about to leave.

But Riley, like a terrier who wouldn't let go, pressed her for more information, asking if her husband had kept a diary.

Abruptly, Shirley cocked her head, looking like a startled bird. Why hadn't she thought of it before? "Yes, he does—I mean . . ."

"Would it be possible to have a look at it?"

She frowned, coming down now from the happy realization that there was something of his she could touch, hold to her bosom, as it were. She spoke softly: "I'm sorry, I don't think he'd want that. After all, it is—"

"We understand," Ma interjected. "It's no one else's business. All I'd ask is that you could check to see it's still where he normally put it. That it's safe?"

"Safe? I'm . . ." She walked into the bedroom, just a few feet down the hall from the living room, pulled out a drawer from an old-fashioned lowboy table by the bed, then shut it.

"It's safe," she told them, returning to the living room.

"Good," Ma said. "When you feel up to it, Mrs. Kozan, would you be so good as to have a look at the entries when your husband had the first run-in with the militia? If you see anything you think we should know, anything at all, would you be good enough to contact the Bureau? I've given you my—"

"Yes," she replied, her left hand feeling for the chair as if she couldn't see it.

"Are you all right?" Ma asked, helping to lower her into the chair.

"A bit woozy," she conceded.

"Can we get you something?"

"No, I'll be all right. I'll call if I—"

"Don't worry about that," Ma said. "Look after yourself first."

She smiled. "I don't know whether I'm up to reading his diary. I'm . . . to tell the truth I'm not sure I want to—just now."

"Of course," Ma told her.

"But if I think of anything—"

"Fine," Ma assured her, then followed Agent Riley to the door, when he turned back and advised her that she should have someone stay over to help.

"Thank you," she said drowsily, feeling for the first time since the memorial service that she might be able to sleep, to escape the horror of her life, if even for a few minutes.

* * *

"Well," Riley said as they got into the rental Plymouth Breeze. "What do you think?"

"Zilch," Ma replied. "I don't think her husband saw anything we'd be interested in."

Riley turned the ignition. "That guy he shot must've thought he did. Otherwise why'd he shoot at Kozan?"

Ma shrugged. "Maybe he'd had a bad day's fishing. Got real pissed off when the ranger shows up. Hates the world maybe?"

"Could be, but the chief'll want a report anyway."

Riley saw a snake slither down from the dike into the drainage canal. "In that case you should have told her to *give* you the diary."

"Didn't want to frighten her."

"Yeah, well what are you going to report?"

"Nothing. Not till I check it out."

"And when will that be?"

"When she's more compliant."

"Com—what?"

"Compliant. Willing."

Riley shook his head. "You're pushing the envelope, Daddy. We've got a time line on this thing, you know—before the opposition starts sniffing."

"Tonight," Ma said.

"Tonight? What makes you so sure she'll be com—"

"Com*pliant*."

"Yeah."

"The tranquilizer. She's on something. She'll be asleep."

"Now that isn't nice," Riley joked. "Illegal, in fact."

"Extraordinary times," Ma riposted. "And extraordinary times call for extraordinary measures."

"Yeah, right. Gators come out at night."

"Oh not me," Ma said, affecting surprise. "*You*, buddy boy."

In a Valium-induced torpor, Shirley Kozan, lying in the cloying heat of her bedroom, imagined she could hear the grass river, called the Everglades, moving slowly but inexorably under the full moon around the islands toward the sea. But what she was hearing was the last of the rain shower running off the galvanized tin roof and down the levee's slope behind the bungalow, toward the water-lily-choked bayou. Despite the coolness in the wake of the storm, she was perspiring heavily, the air thick and unpleasant with the odor of her sweat, the bedspread below her damp, giving off its unaired smell. Mixed up with this body odor, the heat, and the buzzing of mosquitoes outside the mesh-screened windows, she detected yet another odor, that of stale cigars, which was odd because her Bobby had never smoked. She'd heard it said that during emotional crises one or more of one's senses can become particularly acute. Perhaps, she thought, someone was smoking outside.

Despite her heavily drugged state, she propped herself up and looked out the window toward Sandfly Island. There was no one, though she could hear the distinctive slap as a gator or a crocodile hit the water nearby. Only a week before, a tourist, ignoring posted warnings not to venture forth from the boat, had been taken up in Fakahatchee Bay. Just for a second, in her tranquilized brain, when she'd glanced out the window, she hadn't been thinking of her husband's death, but now the full force of it washed over her again and she felt nauseated—so much so that she half walked, half stumbled, in the moon-shafted room toward the bathroom and, hanging her sweat-soaked head over the toilet bowl, began retching. She hadn't eaten since the day before, and nothing came up, her throat already aching from the violent spasm. Despite her own noise, however, she heard the slap of another gator before all outside noises were momentarily drowned by the flush of the cistern toilet.

Later, her consciousness passing in and out between a fitful dozing and wakefulness, Shirley Kozan wasn't fully cognizant of either where she was or what time it was. In a moment or two of wakefulness, though even this was clouded by a thick headache and marked by another wave of nausea, she again became aware of cigar smoke.

Though wobbly on her feet from the tranquilizer, using the edge of her bed, she helped steady herself and she took the flashlight and Bob's .38 from the wallpaper-covered box that served as a bedside table. She moved down the moonlit hall-way, eschewing the use of the hall light, knowing it would only make her thudding headache worse. The cigar stink was coming from the living room. Her flashlight beam swept across the worn carpet. She shifted the beam and gasped—a white face in the beam. The man with the Chinese name. Ma. She hesitated, heard a sound as if someone had spat, and fell back, crumpled sideways, striking her head on the doorjamb, the flashlight rolling across the floor, her finger convulsing, sending off a shot even as she was dying, the blood from her temple a shiny black smear in the moonlight.

"Let's get out of here!" said Riley, who'd fired the kill shot. "Whole fuckin' neighborhood'll have heard that."

"Don't panic," Ma said. "There's no neighbors. C'mon, grab her feet."

"We'd better—"

"Grab her feet!"

Halfway out of the house, moving toward the slough, Ma asked Riley if he'd got the diary.

"Yes. Jesus—what about the crocs?"

"Just keep your eyes open," Ma told him.

"I fuckin' am keeping my eyes open. Goddammit, she's heavy."

Two minutes later as they walked back to the car, parked a hundred yards down the levee from the bungalow, they could hear a furious splashing of water like children playing in a pool as the reptilians' feeding rose to a frenzy.

"Better be something in that diary," Ma said. "After all this."

CHAPTER EIGHTEEN

MA AND RILEY sat in their car, Ma tearing the diary's two halves from their bindings, keeping one half for himself, giving half to Riley. "They're numbered, but try not to get 'em mixed up."

Riley dropped his sheaf on the top of the dash. "Won't be anything in them. Last year's entries—you've got the most recent."

Ma grunted, conceding the point, but tried to save face nevertheless. "He might've written something he'd seen—you know, entered it earlier."

"And why the fuck would he do that?"

"I dunno. Maybe he wanted to hide it."

"Yeah, right."

"Hey, if it's too much trouble to read for half a grand, I'll get somebody else."

Sullenly, Riley grabbed the first half of the diary and started reading. "Handwriting's lousy."

"Almost as bad as yours. It'll take a while."

"Then let's have some music at least," Riley said, his mood resentful. He punched the stereo button and the car was filled with Celine Dion.

"Not so loud," Ma said.

Riley turned it down just a tad. There was a mosquito buzzing, and Riley was looking murderously around for the insect. Both of them were on edge. Things had started going wrong the moment they set foot in the house, and now Ma was worried about the footprints they'd left in the mud when they got rid of her body. Well, there was nothing they could do now except hope the forecast rain was forthcoming—wash any prints away. On top of everything, he hadn't come across anything in the latter half of Kozan's diary, though he had a ways to go. The handwriting wasn't that bad really, but it was small and, being products of the computer age, neither Ma nor Riley had had much practice deciphering something written by hand. Kozan's a's and o's were almost the same.

Ma's frustration increased as he thought of his client, a man in Miami whom he and Riley had communicated with only through a cutout. The man, José, had given them a thousand down—a thousand to come after the job was done. An extra grand apiece had been promised if they found anything at all that indicated Kozan had seen something unusual the day of the heavy rain in Ten Thousand Islands when, after cutting his engine, he'd crept up through the mist and shot the militiaman.

"What kind of thing?" Ma had asked José.

"Anything about the militia."

"Bit vague, isn't it?"

"Yeah," Riley had chimed in. "Too fucking vague for my liking."

José shrugged. "Then don't take the job. Plenty other investigators."

"We'll take it," Ma said. "But can you give us a hint?"

José shrugged. "I don't know."

"Horseshit," Riley said.

"Something unusual," José answered. "That's all I know. She told you he kept a diary. If he saw something unusual, he would be sure to put it in a diary. Yes?"

"Maybe," Riley said.

"You'll be met in Miami. Four o'clock tomorrow afternoon, Morley's Hotel. You know where it is?"

"We know," Riley had said unsmilingly.

Now they were sitting in the car off the 41, halfway to Miami, east of Everglades City, poring over the leaves of the diary.

Riley exhaled heavily and took out a packet of Marlboros.

"Thought you were giving 'em up," Ma said, turning a page.

Riley lit up and took a long drag. "We could tell this José any fucking thing we like. Make up something." The nicotine was relaxing him already. "You ever see that movie *Our Man in Havana*? That limey guy in it. He was supposed to be a spy so he made up things, like he drew a new vacuum cleaner from the States and flogged it off as a hush-hush Russian rocket."

Ma turned another page. "You sayin' we should make something up?" Before Riley could answer, Ma was explaining that whatever the militias hadn't wanted Kozan to see must be known to the militia—anything else they wouldn't be interested in.

"Just a thought," Riley responded.

"It's something that would've surprised him," Ma reiterated.

"And it's so fucking hush-hush they won't even tell us."

"That's right, and the sooner—" Ma stopped, his gaze fixed on the page:

Something happened today that has shaken me up. I killed a man. Was out in the glades with Laddie on the airboat—love those things—you sit high up in the chair, this huge fan behind you, pushing you along and you in command of it all. At first you think you might tip over if you turn too quickly—you're sitting way up there like you're God of the Everglades—the river of grass going on forever. Anyway, Laddie was sniffing the air standing way up front—thought he'd fall off but no he hung on and was having the time of his life. Suddenly the sky started to go black and blue and it wasn't long before I saw long streaks of lightning and instead of heading back through the saw grass—which actually has little saw teeth on it by the way and can do a pretty good job of lacerating your arms, legs, face if you're not careful—I headed out to the islands because I figured that in the river of grass where there was nothing higher than the occasional hammock of stunted trees and the like I'd be the highest thing out there—or rather the airboat would be—and it'd become one hell of a lightning rod. We'd only gone a way into the islands and I saw this other airboat—the driver was dressed in fatigues—a militiaman—in fact he looked like a soldier and had one of those floppy camouflage hats they wore in 'Nam. No one else other than park rangers and the local Indians are allowed to go around in that area in airboats. I think he got the fright of his life when I suddenly happened upon him. Before I knew it he was firing at me. I swung the boat about and took off and he came *after* me! Talk about aggressive! You'd've thought I'd caught him robbing a bank! It started to rain—thank God—because if it hadn't I wouldn't be alive to write this. The rain was the heaviest I've ever seen it. Dad used to tell me about rain up in the Northwest—said it didn't rain on you, the sky just plain collapsed on you like a cow peein' on a flat rock. Well that's what it was like and it saved my life because it covered the noise of my boat when I throttled down. I left Laddie tied up near some mangroves—he was barking and whining and it was this noise that the militia guy followed while I circled back around him. I called out for him to put down the gun— at least I *think* I did—like an auto crash it's so hard to remember just what happened. I mean in what sequence. I saw him turn, the gun in his hand, and I fired. The damnedest thing is that I wasn't aiming—at least not with my eye. I know that sounds queer but the best way I can describe it is that I fired without lining up the gun—you know the way they crouch using both hands with the gun way out in front. I fired at where I was looking if you get what I mean— *without* looking at the gun—it was kind of instinctive. I know you're supposed to be sick and all that after you've killed someone but I didn't—I was too damned mad at someone trying to kill me. It was only later when I heard that he had a wife and a couple of kids that I felt bad and now I can't get rid of the feeling that if maybe I gave him more warning or something and the more I think about it the less clear it is what happened. Tonight I tried to make love to Shirl but I couldn't. I got a hard-on—I mean really hard but I couldn't come. Course it's alright for Shirl—well not really—it upsets her to see me upset about it—but she has an orgasm no trouble and meanwhile I'm cussing the purple topped thing like it doesn't belong to me. I know it's childish but it makes me so mad—so wild at myself I could chew steel. Maybe I'll rent myself out as a stud. "Have Dick Will Travel." I guess you've got to laugh about it because if I don't I'll go crazy. But I can't help thinking God's punishing me for killing another human being. "Thou shalt not kill—" "You mean God unless there's a war or—" "No," God says, "no ifs buts or maybes—no relativism. Thou shalt not kill PERIOD!"

"Damn!" Ma said. "I thought he was going to tell us he saw something." Ma's eyes roved quickly over the rest of that day's entry. "Rest of this shit's about his wife . . . he didn't see anything—not a trace, nothing unusual enough for José, I bet."

Riley was lighting up another cigarette. "Why don't we just give him the pages? They can go through 'em."

Ma nodded. "Yeah, if it's in here, we've missed it. Anyway, we've got another grand coming."

Ma glanced over at the pages Riley had been looking through. "Nothing in your lot?"

"Squat."

"Any militia stuff at all?"

"Nah—just a lot of sloppy shit about his wife. Lovey dovey. She had him by the balls."

"Okay," Ma said, hitting the cab light switch to off. "Miami, here we come."

They drove in silence for a while, the sea of saw grass stretching out on either side of them. Riley was hunched down in his seat, which he'd moved farther back. "What d'you think the militia's so uptight about? I mean, what're they pissin' their pants for?"

"Smuggling operation," Ma said. "Maybe they're refining it back there. A million hiding places."

"I don't think so," Riley said, with all the gravity of a Supreme Court Justice. "Militia isn't normally into drugs. One of the things they're dead set against. 'Specially down here in the Bible Belt."

"You know," Ma said, "one of the wealthiest guys around here during Prohibition was a teetotaler." Before Riley could respond, Ma went on, "It's all about money, Riley. Whatever makes money."

It started to rain over the entire seventy-mile-wide, hundred-mile-long subtropical vastness of the 'glades, and Riley said, "You beauty"—their footprints erased forever.

Upon hearing of the murder—the local sheriff had found blood-spattered remains of Shirley Kozan's nightdress and blood in the bungalow—U.S. Attorney General Helen Wyeth, because the murder had taken place in a national and not state park, ordered the Florida National Guard to conduct a sweep of the Everglades adjacent to Ten Thousand Islands, and the islands themselves.

Marte Price's cell phone rang, and she was torn between covering the events unfolding where she was, in the Northwest, and in the southeastern corner of the continent in Florida.

CHAPTER NINETEEN

Washington State

LINDA SETH HADN'T been gone for fifteen minutes when McAllister, having stayed awhile in the Chinese restaurant for some serious drinking, began to worry again about her.

Ah, he told himself, maybe the vodka martinis had pickled his brain, but he couldn't throw off the feeling that there was something odd about Merk's decision to sell—especially to the

Japanese. What if he, Randy, had been right when he warned her that old Merk might be suspicious of her, of who she really was? Old Wong brought him a whiskey with an Oly beer chaser. McAllister swirled his scotch, staring at the ice cube.

Keen as she was to see Merk, and hopeful to find out more about the Washington State militia, Linda kept the needle on the speed limit, not wanting to be pulled over by a speed cop again. The Bureau would of course get her out of any jam with the local police, but it would mean divulging that she was FBI, and the fewer people who knew, the better. It was stuffy in the car, and she wound down the window, letting a blast of snow-cold air wake her up. She turned the radio to FM and was scanning the dial when she saw in the rearview mirror a pair of headlights swing out from a side road, coming onto the highway about a quarter mile behind her.

In Yakima, McAllister was now gazing vacantly into his beer, trying to feel sorry for himself, but it wasn't working. He knew that his wife, Melissa, wasn't as cold as maybe he'd implied to Linda, or maybe he hadn't implied that at all. To tell the truth, he told himself in a moment of drunken honesty, he couldn't remember exactly what he'd told Linda Seth. Did he tell her she was the most desirable woman he'd ever met? He hoped not. Such a clichéd sentiment was bound to turn a woman off, particularly one as bright as Linda. Couldn't get her out of his mind.

A country-western song of unrequited love was wailing through the restaurant, and for a moment McAllister felt half in the song and half out, trying to figure out Merk. Maybe the old guy was plain horny and wanted to drool a bit more over Linda. Be difficult, though, with old Frau Merk at the helm. If she saw her hubby going goggle-eyed, she'd bust his balls with a rolling pin. McAllister didn't know too much about the old boy, but his frau's reputation was known throughout the valley. Fill your pants full o' buckshot quicker'n look at you. Joke in town was if we'd sent Frau Merk to Iraq, Saddam Insane would've thrown in the towel immediately.

Through the smoky atmosphere of Wong's restaurant—old Henry Wong having refused to post No Smoking signs—McAllister surveyed the other customers, several couples talking animatedly with one another, their conversation punctuated now and then by raucous laughter, and he thought of how pleasant it would be to have Linda sitting across from him. Obviously she didn't feel the same; otherwise she wouldn't have been so keen to go off to the Merks' place. If Merk had invited Linda back, his missus would have had to okay it, and why would she want a good-looker like Linda on the property? It didn't make sense, unless . . .

"Holy Jesus!" McAllister, not bothering to wait for the bill, extricated himself from the cushioned grasp of the booth, went over to the cash register, gave old Henry Wong a fifty, and left. The moment he hit the cold, bracing air, McAllister felt a lot drunker than he had inside the restaurant. Nevertheless, after fumbling with his keys, he got into his '92 Mustang and drove with extreme caution till he was out of town on the 410, then he let her rip. In Cantonese, Henry Wong told his wife in the kitchen that he was "in the stew!"

"Why?" she asked him, too busy with the wok to pay him much attention.

"One of our best customers is driving blind drunk." He didn't say McAllister's name—never could handle the *Mc* sound in English.

"So?"

"So we should help him," Wong said. "We should call the police."

Mrs. Wong tipped the wok and gave it several quick stirs, keeping her eyes on the slices of green pepper going close to the edge. "Are you crazy?" she asked. "You eat something funny in your rice?" Henry was recalling those old Drive Safely spots on TV where you saw a little girl's room, her favorite stuffed animals, her swing where she is now and where she is the next second, riding her tricycle out on the road and the terrible squeal of brakes. It was irresponsible to knowingly let a drunk drive. And in litigious America, maybe the Wongs could be criminally liable for their client's drunken state.

"He wouldn't have to know," Henry told his wife. She didn't answer because he knew the answer—try to keep something like that quiet in Yakima.

"You would lose him as a customer," she said, tapping the stir fry onto a plate, "and anybody else who comes here for a few drinks."

Henry was getting angry. "You think I haven't thought of that, but my English is good. They wouldn't know it was me." Mrs. Wong was lost for a moment in billows of steam from the huge bowl of rice. "Say 'McAllister,' " she said. Henry said it and heard his pronunciation mangle it. He paused for a minute and a waitress came in. "Two Tsingtaos." Henry took two beer glasses down and opened the fridge. After the waitress had taken the stir fry and the green bottles of beer, Henry told his wife he wouldn't have to mention any names. All he needed to do was tell the police it was a green Mustang, heading north. "They mightn't find him," Henry said by way of compromise. "I mean I don't know what highway he's on. Could be the Twelve, or the interstate, or Eighty-Two." She said nothing, which meant she still disapproved.

"What if it was our daughter playing on the road?"

She scoffed at him. "At this time of night? Besides, we look after our children. We know where they are."

"Oh yes," Henry said. "How about Johnny?"

"He's staying over at a friend's for a few days." The moment she said it she could feel a trap closing.

"Where?" Henry demanded.

"Johnny's old enough to look after himself."

"It's not Johnny's driving I'm worried about. It's a drunk driver on the same road maybe."

"Do as you wish," she said grumpily, which meant she had seen his point. Henry went out the back and used a public phone two blocks away. He felt uneasy, but was convinced he was doing the right thing. He'd seen too many people killed or crippled for life from such accidents. The older he got, the more he thought about how hazardous life was. He liked Mc-Allister, but what if he killed someone, nodded off and went off the road, killing himself? Henry believed he was doing him a favor.

Linda spotted the vehicle moving up behind her Taurus through her wake of blown snow, saw "Blazer" spelled backward in her rear vision mirror, and looked for the license plate. There was none, and her training took over. She drew her .38 from her waist holster, putting it on the passenger side, sticking its barrel between the seat's back and seat proper in case she had to brake hard. She pressed her cellular's memory button for Bill Trey at the FBI office in Spokane. "C'mon, Bill." Nothing but static; she was out of range.

The next instant she was flung violently forward, jerked to a stop a couple of inches from the windshield, the safety strap across her torso cutting tightly across her breasts. The green Chevy Blazer hit her again as she pressed down hard on the accelerator, then hit her yet again, slamming against her Taurus. She tried to correct, but then found herself off the road in a frozen drainage ditch and rolling, the Blazer speeding by, then braking hard, its taillights like two huge red eyes in blowing snow.

As Latrell executed a U-turn he shouted over the noise of the hot air vent to the Nazis behind him, telling them that this was as good as "goin' after that nigger and those other snoops they sent up." Norman, getting excited, snatched the nine-millimeter from the glove box.

Andrew reached over. "Hey, you don't want to kill her. Not right off. Maybe we can have some fun."

"Yeah," Norman said. "But what if she starts shooting, eh?"

Latrell pumped the brake. The Blazer stopped in a controlled skid, and the Nazis, Latrell following, and a beer bottle, spilled out of the Blazer into the darkness. "A flashlight," Latrell demanded. "Hurry up." They smelled gasoline, its odor over-coming all others, and when, with some difficulty, they yanked open the driver's door, they could see that her face, though pressed up against the air bag, had been cut by flying glass. She was groaning in pain. Before Latrell knew it, one of the Nazi skinheads had slipped his hand under her skirt and was feeling her.

"What in hell—" Latrell said, pulling the skinhead away from the door. He saw more blood, then two headlights dipping and reappearing less than a quarter mile south of them on the highway, coming their way.

"Hey!" Andrew shouted. "We got company."

"Shit!" Latrell said. "Let's go. C'mon!" He struck a match and dropped it. Within a minute they were back in the Blazer, speeding north. Looking back, Latrell couldn't see any flames. "Damn match must've died."

"You think she saw us?" Zane asked, panicking. "I mean got a good look—"

"I had the flashlight on her," Latrell said. "She was blinded—she couldn't see anything. She won't be doin' any snoopin' for a while." Latrell was perspiring, stinking up the Blazer like a mixture of skunk and onions.

"They'll send someone else," Andrew said.

"It'll take time," Latrell said. "By then it'll all be over."

"What'll be over?" Andrew pressed. Latrell could see the headlights behind him about a half mile away now. They seemed to be weaving along the road instead of coming straight.

"You're sick," Latrell told the skinhead. Andrew said nothing. "Back there," Latrell continued. "What in hell you do that for?"

"Oh I get it," Andrew said with uncharacteristic confidence after his panic of a moment before. "It's all right to run the bitch off the road but not to touch her pussy. Right?"

Latrell's eyes narrowed. "I told any of the militia boys you were messin' with a woman like that, know what they'd do?"

"Yeah," Andrew said, his lust still in overdrive. "They'd be lining up behind me."

"The hell they would," Latrell countered. "They'd take you out back an' shoot you."

"Yeah?"

"Yeah."

"How 'bout a black woman?" the Nazi asked.

"I'm talking 'bout Aryans."

Andrew wasn't listening to him. Now he too was watching the lights way back. Looked like they had stopped. Latrell asked Andrew what the hell he was doing last night at Merk's.

"What d'you mean?" Andrew asked. "I was drinkin' like you."

"You don't remember us talking about Spokane?"

"No."

"Gonna be one hell of a get-together. More'n four thousand, the colonel reckons."

The skinhead didn't answer. Instead he asked Latrell again, "What if it had been a nigger back there?"

"Why don't you look for a nice white woman?" Latrell replied. "Settle down, get married."

"Like you?" the skinhead said.

Latrell either didn't get the irony in the other's tone or he didn't care about it. "Yeah, like me. 'Cept I didn't tattoo 'Mommy' on my chest."

"Fuck you. It's M.O.M., not Mommy. Militia of Montana."

The headlights behind them, Norman told Latrell, had definitely come to a stop, receding from view.

When McAllister reached the gray Taurus, he too smelled the overpowering odor of leaking gas. Despite being half drunk, he did battle with the air bag, leaned over her and quickly released the seat belt, put his hands under her arms and pulled her out headfirst, struggling to get her up the side of the ditch before the gas was ignited by a spark or something. He had just reached the road when the car exploded in flame, the heat wave searing his face and singeing his hair.

Latrell and the Nazis could see it as a quick flash of orange light.

"Good riddance!" Latrell said. Andrew was sniffing his fingers like it was a line of coke. Then he sucked them.

Not knowing how serious her injuries might be, McAllister dragged her into the Mustang's passenger seat, set it to recline, made a pillow of his jacket, and started off back as fast as he could toward Yakima, eighteen miles away, praying along the way. When he saw the flashing red light coming toward him, he began flicking his headlights from high to low beam and slowed, driving close to the center line. The police car slowed. McAllister told the cop that the gray Taurus had gone off the shoulder into a ditch and that he'd pulled Linda Seth out. He pointed back along the road. "I think her car's on fire—saw a glow in the rear—"

"You been drinking?" the cop cut in, McAllister's breath confirmation of old Wong's call. The cop's tone had abruptly changed from sympathetic inquiry to accusation.

"Yeah," McAllister said. "But this woman's hurt bad. She—"

The cop was already calling for an ambulance to rendezvous with him farther back toward Yakima, and a fire truck for the car. He had a close look at Linda. She was breathing all right, blood on her left arm and blouse and face but no sign of any deep cuts or continued bleeding.

"Can you help me get her in the patrol car?" the cop asked.

"Sure, but should I—"

"Buddy, help me get her in the car. Now." When he'd done that, the cop told McAllister to hurry up and turn around against the car.

"Hey—"

"Keep still," the cop bellowed, and McAllister felt himself being frisked. "Put your hands behind your back." He felt his arms wrenched and heard the click of the handcuffs. "You're under arrest. Driving under the influence. Get in the back."

"Hey, man, I dragged her from the friggin' car."

"Yeah. Maybe you were the cause of the accident."

"Hey, I was tryin' to—"

"Shut up and get in the *back*! *Now!*"

The cop put out four flares—driver's side, front and rear of the Mustang—and took out the keys. The moment he got back in the police car and started off, he hit the siren. Its wail seemed to fill the valley. The cop rattled off his prisoner's Miranda rights and asked if McAllister knew the woman.

"Yeah," McAllister said, unable to suppress a burp that added to the beery smell of him. "She works for me."

"Beautiful," the cop said. "You both drinking?"

"No. Only me."

"Uh-huh. She your girlfriend?"

"No. Wish she was."

Linda started moaning, saying something, but neither of them could make it out. Sounded like a question.

"We're taking you to the hospital, ma'am. Hang on, all right?" She moaned again.

"How many'd you have?" the cop asked McAllister.

"I dunno. Six—maybe eight."

"Maybe ten or twelve?"

"Maybe," McAllister said. "I'm over the limit anyhow."

"No kidding!"

"Don't have to be a smart-ass."

"Watch your mouth!"

"I'm worried about her."

"Yeah, well you should've thought 'bout that before you got drunk. Right?"

McAllister said nothing for a few moments to show he wouldn't be baited, and then decided to break the rules and told the cop about her being an FBI agent, how her working for him was cover, and how he believed militia wackos might have run her off the road.

"Yeah, right," the cop said. "How many beers was it? Twenty?"

* * *

The Chevy Blazer with Latrell, Vance, and the four Nazis aboard continued on its way to Spokane. The colonel had already forgotten Linda Seth. A commander had to concentrate on the big picture in his determination to take America's breath away, to show, as he faxed his Spokane agents, that the militia was far from being defeated, that the so-called surrender to which Nordstrom had agreed was no more than a pause in the war. What had Patton said? "America loves a winner and will not tolerate a loser."

In Yakima, the sheriff told his deputy, "Lyle, I don't want that car Linda Seth was driving—what's left of it—touched till forensic's gone over it. The fact we know this woman's FBI means we can expect the federals to want to go over her car with a fine-tooth comb. And I don't want FBI types tellin' us we interfered with evidence."

"No problem, Sheriff," Lyle assured him. "I'll head out there now and put out the yellow tape. Any son of a bitch touches it, I'll blow his head off."

The sheriff had a toothpick between two bottom teeth. "Lyle, just tell 'em to stay the hell away from it."

"You betcha!"

When Lyle reached the Taurus, it was a burned-out shell still giving off toxic fumes from the burned plastic fittings, the glove box empty.

It gave him an eerie feeling being alone out there at night on the highway—maniac Nazis on the loose. He got back into his car and made sure the doors were locked. He even put the inside light on and looked through the cage grill into the backseat. Lyle remembered that the real estate guy in the drunk tank had been right about the injured woman, Linda Seth, being FBI. McAllister had also mentioned that she'd been on the way to see an orchardist—Merk. Lyle called through to Yakima and suggested he go talk to this Merk right now. The sheriff told him to go ahead. Lyle felt a little guilty about the request because the real reason he wanted to go see Merk was to get the hell off the highway. It was spooky out there.

* * *

"Green Chevy Blazer?" Stanley Merk responded to Lyle's question. "Nope, can't say I have." He turned from the front door toward the kitchen. "May, officer here wants to know if we've seen a Chevy Blazer 'round here in the past few days." Merk turned back to the officer. "What color you say it was?"

"Green," Lyle said. "We'd like to talk to anyone who might've seen the driver."

"Green Chevy Blazer," Merk called out to May.

May Merk came out wiping her hands on an apron with *Mother* spelled out in embroidery. "Green Blazers? Let me see now. We seen a few yellow jackets!"

Stan nearly fell over. By God, first joke she'd made in years. Just when he figured he knew her inside out, up she comes with a lulu like that. By God, she could've been on *Jay Leno*.

Lyle had a big grin on his face. "So I guess you haven't seen one, ma'am?"

May was serious now, her leathery face creased with concentration. "One of them four-wheel-drive jobs, kinda high off the ground?"

"You got it," Lyle said.

"You'll have to forgive Stan here. His memory ain't what it used to be." Stanley looked bemused, like Pa from the old Ma and Pa Kettle movies. "We seen one t'other day. Passed it on the highway not far from here. Changing a tire, they was."

"They?" Lyle said.

"Yep," May said, "far as I recall. Two fellers."

"You sure it was a Blazer?"

"Yes," May said. "Think it was. I remember 'em 'cause they had no plates. I always have a look to see if cars are out of state."

Lyle was writing it down. "Two fellers, you said? Can you give us a description?"

May thought for a second. "No, just two fellers. I think one had a hat—that's all I remember. Why, they steal somethin'?"

"Don't know, but they could be involved in an attempted murder."

"Lordy!" May said. "That real estate woman I heard about on the radio?"

"That's the one," the patrolman said. "Name is Seth."

"Linda," May said. "*Linda* Seth?"

"That's her. You know 'er?"

"Lordy—attempted murder? She was supposed to come out to see us," May said. "We wondered why she didn't show up."

"I know," the patrolman said. "Her boss, Mr. McAllister, told us you rang through for her."

"World's full o' crazies," May said.

"You can say that again," Stanley said. May and Lyle ignored him.

"Can't remember anything distinctive about them?" Lyle pressed.

May was thinking, shaking her head slowly. "Only the hat and the sign."

"Sign?"

"Yeah," May said. "You know how people have those stupid signs. 'Seattle or bust.' "

"Is that what it said?"

"No, it was 'Snoqualmie or bust.' "

"Then they were heading west into the Cascades?"

May shrugged. "Guess so."

"The sign said Snoqualmie?"

"Sure did."

"Uh-huh. How 'bout you, Mr. Merk. You recall anything about 'em?"

"I don't even remember the vehicle. Guess I was too busy driving. We were coming back from Spokane."

"Huh," Lyle grunted. "That'd mean they were headed west through the mountains."

"I guess," Stanley said, asking eagerly, "That help you any?"

"Yeah—yes it does. We thought they'd be headed for Spokane. Did they look like militiamen? I mean were they dressed in fatigues? You know, army type uniform?"

"Nope," May said. "You recall, Stanley?"

"I told ya—I didn't see 'em."

Lyle flipped his notebook shut. "Well, thanks, folks. You've been very helpful. We hope we'll get 'em pretty soon. You remember anything else, you give us a call." He gave them his card.

"Sure will," Stan said.

As the patrolman drove off down through the apple trees, they could see him talking into the radio.

"Why d'you tell 'im anything?" Stanley asked her. "Why didn't you say you'd never seen 'em?"

"To throw the federals off the scent. What would you do? Tell 'em they were going to Spokane? I don't trust those skinheads. Cops get hold of 'em, might spill their guts. I'd rather they got clean away, us pointin' the federals in the wrong direction."

"I dunno," Stan said, starting to rub some more navy cut in the palm of his hand. "I would've stayed quiet."

" 'Course you would. You don't think ahead, that's why." She paused. "That woman's trouble."

"She had a concussion," Stan said. "It was on the news."

"People recover from concussions, Stanley. They start rememberin' what happened."

"So?"

"So if the federals got one of those skinheads and confronted him with her, he might start blabbin'—drag us in with him." She suddenly stopped, sniffed the air, and ran into the kitchen. "Darn, I've burned the cookies."

"I thought Fred Latrell would fix her good 'n' proper."

"Well he didn't, did he?" she said sharply, adding disgustedly, "*Men!* Drooling over her. Hadn't been for me, you'd never even known she was a federal. Should've done it myself."

Well, Stan thought, if *you're* so goddamn smart, why the hell didn't you? Trouble was, May wanted to control everything in her life, and sometimes you just plain couldn't. There were too many things outside one's control. "Just have to go with the flow, May."

She came out of the kitchen and stood there, as formidable as a tank, arms on hips, blocking the passage between living room and kitchen. "And what's that supposed to mean? They start searching this place, Stanley, they're going to find more than cider stashed in the basement and you could spend time behind bars. Now given that, don't you think it's time you faced up to reality?"

Stanley was lighting the pipe, his speech punctuated by sucking hard to get a fire going in the bowl. "What—the hell—can I do—about it?" She waited until he got the stupid thing smoking.

"You remember coming home from that militia meeting, not so long back, telling me what the colonel said, that you had to stop leaks with 'extreme prejudice'?"

Stanley nodded and got up.

"And where d'you think you're going?" she challenged tartly.

"I need a drink."

"You need a clear head."

"You think the cop will come back?"

"What d'you think, Stanley?"

He poured himself a half glass of bourbon. She strode over, taking the glass away. "Well, hell," Stanley said. "We can't move everything."

"I know," she cut in. "We'll just have to be ready to do what's necessary. Can't go all jelly belly and flinch from it. Can we?"

CHAPTER TWENTY

MARTE PRICE, HAVING made a quick trip to Florida and reporting from Everglades City on the latest murder in the 'glades, arrived at Seattle's Sea-Tac Airport, immediately called CNN headquarters in Atlanta, and suggested she continue on to Spokane. Her boss couldn't have agreed more. The phones were ringing off the hook. The Eleen/Irwin fight, the murder of a park ranger and shooting of a militiaman in Florida, the vicious attacks on agent Seth near Naches, and the hunt for her would-be killers, presumed to be militiamen, were all coalescing into the biggest militia story since the Oklahoma bombing. Already the militia convention in Spokane was going ape—billboards covered with "Remember Waco," "Remember Ruby Ridge," "Remember Mant"—and signs carried by the conventioneers parading through the streets were everywhere.

And as if this wasn't enough, the President was due to arrive in Spokane in forty-eight hours. For Marte Price it was, to use Socrates's phrase, mind-blowing.

"You think the President'll still come?" she asked her boss.

"Has to, Marte. He backs off now, he's in big trouble politically. He can't be seen running away from the militias. A lot of Americans want them brought to heel. I was on the phone with Attorney General Wyeth. She wants the Army to call out the entire National Guard up there in Washington State, like they have in Florida. The President says no, it would only inflame the situation."

"Can it get any more inflamed?" Marte asked.

"Marte, you have to be on the militiamen's enemies list. You be damned careful. We're sending a full team up to you. Meanwhile, we've got an affiliate crew standing by. Got a pen?"

"Yes."

"I've got the phone numbers you'll need. Oh, and another thing. Don't mess around with scheduled airlines—all booked by militias anyway. Lease a Lear, lease a Tiger Moth, but get there! You beat the networks on the Kozan business, so let's keep ahead."

Her story about the murders in Florida, also carried by Larry King, was largely responsible, along with both Spanish and English editions of the *Miami Herald*, for getting the governor to request a National Guard sweep of the Everglades for illegal militia activity.

* * *

Going through the burned-out hulk of the Taurus, an FBI forensic agent found nothing of interest except a few Coke cans blackened by the fire, and a couple of broken bottles nearby. One of the bottles had obviously been a fifth of bourbon or something similar, the label nearly destroyed, though a small piece of it, made of raised aluminum type, had survived. But the sheriff still couldn't tell what label it had been. The other bottle, broken at the neck, was stubby, an old Budweiser bottle with what looked like black ash sticking to the bottom. After the FBI left, the sheriff pulled a ballpoint from his pocket and fished around the bottom of the bottle, loosening the detritus, whatever it was, then tipped a scab of it, no bigger than a dime, into an envelope and told one of his deputies to FedEx it to Seattle—see if forensics could come up with anything.

In the war of words, both domestic and international media were getting an earful. In particular, militiamen who had driven to Spokane from other parts of Washington State and from Oregon, Idaho, Montana, and Wyoming, were complaining bitterly about the roadblocks, as if, one militia spokesman said, "We were a bunch of criminals."

"And don't forget what the federals are doing down our way," a commander of a Florida contingent interjected. "Buddy o' mine, Harry Morgan, was shot down in the Everglades because he was *fishin'*. Just sittin' there in his airboat, *fishin'*. Next minute he ends up dead! I'm tellin' you, the federals are outta control."

"And now," a rifleman from the Eastern Michigan militia griped, "ain't enough that we have to have a license to drive, a license to hunt, pay county tax, state tax, federal tax. There are those goddamn photo radar traps. Man never knows when he's being watched. Spied on. Next minute the sons of bitches fine you in the mail. 'Course *your* photo's on record, but you never get to see *their* faces. I'm tellin' you, it's Big Brother all over."

"You're right," a Texas militiaman concurred. "Just another money grab by government."

One young reporter, new to his business, felt overwhelmed by the sheer numbers of militiamen descending on Spokane for the annual convention. "It's like living in an armed camp," he excitedly reported for the Larry King CNN feed in Seattle.

General Douglas Freeman was holding the TV remote, shaking his head. "This kid is right, Marjorie. It *is* an armed camp, like a stack of kindling just waiting for the match. I hope those paper pushers in Washington are watching this."

"I'm sure the police have it under control, Douglas."

"I'm sure they don't. That CNN woman, Marte Price—now there's a looker—says there are about four hundred policemen there, four thousand militia. If my math's correct, that's ten militiamen to every cop!"

"Won't there be a lot more policemen when the President arrives?"

"All right, make it a thousand cops. They're still outnumbered four to one."

"Well, I'm sure everything'll be all right."

The general lowered the TV's sound. "You ever see pictures of the Chicago Democratic Convention in 'sixty-eight?"

"No."

You couldn't talk to the woman, he thought. Her answer to the Holocaust would've been, "Everything'll be all right."

"Chicago Convention," Freeman told her, "was an unmitigated disaster. It was a war. Protestors—hippies, most of 'em—went crazy. Cops went crazy. You know what would happen if this turned ugly—and I can't see how it won't with all these guns around. Overseas, especially the Chinese leadership and the Japanese, would see the President's visit being taken over by a riot between the militias and cops. They would conclude—*correctly,* I might add—that this President has lost it! Has no authority. No control over rebellious forces. And so to hell with his foreign policy, including trade. He'd be perceived as a man who can't manage his people, so how the hell can he be expected to manage the economy? Our foreign policy'd be treated with contempt—empty words by a President who can't back it up with a consensus among Americans."

She wasn't listening, dusting in the hallway.

"Then," Freeman said, his voice rising, "all your invest-ments would take a hit on the stock exchange—"

"What?"

"Well, it would affect the stock market straight away."

Marjorie appeared in the doorway. "The President should get those people under control!"

"Not with police," Freeman said easily, almost nonchalantly.

"Douglas, you have to do something."

"Me? I'm retired."

"But you don't want to be."

"True."

"Then tell them at the Pentagon."

"I have—indirectly—told the C.O. of I Corps at Fort Lewis up there in Washington State that he should move an armored column through the Cascades. But no—the White House thinks it would be too 'provocative.' "

The head of Seattle's forensic lab phoned the Yakima sher-iff and told him that a mass spectrometer analysis of the glass bottle had revealed traces of apple.

"Juice?" the sheriff asked.

"No, I'd say cider. There were indications of fermentation. I think it was a cider bottle. Home brew."

"How's that?"

"Well, I'm not a big cider drinker, but I don't remember cider bottles in stores being corked. Except for wine, most bev-erage containers these days have screw or metal caps on them."

"So someone bottling their own cider?"

"I think so. That any help?"

"Yes and no," the sheriff answered. "Probably half the or-chardists in the state brew their own cider. Problem is, which one?"

The sheriff and his deputy, Rayleen, went to the hospital to interview the FBI agent Linda Seth. Rayleen was only one of a handful of black female cops in the Northwest. A plain Jane look but a great figure—about five-foot-six, with a set to her shoul-ders that said she wouldn't take any guff. The sheriff lusted for her but had never let on—or so he thought, trying his damnedest to keep everything strictly professional.

Linda Seth's face was bandaged, a large patch of gauze high on the back of her neck where they'd had to shave her. Her left arm was in a plaster cast and sling.

"How you doin', Miz Seth?" the sheriff asked her.

"I'm okay. Mending fast."

"Glad to hear it." The sheriff took off his hat and used a khaki handkerchief to wipe the inside band. "Last time I saw you, you were under the weather."

Linda managed a smile. "I'll be out of here in a day or two." She looked around cautiously. "Food in here is terrible, and the coffee . . ." She made a face.

"I believe you," the sheriff said amicably, putting his hat back on. "Talking about food and drink, we found a bottle that had apparently fallen out of that Blazer. Cider bottle—home brew, we think. You been anywhere near—"

"Merk's orchard," she cut in. "Stanley Merk—the man I was going to see about selling his orchard. I was given cider there." She looked at the sheriff and knew he was thinking the same thing—that it could well have been the Blazer that ran her off the road had been at Merk's too, which meant May Merk had told Deputy Lyle a pack of lies.

On the way up to Merk's place, the sheriff told Rayleen that when they reached the orchard he wanted her to look around outside the house while he went in.

"Okay."

"I hear that the Merk woman is a bit of a Tartar."

"*Tartar?*" Rayleen asked.

"Yeah," the sheriff said. "You know, tough."

"Uh-huh."

There were KEEP OUT and TRESPASSERS WILL BE SHOT signs at the turnoff to Merk's place.

"Friendly," Rayleen said.

The air was redolent with Rayleen's perfume, Maui Rain, and the sheriff took a deep breath, visualizing the air going deep inside him, then exhaled slowly, a relaxing technique he'd picked up from some Chinese guy on the PBS channel. He stopped the car in front of the spring down/up gate, having already seen a man moving off to his left, coming out of the first line of trees. "Damn fool gate for someone who doesn't want trespassers," he told Rayleen.

The man waved. "Straight ahead, first turn on your right."

The sheriff nodded and slipped the gun to automatic. "So Mr. Merk knows we're here. That guy probably stands near that gate all day."

"We probably broke an alarm beam the moment we turned off the highway," Rayleen said.

The sheriff grimaced with pain.

"You all right?" Rayleen asked.

"Fine," he lied. "Bit of a cramp—been sitting too long. You okay?"

"Don't get cramps," Rayleen said. " 'Least not that kind."

" 'Course, you work out," the sheriff said.

"Uh-huh."

"No gain without pain. That it?"

"Uh-huh."

Merk's pipe was streaming with smoke, a sure sign to May that he was worried. "They're here!" he called out, watching the car approach through the front window.

"Don't have to shout," May said. "I'm right behind you."

"I don't like this, May, not one little bit."

"Just be calm."

"Second time they've come out. First that Lyle feller, and now—"

"Just tell 'em what you told the last one. We saw a green Blazer, that's all. I'll put on some coffee. Just don't go shooting off your mouth. You do that when you're nervous. Start blabbing about nothing. Think before you say anything."

"They'll think I'm hiding something if I don't answer."

"I didn't say not to answer—just count to three before you open your yap."

The police car stopped, and Merk watched the two of them get out, the sheriff and a black woman. Opening the front door, Merk raised his pipe, a stand-in for a welcoming wave. "How you doin', Sheriff?"

"Just fine."

The sheriff introduced himself, then Rayleen.

"Come on in," May said, smiling, friendly as could be. "You folks like some coffee?"

"Love some," the sheriff said, "but first I'll use your bathroom—if I may?"

"Surely," May said. "Down the hallway on yer right."

The black woman hadn't come in with the sheriff. Merk noticed that she'd gone around the corner of the house. His heart just about crashed through his chest, panic-stricken. And how in hell did the sheriff know he kept a handgun in the bathroom? Or *did* the sheriff know? Maybe one of the Nazis had found it?—He'd been in there a lot, throwing up. Maybe the federals had caught the Nazi and he'd blabbed? Maybe—What the hell was goin' on?

Outside, Rayleen walked slowly around the cream-colored house. The back of it was more exposed than the front, showing a much deeper facade that formed the wall of a basement, its two black-trimmed windows like malevolent eyes. Maybe she was a bit spooked because of the sheriff's suspicions about the cider bottle, she thought. There was a lock on the basement door—no rust or other sign that it hadn't been used for a while. The cement steps were also clear, swept, with no leaves or brambles blown in from the orchard.

She heard a toilet flush, the high bathroom window half open. Apart from that it was so quiet around the house all she could hear was the wind in the trees, sounding like running water. She couldn't see inside through the two windows since the sun was hitting them flat on; all she could make out were mirrored glass images of herself. She caught a whiff of a vinegary apple smell, moved quietly down the outside basement steps and up closer to one of the windows, cupping her hands around her face to beat the glare.

"Can I help you?"

Jesus Murphy! She just about died of shock. It was the Tartar herself, a thin mustache line above her lips, her teeth bared in a forced smile. If a wolf could smile, Rayleen thought, flat against the wall, her right hand on her holster, this is what it'd look like.

"Mrs. Merk!"

"Yes."

"I was just looking around."

"Yes."

"Ah, nice place you have here."

"Yes."

"Maybe I'll go inside. Join the sheriff."

As the two of them entered the house, Rayleen was feeling guilty, as if she were back in her childhood, caught stealing apples. The sheriff gave her a sidelong glance that asked if she'd found anything. She remembered the vinegary odor.

"I'd like to search the house," Rayleen said.

The sheriff nodded. "You mind, Mr. Merk?"

Merk looked about frantically for his wife. She wasn't there.

"You have any objections, Mr. Merk?"

"Damn right I do. You got a warrant?"

"No. You figure I need one?"

"Damn right. May . . . ?" he called out.

"You got guns in the basement," the sheriff asked, "as well as illegal brew?"

"What—hell, no. No guns."

"Cider?" the sheriff pressed him.

"Fer Christ's sake, everyone makes their own hooch around here."

"You sell it?" the sheriff asked.

"No," Merk said. "May . . . ?"

"So you do make it?"

"You—you people have no right here."

"We've got probable cause," the sheriff said.

Mrs. Merk reappeared. "Maybe, Sheriff, but it could get around this county that you come bustin' into folks' houses without a warrant—or maybe you ain't thinking of running for reelection again."

The sheriff knew the old bitch was right. Merk and all his militia buddies and their buddies made a sizable voting bloc. "I'll be back," he said. "Meanwhile, I'm gonna leave my deputy here, at your gate."

"Why?" Merk asked. "You don't trust us? Think we'll skedaddle out of here? Think we're scared of the *law*?" He said *law* like it was a disease.

"C'mon," the sheriff told Rayleen, and she followed him out.

Inside the house, Merk, despite his last minute bravado, was sucking air through his pipe, not yet realizing the fire had died. "Where was you, May?" he began. "I turned around and you—"

"I was calling your friends, you fool. You're sure as hell gonna need 'em. And most of *them* are up in Spokane."

"Ah, the law won't find nothing in the basement 'cept the cider."

"And what about the shed in the orchard? You think they're just going to search the house?"

There was silence for a few moments, during which they could both hear the ticking of the clock set in the elephant gun's stock.

"We've got to move it, May."

"I told you we don't have time. Besides, that black slut's at the gate now." May was taking off her apron in a fury. "Hadn't been for you and your militia we wouldn't be in this fix. You lost your head, and that's all there is to it. Moment they came in you started to panic."

Chastened, Stanley Merk looked at his wife. "Shit, May, what're we gonna do?"

CHAPTER TWENTY-ONE

EXCEPT FOR THE city's annual Spring Lilac Bloomsday Run, Spokane hadn't seen anything like this since the World's Fair in '74, especially if you were a military type like Douglas Freeman. The parade he'd seen earlier on TV, the arrival of "amnestied" militia units from all over the country, was a mere curtain raiser to what this was going to be: over four thousand militiamen—and several hundred militiawomen—readying for a preconvention afternoon march in column through the city in a hopefully quiet protest against the federal government. CNN and the three TV networks had staked out strategic viewpoints atop buildings throughout the route, with a helo overhead. The militia had held their annual convention here for years, and the fact of their recent defeat in the field wasn't going to stop them this year. They knew that the President knew as much, which was why he'd scheduled a visit for the following morning, a ballsy stand-up to the military convention that he probably hoped would impress the country.

Among the civilians making their way through the early gathering crowds and lunchtime spectators was ATF agent Bill Trey. He wasn't interested in how military-looking the militia was; he was concerned with faces, one in particular, the militia-man Frederick Latrell. The lab in Washington, D.C., had discovered that Latrell's dental records and those of the corpse Hearn had said was Latrell didn't match. Which meant Latrell, still wanted for murder and attempted murder, was still at large.

The throng didn't overwhelm Trey; he was used to it. He'd spent weeks in training, watching news videos of crowds pressing in to see the President. Working a real crowd, however, was a lot different than eyeing videos, for faces were in constant motion, turning, laughing, grimacing, some just staring, waiting. And among them were other agents doing the same thing as Trey, both men and women, their only ID to each other being a common lapel pin and the way they'd look down as if watching their shoes as they listened intently to the steering information coming through from control to their earpiece.

Trey's appearance was not that of most other agents, however: he knew one of the first tip-offs that you were an agent was to wear sunglasses and a suit. If you had to cut down on the glare—and in big sky country like eastern Washington, Wyoming, and Montana, glare was a problem—you were better off, he figured, to wear a pair of the old hippie shades—round lenses in silver wirelike frames. Cool, man. Traditions died hard in the ATF or any other government agency, but with domestic and international terrorism on the rise, agents were allowed more latitude in matters of dress. Any terrorist over the age of twelve could spot a traditionally dressed agent in the blink of an eye.

God, it was tiring, Trey thought, what with hundreds, thousands, of faces. But he kept working the crowd. Now, he could smell candy floss and fries, which made him hungry, and the stink of police motorcycle exhaust as the cops moved along the militiamen's parade route, keeping the growing crowd back behind the barricades. What with the conference tomorrow coming on the heels of the President's visit, Trey mused that the Spokane police headquarters would go broke just paying the overtime.

A band struck up, and he sensed the wave of the crowd's excitement. He glanced at his watch. It wasn't yet noon—a quarter to. A protest had begun—students from across the Spokane River at Gonzaga University, carrying placards denouncing the militias. TO HELL WITH RIGHT-WING NUTS and SCREW THE MILITIAS were two of the signs.

Jesus, now it's gonna hit the fan, Trey thought, and within five seconds there was a fracas outside the opera house, spilling west toward the park near the eastern arm of the intersection of Washington and Trent avenues. Militiamen, about thirty of them en route to the parade's marshaling area a quarter mile away, waded into the stream of students, where fists and epithets were flying. One sign was already wilting as the students, though there were more of them than militia at that point, were overwhelmed. And then the militiamen were joined by a small Nazi skinhead contingent from Hayden Lake, Idaho, Aryan headquarters in the Northwest. The biggest of the Nazis was laying waste to the students around him. One of the placard sticks snapped and a student used it to hit the big Nazi in the back of the head. The Nazi turned around, his fist coming down on top of the student's head like a club, felling him instantly, the wooden stick clattering to the street as eight police outriders entered the fight, black nightsticks drawn and chopping.

It was made for TV. Chaos. Bill Trey spotted Marte Price, CNN's ace correspondent, leaning precariously over a four-story building's guttering, animatedly describing the fight, the crowd roaring its approval. The zebra-striped police barriers were tipped over, the legs of the wooden trestles sticking up like dead horses, as pockets of the crowd swelled and broke from the sheer momentum of those behind, spilling out into the street and the fight, turning what was already a chaotic punch-up into absolute bedlam, people screaming, motorcycles crashing over, the university students' signs sinking into the mass like the flags of a defeated army.

Police and ambulance sirens wailed, the vehicles failing, however, to make any headway into what was now a sea of people choking the parade route. Not even the mounted police could penetrate the mass of bodies, everybody running every which way, forcing Bill Trey into the shallow recess of a storefront, the plate-glass windows behind him trembling from the shock waves of the crowd. He saw a girl of about six or seven in a pink track suit panic-stricken, like so many others, screaming, "Mommy! Mommy! Help me! Help me!" Trey thrust up his left arm as a protective barrier, grabbed at her, missed, and was knocked to the concrete pavement. Before he could be trampled underfoot—

the noise, the screaming, was unbelievable—he heaved himself up, pushed violently forward, and reached for the girl again. He got her in his grip and quickly sidestepped into the storefront's recess. "It's all right, honey, I'll look after you," he said, trying to calm her.

The girl was hysterical. To her, Trey was a strange man who had attacked. Her scream attracted the attention of a man in the passing current of people, and he threw a punch at Trey, connecting with his left eye, knocking Trey back into the glass door, where he struck the back of his head on the aluminum push bar. Trey crumpled to the ground, everything turned dark, and the girl reached out to her rescuer, who by now had been swept away.

When Trey sat up again, he pressed his hand to the back of his head, which was numb, and felt wetness. Looking at his hand, he saw it was covered in blood, the wound bleeding profusely. He looked up at the feral roar of the thing that was a crazed mob, and heard a loud splitting noise and the unmistakable crash of glass breaking. The storefront window had given way, and people were being shoved aside into the stalagmites and stalactites of glass shards. There was more screaming as several people were impaled on the jagged glass of the window, which now looked like the savage mouth of an enormous shark, its teeth gouging and slicing into the crowd. Trey heard more glass splintering, then collapsing, headless and limbless mannequins toppling over, glass and bodies crashing into them. Blood.

That evening the guests' spot on *Larry King Live* was cut to a half hour so the Spokane riot could be covered. Marte Price's narration, cool yet intense, accompanied the shots of utter confusion that had filled Spokane's main street only a few hours before. So far, hospitals reported seven confirmed dead, scores injured—some seriously—and among the dead, two children, a boy age eight and a seven-year-old girl, her pink track suit visible under the blanket that covered her body in the makeshift morgue. Distraught people, many sobbing, were still wandering around stunned, unable to get their bearings, harried-looking police officers standing guard in front of broken store windows, several of the stores spray-painted with NIGGERS UND JUDEN RAUS!

Linda Seth watched CNN from her hospital bed in Yakima. Following the video of the riot and its aftermath, Larry King had a video hookup with Marte Price, Spokane's chief of police, an "amnestied" Colonel Somer of the militia, and a woman, her neck bandaged, the cut caused by flying glass. Larry King began with the woman, Laura, who had been in the crowd close to the initial fracas between the university students and the militia and Nazi attackers. She told King that there had been some verbal altercation between several of the Nazis and the university students. "There was a lot of bad language and someone threw a punch and—"

"Who threw the punch?" Larry cut in. "Did you see—"

"No, but I think it was one of the bald-head—"

"Skinheads," King said. "Nazis."

"Yes—that's what I mean. I think it was one of them."

"But it could've been one of the students?" King proffered.

"Yes," Laura conceded.

"Go on."

"Well, a fight started, and a few seconds later there was a shot, and one of the students holding a sign—or rather, one end of it—just fell to the ground. There was another shot and then all hell broke loose."

King turned to Marte Price. "Marte, did you hear shots?"

"I heard one, Larry, but after that, as Laura says, everything went crazy, so I never heard the second shot."

King turned to the police chief. "Chief, have you any information on the shooting?"

"Yes, Larry. At this point in time we have two gunshot fatalities, one a student and the other a militiaman."

"Is—I should say, *was*—the militiaman a skinhead?"

"No, ah—he was regular militia. I believe he was on his way to the marshaling area where most of the militiamen were—ah, assembling for the march."

"Anyone arrested?"

"Not as yet."

"Now is that because you don't know who the perpetrator or perpetrators are, or—"

"We have one good description, Larry, a militiaman identified but not yet apprehended."

"You think the militiamen are hiding him and any other militiamen involved?"

"Absolutely."

"Chief, I would imagine that this riot—stampede, whatever we want to call it—means a cancellation of the President's visit tomorrow."

"That's been my recommendation. Ah, I should add, Larry, that we're seeking the public's help with these shootings. If they recognize anyone in the news reports that we might want to talk to, they should contact us. In particular we're still looking for a militiaman named Frederick Latrell, who is wanted on a federal warrant for murder. We've had roadblocks up, but as you can understand, we've only been able to mount a handful of those because of the shortage of police officers."

"Larry . . ." It was Marte Price, her full-bosomed white cashmere sweater filling the screen. "If I can jump in . . ."

"Sure. Go ahead."

She was adjusting her earpiece. "I've been talking with presidential aides in Seattle, and it's not clear what the President will do. One of the reasons the President is in the Northwest is to mend some political fences, to shore up support here for the forthcoming elections."

"So you're saying it might still go ahead?"

"It could go either way. If I could ask the police chief a question . . . Chief, it's been rumored that you've requested assistance by the National Guard in the event that the presidential visit goes ahead?"

The chief was visibly uncomfortable. "That's a possibility. Nothing's been decided yet."

King turned to the other woman. "Laura, do you think the President should come to Spokane?"

"No. We've got a bunch of kooks running loose up here, and after today I think it's too dangerous."

"Kooks? You mean the militia or the skinheads?"

"Both. Skinheads are part of the militias and—"

"Hold on a minute," King interrupted. "Sorry, ladies and gentlemen, Colonel Somer, spokesman for the militias, apparently has been disconnected and has something to say. We'll take a short break, give our technical crew here time to sort things out. Don't go 'way!"

Vance, registered under the name "Fraser," was watching the show from his room in the Holiday Inn. It was obvious to him they were determined to get Latrell no matter what.

Larry King was on again, and Colonel Somer came on screen. "Colonel Somer," King said, "why a militia conference in the first place?"

"Larry, this is supposed to be a free country. No one complains when the Shriners or—"

"C'mon, Colonel, the Shriners don't send four thousand troops into town."

"Neither do we, Larry. We're unarmed, under the President's antiterrorist law. So we can't parade through a city bearing arms, even though, Larry, we have the constitutional right to bear arms. We obeyed the city ordinance—no guns on the street and—"

"Then how come there were gunshots?"

"Because, Larry, someone had a concealed weapon."

"A militiaman?"

"We don't know that. Could've been a policeman. *They're* armed."

King was trying hard not to show his exasperation. "All right, then, what's the point of this conference?"

"Same as any other conference, Larry. To exchange ideas and—"

"Ideas about what?"

"All kinds of ideas. How to defend your home, how to survive in the event of a natural disaster or unauthorized attack."

"Attack by whom?"

"Rogue government forces."

"Can you give me an example of a 'rogue' government force?"

"Sure, Ruby Ridge, the attack on Waco. The use of CS gas there."

"What's wrong with the use of CS gas?"

"You *see*, Larry, you people in the media don't understand. CS gas has long been banned by the international community—by more than a hundred countries. Former attorney general Janet Reno was nothing less than a war criminal for authorizing the use of CS against women and children."

"Against a heavily armed cult," King said.

"The Davidian sect wasn't doing any harm, Larry, and the government in its attack on the sect used CS gas, which is outlawed by international agreement."

"Chief, what's the situation now?" King asked. "Will the militia parade and the annual conference still go on? *After* the President's visit maybe?"

"No, Larry," the chief said. "Not if I have anything to say about it."

"You overruling the city council?" King pressed.

"There's been no formal emergency meeting of the council scheduled as yet. We, ah, haven't had time, but I think I could speak for the council that, ah, no permit would be issued. Certainly not for tomorrow if the President's visit proceeds—not after this."

"You think it'll go on, Marte?" King asked. "The President's visit, I mean."

"It's difficult to tell. I'd say it was fifty-fifty at the moment."

As the President's aides watched the King show, they welcomed the chief of police's response.

"I don't think we should," White House chief of staff Delorme said. "Not after today's shootings. Tempers are up, militias are frustrated as hell, not being allowed to—"

"We're going," the President said calmly, quietly. "As planned. As far as public relations go, it would be disastrous not to. It'd look like cowardice in the face of the enemy." Apart from the political cost of not going, he reminded them that he was President of Spokane as well as the rest of the United States. Just as the civil rights workers went into the deep South, he said, he had to go into the deep Northwest and show leadership. It was a matter of personal honor.

"All right, Mr. President," his National Security adviser told him. "But let's at least bolster the police forces in Spokane. Let's put the National Guard along the route."

"No," said the President emphatically. "That'd signal alarm on our part."

"I disagree, Mr. President," the head of his Secret Service detail said. "We have the perfect rationale. Looting. Police chief hasn't mentioned it because it'd make his town look bad, but we've already had reliable reports from our agents in Spokane that looting was a problem. Heck, after a flood, fire, whatever, it's quite common for us to call in the Guard."

"He's right, Mr. President. Matter of fact, we—the government—could be seen as derelict in our duty if we didn't call in the Guard. And those policemen in there sure as heck need reinforcements, if for nothing else than just to spell them off. A lot of those guys have been on duty twenty-four hours straight."

"How many?" the President asked. "I mean National Guardsmen?"

"A battalion," an adviser said. "Eight, nine hundred men. Station them along the route."

"Sir," the ATF director said, "one of our agents tried to catch a little girl in that stampede. He had her one second, she was gone the next. We need a *wall* in front of that crowd, and there's gonna be one heck of a crowd. You're more popular than the militias."

"You think so?" the President asked laconically.

"Know so, sir. Mr. President, after what's happened, the police have shown they can't control that big a crowd. It's no reflection on them, but we need more men."

"Besides," adviser Delorme added, "you have a precedent. The Attorney General's already called in the Guard in Florida."

The President thought long and hard and finally acquiesced. "All right, boys, you win. But one battalion, no more."

"Still leaves the militia with a four-to-one advantage, Mr. President."

"For God's sake, Jerry, the war's over."

CHAPTER TWENTY-TWO

IN THE SPOKANE hotel, Latrell was swearing like a trooper, pumped up on coffee and still coming down from the excitement of the riot. "To hell with the latte," he told Norman, his roommate. He wanted lots of espresso—dark as sin and sugared to boot.

"Shit!" he complained, poking his nose like a ferret into the hotel room's refrigerator. "Bastards've drunk all the booze." He meant the other three Nazis, currently on guard up in Vance's room and watching the local TV station announcing the imminent arrival of the National Guard.

Norman slumped in the lounge chair, thinking about the "unofficial" maneuvers the militia had planned for after the conference. It was an annual event, and he and the other three Nazis were thinking of joining in, having some fun after guarding Vance all this way, but they were used to handguns, not rifles. "An M-60," he said to Latrell. "Is it hard to operate?"

"You kidding?" Latrell quipped. "Fucking moron could fire it. Why?"

"Aw, nothing. Thinking about the maneuvers. Is it easier than a shotgun?"

"For my money, shotgun's best close up. You oughta know that by now. Don't worry 'bout the maneuvers. Militia'll have what you need. Jesus! Look at this, they've drunk all the pop too. All they left are fuckin' tortilla chips. Smell like fucking mice."

"It ever rain in this burg?" Norman asked.

"Hardly ever. Semidesert here. Snows now and then. Why?"

Because if it rained, the Nazi thought, the National Guardsmen that the feds were bringing in would all be wearing capes. "No reason," the Nazi said. "Just wonderin'. Never been in this part of Washington before."

"God's country, Norman. Big sky. Not like all that rain you get in the Cascades."

No rain. An open limo, right! Pop! A grenade. Or two. Bang. Damn! It was like a cocaine rush. Norman turned abruptly away from the window. "What about your wife?" he asked Latrell. "And your kids. Aren't you worried?"

"She knows how to take care of herself. Kids too. 'Sides, militia boys stick together. We've always got contingency plans. Like Randy Weaver's family—all knew how to handle themselves."

"Yeah. Two of 'em got killed."

"Well, that won't happen again. We got that covered. Friends'll move 'em outta state if necessary."

"You guys use smoke grenades?"

"In maneuvers?"

"Yeah. Any of the boys here have some?"

"Boys here got everything. You take the rocker panels off half the boys' pickups, you'll find everything from condoms to AK-47s."

"Could I be outfitted before we go to the Cascades?"

"Why bother?"

"Because the federals are after us, or didn't you know? One of 'em shows up at the door, I don't want to be left holding my dick, that's all."

"What d'you want?"

"Your Browning. Couple of mags, couple of grenades. A smoke one too. Could you get 'em for me?"

All Latrell could find in the ice box was a small bottle of Schweppes tonic water. "I hate this stuff."

"You don't have to drink it."

"I'm thirstier'n a dry crick. 'Least it's fizzy."

"Have some more coffee."

"No—I want somethin' cold."

"Can we get those grenades and ammo?"

Latrell shrugged. "I guess."

"Good."

"They'll want to know what you want 'em for. Might think you're paranoid."

That's a good one, Norman thought—the militia thinking you're paranoid. He smiled. "Tell 'em I'm gonna whack the President."

"Yeah."

When Latrell, making sour faces from the tonic water, began dialing room service, Norman saw the number on the telephone's dial card: 555. He closed his eyes, his heart pounding, trying to calm himself. It was like the excitement before an orgasm. Five five five was Adolf Hitler's membership number in the National Socialist Workers Party. It was a sign.

Yakima's sheriff had been delayed by urgent requests for some of his deputies to help man the roadblocks outside Spokane, in order to relieve the Spokane police for city duty following the aborted militiamen's parade. By the time he'd sorted out the complex problem of scheduling, even with the help of the station's computer, he knew he was going to be late driving back to the Merk house with the search warrant, especially since he wanted to pop in and see how Linda Seth was coming along.

When he arrived, he saw another man there, Bill Trey, standing by her bed. The sheriff introduced himself before speaking to Linda: "You better since this morning?"

"I always feel better once I get through the mornings. Broken arm or not, I'm out of here tomorrow."

"I'd say you're due for sick leave." He paused. "Still think you should take more time off."

She smiled. "And since when are you director of the FBI?"

"I'll squeal on you," he said, winking at Bill Trey.

"Thanks a lot," she said, still smiling. "No, really, Sheriff, I'll be fine."

"That's because you're in bed now," Trey cut in. "You start moving about, you'll feel the difference."

"I'll sit down if I'm tired," she said. "No way I'm staying cooped up here, though. I'll be up in Spokane for the President's visit."

"Oh, sure," Trey said. "A one-armed FBI agent working the crowd."

The moment Trey said it he realized what a good cover it would be, and he could tell she'd already thought of it. "All right," he said, "I see there's no stopping you."

"The President's nuts to go," Linda told the sheriff and Trey. "Just between you and me."

"I know," Trey said, "but—" He spread out his arms. "—politics."

" 'Course," Linda added, "I have to admit the White House hasn't exactly been the best place to be these last few years. In 'ninety-five a plane crashed into it. In 'ninety-six a guy fired an AK-47 into it, and another crazy got over the wall."

The sheriff looked at his watch. "Got a deputy waiting for me. Have to go." He pointed at her. "Don't be a martyr now, Linda. Nobody'll thank you for it. If you don't feel up to it, stay put for a few days."

Bill Trey was on the phone to Washington, D.C., and was told to return to his assigned duty in Spokane. "Keep working the crowds," his boss said. "Hotel lobbies, et cetera. Usual stuff."

"Problem is," Trey countered, "since that incident with the little girl, every news hound in Spokane is trying to nail me for an interview. I'm not that hard to spot with a gauze patch on the back of my head. Big as a fist!"

"You can manage to fend them off."

Wasn't the guy listening? "No. You know what reporters are like—gum on your shoes. Marte Price from CNN—she wouldn't go away until I gave her an interview."

"Marte Price. Poor you—my heart bleeds."

"Yeah, yeah, but having my face plastered all over America—"

"All over the world, Bill. What's your cover up there?"

"Insurance salesman." He paused, and his tone changed. He remembered the little girl. "I just couldn't hold onto her."

There was a heavy silence on the line. "Hey, Bill, it's not your fault. Shit happens."

CHAPTER TWENTY-THREE

Fort Lewis, Washington State

"GENERAL," DAVID READ'S secretary said, "it's General Freeman on the line."

Read, C-in-C of I Corps, Fort Lewis, sighed and negotiated his way through piles of packing boxes full of documents that would accompany him to his new job in the Pentagon. "Hi, how you doing, Douglas?"

"Fine, Dave. You?"

"Up to my ass in files. All this crap was supposed to be on disks months ago."

"Well, I know how busy you must be so I won't keep you, but I had to call someone about this schmozzle in Spokane."

"What's that, Douglas?"

A thousand miles to the south, Freeman was trying to make himself heard over the whine of his sister-in-law's mixer. She was always doing something. Friggin' thing made more noise than a Tomcat going off a carrier. "That riot in Spokane," he told Read, "then Washington—sending in the National Guard."

"Well, Douglas, those boys are well-trained for this type of situation."

"Against four thousand militiamen?"

"Have the militias taken over the city?" Read asked, winking at his secretary.

"Not yet, but we have to show them we won't put up with any trouble. I know the antiterrorist bill bans them from carrying weapons, but do you really believe that—"

"Douglas," Read cut in, "that's precisely why the Guard's been sent in. Calm things down—show the flag, put the militias on notice."

"Notice of what? They outman the Guard four to one. No offense to the Guard, but we ought to be having regular Army combat troops along that route."

"C'mon, Douglas, this isn't some banana republic, it's the United States of America."

"United?" Freeman countered. *"United?* Jesus, Dave, militias and the federal government are two separate countries. What we need—"

"Douglas," General Read cut in, "I don't mean to sound rude, but you're talking to the wrong man. You should voice your concerns to the Pentagon. Up here I'm a big fish in a small pond, but in D.C., I'll be a small fish in a mighty big pond. You give me credit for more influence than I have. Why don't you fax the Joint Chiefs?"

"I have. I get 'thank you for your advice' letters with those goddamn phony personal signatures on the bottom so they think I'll believe it's been signed by them 'stead of some machine. They must think I'm senile. Christ, I've fought more wars than half those bastards've even heard of. In 'Nam, the Gulf, and—"

"I know, Douglas. Look, I'll raise the matter with General Shelbourne. He's a good man."

"Not bad for a pen pusher. But Dave, by the time you raise the matter, these jokers up in Spokane—"

"Douglas, I'll bring up your concerns at the Pentagon. That's all I can do."

"All right," Freeman said with resignation. "Thanks for taking the call."

General Read thought for a moment. He didn't at all like Stan Black, the man who would take over command at Fort Lewis. "Douglas, I tell you what, soon as Black, my successor, arrives, why don't you call him? He might be more in your ballpark."

"All right," Freeman said. "I will. Thanks for listening."

General Read smiled as he put down the phone, and his secretary caught him. "General, that was mean. Freeman'll hound the poor man to death."

"I *know*."

"General, that's awful."

"I know."

"But do you think General Freeman has a point—about the militias?"

"Hmm . . . mountain out of a molehill. Besides, the militia's whipped. Look at Packwood. Nothing'll happen."

By the time Yakima's sheriff headed northwest back along the Naches River toward the Merk place, the temperature had dropped to near freezing. He felt guilty about having left Rayleen out in the cold. She'd be all right with her parka, but he'd bet a dollar to peanuts that old Merk and the Tartar wouldn't invite her up to the house. The sheriff hadn't liked leaving her alone, but hell, they'd wanted equal pay for equal work, and now she had it. Cold feet came with the territory. He had the commercial radio band on from Spokane as well as the police radio. Loretta Lynn was singing "Secret Love."

Without even trying he began fantasizing a scenario with Rayleen. Maybe they'd be called out to a domestic dispute at one of the farms, wife calls in an emergency and it's tense the moment they get there—husband drunk, maybe on some of Merk's cider, and making a racial remark about Rayleen. Then he would step in: "Hey, buddy, enough of that! I want an apology right now!" And the drunk, faced with jail, would say he was sorry, and on the way back, in the velvety warmth of the car, redolent with her Maui Rain, he'd risk touching her shoulder. "You okay?" She'd say yes and there'd be silence for a while and then, like a butterfly landing, her hand would touch his thigh and stay there. He'd put his right hand on hers and squeeze, and then, not too fast now, he'd coax her hand closer to him. By then he'd be hard as steel, and he'd pull off the road, unbutton her shirt, make some comment about this being strictly against regulations, and she'd agree. Then she'd say she wanted to do it for him and unzip him, not looking down but smiling at him, then she'd squeeze it. "Put the seat back," she'd say softly, and he'd do it—back the seat right up against the cage—and before he knew it she'd be down on him, her warm, moist tongue slippery, curling around it, her dark cherry-red lips closing.

As the sheriff turned onto the side road, he had an erection.

At first he didn't see her by the gate, and thought that perhaps old Merk had relented and let her go up to the house. But she was to the left of the gate, sprawled out, facedown in a patch of nettles. He immediately put the spotlight on her and could see bloodstained white panties around one ankle. Getting out of the car, he unclipped his holster, and could smell spilled cider, then human excrement and urine. There was no pulse, and a closer look at the back of her head with his flashlight revealed a huge lump swollen right across the base of her skull, frost already settling in her hair, making it stiff. Surprisingly, there was no blood.

He suddenly felt his esophagus on fire, ran several yards from the body and threw up.

Up in the house, which he couldn't see from the gate, he heard the frost warning bells ringing like crazy, giving him the same kind of involuntary panicky feeling as when his wife was cooking at home and the damn smoke alarm kept beeping till you had time to tear out the batteries.

Gun drawn, the sheriff cautiously entered the house. The Merks had vanished. Outside, he heard a tractor approaching in the near distance, its lights like huge eyes flitting through the orchard. Shading his eyes from the glare, he stepped out of its beams. There was a crack and, eyes agog, he fell to the ground, dead.

For the paranoid gatekeeper it was déjà vu—the first federal snoops had met their end at his hands. Calmly, he put down the .30 Sporter rifle, shut off the tractor, walked over, got into his battered Chevy pickup loaded with survivalist supplies, and didn't look back as he ran down the gate on his way out. The Good Book had foretold it all in Revelations—the end for those who transgressed against the divine will—and a white policeman who rode around with a black woman had unquestionably transgressed, polluting the gene pool. He didn't put on his headlights until he reached the highway.

"Colonel Somer," Marte Price said to the Spokane spokesman for the militias, her legs arousing his lust, "why are your militias about to carry out maneuvers?"

"The militias, Ms. Price, are made up of people, men and women, who feel that individual freedoms in this country are increasingly under attack by a government, a bureaucracy, out of control. And I don't care if it's Democrat or Republican. Bureaucracy has a life of its own."

"But isn't government trying to protect civil rights? The courts—"

"The courts are obsessed with minority whining. They protect everyone except white males. We're held responsible for everything from the great flood to prejudice against women. Then how come we've got women in the militias, and the highest rate of crime is amongst young black males?"

The reporter's response was another question. "Militias in this country used to be, I think you'll agree, more or less run by consensus, but commentators have noticed that in the past few years they seem to be run much more along military lines. Why is that?"

"Size."

"Could you expand on that?"

"No."

"Why not?"

"Because you've already got your mind made up that we're a bunch of bigots, and no matter what I say you won't change your opinions. Besides, militias in this country have always been run on military lines, so I don't agree with your original premise."

"But many people say your General Nordstrom, whoever he is, is a dictator."

"So?"

"How do you answer that?"

"I don't. Ask the men."

"You think they'll say otherwise?"

"I don't know. My men aren't computer-run automatons. They don't live in cyberspace—they're flesh and blood individuals. They're not brainwashed like your regular Army."

"Brainwashed by whom?"

What she needed, he thought, was a bit of stick. "Brainwashed by the government," he replied.

"To believe what?"

"To believe they're defending the United States. What they're defending is big business, big banks, and moral decay."

She cocked her head like a surprised bird seeing a worm, as he'd seen Mike Wallace do on *60 Minutes*. "Moral decay?" she said.

"Legalized prostitution, drugs, child pornography, abortion. Free enterprise and liberal dogma gone mad, meetin' one another in a central doghouse."

"What would the militias do about it?"

Somer smiled. Oh, you beautiful, big-titted woman, he thought, you just gave me a pulpit. He paused, affecting a look of grave deliberation. "The militias would prohibit prostitution, abortion, shoot drug dealers and other criminals for anything above petty theft. *One* strike and you're out. We would shoot pornographers."

"You mean child pornographers?"

"I mean pornographers."

He saw her shift position. Pussy getting too hot, he thought.

"But that might mean—depending on your definition—some, let's say, Hollywood directors."

"Yes," he said.

"You would shoot directors?"

"If they're pornographers, yes. I'd shoot them quicker than that federal shot Randy Weaver's wife."

"You'd shoot every criminal who—"

"Anything above petty theft."

"Like what?"

"Stealing your automobile."

"You'd *kill* a man for stealing an automobile?" she asked incredulously.

"You watch grand theft auto go way down—if we're in power."

"So you're after power?"

"No. We're for being left alone, for much more decentralization, for much more local government *by locals*. And we don't like to see our tax dollars being wasted—being used, for example, to give murderers a nice cozy cell with TV and conjugal visits while we let victims suffer."

"Would you call yourself dictatorial?"

"This afternoon General Nordstrom told the men that if any of them wanted to stay in Spokane for the presidential visit tomorrow, they could. If they don't want to, they don't have to. Some dictator."

"This son of a bitch," General Freeman opined, watching the interview on Marjorie's TV, "is smarter than a shithouse rat. Marte Price isn't going to trap him. He gave it to her straight between the eyes. One tough cookie."

"You sound as if you admire him," Marjorie said disapprovingly.

"I do. Same as Patton admired Rommel. He's on the wrong side. We can't tolerate private armies in the United States—end up like Bosnia and Serbia. Everybody fighting everybody else. Black against white, Christians against Farrakhans. But this Colonel Somer is no fool, even though he's full of himself.

Promoting himself to colonel. That's rich. Son of a bitch was a major in 'Nam."

"I've asked you before, Douglas, to refrain from using bad language in this house. I suppose you think it's very macho. I don't."

Freeman thought for a moment. "I'm sorry, Marjorie, been in the Army too long." He paused. "I *was* in the Army too long."

Norman sat on his bed doing a blindfold test after stripping an M-16, another militiaman, from Arizona, timing him. The Nazi wasn't doing well. The grenades—one stun, two H.E.'s, and a smoke grenade—were given to him by one of the Michigan militia. Yakima's Channel 7 was showing confused, jerky weather satellite shots that bothered Norman's eyes. The bottom line seemed to be that there was a sixty percent chance of rain tomorrow, snow to the south of Spokane. Norman was thinking that if the National Guardsmen had to wear their ponchos against the rain or whatever, it would probably mean a covered limo, a plastic bulletproof bubble. Piss on that. On the other hand, if the weather was fine, then using a Guardsman's cape to conceal a weapon was a no go. Best break would be to have it rain just before the motorcade rolled down Riverside Avenue at ten A.M. Then the sun comes out, the Guardsmen still wearing ponchos, not having time to take 'em off. A shotgun under a cape, and blinding smoke from the smoke grenade pouring out all around. Chaos.

There was a lot to think about. He rang through for a porno flick, and pretty soon he was watching this movie about the Bobbitt guy whose wife cut off his prick with a pair of scissors. Bobbitt had told *Extra*, or was it *Hard Copy*, that he'd had restorative surgery and that it was as good as ever. Norman remembered how the Führer had only one testicle and had got all these bastards who tried to kill him and had them all hung on meat hooks so they'd take a long time to die. That's what he'd like to do with the President and his nigger aides, he thought, but hey, you had to play the hand you were dealt, right? And he figured he'd never get this close to the man again, and there was a real possibility of escape with such a crowd. Anyway, it was better to live one day as a lion instead of a lifetime as a fucking sheep.

On TV, CNN announced that the President, under increasing pressure from his Secretary of Treasury, Nanton, and southern congressmen, regarding uncertainty in the money markets because of the "militia crisis," had ordered more of a National Guard presence, not only in Washington State but in southern Florida, where federal authorities were said to be encountering increasing opposition from what were believed to be nascent militia groups. As part of the National Guard sweep ordered by Helen Wyeth, a company of approximately two hundred men was being dispatched immediately to the Everglades, to be followed in a day or two by the remaining three companies of Tampa's 53rd Brigade's First Infantry Battalion.

CHAPTER TWENTY-FOUR

The Everglades

AT FIRST COLONEL Armani, C.O. of the First Infantry Battalion, ordered an unmanned aerial vehicle to recon the area for sixteen square miles around the Kozan bungalow. The UAV's digital real-time camera relayed its topographical pictures of where the 'glades met the sea, but all that came back were shots of the verdant green islands, some over seventy yards across, the smaller hammocks like clumps of green grass against the blue, sometimes green and brown, watery expanses where the

Everglades met the sea. Now and then a deserted campsite could be seen beneath the thick foliage of gumbo trees, oaks, and the ubiquitous mangroves of the coast, and here and there the fine, white sands of a plethora of creeks that brought the vital freshwater of Florida's interior down to the Gulf, with occasional rafts of dead mangrove leaves floating near the estuaries, trapped by the jungle of roots.

Armani wasn't surprised—he hadn't expected anything from the UAV. They were good at picking up anomalies on more open ground, but he knew that not even their infrared vision could detect anything of significance in the already hot glades, where men's body heat could be lost in the cloying, muggy world of islands. Besides, a UAV could cover only a strip at a time.

Armani knew you could hide an army in there. He told his second-in-command, Major Gill, "If the militia won't give up the suspects we've come for, no way I'm going to disperse my men to hell and gone in this damn jungle—let them get picked off one by one. We'll go in, in force—deliver high concentrations of fire if necessary."

"Militia might not want to fight, Colonel," Gill said. "They may decide that discretion is the better part of valor—pressure the men who killed Kozan and his wife to give themselves up. Won't do them any good publicitywise to be accused of hiding fugitives."

"Major, you're from where? Pensacola, isn't it? Up on the panhandle?"

"Yes, sir."

"Redneck country, right?"

"Yessir."

"And I'm from Tallahassee. You and I probably got kin in the militia."

Gill was no slouch. He'd seen it coming a couple of seconds before. "All right, sir—they won't give up kin."

"Especially," Armani added, "if they think Kozan shot first, and from what I'm hearing from my G-2, the consensus in the militia—here and 'most everywhere else in the country—is that the rangers—federals—started it."

"How about his wife?"

"We don't know about that, do we?" Armani replied.

"But it's a pretty good assumption that she was murdered too."

"Agreed, but t'ain't no body, Major. It's an assumption, and we're not going to convince the militia or anybody else, except maybe his wife's parents, that she was killed by the militia." Armani pointed to the TV screen. "UAVs—a goddamn waste of time. All it does is alert the militia that we're looking for them." He knew what was on Gill's mind—they had served long enough for that. "So, Major, you're asking why I did it. The UAV?"

"CYA," Gill suggested. He meant "covering your ass."

"Precisely."

"Some of the men are a bit uptight," Gill told Armani, "at the prospect of wading through the 'glades."

Armani, a fit fifty with salt and pepper hair, affected surprise. "You mean alligators and stuff? They've got boots, haven't they?"

Surely he was jesting? Gill thought. The vast river was no more than fifteen inches deep, except for the gator holes, but in a tangle of saw grass it was difficult to see a gator. Even the guys in the battalion of nine hundred who'd had experience in the 'glades wouldn't want any part of doing a sweep through the reptile-infested country. Hell, the National Guard were volunteers. It was Gill's firm conviction that if he ordered men to wade through the swamps, he'd have to face mass insubordination. And anyway, an officer was supposed to lead by example, right? Without realizing it, he was looking down at his boots. Armani, however, was thinking of boats—airboats—the big kind used *outside* the Everglades National Park.

But first he'd have to navigate the shoals of the powerful, essentially upper-middle-class environmentalist lobbyists for whom any machine *in* the Everglades National Park, *near* the Everglades National Park, was anathema. And yet his plan would have to accommodate the sudden impatience of Washington,

D.C.—the latter's determination to be seen flexing muscle against the militia, to show American voters and overseas investors that Washington was firmly in control. In short, Armani had to be at once a diplomat and a soldier.

Armani, with Major Gill as his erstwhile assistant, achieved such status by arguing with a covey of "enviros" and the President's Pentagon advisers for a compromise: allow him some fast airboats for recon in order to speed ahead of the main force to identify militia positions so that helos, unarmed, could descend with loudspeakers and/or leaflets, offering the militia here the same kind of amnesty that had been offered in the Pacific Northwest, if they surrendered their arms. This would simultaneously satisfy the American public's sense of fair play, limit damage to the admittedly delicate ecosystem of the Everglades, and could be done fairly quickly.

"How many airboats?" they asked him. He told Gill he needed at least twenty-five, and so he asked for thirty-five. *Thirty-five!* The advisers suspected that the environmental lobby would have a fit, and told him they couldn't possibly allow more than twenty-five in the delicately balanced ecosystems. "All right," he told C-in-C Shelbourne over the radio in a heavy, resigned tone, winking at Gill. "Very well, General. I'll just have to work with twenty-five."

"That's the spirit, Colonel," Shelbourne said. "When do you anticipate you can move?"

"As soon as the airboats arrive."

There was a short delay before the general came back on the scrambler. "You'll have them tomorrow. No later than noon. We'll send them across from the east coast via Tamiami Trail."

"Good," Armani said. "Ah, there is one small detail, General."

"Shoot."

"I didn't specify the size of the airboat."

"They're standard, aren't they? Two seats—about five feet wide, ten feet long?"

"I was thinking of four of those, fast boats, and twenty-five tourist class. Enough to take in several companies. There are two hundred men per—"

"I know how many men are in a company, dammit! Armani—are you Jack Armani's son?"

"The same, General."

"You were an aide-de-camp to Douglas Freeman. Correct?"

"Correct, General."

"By God, so that's where you learned to be so damned cunning?"

Armani said nothing.

"Freeman's been trying to tell us how to run this operation as well as the Northwest Theater."

"I'm not surprised, General."

"Neither am I, Colonel. You've picked up some of his bad habits, like bullshitting my advisers. If they knew you meant twenty-five jumbo size, they would never have okayed it."

"I figured that, General. Do I get the boats?"

"All right. But you're going to have to specify the size to Miami. I'll sign the requisition for twenty-five airboats. But if it hits the fan, it's your ass."

"Thank you, General."

"Armani?"

"Sir?"

"Expeditiously. We want this done ASAP. Get that damn militia out of that swamp."

"I will."

It had stopped raining. Moving east from a levee, four hundred men, Armani's newly constituted advance force of Alpha and Bravo companies, took the left half of a two-thousand-yard front facing the Everglades, while the four hundred of Charlie and Delta companies took the right half. Although the murder of Kozan had taken place in Ten Thousand Islands, it was assumed that any major militia concentration would be found in the Everglades or Big Cypress National Preserve east of the myriad islands. Accordingly, the four smaller, faster, three-man search airboats acquired by Armani were dispatched ahead. If the enemy was discovered, the big boats carrying up to thirty to forty National Guardsmen could quickly ferry several companies from the levee to the spot and bring concentrated fire to bear.

"At 1500 hours," Armani told his four company commanders and Major Gill, "any force we've sent out will have to stop and start to bivouac."

The company commanders were taken by surprise.

"It's no damn good coming all the way back to this levee to make camp," Armani explained. "We'd only have to cover the same distance tomorrow before we could resume the sweep. Whoever we send out this afternoon will have to camp on the nearest hammock." He meant the bayheads, or islands of hardwoods and bush that, through the accumulation of vegetation, had been raised several feet above the river of saw grass. The water there, except for deep holes, was no more than fifteen inches deep. Still, it would be hard slogging for the troops ferried to any suspicious area. Once out of the boats, their boots would quickly be soaked, and they'd have to make their way through the sharp-edged, shoulder-high saw grass and the peat-colored marl that lay above the bedrock and tangles of roots.

The normally decisive Armani, his face creased by glare, pointed toward the watery plain of hammock-dotted saw grass, some of the hammocks only twenty yards or so long, others ten times as big, and the gray blur that was the forest of cypress beyond. "They might be in the cypress."

Gill hoped not. It would be a logistics nightmare just getting enough MRE—meals ready to eat—out, let alone other supplies.

No mass movement of the Florida militias had been reported, and nothing militialike had been seen on the cross-peninsula Tamiami Trail on the over-forty-mile-long straight section of Highway 41 that ran parallel to the Tamiami Canal from the Miami area to the Big Cypress National Preserve.

Typically, Armani took the first of the four "scout" boats and headed out into the saw grass. Jory Thomas, the driver, in the high chair, was a Guardsman who'd grown up in the 'glades, and Ainsley, the radio transmission officer, had jury-rigged a sponge rubber seat for himself just forward of Armani. Despite the cushion, however, Ainsley's butt was soon sore from the bumping of the airboat over the saw grass. Since he was the farthest forward in the boat—no cover in front—he felt extraordinarily vulnerable, and was praying there was no militia. In fact it was Thomas, the driver behind him, high up in the topmost chair, who was in greatest danger. In most circumstances, with his unparalleled view, Thomas would be the first man of the three to spot anything unusual in the onrushing sea of hammock-dotted green-brown grass. Right now, he was watching the grass for any sign of recent channels where grass temporarily flattened by an airboat had not yet sprung back to its original position. The zephyrs that blew across the sea of grass caused only a slight swaying motion here and there, but in the next moment this phantom breeze had passed.

For a while the sun beat down hard on the saw grass, its green-gold sheen shimmering in the heat until a chilly breeze, smelling of impending rain, came in from the Gulf behind them, the great towering white cumulus having turned into what Armani's weather officer called a line of L3s—anvil-shaped thunderheads stretching along the horizon like enormous battlements, those directly south of them plum-purple, their centers black. Armani surveyed them like a second front—arrayed against him. Rain, he knew, would favor the militia and their local knowledge—if there were militia ahead. A tornado would be disastrous. Thomas was concerned too. He had a vivid memory of a tornado a few years back, and watching helplessly as his passenger, seat-belted in a Taurus, was literally sucked out of a car into the maelstrom, never to be seen again. Thomas had seen him screaming but couldn't hear him, the roaring-train sound of the tornado muffling all other noise. The more religious amongst Thomas's folk had claimed that Jory had been saved by a miracle. Jory said it might have been the good Lord who saved him, but where was the Lord when it came to the passenger? Oh, they'd said, he must have been a better man in the Lord's eyes. Jory replied that it was his grip on the steering wheel in those few seconds that had saved him. Afterward, he felt guilty about what he'd said. In fact, ever since then, he'd feared that the good Lord might punish him someday for doubting His goodness.

Now, Jory was also thinking that if they were hit by a big storm, the rain and wind would wipe out any trace of recent channels formed by the passage of airboats or any other craft. On the other hand, that would put the kibosh on the search and they'd have to call it off. Dear God, he prayed, let it rain—not a hurricane, but enough to wash out the search.

It was the birds, or rather, their profusion on two large north-south, tear-shaped hammocks, that caught Jory's eye. The island, he guessed, was three or four acres in size, between two other hammocks and was devoid of the long, sharp-beaked, snow-white egrets. Whenever you saw that, it meant that a predator—anything from a Florida panther to a black bear—could be passing through. Jory shouted down to Armani and RTO Ainsley and pointed at the hammock, a thick growth of stunted pine now visible together with bright green palmetto plants that grew in spiky clumps. Here and there, floating dead-heads had to be avoided.

"Call in our GPS!" Armani shouted over the sound of the engine and propellers, the latter a translucent circular blur against the bruised sky. Ainsley punched the buttons on the geo-synchronous positioning system that got their exact location from the satellites within seconds and radioed it back to the four company commanders and Gill on the levee.

Armani heard a *thwack!* then a *bang!* The airboat swerved hard to the left then, almost tipping him out of the seat, clouds of white egrets filling the air. RTO Ainsley's helmet hit the deck and Ainsley was flung back, then slumped forward, dead in his seat. There was a neat hole in his forehead, and a bloody, gaping hole the size of his fist in the back of his head excreting a pinkish ooze of brain.

The boat swerved again hard left, the radio gone—another bang. Jory shouted an obscenity as he tried to curl himself into a ball in the high seat while still steering the accelerating boat as it hit its own wake. He hoped the fast up and down motion of the flat-bottomed boat would make it that much harder for the sniper. Another bang was followed by a grinding lawn-mower noise as the prop's blades, thrown off kilter by the second bullet's impact, crashed against the fan's circular cage. The boat immediately slowed as Jory cut power, heading into a smaller football-field-sized hammock on the off side of the three larger hammocks. But despite slowing, the airboat struck the hammock with such force that Armani felt himself momentarily airborne, thrown hard across the forward decking into a clump of palmetto. Grass teeth lacerated his forearms as he tried to break the fall, his shoulder dislocating an insect nest from the trunk of a stunted cypress. Within seconds thousands of wasps were swarming on him and Jory Thomas, covering Armani's neck, face, and bloodied arm like a thick, seething blanket. Thomas was screaming in a panic as hundreds of wasps stung him mercilessly. He jumped down from his high seat onto the decking, slipping in Ainsley's blood, the dead man sprawled on the deck, partially wedged between the metal boat's blunt rectangular bow and the saw grass growing out from the island. Amazingly, Ainsley's body was untouched by the wasps.

Armani dove into the water to escape the swarm, but with the water no more than fifteen inches deep, he found it almost impossible to keep himself under, his nose crawling with wasps, and the thickness of his front load vest preventing him from getting his torso completely submerged. The wasps were also attacking Jory Thomas, who was thrashing the air, also trying to get submerged, his lips and cheeks puffed up, eyelids swollen shut as he went into anaphylactic shock.

Armani, with superhuman effort, managed to keep his head despite the mass injections of red hot pain from the wasps' stingers, and thrusting his arm above the now muddied water, he pulled the tab of a smoke grenade, its purple smoke rising quickly above the green island into the ever-darkening sky. A mile back on the levee, Major Gill spotted it and dispatched one of the bigger boats under the command of A Company's Captain Mallory.

* * *

Through his binoculars, Mallory, along with the thirty-man platoon of infantry aboard his boat, could see Jory Thomas's bloated body, his grotesquely swollen face barely recognizable as human, eyes no more than slits, and his tongue, enormous and blue, protruding obscenely as he floated, dead, a few yards from the hammock. Armani, his face almost as swollen as Thomas's, still lay in the shallow water. Approaching in the big thirty-man boat, Mallory adjusted the focus on his binoculars and could see the swarm of wasps. He signaled to the driver to kill the engine so he could be heard. "Insect repellent!" he shouted, pulling the tube from his load vest pocket. "Put it on *now*!"

The men didn't need a second order.

"Medic?" Mallory called.

"Sir?"

"We've got a possible survivor. Massive wasp bites. You handle it?"

"Affirmative," the medic said.

As Mallory ordered the big airboat ahead, using the protected side of the island, not knowing why Armani's search boat had ended up there, he realized that even with the purple smoke, they would have spent more time finding the island amidst so many hammocks had Armani's RTO not radioed in their exact GPS position.

The medic, using one hand to wave off the wasps, injected the atropine into Armani even as two other Guardsmen prepared to lift him aboard the big boat. "Jesus!" another soldier muttered upon seeing the colonel's face.

Mallory saw Ainsley's floating body turning slowly farther out and tried to piece together what had gone wrong, Colonel Armani in such bad shape that no one could understand what he was trying to say. Mallory recalled that he and the other three company commanders had heard a *crack* or two like the sound of a rifle in the distance, but some of the men had thought it was the sharp sound of thunder following a lightning strike farther south. But now, through his binoculars, Mallory could see Ainsley's body more clearly from a different angle as it turned in the slow-moving current to reveal the RTO's massive head wound, a dark cloud of insects buzzing about it. It looked like a bullet wound, but he couldn't be sure. Not wanting to waste what was precious time for Armani, he ordered the big boat back to the levee, leaving most of A Company's first platoon with him at the hammock, though no one among the National Guard, including platoon leader Lieutenant Houseman, was quite sure what they were supposed to do.

"Look around," was all Mallory told them, which did nothing but confuse them further. What were they looking *for*? Armani, his RTO, and his driver, Jory Thomas, had obviously been attacked by a swarm of wasps. But where had the shot come from? Mallory had told Lieutenant Houseman that beneath the mass of insects on Ainsley's body they'd probably discover he'd been shot, and that Armani and Jory Thomas had been thrown into "harm's way" while trying to "exit the situation."

Exit—that was the way Mallory talked, much to the annoyance of Lieutenant Houseman and the other three platoon commanders in A Company. If there was a way of tarting up a straightforward explanation, then Mallory would take it. He also liked posing as the no-nonsense, kick-ass and take-names officer of the battalion, but his attempt to create the impression of a hard-ass lone ranger was usually undermined by his concern for his men. And today this concern reined in what in another commander might have been a decision to press forward immediately, into the Big Cypress preserve. Instead Mallory was keeping his first platoon on the hammock until he and his fellow company commanders could get more information from Armani.

"Secure the island," he told Lieutenant Houseman.

One of the four men equipped with a SAW in the first platoon quipped to another, " 'Secure the fucking island.' He thinks he's in the fucking movies. This is the worst fucking bush I've ever seen. I never joined up for this crap. Palmetto, saw grass, crippled trees—all thrown in together. You can't move a fucking inch without a machete."

"Then quit your squawkin'," said the platoon sergeant, an accountant from Mobile, "and get one." The SAW gunner, PFC Johns, surprised at being overheard, whistled to one of two men in each section designated to carry machetes.

"Johns!" the sergeant said. "Don't whistle like that. Hear you a mile away. Think you're in Disney World?"

It would be said afterward that PFC Johns's whistle told the militia east of them exactly where the platoon, now disembarked, was situated—midway along the western side of the hammock. In fact it was only sheer coincidence that a few seconds after Johns's whistle the militia fired its first 81mm mortar rounds. In a perverse stroke by the militia, the rounds had been fitted with "Stuka caps" that announced their impending arrival with a high, nerve-shattering Stuka dive-bomber-like scream, more unsettling to neophyte National Guardsmen than the sound of the mortar bombs' explosions in the thick growth of the island.

The militia on the middle of the three teardrop islands, which egrets had long vacated, were waiting until the big airboat bearing the wounded Armani was well away, leaving Houseman and his men without a quick means of evacuation. Only a few of the mortar rounds landed wide in the boat's wake, sending up marl-blackened geysers, the range obviously known to the militia mortar crews who now rained down fire and destruction on the hapless National Guard platoon. The Guardsmen ran, or rather stumbled, over tree stumps, branches, into hidden water holes as they frantically spread out and sought cover, as if the farther they were from their comrades, the safer they'd be. This was an illusion, for the militia mortars were so carefully laying down fire that every sector of the hammock was being hit simultaneously, eruptions of pungent, uprooted green foliage, black soil, peat, and limbs from stunted slash pine filling the air, pulverizing the small island.

Dried wood on the hammock became deadly additional shrapnel as the thirty-man platoon sought refuge. Some, in a blind panic, began digging furiously with their entrenching tools, but to no avail, the plant growth so prolific and intertwined that it defeated any quick excavation. Besides, any hole, if dug more than a foot or two deep, was quickly flooded, like those recurring pools of seawater that thwart children's attempts to dig deep holes on a seashore.

One desperate squad of ten men turned westward, fleeing from the island as fast as the water and soft marl of dead roots, leaves, and black mud would allow them, escaping, or so they thought, the deadly rain of explosive coming down on the hammock. Their illusion of having escaped was shattered, however, by a salvo of six mortar rounds that radiated out from the island, catching them in the open with only water and saw grass as protection, which was no protection at all. The explosions and singeing shrapnel of the high-explosive 81mm rounds cut them down as if some huge scythe had swept west of the island. Six of the ten men were killed outright, the four others so badly wounded they could barely move, their noise and their blood arousing a brood of alligators ashore on a small hammock.

One of the Guardsmen caught in the saw grass sea about seventy yards west of the hammock was Private Johns, whom the platoon's sergeant, Abrams, had bawled out for whistling. Not only was Johns, a bus driver from Tampa, severely wounded, his left arm hanging uselessly, but he was experiencing a panic attack, convinced he was going to die, that his frantic heart would simply stop from utter exhaustion. His indecision, not knowing whether to go back or forward, literally paralyzed him, until the Stuka scream of an 81mm round passing high over his comrades on the island zeroed in on him as if it had been personally programmed to hit him, exploding in a black rush of marl and shrapnel only three feet away. The shot decapitated him, blood bubbling from his stem as, headless, his body walked a few feet and collapsed, disappearing in the wind-bowing saw grass as though he'd never been there. Houseman, the platoon lieutenant, saw Johns go down, some of his body parts flung into the saw grass like a gutted chicken. The lieutenant had joined the Guard because he liked the camaraderie and the idea of being paid for it. He hadn't signed up for this.

Mallory, crouching down on the interface between the hammock and the sea of saw grass, his left hand pressed hard over his ear, was shouting into the phone of his RTO's PRC-1 radio, telling Major Gill back at the levee that he was taking heavy mortar fire and, he thought, possibly machine-gun fire, though he wasn't sure of the latter. It could be one of his M-60s, its burps muffled by the heavy growth.

"Mallory," Gill informed the infantry captain, "I'm sending out two of the big boats—a driver and six men apiece—to evacuate Houseman's platoon."

"Roger that," Mallory answered, shouting louder than he needed to be heard above the crash of more mortar bombs. "The two big boats should be careful not to expose 'emselves too much in the gaps between hammocks."

It was then that the stranded platoon's second lieutenant, Cade Raleigh, believed he was witnessing the answer to his prayers—a miracle—as the oncoming Gulf-brewed storm from the southwest broke in a torrential rain. It would provide excellent cover for the evacuation of the platoon, or at least the nineteen out of the original thirty, a greater than thirty percent rate of attrition. The slaughter had taken less than a quarter hour. Catastrophic. At this rate the entire platoon would be wiped out in thirty minutes or less.

He ordered the nineteen men into two groups for the two big airboats, telling one group of ten men to head due north, the other nine men due south, away from the east-west tear-shaped island. It wasn't the shortest route back to the levee for either group, but one that would best avoid the mortar fire landing west of the island.

On a clear day the two big airboats would have been spotted as soon as they began to move as they dragged their hapless comrades from the saw grass, but under the obscuring protection of a tropical downpour, they headed off unseen, motors killed, the survivors who could manage and the six men assigned by Gill to each rescue boat using their M-16s and other weapons to, in effect, pole the airboats. But one of the newer Guard recruits had the safety off his M-60, and a stick stuck in the marl of silt and other debris got caught up in the trigger guard. The bullet entered above the Guardsman's right ear and blew out part of his skull over the right eye, which then hung loosely by the optic nerve, freaking out everyone in the boat, the sound of the shot barely audible above the heavy hiss of rain. Even so, it was heard, albeit faintly, by the militia on the middle of the three larger islands now lost to view, which led to another Stuka-shrieking mortar salvo that blew out large clumps of saw grass. The upheaval released a putrid, rotten-egg swamp smell of hydrogen sulfide that panicked some of the Guardsmen in the two rescue boats who, for a terrified moment, thought the militia was using chemical warheads on the mortars. "No sweat," the platoon's sergeant announced in the second boat. "The lieutenant just farted."

This produced a hysteria of relief out of all proportion to the comment, several Guardsmen in tears, they were laughing so hard in the tension-releasing moment. The lieutenant's reply to the sergeant, "You're welcome, *Corporal!*" added to the laughter, one of the men remembering how a Marine, in the bloody fight for Mount Surabachi on Iwo Jima, had been sitting in the fetal position out of range of the Japanese artillery when, as a result of American artillery fire, a Japanese soldier was hit, only his buttocks intact, coming down on the Marine in a shower of dirt—plop!—right on the Marine's arm-locked knees, and how the American squad had broken up, several laughing so hard they were useless for the next half hour.

But on the first boat heading south in a semicircular path to the levee, there was no such laughter as a squad leader, hands trembling, kept his eyes locked on the GPS in order to get back without spending any more time in the saw grass than necessary. One of the other men in his boat, a nineteen-year-old, was blubbering like a child. No one offered comfort, on the edge themselves, not daring to risk empathy lest they crack too. Before this debacle, none of them had ever seen a man die, let alone one of their friends. The squad leader, barely older than the traumatized teen, heard a low hum off to his left by the gradually emerging shape of a small hammock. He knew it couldn't be the first rescue boat, not unless they goofed and had doubled back in the storm, the rain now drumming so hard on the aluminum boat it could have been mistaken for hail. "Someone's coming," he hissed, flicking his M-16 to automatic. He saw the blunt nose of a boat, but much smaller than the other rescue boat. "Fire!" he yelled to his comrades, and let off two three-round bursts.

The first was too high, hitting aluminum superstructure, the second on target, knocking the driver right out of the seat, the long joystick by his side, no longer under tension, sliding forward, the boat dead in the water, someone screaming to "Hold your fire! Hold your—" before he too fell on what turned out to be one of the four three-man scout boats Armani had sent out earlier. It shouldn't have been there, having come out of its search zone to offer what assistance it could, only to be mistaken by the stressed-out squad leader and the other men on the bigger rescue boat as another militia attack.

CHAPTER TWENTY-FIVE

Camp Fairchild

IN THE SAME way as a tourist sometimes feels that the details of the last country visited now seem so far back in time, Jeremy Eleen's battle against the federals in the Cascade blizzard was receding in his memory, or at least merging into all the other battles he'd fought north of the Oregon-Washington line. One memory of that battle, however, was still with him, and, he was sure, would stay with him until the end of his life: crouching in the chopper's open door as Mulvane held him back from leaping out to help the wounded Rubinski, and Rubinski's look of desperation and fear, of having been deserted. It was an incident that had not been absorbed into the train of Eleen's other war memories. It stayed with him night and day because self-doubt, fueled by his militia's humiliating defeat at the hands of federal Major Irwin, continued to plague him. Was there something he could have done for Rubinski, or had Mulvane's restraining grip provided a convenient excuse for not going back? Had Jeremy Brigham Eleen, son of one of the Marines who'd fought their way, *with* their wounded, from the Chosin Reservoir to the sea, turned coward?

Eleen wasn't sleeping well, despite the fact that the POW barracks, while not exactly warm, were at least heated, the electric radiators keeping the hut in the low sixties. He was so exhausted that he would frequently nod off, only to find himself jolted awake, his hand outstretched. It was annoying to the other thirty-nine men in the hut too, because his snoring, then sudden awakening from nightmare, was as often as not accompanied by an unintelligible exclamation of his fright. Who was it who said, "Laugh and the whole world laughs with you; snore and you sleep alone"?

Unlike most POW camps, at least those he'd heard about, militia officers were not segregated from NCOs and privates, the federal government decreeing that insofar as the militia was not recognized as a "legitimate" force, distinctions between so-called militia officers and ordinary militiamen were "illegitimate." Civil libertarians interviewed by Marte Price, who was annoyed at having missed the federals' "screw-up" in Florida, as her editor had described Armani's ill-fated attack, claimed that not treating the militia captives as "legitimate" POWs would mean that the accords as laid down by the Geneva Convention would not be enforced, that POW commandants would therefore "feel unconstrained."

In fact, Major Schmidt, administrator of the Fairchild POW camp, had gone beyond requirements of the Geneva Accord in having the barracks provided with radiators at "government expense," rather than installing barrel-bellied wood-burning stoves, as in other countries. And he pointed out in Marte Price's interview of him, "We have also installed hot water in each hut. It's hardly what you'd call 'primitive.' "

"How about toilet facilities?"

"There are two for every hut."

"Flush toilets?"

"I don't think the American taxpayer wants us to run federally funded *resorts* for people who are actively trying—or I should say, *had* actively sought—to overthrow their democratically elected government," Schmidt snapped. "Do you?"

When the interview ended, Schmidt flashed a smile at Marte Price. "Can I tell you something?" he asked. "Off the record?"

"All right."

He leaned closer. "If I had my way, I'd have the fucking ringleaders shot. You media types think this is some kind of game. If the militia were to get their way, you'd be the first fucking people to be silenced. Have you thought of that?"

Marte didn't retreat an inch. "I thought the fight was over?"

"Then you thought wrong. Those militia bastards are just licking their wounds. What d'you think all this business in Florida is? They're starting up again. Well, we're not going to turn *this* camp into a fucking rest home for those pricks. Any one of them goes near that fucking wire, they'll be shot."

"Do you always speak so elegantly—*off the record*?"

"Sometimes it's necessary to make a point."

"And here I was thinking you were a defender of democracy. Instead you're just another run-of-the-mill fascist."

"You know what you need, don't you?"

"Not from you I don't." She paused. "I'll be watching this camp with great interest."

"Yeah, well, you watch. Whose side are you on?"

"I'm on no one's side. I'm a reporter."

"No you're not, you're a bitch with ambition. You're for yourself, and screw everyone else."

"I'll be watching this camp with great interest," she repeated.

Marte Price wasn't being entirely truthful. What she really

wanted was to get the heck out of the place, go down south and interview Armani—if he was well enough, and even if he wasn't. Find out why the militia had put up—was putting up?—such a fight in the Everglades. After all, wasn't it just a big swamp?

In Miami, Riley and Ma were booked in the Morley's Hotel over the causeway and down three blocks from Collins Avenue, where the hip and beautiful people could be seen, sipping lattes and Bacardi rum, and paying outrageous prices for cracked blue crab. In Morley's, an old hotel that had seen grander days of art deco, the ceiling fans and rattan chairs conjured up visions of Sydney Greenstreet perspiring, and Peter Lorre holding his cigarette between thumb and finger in the Continental fashion. In the bar, where Ma and Riley were waiting, no one was in attendance, and Riley was grumbling. He wanted a Coke with lots of ice, and he told Ma he didn't want it out of a fucking spout. He wanted a can or, better still, the old eight-ounce bottle, which he said you paid through the nose for but which was just the right amount. "Know what I mean?"

"You sure you read those pages right through?" Ma asked him.

"Yeah."

For Ma, it didn't have the ring of conviction—same tone as a kid telling you he's brushed his teeth.

"Yeah," Ma said, "did you read 'em or did you just glance over them?"

"I fucking read them. Get off my back. There was nothing there about the militia. You read *yours*?"

"Yes. All he said about the militia was how he felt bad about waxing the guy he'd surprised."

"Like I said," Riley grumbled, "it'd help if we knew what *exactly* we were looking for."

"I told you we do—anything about the militia."

"You know what I mean," Riley retorted. "Something . . ." He had to search for the right word.

"Something specific," Ma said.

"Yeah. Specific."

"Well, they told us to note anything he said about the militia. Anything unusual."

"So there's nothing unusual," Riley answered. "Don't worry, we'll get paid."

A man in a dirty T-shirt—HILVERN'S MARINA—and faded stone-washed jeans came in smoking a hand-rolled cigarette.

"Hey!" He glanced at the bar, then called out to the teenage girl at the nearby registration desk. "Y'all gone on strike or somethin'? Where's Larry?"

"Changing a bulb," she said. "You want a drink?"

"Yes, ma'am. I'm drier'n a bush turkey."

"He'll be back," the girl said. She looked anorexic.

"Next year?" the man joshed, sliding up to the bar. "How y'all doin'?" he inquired of Riley and Ma.

"Hot," Ma said.

"This ain't hot. Wait till it gets over the hundred."

"Air conditioner doesn't work," Riley griped without looking at him.

"Sure it works," the man asserted. He was of medium build, tanned, with a creased, middle-aged face, though his eyes and energetic demeanor were those of a much younger man. Bluish-gray smoke streamed out of his nostrils. He smiled, jerking his thumb up at the fans without looking at them. "Best air conditioner in the world." He looked over at the desk. " 'S' at right, Bess?"

"Whatever you say."

The man sat on one of the bar stools, plonked down his tobacco tin and rice paper, and slapped a couple of dollar bills on the bar counter. "Help myself?" he asked the girl jokingly.

"Larry wouldn't like it."

"Well, you tell that ol' boy—he don't get his butt on down here, I'm helpin' myself." He winked at Ma, who was patting his pockets, a worried look on his face.

"Lost your wallet?" the man asked.

"No. I'm out of smokes."

The man indicated his tobacco tin and papers. "Help yourself to mine if you like."

"No thanks. I like tailor-made. No offense."

"None taken." The man smiled. The contact had been perfect. "Tailor-made." He put out his hand. "I'm Billy Joe Hurst."

"Ray Ma. This is Dan Riley." Riley didn't shake hands, nodding perfunctorily.

"Pleased to meet you," Billy Joe said.

"Larry's comin'," the clerk announced hopefully.

"So's Christmas!" Billy Joe joshed with an easy belly laugh. He turned to Ma—it was clear to him that Riley was a moody son of a bitch. "You boys down here on business?"

"Nope," Ma said, easily adopting Billy Joe's mood. "Just trippin' around."

"Uh-huh . . . here's the man. Larry, where in hell you been?"

"Lightbulbs. They put a man on the moon—can't make a goddamn bulb that'll last more'n a month." He walked behind the counter. The bar itself was nothing fancy, just a row of bottles, a couple of flies on reconnaissance, and a cold chest below for the bottled beer and pop. "What can I get you boys?"

"A beer, a Coke—lots of ice," Ma said, "and . . ." He looked at Billy Joe. "What'll it be?"

"Jack Daniel's on the rocks."

While Larry shuffled about getting the drinks, Billy Joe asked what they'd seen so far.

"Everglades," Ma said.

"Any wildlife?" This was the key question.

"Lot of gators," Ma replied.

"Uh-huh. You see any gallinules? Purple-chested bird, big feet, walks across the water on the lily pads?"

"Yeah," Ma said, smiling. Riley was getting mad at the ice.

"Anything else?" Billy Joe asked.

Ma looked as if he was thinking hard. "I don't think so. D'you, Riley?"

"Nothing," Riley said. "Nada."

Billy Joe, who'd been sipping his Jack Daniel's, downed the remainder, an "Ahhh" of satisfaction coming from him as he put the glass down sharply on the counter. "Well, I'd like to chat some more with you boys but have to be heading off. Thanks for the drink."

"You're welcome," Ma said.

Larry asked Ma if there'd be anything else, and when Ma said no, he shuffled out of the bar and disappeared into the back of the hotel.

"I don't hold with all this secret shit," Riley said.

" 'Course you don't," Ma shot back. "That's because you don't give a shit about their security."

"So you *do*?"

"I want to get paid—and we don't get paid if their militia is penetrated."

"Yeah, I care about their security. So let's get the hell out of here."

"We will. Tomorrow," Ma said.

"How 'bout right now?"

"I want to stroll down Collins."

"See the stars at the Colony?"

"Anything wrong with that?"

"Seen one, you seen 'em all."

Ma knew that Riley's mood wasn't about the sameness of the stars as much as the fact that he'd pulled the trigger on the Kozan woman. Ever since he'd read in the *Herald* that she'd been pregnant, Riley had been feeling remorse. He didn't want to admit it for fear of being thought a bleeding heart. Ma told him that a walk down Collins would do both of them good— "lots of tit and ass."

Schmidt had ordered a sweep of the POW camp for the seizure of all cell phones, radios, Walkmans, any flip-open, flat-screen digital pocket TVs—anything that the prisoners could use to send or receive communications with the outside world. He well knew, however, that his men were bound to have missed some prisoners with radios and phones, because a quick call by one cell phone to another, or a hand signal, would have alerted many of the prisoners that a search was under way.

At three A.M. the next morning, as the bitterly cold wind from the snow across what was normally semi-arid desert howled across the bleak tarmacs of Fairchild Air Force Base and around the huts of Camp Fairchild, Schmidt ordered a search. He had borrowed Air Force men from the air base so he could hit every one of the fifty huts simultaneously, giving no one time to hide anything. The POWs were roused abruptly from their REM sleep by the deliberate din made by guards shouting. Schmidt knew that between two and four A.M. human beings were at their lowest psychological ebb, more vulnerable than at any other time.

As the hundreds of POWs stumbled out of their bunks, dull-witted and cursing, the search began, the dogs sniffing bunks and the open baby-bath-sized plastic tubs that served as lockers at the end of each of the three-tiered bunks. Some men, confused by the sudden wake-up, the shouts of the guards, the heavy stomp of boots, and the skittering of dog feet on the bare, cold, wooden floor—the heaters having been turned down to sixty at night—all but fell to the floor still half asleep.

Schmidt, however, despite his haul of twenty-six radios and Walkmans and two digital "liquid" flat-screen TVs, was under no illusion that he'd retrieved them all, and had signal experts from the air base set up a detection center in the commandant's office, a hut a hundred yards east of the main gate. There, a signals squad of eight privates and a sergeant set up shop with equipment to monitor the air waves for any outgoing or incoming signal traffic and to detect, via silver-dollar-sized sensor caps whose probes penetrated the earth a few inches on all four sides of the camp, any "unauthorized movement," particularly at night. Schmidt could thus discover any attempt of the prisoners to contact the outside world with either cell phones or small radio transmitters, while the motion sensors in the ground would detect any attempt at tunneling out. Within twenty-four hours eleven more cell phones that had been squirreled away by POWs, and eighteen small transistorized headphones and other small radios, had been detected by the "ferrets," as the signals squad was known.

During the six A.M. head count next morning, Schmidt, his Army greatcoat dusted by snow, announced to the assembled nine hundred militia prisoners that two of their number, impersonating officers, had been stopped at the gate by a guard who discovered they did not have the correct identity card.

"And if you think," he continued, "that that guard was especially alert, you're sadly mistaken. *Every* guard has been selected on the basis of his record in the military police, many of them police in civilian—" There was a spontaneous booing at Schmidt's mention of "police."

"Federal suckholes!" someone shouted, a sentiment greeted with cheers, and, in Eleen's hut, by loud clapping. "Right on!" Corporal Mulvane shouted, adding "Assholes!" for which he was immediately taken to the "cooler," a blockhouse of gray cement bricks by the main gate and guard tower. There, he was rudely shoved into one of the ten solitary cells, next to Hearn's. All of Eleen's hut POWs had cheered Mulvane on his way. One POW called out, "Hey, Schmidt—who's screwing your wife?" For this, Commandant Schmidt issued hut 5A a CTH—confined to hut—for three days.

Glen Autry, a militia M-60 machine gunner in Eleen's hut, and known not as Glen but as Gene, asked a grim-looking Eleen why he wasn't joining in the fun.

"It's counterproductive," Eleen grumbled, sounding much older than his twenty-eight years, pointing out how being stuck in their hut for the next seventy-two hours wasn't going to help anyone except Schmidt, who now wouldn't have as many POWs to watch in the yard.

"Good for morale, though," Autry pointed out. "Piss off the federals."

Eleen, his Mormon faith as strong as ever, never swore, but he told Autry that annoying the federals would only make them more alert, more determined on payback. Autry didn't say any more. Lieutenant Eleen was decidedly moody these days, and Autry knew why. It was Rubinski—Eleen carrying his guilt around like a man weighed down with a hundred-pound pack. Several of Eleen's men who had survived the Cascade battle, and other POWs in his hut, had commented on how down the lieutenant looked. A few of the men from the hut recounted how they had said good morning to him and gotten no reply, as if he hadn't even seen or heard them. Others in the hut who hadn't known Eleen before he was captured thought him stuck up, as if he was silently bemoaning the fact that he, a militia officer, had to bunk with NCOs and other peasants.

"Ah, bullshit!" Autry told them. If there was one militia officer who couldn't care less about differences in rank, it was Jeremy Eleen, and there wasn't a prejudiced bone in him. If anything, Autry posited, Eleen was as downcast about the rumored possibility of being separated, along with all other militia officers, from his men, Schmidt still weighing the merits of treating all militia POWs with the same contempt versus the advantages, "securitywise," to his federals of depriving the ordinary militiamen of their leaders, the latter more likely to try to organize escapes.

"Well," a PFC machine gunner's mate said, "he's still a moody bastard. He better snap out of it, man, 'fore he cracks up. Seen a guy like that in the fight for that fucking bridge over the Columbia River. Moody as fuck. Know what happened to him?" Before Autry could answer, the gunner's mate told him, "Shot himself. A fucking .45—went in one side, came out the other. Should've seen the mess, man—fucking awful."

"Ah," Autry began in his usual fashion, "the lieutenant isn't gonna shoot himself."

"Ten bucks says he does."

"You haven't got ten bucks. Federals took all our money when we come into this shithouse."

"My ration of cigarettes, then."

"I don't smoke," Autry said.

"No, but you can use 'em for trade."

"Listen, Marty, he won't kill himself. All right?"

"One pack of cigarettes?" Marty persisted.

"Oh, all right."

"Shake on it?"

"Betting's illegal," Autry joshed. "Orders of Mein Führer Schmidt."

"Shake on it!" Marty insisted.

"Ah, all right, but he won't kill himself, Marty."

" 'Course not."

They shook hands.

If anyone was more depressed than Eleen, it was his supreme
commander, Colonel Vance, alias "General Nordstrom." The
reason was simple, yet disturbing. Freeman's earlier capture of
Hearn, a militiaman whom Vance personally detested, had become the federals' big catch. Hearn's acerbic interview with
Marte Price, an interview federal officials had been kicking
themselves for ever since, resulted in an enormous rush of volunteers for the militia among millions of dissatisfied Americans, especially among the unemployed, the underemployed,
and the young. As Hitler had appealed to the dissatisfied Ger-
mans in the 1930s, Hearn had rallied a portion of the dispos-
sessed to his side, to his black and white vision of an America
seized by greedy rich film stars and the "Jewish leeches" of
Wall Street. These, Hearn had charged, flaunted their wealth in
the face of a nation, particularly in the face of a middle class
that felt perennially overtaxed and oppressed by a government
pouring millions, no, *billions,* into affirmative action, and which
allowed masses of Hispanics to cross the borders of the "dis-
united States" to suck at the teat of "pinko liberal largesse." It
didn't matter that such political proclamations by Hearn didn't
make sense when coolly, calmly evaluated, many of them plainly
contradictory. What mattered, Vance knew, was that Hearn had
succeeded in pushing all the right buttons of a volatile cross-
section of white America. What was badly needed now, in
General Nordstrom's view, was a decisive military victory to
capitalize on Hearn's propaganda victory and the windfall of
new recruits.

CHAPTER TWENTY-SIX

The Everglades

COLONEL ARMANI, STILL recovering from the effects of the wasp attack, looked grotesque, his face swollen, his eyes all but closed, his cheeks a vivid pink, his lips fat and protruding like a gopher fish. He hadn't seen himself as yet in a mirror, and no one was about to suggest he should, but his four company commanders needed to hear from him, to learn precisely what had happened to his RTO and to his airboat's driver. Where had the militia fire come from? Armani's tongue was twice its normal size, threatening to choke him, and his speech was unintelligible. They gave him pencil and paper. His fingers too were swollen, but holding a Day-Glo marker in his fist like a young child and using big letters, he managed to convey the essential military aspect of his experience in the 'glades east of Ten Thousand Islands; namely, that he'd come under fire from the *middle* of the three islands, no more than a quarter mile from the hammock on which he'd sought refuge.

If nothing else, the information relieved any anxiety the company commanders had about this mission's rules of engagement. The militia had clearly initiated hostilities, so now it was a simple case of returning or initiating fire the moment any militia was spotted. There was the rub, however, for Armani. Despite his bone-deep agony from the hundreds of wasp stings, his body still coursing with poison, he had not seen a single militiaman. Could it have been a *single* sniper who had killed his RTO and forced them to take shelter from the mortar squads hitting them? The four commanders' assumption that there was a large militia force at hand was just that: an assumption.

There was only one way to find out, only this time Armani's second-in-command, Colonel Gill, had a definite target, the middle island of the three. This time Gill ordered men of the 53rd Battalion, the four hundred of Alpha and Bravo companies on the left flank, the four hundred of Charlie and Delta companies on the right, to proceed in two channels of water lilies approximately a hundred yards apart to the off side of the football-field-sized island to which Armani, Ainsley, and Jory Thomas had fled and designated "Echo." It meant that instead of approaching the middle "White" island of the three islands beyond Echo designated "Red," "White," and "Blue," as Armani's three-man scout boat had done in the relatively open saw-grass water, Alpha and Bravo on the left with Charlie and Delta on the right would advance toward White Island using Echo Island as a blind. Once in close to the western side of Echo, the two companies could sweep out quickly from the northern and southern extremities of the island, Alpha and Bravo taking Red, Charlie and Delta taking Blue, before the enemy could launch an effective mortar attack. But even if the enemy launched another small arms and mortar attack, they would have to split their resources in order to bring fire on the two National Guard forces. Once reaching the security of Red and Blue, the two Guard forces could begin *their* mortar attacks on White Island, halfway between Red and White.

Admittedly there was the danger of overreach, of Alpha-Bravo mortaring Charlie-Delta and vice versa if they weren't careful, but Gill and his four company commanders stressed keeping the mortars tight, meaning at acute angles. In any event, the three remaining three-man scout airboats, an RTO aboard each, would stay wide, scout boats one and two guiding the fire of Alpha-Bravo from Red to the north and the fire of Charlie-Delta from Blue to the south. Gill's intent, as he succinctly put it, was "to pound the shit out of White Island," to rain down such a thick, rapid concentration of fire that the militia, no matter how many of them were there, would be annihilated. The most dangerous part of the plan, he conceded, was to reach Echo a mile from the battalion's levee without encountering opposition, for here, while both forces would be using the lily pad channels, the latter relatively unobstructed by saw grass, they would nevertheless be in the open.

Armani, trying to listen to Gill's preparations, was vomiting violently, but through a Herculean effort he managed to scribble the letters NVG with his Day-Glo marker. Gill, however, doubted the militias would be equipped with night vision goggles. Even in the National Guard units, only two men in ten—a squad—had them, the point man and whoever was tail-end Charlie on a patrol. Gill would give Alpha-Bravo and Charlie-Delta the green light when there was just enough gray light to launch and be over behind Echo by dawn. He would need full daylight for the two short, dangerous end runs from north and south Echo toward Red and Blue. But his force wouldn't blunder on militia as Armani had. They'd be ready to return fire from the boats, and he'd already given orders for each boat to have a mortar forward and those men of Alpha-Bravo on the starboard side of the boats to carry LAW antitank missiles, potent close-in artillery, the choice of which Armani had been laughed at for adding to his equipment. "First of all, the militia don't have tanks, and even if they did, you're not going to see any tanks in the swamp, Joe," a colleague had scoffed. But Armani had seen the psychological effects of a squad being hit by a LAW missile. It was nothing less than devastating, and got people's attention in one hell of a hurry. And Gill knew the LAWs would come in very handy if the militia dared launch its own airboats. One LAW hitting an airboat would do the job nicely. What had been an airboat would be scrap metal.

"Look at that!" said Harold Mead, one of the riflemen among Eleen's survivors of the Packwood fight. He'd been watching Schmidt's men placing more sensors into the ground along the inside of the ten-foot-wide "No Go" strip of carefully raked ground that ran like a moat around the POW camp's barbed-wire perimeter.

"What d'you mean?" inquired another POW, who thought Mead was commenting on Commandant Schmidt, finishing his morning run outside the wire.

Mead had to think quickly. In an unguarded moment he'd almost given away the secret of Eleen's hut. "Ah," he began, "I mean that if any of our boys try snipping through the wire, those sensors'll feel the vibrations."

"Oh yeah," said the man, a PFC Browne, from a couple of huts up from Eleen's, his hands thrust deep in his pockets to keep them warm in the freezing weather. He stamped his boots on the frozen ground, his breath visible in the early morning air. "Maybe our guys can build some kind of ladder. Run it out at night from under one of the huts near the wire and rest its other end on top of the wire. That way you wouldn't disturb the No Go strip. Simple."

Mead, a short, wiry plumber from Portland, looked at Browne to see if he was kidding. Browne showed no sign of it as he kept stamping his cold feet. "Have you had breakfast?" Mead asked him.

"Yeah," Browne said, puzzled at Mead's question, "if you call that oatmeal muck breakfast. Why?"

"Because I figured you might be delirious from hunger."

"Why?"

"Fucking wire would vibrate, wouldn't it? Sensors'd register the vibrations."

Browne pouted. "Not necessarily. Not the high fence. You wouldn't let it touch the wire."

"Where else would you put it?"

"On one of the fence posts."

"Not unless you want to die," Mead said. "Vibrations would be felt by the wood. Sensors'd pick it up."

"Maybe, maybe not," Browne mused. "Wood doesn't pick up sound."

"Why not?"

Browne, a medium-sized man, had stocky features that made him appear overweight, but most of it was muscle. "Vibrations through wood get muffled." He looked across at Mead. "Used to run a lumber store," he said by way of explanation. "We could use a ladder."

"Well, you won't find me on any friggin' ladder atop a post or anything else. Even if the sensors wouldn't pick it up, haven't you heard of searchlights?"

"You mean you wouldn't want to give it a try?" Browne asked, his tone close to accusatory. "Don't you want to get out?"

"Listen," Mead retorted, "when I go, it'll be something that's got half a chance."

"Such as what?" Browne challenged.

Mead fell silent for a few seconds. They heard an announcement from the commandant's office that it was coffee break. The POWs hated it. The coffee was a weak and bitter swill, and they suspected it was used as a front for carrying out an unofficial head count. No one had yet escaped from Camp Fairchild, and Schmidt was determined to keep it that way. As Browne and Mead went to their separate huts, Mead was glad of the opportunity to talk to Eleen. "Sir," he said, "I think Archie's had it."

Eleen nodded morosely, not realizing how obvious his state of mind was to others, just how much his black mood infected them with a kind of malaise, a loss of hope. Nevertheless, despite the burden of his guilt over Rubinski, he had still been grounded enough in the obligations of a leader as defined by his father to know that idle hands and minds lead to serious problems of morale. It was for this reason and not because he had much confidence in its eventual efficacy that he'd agreed to let his hut, all twenty-nine POWs in addition to himself, participate in "Archie," the name used in the yard for the tunnel they'd started, fourteen feet down and fifty to go to get under the carefully raked No Go zone and wire. And now Mead, who, along with Sullivan, a short, thickset "sandhog" from New York who knew all there was to know about burrowing under Manhattan or any other place, was telling him that Archie was kaput. Mead and Sandhog Sullivan had another word for it, but didn't say it in front of Eleen.

"I guess," Eleen said, "you're talking about the sensors they're putting in?"

"Yes, sir."

Eleen was swilling the weak, lukewarm coffee, staring at it as if it was a whirlpool, dragging him down. As a young man, his Mormon mentors had warned him against so many dangers, possible addictions—including coffee and tea. Well, he could tell his forebears in absentia that there wasn't the slightest possibility of him getting addicted to this apology for coffee. "Have you got any other ideas?" he asked Mead, his voice trying to convey genuine interest.

Mead hesitated but then thought, What the hell? "Well, sir, one of the guys in hut four reckons you could use a ladder and—"

Eleen shook his head. "Uh-huh, and what does he think the dogs'll be doing? Sitting nicely in a row?"

"Yeah, I told him it was crazy. And there are the sensors."

"Exactly."

" 'Least he wants to get out," Mead said.

"We all do."

"Yeah, what I mean is, he's keen. Some of the guys are just content to sit it out."

"Not many," Eleen ventured.

"No. I guess I was just thinking it'd be nice if we'd had a few more like him. Could hurry up Archie a bit."

Eleen was thinking about Korea—not the Marines' fighting retreat from Chosin Reservoir, but the later discovery by the South Koreans of North Korean tunnels burrowed right under the DMZ. And the American Army had had sensors all along the razor-wired DMZ that ran like an ugly scar across the peninsula. Eleen remembered that it was the federal general, Freeman, who'd solved the riddle, and for the first time since his fight against the federals under Irwin, Jeremy Eleen allowed himself a smile. "I think," he told Mead, "we have a way of finishing Archie after all. And you're right, we could use more diggers—like this Browne from the next hut. Tell him to forget all his crazy ideas about ladders unless he's bent on getting shot."

"But, sir, how're we going to—"

Eleen was walking toward the No Go zone. Someone, alarmed that Eleen had gone stir crazy and was bent on ending it all—one militiaman had already committed suicide this way—called out for someone to stop him. But Eleen stopped himself just short of the trip wire that marked the edge of the carefully raked ten-foot strip. There had been rumors that the strip was mined. No one wanted to test it, and the stir-crazy militiaman who committed suicide had taken only one step beyond the trip wire into the NG zone before he was shot by one of the tower guards. Someone had accidentally-on-purpose lobbed a baseball into the zone during one of the yard periods to see if anything exploded. It didn't, and Schmidt, to thwart any other probing attempts, personally announced over the P.A. system that any object entering the No Go zone would remain there. Baseballs were hard to come by, there being only four in the entire camp. Schmidt didn't have to worry about his guards enforcing the order—bored, recreation-starved POWs did it for him. Hit a ball out of bounds into the NG zone and you were suspended for two weeks from the team. Do it a second time and you wouldn't be allowed to play, period. It was a classic Machiavellian movement—divide and conquer—by Schmidt, getting the POWs to enforce *his* rule.

Eleen, stopping just short of the trip wire, the nearest guard tower's .50 caliber machine gun pointed at him, held up his right hand and requested an audience with Schmidt. Eleen could see the machine gunner's mate on a field phone, and after a couple of minutes the man put down the phone and told Eleen to go to the main gate, about a hundred yards on Eleen's left. The Mormon militiaman wasn't surprised. He knew Schmidt's type. Schmidt would be intrigued by the request.

Mead was talking to Browne when the latter had seen Eleen

raise his hand for permission to speak to the commandant. "What's the suck-holing up to Schmidt for?"

"He's not suck-holing," Mead answered.

"Then what's he want to see him for?"

Mead didn't know.

As the move of Alpha-Bravo on the left flank, Delta-Charlie on the right, toward Echo got under way in the predawn light, Private First Class Ernesto Rafael, with Alpha-Bravo, was in the midst of the "frights." Rafael was a rifleman, and a designated runner should intercompany radio communication fail. Other than that, he was just another Guardsman under Gill's overall command. Maneuvers had been one thing for Rafael, but this operation, code-named by Gill "Southern Stealth," was, in the words of Rafael's sergeant, "frightening the living daylights" out of the private. His whole body was atremble as he stepped noisily aboard one of the big airboats, his platoon buddies hissing at him to be "Quiet, goddamn it!" as he clumped on the aluminum gunwale before sitting at the end, on the starboard side of second squad's row.

The big boat hadn't pushed off more than ten feet from the levee when Rafael began dry heaving—nothing coming up because he'd been so uptight before H hour he hadn't been able to eat anything. Someone, strictly against regulations, had offered him an Ornade, a nasal decongestant that they said had a side effect of "calming you down." Swallowed on an empty stomach, the pill made him sleepy but didn't calm him. His shaking ceased, or at least was reduced to intermittent bursts of tremor, and he began saying the Lord's prayer: "Our Mother/Father who art in—"

"Hey!" someone hissed, "knock that off!" Rafael either didn't hear or didn't care. He kept it up and after he said, "Amen," he started up again. "Our Mother/Father—"

"Hey, puss nuts!" another Guardsman said. "It's our *Father*— what's this Mother/Father bullshit?"

Rafael kept on, and the sergeant could see he was upsetting

some of the younger guys. He jabbed Rafael hard with his elbow. "Say it quietly to yourself!"

Rafael stopped, but a few seconds later as the boat scraped noisily over a particularly tall stand of saw grass toward its designated channel, he had the dry heaves again.

"Jesus Christ!" someone whispered. "He'll get us all killed. Fuckin' militia'll hear us a mile—"

"Keep quiet!" It was third platoon's Lieutenant Ambleside from the 53rd Battalion's Alpha Company, whom the men had dubbed "Sides," working his way along the starboard gunwale, using the shoulders of his soldiers for balance. "Now breathe deeply," he instructed Rafael calmly. "You'll be fine. Just take a deep breath . . . hold it . . ."

Rafael had already exhaled. He was still trembling, but the lieutenant's intervention had at least brought some measure of self-control, though the smell of his urine dominated that of the humid saw grass swamp as they neared the halfway point in the channel between the levee and Echo. Lieutenant Sides crouched in the well between rows of the airboat, consulting his GPS and backlit, ruggedized, black aluminum-encased 486 handheld computer, removing the rain-proofed cover of the LCD display to check his platoon's position in relation to the rest of the airboat flotilla. Up forward a sergeant's helmet seemed welded to the tripod-mounted Nite Ranger optical scope filled with a forward looking infrared sensor that was now scanning Echo for any signs of the enemy.

Ashore on the levee, one of the battalion HQ group was using a ruggedized 760R fax machine to send a coded situation report directly to the Pentagon: "Mission progressing as planned."

CHAPTER TWENTY-SEVEN

Camp Fairchild

SCHMIDT WAS IMMACULATE in a newly pressed uniform, his office utilitarian. Its almost fanatical cleanliness and orderliness told Jeremy Eleen that Schmidt was a stickler for organization—a place for everything and everything in its place. In this aspect, at least, he reminded Eleen of himself, for he too was a stickler for details. Because of his Mormon upbringing, he'd embraced the notion and its attendant worldview that cleanliness was indeed next to godliness. But Schmidt had apparently not followed any attendant notion of humility: his desk was on a raised dais, at least a foot above floor level. Even if you knew that the commandant used the raised desk in order to intimidate, it still worked, especially if, in addition to the shame most men felt at being taken POW, they looked and felt ragged, defeated, because of the lack of razor blades. Having to look up at Schmidt induced in many, guards as well as POWs, the kind of subservience a child might feel having to look up at a pharmacist behind his raised counter, waiting to be recognized.

"Who are you?" Schmidt demanded.

"Lieutenant Eleen. I'm—"

"*Lieutenant!*" Schmidt sneered. "*Lieutenant.* You have no rank! You have no legitimacy whatsoever in the eyes of the government of the United States." He paused for effect. "You're *nothing—nothing* but a rebel. Hut 5A, correct?"

"Yes," Eleen said quietly.

"Yes, *sir!*"

Eleen thought about it for a couple of seconds. He knew what he would like to do to Schmidt—shoot him cleanly between the eyes, blow his arrogant head off—but as an officer, even if Schmidt didn't recognize him as such, Eleen couldn't always do what he felt like. He had to think of his men. He thought of the militiaman who'd committed suicide by walking straight into the No Go zone. Eleen told himself, as he knew his corporal, Mulvane, and Mead would have advised, to keep cool.

"Yes, *sir*."

Schmidt couldn't hide a smirk of satisfaction. "What do you want?"

"The men are pretty bored, sir. I'd like—"

"Your men, Eleen, are prisoners. They're lucky they're bored and not dead."

Eleen took a deep breath. "My concern is their morale, and I was hoping you'd be good enough to allow us to organize some kind of physical fitness programs?" It was then that Eleen had a sudden inspiration, which he attributed to God. He recalled how Schmidt was a runner, having seen him doing laps around the camp perimeter.

"You're an athlete," was the way Eleen put it. "You know how important it is to keep fit. Even if you don't care about them being bored, it's going to look bad in the press and in Washington, D.C., if men, prisoners, are out of shape, fall ill and start costing the government money."

Schmidt had picked up a pencil and was holding it in both hands, twiddling it. "You don't have to suck up to me, Eleen."

Eleen's face reddened. "I wasn't—"

"Maybe," Schmidt continued, his face impassive, "that's how you get things done in the militia, but not here. I'm a professional. I'll grant your request because I'm tired of seeing your rebels moping around the camp like bums. Unshaven, slovenly—"

"It'd help," Eleen cut in, "if we were issued proper toilet kits and clean—"

"You think I'm running a holiday camp here?"

"You force men to look like bums, pretty soon they'll act like bums. It's axiomatic."

Schmidt sat staring at Eleen, who realized Schmidt didn't know what the word axiomatic meant. "I'll issue ten disposable safety razors per hut," he finally said, "but after three days I want them returned. Any missing and it's a punishment for everyone in the guilty hut. No privileges, no sports. As far as clothes go, you have washtubs in every hut. Use them!"

"We haven't got any wash powder."

"You can still wash. Use the shower soap." With that, Schmidt put down the pencil. "You're dismissed."

"We need more sports equipment. Baseballs, gym—"

A soldier appeared, complete with .45 sidearm band and MP on his helmet. "Take this rebel back to the compound," Schmidt ordered abruptly.

"Yes, sir. C'mon, you." He put a hand on Eleen's shoulder. Eleen shucked it off, but knew he had no option but to do what he was told. *For now.*

As he passed through the east gate he saw that Browne from the next hut to 5A was in a shouting match with a guard in the nearest tower, the guard telling Browne to get back from the trip wire, Browne telling the guard he was nowhere near "your friggin' wire!" Mead, anxious to learn what Eleen had been up to, was walking toward him when Eleen told him to get Browne away from the wire. "He's just goading 'em," Mead explained.

"Yes, and if he keeps up he'll wind up in the hole along with Mulvane."

"Helps keep up morale, sir."

"I told you," Eleen said, his voice subdued and projecting what was, to Mead, an unexpected tone of authority, "to get him away from the wire. He can't help us with Archie if he's in solitary. Take him to our hut."

Mead walked over, holding up his hand in a placating gesture to the guard, and told Browne that Eleen wanted him to get away from "the fucking wire." With a defiant look back at the guard in the tower, Browne reluctantly did as he was ordered by Eleen. Eleen walked back into 5A, where he waited by the electric radiator bar by the washroom.

When Browne came in, Eleen put out his hand and, for the first time in weeks, had something akin to a pleasant expression on his face. "So, you don't like the guards?" he asked rhetorically.

"Fucking goons," Browne replied.

Eleen's expression darkened. "We can do without the foul language, Browne." There was a second where Mead thought Browne was going to talk back to the militia officer, but Browne stopped himself. "If you'd like to work off some of your hostility against them," Eleen told him, "we've got a job for you."

"Doing what?" Browne asked, his tone verging on insubordination.

"Getting out of here."

Browne's mood shifted as quickly as Eleen's had after he'd seen Schmidt. Mead had noticed the change. Ironically, Schmidt had been the best medicine for Eleen. Clearly, the federal commandant had said something to Eleen that deeply angered the Mormon and snapped him out of his unhealthy preoccupation with what had happened to Rubinski. Knowing Eleen as he did, Mead doubted the incident would stop haunting Eleen, believing instead that his self-doubt had been supplanted by attention to the details needed to run an effective escape.

"How're we going to bust out?" Browne asked, turning to Mead. "You're going for my idea with the ladders?"

"No," Mead said.

"Why not?" Browne persisted.

"Because it's crazy."

Eleen shrugged. "It might work for two or three men, but not for more. The searchlight would pick it up on the second sweep, unless you pulled the ladder back and—"

"I've timed the light," Browne cut in. "It goes around every two minutes. You put the wire up. Two guys go up and over. You snatch the ladder back before the sweep comes around again, then put the ladder back up soon as the light passes."

"Not enough time," Eleen said. "And what about the ground sensors?"

"Exactly," Mead put in. "That's what I told him."

"And I told *you*," Browne said, "that I don't think the sensors'd pick it up if you put the ladder against a post instead of the barbed wire."

"Are you certain of that?" Eleen asked.

Now it was Browne's turn to shrug. "Not absolutely. Nothing in this world's guaranteed, Captain."

Eleen believed God was, but this wasn't the time for a lecture on the Book of Mormon. "Maybe not," Eleen conceded, "but I'm not going to risk men's lives unnecessarily. I've seen these sensors before. They're pretty darn sensitive to movement."

"I'm willing to try," Browne said, "alone. All I need is someone to hold the ladder."

Eleen was impressed with the man's courage, or was it his desperation to break out? Some POWs in Vietnam, he knew, had gone insane from being imprisoned. For some men, who never knew it themselves while living as free men, the experience of being locked up in a camp was so claustrophobic that it undid them.

"This hut has got a better plan," Eleen told him. "We've started a tunnel—we call it Archie—but progress isn't fast enough, not with the soil semifrozen under the surface. We need more men."

Browne shook his head. "No way, sir. Can't stand confined spaces." As firm as he sounded, however, he was clearly embarrassed at what he knew might be perceived as weakness by others. "I'm—I'm sorry, I couldn't do it. I—"

Eleen nodded and put his hand on Browne's shoulder. "It's nothing to be ashamed of, Browne. I can't wear anything made of wool. Some people think I'm crazy, but I'm allergic to it— skin breaks out in red welts. Itchy as heck. We all have our Achilles' heel. But we can still use you. We need extra lookouts to warn us of the goons. We need men on our bellows."

Browne looked puzzled.

"Air bellows," Mead explained. "Got some leather jackets from the guys, sewed them up, put 'em on a wooden frame made from apple boxes we stole from the mess truck. Sit down and push it back and forth like a piano accordion—keeps pumping fresh air into the tunnel. It's hard work."

Eleen smiled. "Good for shoulders and abs! A few weeks of that, you'd look like Arnold Schwarzenegger."

Browne was grateful. The Mormon had reached out and rescued him from personal humiliation. Now he understood why, the helo incident notwithstanding, Eleen's men would do anything for him, why they had refused to give in to the federals' demand for surrender and gone the distance. "Well, sir, my abs *are* pretty flabby."

Mead nodded. "It's all that good goon MRE cooking." He meant the meals ready to eat, commonly referred to even by the federals themselves as "Meals Revolting to Everyone." It wasn't true, but anyone could get tired of the same thing day after day.

"All right," Browne said. "I'm in."

"Good," Eleen said, and shook his hand. Browne on the bellows would free another man to dig.

CHAPTER TWENTY-EIGHT

The Everglades

THE ADVANCE OF Gill's National Guard battalion was proceeding well, Alpha-Bravo having obtained the northern end of Echo, Charlie-Delta the southern end. AB was now readying for its five-hundred-yard dash across saw grass toward Red Island, a quarter mile off to the left, and CD was going through its last minute check in preparation for a simultaneous dash toward Blue, the island off to its right.

Lieutenant Sides was particularly worried about his platoon. Rafael, with his dry retching, reeking incontinence, and trembling limbs, had rattled several other men in the forty-man boat. At one point two of Sides's riflemen spotted ember-red eyes in the predawn light. Protected by federal law, unless raised in controlled farms for the handbag trade, the two saltwater crocodiles had come in from the intertidal zone and were lying submerged, except for the bumps of their red eyes and the hump of their armor-plated back. A good ol' boy from Memphis whispered, "They ain't gonna mess with you 'less you mess with them."

"Yeah, right," another said disbelievingly.

"Shut up!" Sides hissed as their airboat, the fifth in a row of eleven boats, proceeded from Echo, some men remaining on Echo as traffic cops to coordinate AB's boats with those of CD's force off to their right on the southern end of Echo. When Rafael glanced back at the murky receding shore of Echo Island, he caught a glimpse of the crocodiles, stopped shaking and went rigid with fear. All he could think of as the eleven boats formed two lines, each boat with a .50 caliber machine gun on its prow, was dying. All the men, including Rafael, were now hunched down, and all that could be seen were rows of helmets and the spikes of weapons moving into the dawn. It was that time, so beloved by military assault forces throughout history, when the shapes of things were difficult to define. A time, Lieutenant Sides knew, of indistinguishable shapes, a good time to attack. But it was also the time when the probability of blue-on-blue accidents was high unless strict tactical discipline was observed. It was not a time for cowboys dashing off here and there in the indeterminate gray light that would not last long before the sun rose, hard and unforgiving, in the unrelieved blueness of the Florida sky.

At any moment Sides expected to take fire from White Island. Surely it wasn't possible that the noise of the two airboat flotillas wouldn't be heard by the militia. He wondered about the awful possibility that he might be approaching an enfilade of fire now that they were beyond the halfway point, both AB and CD beyond the point of no return, their boats closer to Red and Blue than to Echo. For a moment he felt an icy chill in his bowels and could hear his heart thumping so loudly he was sure Rafael and the others nearby must be able to hear it too. But rather than dwell on his own fear, he placed his hand on Rafael's shoulder. "You'll be fine," he told the nineteen-year-old. "Don't worry." Sincere utterances that gave the boy no reassurance whatsoever, Rafael ruing the day he'd volunteered for the National Guard.

The boat suddenly stopped, a thicket of saw grass too much for its low speed. As the driver carefully but of necessity noisily increased the boat's power, Rafael couldn't breathe, convinced now that he was in the throes of a heart attack. CD force, five hundred yards to their right, was slightly ahead of them.

Hearn hadn't been given any warning, not even the usual curt instruction to use his toilet bucket before leaving. Rather, at three in the morning, a cold wind wailing about the cement blockhouse near the east gate, his solitary cell thick with the stench of his own body wastes in the metal-lidded pail, he suddenly felt a guard's boot against his thigh, waking him. As his head rose slowly off the palliasse from a deep sleep, he shaded his eyes against the harsh explosion of white light, temporarily blinded. From the corridor he could hear one of the guard's transistor radios squawking.

"C'mon, get up!"

"Yeah, Adolf!" the other guard shouted. "Move ass."

"Wha—" Hearn began. "Where're we going?"

"Move your ass, sonny boy. C'mon, let's go!" This second guard, his M-16 held across his chest, moved menacingly closer as he spoke but was restrained by the other guard's outstretched arm. "We kick him again he'll bruise. Remember what the old man said?" The old man, Schmidt, though hardly old at forty-seven, had issued strict instructions to all the guards who would be involved.

"He said," the second guard replied, "he didn't want to see any bruising. No outward signs of interrogation. *Outward* signs. I remember that's exactly what he said."

"Fuck you, Johnno," replied the first guard, whom Hearn now recognized. He was a big, red-faced Irishman who was known in the camp simply as "Thug."

Johnno helped Hearn to his feet. "Bring your jacket, Adolf. It's cold out there."

"Yeah," Thug added. "If I had my way, I'd set you free—let you roam around in the snow till you were frozen, then I'd—"

"What's the problem?" It was the booming voice of another federal, a sergeant major, echoing down the narrow, well-lit corridor.

"On our way," Thug replied on one side of the half-awake Hearn, Johnno on his right, cuffing Hearn's hands behind his back. There was barely enough room for them to walk three abreast down the corridor.

When they opened the cell block door to the outside, a blast of frigid air stung Hearn's bearded face. Unlike all the other POWs, Hearn had been ordered not to shave, and took it to mean that they were afraid of him committing suicide should he be given anything sharp. But Schmidt's real reason was that if any press photographer were to be permitted in the camp by the fools in Washington, D.C., a bearded man, like Unabomber Ted Kaczynski, always looked like a crazy radical, evoking little if any sympathy from viewers. But this morning there would be no pictures, no vicarious glory offered up to the militia and their sympathizers. This morning was still dark and star-studded in the Northwest, while thousands of miles to the southeast in Florida the sun was already starting its climb.

It was only two hundred yards from the blockhouse near the camp's east gate to Schmidt's hut, but under Schmidt's orders, despite the fact there was an armored MP on either side of him, Hearn had to march, or rather shamble, along the snow-dusted gravel road in chains and leg irons, with only his chilled hands handcuffed behind to hold his pants up.

"Crappin' yourself, Adolf?" Thug asked, and when Hearn

didn't answer, added, "Ten to one he's gonna beat the shit out of you, Hearn, and there won't be a fuckin' mark on you. You squeal in court, it'll be your word 'gainst his. Who you think the fuckin' jury'll believe?"

Hearn said nothing. This irritated Thug, and when Hearn stumbled over a fist-sized rock in worn truck-wheel ruts that passed for a road near a quickly constructed camp, Thug gave him an elbow in the kidney, knocking Hearn further off balance, driving him to the ground, then kicked him in the ankle.

"Ease up," Johnno cautioned. "You'll bruise him."

"I'd like to fuckin' kill 'im—that's what I'd like to do."

"Hey!" Johnno had raised his voice against the wind that was now blowing up the snow. "If he bruises, man, we'll be in the shit. Major'll give us both K.P."

"Yeah?" Hearn said as he got up. "K.P.'d kill old blubber guts here."

Thug's right hand came back; Johnno blocked him, but it had nothing to do with compassion. "Hey, what's the matter with you?" he asked Thug. He indicated Schmidt's hut, no more than thirty yards off. "We're nearly there."

Inside, Schmidt was aloof, seated behind his desk, looking down at Hearn. "A lot of your fellow scumbags are bound for Spokane."

Hearn waited. Schmidt maintained the steely silence for a full minute. Schmidt saw that it was the two guards rather than Hearn who were showing the strain. Hearn stared back.

"One of those scumbags," Schmidt said, as if there'd been no pause, "has to be the elusive Nordstrom. You agree?"

Hearn hadn't blinked—didn't answer. Another silence. Hearn could hear the moaning of the wind that had blown down from Canada.

"What we want to know," Schmidt said, "what we *insist* on knowing, is exactly who Nordstrom is. A description, aliases?"

Hearn blinked; the strain of not having done so earlier was starting a headache above his temple. He knew that what the federal commandant was really saying wasn't just that they *wanted* to know, but it was what they *needed* to know, *had* to know, if they were going to thwart any coordinated militia activity in the Northwest. He said nothing.

Schmidt, hands clasped, looked down on Hearn with a malevolent smile. "I take it your silence is a no."

"Under the law," Hearn said, "my silence has to be taken as affirmation, not refusal." The guards glanced at one another, astonished. That was the thing that bugged them about Hearn. Unlike the behavior of most of the POWs, his temperament defied prediction.

"If you're trying to impress me with your knowledge of the law, scumbag, forget it. You violate the law, then expect us to extend it to you. You seem to be under the delusion that you're protected by the Geneva Convention on POWs. You're not a POW—you're a scumbag murderer."

"Then what am I doing in a POW camp?"

"Because it's *convenient*."

There was another silence, though not as long as the first. Then slowly but purposefully Schmidt, hands still clasped, leaned forward. "I'm not going to waste time with you. You'll tell me who Nordstrom is or else."

"I'll want a lawyer."

Schmidt laughed, shifting his gaze to Johnno and Thug. "A *lawyer*. The scumbag wants a *law-yer*." Thug was grinning, anticipating a little violence before breakfast. "Hasn't he heard about the antiterrorist bill passed by all those scumbag *lawyers* in Congress?" Schmidt asked the two guards. "Doesn't he know we're on DEFCON Three?" He meant the armed forces' third stage of readiness. "Doesn't he know we can keep him up to three months without a fucking law-yer?" Schmidt, his grin wider now, answered himself: "No, I don't think he does know." With that, he signaled the guards to approach the dais. All he could see was their MP helmets and faces. Hearn, trying not to show it, strained to hear, but Schmidt's monotone was too low. When they returned to Hearn a few minutes later, Johnno held back his manacled hands, jerking the belt chain, and Thug punched him in the stomach. Hearn had anticipated it at the last moment and tightened his solar plexus. But it still knocked him back, and before he could straighten, Thug hit him again. Hearn sagged to the floor, Johnno releasing him so he dropped.

"That's all," Schmidt said. "For today." With that, he dragged over a manila folder from the desk and, unfolding a pair of reading glasses, began to peruse the file.

"C'mon!" Thug shouted. Hearn struggled to his feet, and beyond the pain he was experiencing he was struck by the fact that Schmidt must have said much more than "Hit him!" They'd been up at the dais a few minutes, standing there like two obedient school kids.

The first digger in the tunnel's noon to two P.M. shift was a young militiaman in his twenties by the name of Alan Morse. The son of one of those Virginia coal miners who, like Merk, had migrated to the Northwest when the mines in the South fell upon hard times, Morse had spent most of his summers working in the mines of British Columbia north of Washington State's border. He was used to confined spaces and took pride in being the preeminent digger in Archie's progress.

The presence of the sensors had been nullified by a simple yet brilliant strategy designed by Jeremy Eleen. Eleen, always modest, had refused to take any credit for the ploy, saying it had been the federal general, Freeman, who found the answer years ago, in Korea. Eleen explained to the tunnel escape committee how the U.S. had installed movement sensors all along the trace, west to east, right across what Freeman had unflatteringly referred to as the "limp dink"–shaped peninsula. It was Freeman, Eleen told privates Mead and Browne, who had done his homework after the war, poring over piles of the captured North Korean archives and going over thousands of dull military bureaucratic sitreps. Freeman was trying to divine how it was that the sensors on the trace had failed to pick up vibration from any of the *three* tunnels the North Koreans had burrowed from Kim Il Jong's Communist North to exit points south of the trace where the U.S.-ROK defenders had, more often than not, found themselves trapped, as North Korea's regiments poured over the trace, coming up *behind* them, exiting the tunnels from points well south of the trace.

What Freeman discovered, working at his laptop late one winter night long after the U.N.-Allied victory against the North, was that the dates of all joint U.S.-ROK, U.S., and ROK maneuvers along the trace corresponded precisely with the dates upon which the North Korean Army's Catering Corps used the most gasoline. Why? Because meals had to be transported from army base camps to the tunnel entrances.

"The North Koreans," Eleen explained to Mead, Browne, and others from huts 5A and 5B, "had cleverly used the U.S.-ROK joint stay-alert maneuvers along the trace as cover for their tunneling."

"Cunning bastards," Browne commented, but Mead, Eleen saw, was a little slow on the uptake.

"Our U.S. sensors along the trace," Eleen explained, "would vibrate like crazy during our joint maneuvers with the South Koreans. And so our intelligence guys had no way of knowing the North Koreans were digging like crazy during those times. My dad said that it wasn't till later that our intelligence guys found out the North Koreans had even been using big bore tunneling machines."

"Yeah," Mead said, "but we ain't got no bore machines."

"No," Eleen conceded, "but we can dig."

"All right," Mead said. "But even using our homemade trowels, Schmidt's sensors are gonna pick us up."

"Yeah," chimed in another man, a lookout from 5B. "We ain't got no cover."

Eleen grinned mischievously, something Mead hadn't seen since before their surrender in the Cascades. "Major Schmidt," Eleen said, "has given us permission to exercise after all. He doesn't like the idea of lazy POWs slumping around the camp eating his MREs—getting a free lunch." Eleen looked about at the escape team. "The POWs in this camp are going to become the fittest in the nation."

"How d'you mean?" another digger asked.

"Each hut is going to exercise for an hour a day. There are

fifty huts in all. More than enough for the twelve-hour day dig. We'll vibrate the heck out of those sensors."

"And," Browne said, "the goons'll think it's us exercising."

"You've got it," Eleen said. "I want games of basketball, football—whatever you can organize—going on no matter what the weather."

"We haven't got the equipment," another soldier complained.

"You're on bellows, aren't you?" Eleen asked him.

"Yes."

"How did you get the equipment to make the bellows?"

"We scrounged," another answered.

"Well then," Eleen said, "get scrounging."

Mead looked forward to Mulvane getting out of solitary so he could tell him about the change in Eleen, with the advent of the tunnel promising a mass escape.

CHAPTER TWENTY-NINE

Spokane

THE BIG EARLY morning sky over eastern Washington State was leaden and sullen, everyone hoping rain or snow would hold off until the President's visit was over, *Air Force One* due in from Seattle in another two hours, his motorcade through town scheduled a half hour after his arrival at Fairchild Air Force Base.

In Spokane it was six o'clock in the morning, and in one of the third-floor rooms of the Imperial Hotel, militiaman Peter Mawley, still drunk from the night before, was showing off. A twenty-year-old, Mawley had joined Washington State's militia for no other reason than he *loved* weapons. From modern crossbows to the latest cannon, Mawley was fascinated by them all. He had once heard a Canadian broadcaster refer to the Uzi machine gun as an "ugly weapon" and thought the broadcaster mad. For Mawley, now chatting enthusiastically with Norman, whom he had met only minutes before, there never was, nor could there be, an ugly weapon. One might as well talk about an "unbeddable" woman, a species that the twenty-year-old Mawley had never seen. His enthusiasm for weapons had led at times to security indiscretions, like showing off the brand new upgraded Chinese-made AK-74s and AK-47s to members of other militia chapters who had yet to receive their shipments.

Mawley was slated for a maneuver with his Idaho militia on the Washington-Idaho border less than twenty miles to the east but had decided to stay until the morning and watch the biggest federal of them all pass by. He'd never seen a President before, at least not in the flesh.

Mawley was a wild card, not only a heavy drinker, but, contrary to strict militia antidrug rules, he also liked a snort or two of China white when he could get it. Norman didn't like Mawley, even though the militiaman had given him a couple of lines on top of the bottle of Jack Daniel's. Drunk and high on a snort, Mawley had already made a couple of smartass remarks about skinheads and swastikas.

"Hey, *Kamerad,*" Mawley said conspiratorially, walking to the door, turning the third floor room's dead bolt to the lock position and going back to his suitcase. "Ever seen one of these before?" He unpacked half the suitcase, then took out a tubular cardboard map case, a sixteen-by-three-inch tube about the length of a big sausage but weighing less than three pounds. Excited, he said in a rapid-fire delivery: "Arpac, French anti-tank missile launcher. Rocket included. Neat little job, eh? Disposable. Use it and lose it. Talk about compact. Used 'em on Freeman's armored columns. One shot—a hundred yards. Bye-bye, tank."

Norman, who, like Mawley, had had too much to drink, was experiencing difficulty focusing on the Arpac, but Jesus, with the last snort and swig, he was king of the world. He put his hand out for the rocket-cum-launcher. "Here, let me see that." A hundred yards. That'd take it clear across the road. Fuck an M-16, a shotgun, and the grenades—leave 'em on the bed. "How's it work?" he asked Mawley.

"It's beautiful, man. Sliding barrel recoil. Shoulder it. See this flip-up peep sight—wait till the tank fills it, then wham, bam, thank you, ma'am! Over 240 feet a second. How d'you like that?"

And here he'd been growing despondent, Norman thought, because the weather forecast was for possible rain and snow, which meant the federals'd probably use the bulletproof bubble-top limo. "Have another drink," he said.

Soon Mawley was asleep and snoring like a bull elephant.

"Shit!" It was the first time Marte Price had cursed all week. She'd come all the way to Spokane to cover what was reportedly going to be a demonstration of militia strength, albeit without arms, and all the CNN audience had seen so far was a riot between militiamen mixing it up with the students from Gonzaga University.

Nordstrom's followers from as far away as Florida, Texas, and Alaska had been humiliated because a few dozen of them had precipitated the fracas, along with the Nazis, against the students, and were being blamed for the deaths in the ensuing stampede. A four-by-six picture of the little girl that an ATF agent named Bill Trey had tried to save was on page one of the Spokane *Spokesman Review*. The only militia comment Marte could run wasn't a live interview she'd hoped to get with the mysterious Nordstrom but a short news release from the militia. She had to be content with having to read a militant militia communiqué to Linden Soles and Bobby Batista at the CNN anchor desk in Atlanta, when she would much rather have been covering the situation in Florida.

But being the pro she was, she managed to affect patience while fielding a few questions from the Atlanta desk. Linden Soles asked her whether security officials were feeling nervous about the President's imminent visit—indeed, as he glanced at his watch, "the very imminent presidential visit to Spokane."

"Well, naturally, Linden," she replied, "federal officials here are concerned. I understand that via *Air Force One* the President has spoken with some of those injured here yesterday, particularly with the parents of little Jennie Morgan, the seven-year-old who was an early fatality on the scene, but officials aren't overly concerned about the President's visit. Security is much tighter than usual because it's an election year, but the events of yesterday are the events of yesterday, as it were, and certainly the President's schedule hasn't been altered. The President will arrive in about seven minutes at Fairchild Air Force Base outside the city, make a brief speech there, and then proceed to downtown Spokane, where he's scheduled to make a stop and another short speech while opening a new wing of the Museum of Native American Cultures."

"So," Bobby Batista interjected, "no worries about the presence of—what is it?—over four thousand militia."

"No, not really, Bobby. Many of the militia have already left town for maneuvers which they hold every year and which I'm told will be taking place in the Idaho panhandle. The First Lady, who has been visiting Portland, is now also with the President."

"Thank you for that, Marte," said Linden Soles, who then reminded listeners that the second half of the show would be an interview with two Los Angeles cops who, responding to a 911 call from a local golf course, had intervened in the attempted murder of O. J. Simpson.

Flying high above the snowcapped Cascades, the President was struck by their wild cragginess. They were different from the Rockies and resembled the European Alps. Most of all he was surprised by the isolation of sparse settlements here and there, commenting that those who lived in such small enclaves must be a particularly hardy breed of Americans. In some of the outposts, snow still clung tenaciously to the mountainsides.

After passing over the mountains, the President was impressed by the wide, flat, arid aspect of the Columbia River basin that, though dusted in snow, was in stark contrast to the Cascades. High above *Air Force One*, escorting fighters glinted in the morning sun. But descending now toward Spokane, the President's plane entered the thick layer of gunmetal-gray nimbostratus that formed a vast, bleak blanket over eastern Washington.

"All right for the press to come up front, Mr. President?" Delorme asked.

"Sure."

The First Lady promptly excused herself. She didn't like the press. They built you up only to tear you down, and she avoided them whenever possible.

An ABC reporter wanted to know the President's estimate of the preelection campaign so far.

"Off the record, I'll romp in!" It was met in the spirit it was given and a ripple of laughter ran through the reporters. "*On the record*," the President continued, "I think it's going well but I'm not taking anything for granted. It's early yet, and what I'm doing now is taking the pulse of the American people—finding out what they want, what their concerns are."

"Most people say they want lower taxes."

The President smiled. "You know of any electorate, Sam, that doesn't want lower taxes?"

More laughter.

The *Los Angeles Times* wanted to know if he had any comment about the brouhaha in Spokane the day before.

"My visit here is my statement. I deplore violence of any kind, but particularly when it's perpetrated by messengers of hate."

"You mean the militias."

"When they harbor hatred of other groups, yes. But I'm here to do what I can to bring people together. If I can bring just two people together who yesterday were apart, then I think the visit's worth it."

"What about Senator Reese's claim, Mr. President, that you're not doing enough to control the burgeoning power of the militias?"

"*Control?* Last time I looked at the Constitution, gentlemen, you could freely associate in this country. We don't put people in jail if they're against the government. It's their right to disagree all they like."

"But these are armed groups, Mr. President."

"Yes, and we don't like that. But until they actually preach armed insurrection, there's not a great deal we can do about this. As you know, the Emergency Powers Act notwithstanding, I recognize the individual's right to bear arms, and so long as that's all the militias do and don't infringe on anyone else's rights, we'll have to leave them alone."

A woman from the *New York Times* was given the presidential nod. "Does this include the suspension of civil rights under the post-Oklahoma antiterrorist bill?"

"Well . . . for the moment, yes."

The President's aides could feel the negative electricity in the air. "Does this extend only to Spokane or to the whole of the country? How about Florida?"

"Ah, well, until I receive a full report from the appropriate agencies, I'll have to reserve judgment on that." An aide sighed with visible relief. The President sipped a glass of water. "But off the record I'll tell you this, that any movement—black or white—that argues that the Constitution doesn't allow the military to be used in any police action against the people of the United States is nuts."

"But," the *New York Times* pressed, "the Constitution *does prohibit* the use of the military against citizens of the U.S."

"But clearly," the President said, becoming agitated, "the founding fathers had something else in mind. I mean, er—a completely different set of circumstances, the illegitimate use of power."

"Then it's a matter of interpretation."

"Everything's a matter of interpretation, Jennifer."

"Excuse me, Mr. President," Delorme cut in, fiddling with his earpiece. "Pilot says we're about to run into turbulence. Would you all please return to your seats and buckle up."

In fact, the pilot hadn't told Delorme anything, but he'd seen political turbulence ahead over the military versus citizen question and decided to pull a time-honored trick against the press. The subject, however, continued to be discussed among the reporters themselves.

"When was the last time the government used the military against U.S. citizens?" the *L.A. Times* reporter asked a colleague.

"National Guard against rioters? Alabama? Kent State?"

"No, I mean the regular Army. Ever been done?"

"They've shot looters."

"Who shot looters?"

"National Guard."

"Yeah, I know that, but was the regular Army ever used against citizens?"

One reporter suggested it was when MacArthur used troops to disperse the Bonus marchers in 1932.

"Yeah, and there was hell to pay over that."

Through the moisture-laden clouds, the world outside the President's window was a swirling maelstrom, the starboard wing's green light barely visible, water droplets streaming across the perspex suddenly whipped away by the jet's movement. Once *Air Force One* was below the stratus, the scene was clearer, but no less depressing, the city sprawl of Spokane in the distance, cut off from the sun, taking on the forlorn grayness of the sky. The long slab of Fairchild's east-west runway appeared, banks of dirty snow on its peripheries, looking even less inviting than the city. A small forest of black umbrellas was clustered about the main building, where a huddle of officials and neat lines of bandsmen and Air Force troops awaited the world's most powerful leader. To the south lay the neat rows of Camp Fairchild.

"Think we should've headed farther west, Mr. President," Delorme said. "To Hawaii."

The President sighed. "Looks pretty grim, doesn't it? Still, duty calls."

Was he mistaken, the President wondered, or was the Air Force band's rendition of "Hail to the Chief" a little fast, given the downpour that greeted the arrival of *Air Force One*? He kept the speech short as well, telling the men and women of the Fairchild air base that they had stood on guard through the years of the Cold War and were still on guard to keep the peace. And he wanted them and the families who supported them to know that the nation went to bed that much safer because of their vigilance.

The applause was as vigorous as umbrella-holding hands would permit, the view-obstructing umbrellas hated by the Secret Service. The bulletproof bubble-top, in contrast, pleased the Secret Service people, both those who were with the President and those working the crowds in Spokane twenty-three miles to the east, where it was still overcast but not raining. The agents hoped it would stay that way—no umbrellas up to hide some potential wacko in the sidewalk crowds. The Secret Service had tried to get all windows above ground level closed for the duration of the motorcade, but the mayor, Norma Moffat, said no to that, asking Bill Trey, who'd made the request, "You do that in New York? Close all the windows?"

"Well, no, but—"

"But nothing. You're not there anymore, you're in the wide-open West. Folks out here are honest as the day. Patriotic Christians, every one of 'em. What's good enough for *New York* is good enough in Spokane."

"How about the riot yesterday—the militias?"

"Nothing wrong with the militias either. Those boys just don't want big government telling them what they can and can't do."

"You're government, aren't you?"

"Local. We understand the militias, you don't. Anyway, the motorcade'll last five, ten minutes, if that."

"Ah," Trey said mockingly, "I guess all this openness is good ol' western hospitality."

"You betcha!"

Hick, Trey thought, and had gone on with his business with the other agents, police and Air Force helos overhead—watching for possible sniper positions—the choppers looking like dark gnats against the sullen sky.

As the five-car motorcade—two in front of the President's armor-plated, bubble-topped limo, two behind—left Fairchild, the head of the Secret Service detachment in Spokane alerted all agents that in his opinion the clouds were about to open up any minute over the city. Accordingly, agents on the running boards of the President's limo should keep wearing the new folding sun-cum-rain shades and folding raincoats issued for just such an occasion. None of the agents liked the new shades—they definitely didn't go with a suit. In fact, they looked plain goofy. But they allowed the agents to see better in the downpour.

"I thought we were in the *arid* region of Washington State," the President quipped.

"I told you rain was forecast," the First Lady said. "But you never listen."

"I never pay attention to weather forecasts or polls," he answered good-naturedly.

"Never?"

He smiled. "Well, hardly ever."

Despite the thick insulation afforded by the bubble, the First Lady had to raise her voice over the muffled roar of the police's motorcycle outriders flanking the motorcade. "Did you get the model Boeing 777 in Seattle for Robby?" she asked.

"Oh, shoot! Sorry, hon—forgot clean about it."

"Oh no, you didn't!" she said. "He doesn't often ask us for anything, but he had his little heart set on that."

The President smiled broadly. "I got it."

She poked him playfully in the thigh. "You rat!"

His hand found hers and squeezed.

The Secret Service were receiving the news through their earpieces that in Spokane it remained overcast but still no rain. "Don't tell the man," one of them said, "or he'll want to switch to open limo."

Now and then the limo sailed by clutches of farmers and their children, the President and First Lady waving, but because of the rain-streaked bubble the limo was often past them before they could be seen. "Wish we could see out better," the President said. "I'm always touched by people taking time out, and in this foul weather, to give us a welcome. Hate like hell having to whoosh by as if we're Lord and Lady Muck."

She giggled. "Where on earth—" She had to stop, she was laughing so much.

"What?" he said, smiling, joining in the fun.

"Where on earth did you get that expression?"

"Lord and Lady Muck? Don't know. Must've heard it somewhere." Now he was laughing too. They were still very much in love.

By the time the motorcade approached Airway Heights off the western edge of Spokane, the rain had stopped and the President suggested they switch to open limo. While possible, it was a time-wasting exercise that would throw the timetable off, and the head of the Secret Service contingent opted for the bubble top. "Besides, that sky could open up again at any moment," he said. The President toyed with the idea of being a martyr, driving through the rain unperturbed. It was sure to get press coverage too. But with his wife along in a crisp new outfit, hair freshly coiffed, he agreed to stay with the bubble.

In Spokane, the distant rumbling of the outriders' motorcycles alerted uniformed and plainclothes police and FBI agents in the crowd that the motorcade was only a few blocks away. Children, wrapped up against possible rain, nosed through at the edge of the crowd, waving the Stars and Stripes.

As the first outriders passed, Norman, standing back from the open window of Mawley's third-floor room of the Imperial, flipped up the peep sight on the Arpac. He lifted the tube, sighting on the first limo. He inhaled, held his breath, and the moment the nose of the bubble limo filled the peep sight, he fired, the sliding barrel recoiling, the missile's motor, which gave off no flash, blasting from the barrel at more than 240 feet per second.

A split second later the bubble exploded, belching flame, the Secret Service men blown off the car by the force of the concussion. The car swerved out of control, the President falling back, the limo driver slumped over the wheel, the car plowing into the crowd to its left.

There was pandemonium, Secret Service and police swarming toward the limo with fire extinguishers, streams of white foam coming at it from all directions. The President was already dead, a fist-sized piece of partially melted bulletproof glass embedded in his skull. His wife, with third degree burns, a blackened raw red mass with clothes melted into her, was still breathing, but barely. With ambulance and police sirens wailing, police were forming a ring about the burnt-out limo, its acrid smoke, mixed with the sweet, sickly smell of burned flesh, rising above the crowd.

Up on the third floor room of the Imperial, Norman knew he would have to run, but first he wiped the Arpac for prints, rolled it under the bed, and only then left, via the fire escape stairwell.

In the lobby it looked like another riot. There was hysteria, a mass of people, a good many of them children, flooding into the hotel away from the burning limo. The policemen amongst them were pushing their way toward the elevator and stairwell doors, while terrified clerks behind the counter took some of the children being thrust at them over the counter by equally terrified parents.

"Hey, you!" a cop shouted at Norman, whose tiger fatigues stood out as he emerged from the fire escape.

He looked surprised. "Me?" he said, pointing a finger at himself.

"Yeah!" the cop bellowed. "Stay where you are!" But the cop could only move slowly amidst the crowd of people, and meanwhile Norman pulled out one of the small can-shaped smoke grenades, pulled the tab, dropped the grenade, and went back into the stairwell. There, he pulled the tab on the second smoke grenade, and left it behind him in the stairwell. Then he ran down quickly to the underground garage, where he saw a motorcycle cop coming down the entrance ramp from outside. As Norman dropped out of sight between two of the parked cars, he could hear the police motorcycle's throaty roar subside, becoming more rhythmic, idling now that the bike wasn't moving. Outside, sirens were still screaming.

* * *

CNN's Marte Price, her face ashen despite her makeup, was reporting to the world that the President of the United States had been assassinated and that the First Lady was in critical condition as the result of an explosion. Some eyewitnesses claimed it had been a bomb, possibly beneath the car or inside it, others saying just as certainly it had been some kind of missile.

"The scene below," she began as the camera zoomed in on the street, "is sheer chaos. The police have sealed off Riverside Avenue at Division and Monroe streets and are attempting to keep the crowds back on the sidewalks, many people being forced into shops whose windows have already been smashed from the militia riot of yesterday. We also have smoke—Frank, could you get a shot of—yes, that's it—smoke coming from what appears to be the entrance of the Imperial Hotel. Firemen are running out hoses as fast as they can but don't appear to be making any headway toward the fire that could further compound this tragedy. Police and Air Force helicopters are overhead but I'm not sure what, if anything, they can—"

"Ah, Marte," Linden Soles cut in from the Atlanta anchor desk. "I'm sorry to interrupt, but have we any more information on the First Lady's condition?"

"Linden, there are all sorts of rumors flying around, but until we hear from someone at Sacred Heart Hospital we can't say. It's just too chaotic to know anything for certain at this point."

"But," Soles began, in the toughest line of his career, "we do know for certain the President is dead?"

"Yes, Linden. He was, ah—" Marte Price's voice broke for a second. "—he was pronounced dead at the scene. This, ah, this isn't normal procedure. As you know, such announcements are made at the hospital, but this was so—"

Soles waited for a second, then said, "We understand, Marte, and we thank you for that report. We now go to Washington, D.C., where the vice-president is being sworn in."

* * *

The policeman turned off the motorcycle's engine and dismounted. He drew his .38 and began walking down the rows of cars, checking beneath them, then stopped, walked back to the bike, kicked up its stand, and wheeled it a few feet in order to block the exit. Then he resumed walking back down the rows, stopping now and then to look under the cars. It was literally giving him a pain in the neck. In the background his motorcycle's radio was squawking and crackling, though with the bike in the echoing underground parking lot, it was impossible to hear anything clearly.

"Holy shit!" Norman yelled. "Officer!"

The officer swung around and saw a man in tiger militia outfit.

"Officer, there's a grenade over here. I saw a guy—"

"Who the hell are you?"

"What, there's a fucking—"

"Who are you?"

"Murphy. Rick. I saw a guy running down the fire escape. He dropped this grenade. Fucking pin's still in—"

"Get up against that wall. Where's this gren—"

Norman ducked down behind the car he'd popped up from, grabbing his nine-millimeter. The cop fired and was diving for cover when Norman fired at him, hitting him in the back. The cop fell, his holster, equipment belt, and gun clattering on the cement floor, making more noise than the muffled sound of thousands of people and the sirens wailing outside. Norman was moving fast toward the cop, seeing the man's gun still in his hand. From the *thwack!* of the impact of the nine-millimeter, he guessed the cop was wearing a flak jacket, so he shot him again, and then again, until he saw the cop's body suddenly arch like a landed fish as a bullet hit him in the back of the neck. The cop went limp, and the Nazi, sweating profusely, dragged the body in between two rows of cars and watched the door to what would now be the smoke-choked stairwell. Altogether, he'd fired four shots, which meant he had nine left in the Browning.

* * *

Marte Price's story was so hot that Atlanta okayed cutting in on the vice-president's swearing-in at the White House. She reported that the First Lady had succumbed to massive third degree burns over most of her body and died shortly after arrival at Sacred Heart. A room-to-room search of buildings on either side of the street where the President and First Lady's limousine had been attacked was under way. No suspects were yet in custody.

A motorcycle cop reached the police barricades at the junction of Riverside and Monroe. "You hear the transmit from the chopper?" he asked one of the four policemen, their squad cars parked back to back.

"No, can't hear a damn—"

The cop on the motorcycle didn't wait for him to finish. "There's a suspect in a blue Nissan Sentra heading north on Highway 2. Idaho plates." He gave them the number.

"Well," his partner said, "we can't move from here till we get the okay from Central."

"I know," the motorcycle cop said. "But I can. We're setting up a roadblock in Chattaroy."

"Take care," one of them told him. "Guy who did this is a psycho."

With that, the motorcycle cop roared off.

Twenty-three minutes later a dead, naked man with a Washington State Police Academy signet ring was found shot in the head and neck in the underground parking lot of the Imperial Hotel, his uniform missing.

The policeman who spotted a militiaman in the chaos that had been the foyer of the Imperial was asked to describe the man. He told fellow officers, FBI, and ATF personnel that the man was a skinhead, and proceeded to give them a fairly good description. The roadblock cops at Riverside and Monroe were given the ID, but they couldn't tell whether the motorcycle cop they'd let through their roadblock had been a skinhead, because of the helmet he wore.

"Any blood on the guy's uniform—back of the neck?"

"No, had his leather jacket on."

"Bulletproof vest?"

"Yeah—looked like he was wearing one, but again his leather jacket was zipped up. It was cold."

"Is HQ sure," one of the roadblock cops asked, "that it was the killer in the cop's uniform?"

No, HQ wasn't sure. They'd have to account for where every cop was at the time of the President's death.

"So the cop killer," a reporter said, "who might also—well, who was *probably* the President's assassin—could still be in town?"

"Yes," said the police chief, surrounded by deputies, Bill Trey, and a clutch of reporters. "But I'll lay ten to one it's the same guy."

"Has anyone else seen this skinhead?" another reporter asked.

"Not sure," a distraught deputy said. "But there's an FBI agent down in Yakima who was run off the highway by Nazis. Damn near killed her."

Bill Trey had taken the deputy aside, trying not to grimace from the pain in his head. He didn't use Linda Seth's name, but asked, "If we match the FBI agent's ID with the description from the officer in the lobby of the Imperial, we've got positive ID. Right?" The deputy didn't hear him, so Trey waited till the police chief had finished with the reporters, then asked him privately, this time using Linda's name.

"Yes," the police chief said hesitantly, pausing, the avalanche of rumors in the aftermath of the Kennedy assassination in mind. "But we don't know for sure if whoever ran the FBI woman off the road is involved in the killing of the President, and I don't want anybody speculating about that possibility to the press."

"You're going to have to say something soon," Trey advised. "The press is in a feeding frenzy out there. Some are already hypothesizing that this Latrell we're after is the assassin."

"If you want my opinion, Mr. Trey, first we have to get an ID from your Linda Beth—"

"Seth," Trey corrected him.

"Yes. If her ID matches our officer's up here, we might—I emphasize *might*—have two faces to look for."

"Whatever else, it's pretty clear they're militia," a deputy said.

"Well," the chief said, "we know Latrell is a militiaman. And our cop said the guy he saw in the lobby was militia. So it's a good bet, I agree, but we have to make a positive ID."

"Where is this Seth?" another cop asked.

"In Yakima," Bill Trey answered. "I'll fax them to take an ID computer identikit to the hospital."

"I'll bet you," a detective said, "that the guy who tried to run her off the road *is* the same guy our man saw."

"Sir!" a cop called out, his cellular in hand. "They've found some kind of rocket casing in the Imperial. Room 301. Window on the third floor overlooking the crime scene."

"Tell 'em," the chief said excitedly, "not to touch a thing. Cordon it off."

"Yes, sir."

The clerk who'd taken the militia reservations was shaking. The militia hadn't booked room by room, he explained, but in a block.

"But you must have a breakdown of who was where?"

"Oh yes, sir. But I'd have to call it up on the computer."

"Then call it up, son!"

After using his keyboard and consulting the screen, the clerk looked up again. "Ah . . . only two men in that room," he said. "Mawley and Mawley. Spelled with one L. Brothers, I guess."

"Maybe they're married," the chief said dryly.

"I don't know," the clerk said seriously. "A Raymond and Harold Mawley."

"Part of the militia contingent?"

"Yes, sir."

"All right," the police chief said. "We'll have to wait till we get a description from Mr. Trey's colleague in Yakima. You know Seth personally?" he asked Trey, who was having no luck on the cellular trying to get a call relayed to Yakima.

"Yes," Trey answered. "I do."

* * *

The chief already had his officer's description outlined in the identikit, but he told Trey to make sure that Linda Seth's ID was in no way compromised by her having any inkling of his deputy's description. Even the best trained professional had a tendency to be influenced by another's description if they saw it first.

"Can't reach her by phone," Trey told him after the fifth attempt. "Lines are jammed."

"Damn it," the chief said. "All right, Deputy. Tell Johnny to grab his laptop comkit, then take him and Mr. Trey out to Fairchild and have them flown down to Yakima. We need that description corroborated."

CHAPTER THIRTY

AS THE SPOKANE police car approached Camp Fairchild, its siren howling along the snow-dusted stretch of Highway 2, some of the nine hundred militia POWs stopped what they were doing to see what was up. For a moment Eleen was worried that the sudden cessation of activity might mean any noise his diggers made would no longer be cloaked by the sound of the POWs exercising. But only a few seconds later he could feel the vibrations of three platoons of militia POWs. Their noise on the muddy, half-frozen rain- and snow-soaked ground was more than enough to cover the sound of his tunnelers.

By now Archie was beneath the No Go zone. Initially, Eleen had been concerned that if there were mines buried in the NG zone, vibrations too close to them might set them off, but Browne had noted that the drill platoons' feet had thundered in unison within a foot of the trip wire with no resulting explosions. It wasn't absolutely certain that tunneling vibrations would not set it off, but the consensus of the escape committee was that it was unlikely that mines, if there were any, would be set off by anything but overpressure. Nevertheless, to be sure, Eleen insisted that under the NG zone the tunnel dip down on a fifteen-degree angle before proceeding on a level line, thus decreasing the risk of vibrations from the diggers' trowels and the "roofers," who were responsible for putting in scrounged planking to shore up the tunnel's sides and roof to prevent cave-ins—most of the planking pilfered from apple boxes delivered to the mess.

Whether or not their captors had anticipated escapes by tunnel, the prisoners' bed boards were made of solid particle board, made from the wood chips in the abundantly forested Northwest, rather than planks, a palliasse of thin foam rubber covering the particle board as a mattress. The only way to make planks, which in turn could be sawed up as tunnel supports, was to cut them from the four-foot slab of particle board, and all a guard had to do was run a hand underneath the mattress to find out if the particle board was solid. Thus, other wood was at a premium, and extra cigarettes were authorized by Eleen's escape committee for anyone contributing planks. As a result, the closed-in roof supports of several huts had been so weakened by militiamen keen for the extra tobacco ration that the roofs were in danger of collapsing. Eleen had to issue orders that these huts—five in all—were off limits as a source of wood.

Linda Seth, having overexerted herself earlier, was now in acute pain and getting drowsy from the strong Tylenols. The nurse, a fiftyish, no-nonsense woman of German extraction, had given her the two pinkish tablets only ten minutes ago, but already Linda was starting to feel the analgesic effect of the codeine additive, a kind of warm numbness spreading throughout her limbs, as well as affecting her vision.

Linda had been watching CNN's report on the assassination, but the reception was bad. Some were saying it was sunspot solar flare activity, others that it was the militia trying to jam the signals. Drowsily, she slid farther down on the pillows and switched from CNN to KIRO, but that station's reception was also snowy. She was channel-surfing when a large nurse she'd either not seen before or couldn't focus on, a gold watch pinned over her bosom, came in, vigorously shaking a thermometer. The woman told her to open her mouth, unceremoniously stuck it under Linda's tongue, then took Linda's wrist in her hand, her middle finger on Linda's pulse. As the nurse checked her pulse against her watch, Linda switched back to CNN, which was now coming in clearly. Satisfied with the patient's pulse, the nurse said, "Let me puff up these pillows for you."

Whether it was the woman's voice, or Linda's drowsy recollection of her face, or the FBI agent's realization that up to now the hospital had been using state-of-the-art "ear thermometers" to take her temperature rather than the old mercury stem oral kind the woman had used, Linda sensed that something wasn't right. By then, however, May Merk had turned up the TV and jammed a pillow over her face, pressing into her with all her strength. Linda's right arm felt frantically for the top drawer of the bedside table, pulled it out and probed for her gun. May Merk had two choices: to let go of the pillow with her left hand and go for Linda's hand, or press down harder on the pillows with both hands. She went for Linda's hand just as Linda grasped the gun.

Linda, out of air, was in complete darkness until she felt the pillow loosen as May Merk moved her left hand. With all the fading strength she could muster, Linda tried to roll hard right. She failed, but the movement threatened to throw her attacker off balance, and May Merk had to loosen her grip on Linda's hand, which could now more firmly grasp the gun. Linda, still blinded by the pillow, fired twice, the sounds of the shots reverberating out through the antiseptic hallway.

Linda threw the pillow off her then, hearing a crash, then something like a kidney dish clattering to the shiny floor. Sitting up, she saw May Merk, her throat spurting blood, her face ashen, slumped against the over-bed tray table that was momentarily wedged against the end of the bed. The tray abruptly spun about as Mrs. Merk, her white bosom now soaked with blood, lost her footing. The mobile tray was dragged down with her, collapsing noisily against the wall, the tray shooting off on its own into an orderly who had heard the commotion and now came into the room.

Stanley Merk, who'd been in a car outside, hadn't wanted to leave immediately. But, shaking with fear, he'd recalled May's exact words: "If it goes wrong, Stanley, you git, hear?"

Before Linda had a chance to fully recover from the shock of the attack, Bill Trey and Deputy Johnson had walked in with the comkit, asking her to describe the fleeting but, for Linda, unforgettable image of the face she'd seen in the Blazer. She'd already identified Latrell from the Yakima police chief's Most Wanted list, but now Johnson was working on the image of the Nazi as described by her. Next he went to split screen and compared it with the description provided by the Spokane deputy who'd been in the Imperial Hotel.

"That's him," she said.

"Right!" Trey said. "We'll have this sent every which way we can. Local, federal agencies, media, the lot."

"We've got to be careful to say that this Nazi or whoever he is is only a suspect," Linda cautioned him, "in driving me off the road as well as in the assassination of the President and First Lady. At this point it's all circumstantial. In the press especially we've got to emphasize that they're suspects. We don't want them to get off on due process or lack of evidence."

"Jesus," Trey said in an uncharacteristic outburst. Linda's near murder had shaken him more than he realized. "I mean, he's a suspect in murdering the President of the United States of America. Who in hell is going to put up that sort of O.J. defense? Who would have the money?"

"The militia—if they think he's being framed."

"We'll get him," Trey said, taking Linda's hand. "We've got

to get going." He looked out into the hallway. They'd already posted guards on her room.

"I'll be okay," she said unconvincingly. "I'll join you in a few days."

"No you won't," Trey said. "You'll stay here for a few days."

"We'll see."

By the time Trey returned to Spokane, the new President had announced that emergency measures were being taken. "Emergency measures" meant military force.

"Who's going to hold the news conference?" the Spokane police chief asked, looking at Trey, who refused to be drawn in. The chief indicated the overflowing room. "There's already a hundred or so reporters out there, and the boys at Sea-Tac," he said, referring to Seattle's airport, "tell me they're pouring in from all over the world. Forty-eight hours from now you won't be able to *buy* a room in Spokane."

No one said anything. "Oh, I get it," the chief said good-naturedly. "I have to do it, right?"

"Lot of good-looking reporters out there, Chief," someone said, trying for levity in a situation that up to now had been depressingly somber.

"I'm married," the chief replied.

"I meant the men." There was scattered laughter.

"Cheeky bastard."

The moment the chief stepped outside, he was blinded by the massive staccato of lightbulbs flashing. A thicket of taped microphones was at his throat, plus the eyes of KCTS, King 5, KOMO 4, and Seattle's PBS channel 9, as well as the CNN camera, Marte Price beside it. He held up his hands for silence and glanced down at a sheet of notepaper, the top of it instructing him, in his wife's handwriting, to bring home a loaf of bread—eight grain—and a carton of milk, two percent. He then adopted a disembodied official police tone, talking about "male Caucasians," "suspected perpetrators," and even used the cliché "at this point in time." Then he called upon an officer, who came out with a two-by-four piece of cardboard on which a deputy had taped the driver's license photo of Frederick Latrell, wanted for questioning regarding various crimes, including several homicides in Oregon and Washington State, and the identikit drawing of his suspected accomplice, a Nazi known only as Norman, also wanted for questioning as part of the investigation of the assassination of the President and the First Lady. A million-dollar reward was being offered for information leading to the apprehension and conviction of whoever was involved in the assassination.

Television had taken over the assassination. While radio reports of what was going on occasionally scooped CNN and the other networks, nothing was believed by the American people until it was proclaimed on television.

Feeling cut off, for lack of information about the world outside Camp Fairchild, Eleen and the other four members of his escape committee made the acquisition of a radio a priority. Hopefully, he thought, one of the guards could be bribed. But the imprisoned militiamen had nothing with which to bribe anyone, as all money had been confiscated from the POWs upon arrival at Fairchild, and cigarettes were of little use because Thug, the guard he had in mind to bribe, didn't smoke. Besides, no one wanted to approach him or any of the other guards for fear that any attempt to compromise them would get back to the commandant.

To the astonishment of Browne, Mead, and others, it was Private Martin, a quiet-spoken, reticent militiaman from the Yakima detachment in hut 5B next to Eleen, who stepped forward, albeit hesitantly, with a better idea. "Need a diode," he said in a soft mumble.

"Right," Browne said. "I'll get Lieutenant Eleen to write out a requisition and we can call up Wal-Mart. Oh shit—" He snapped his fingers. "—I don't think they're open this time o' night. Maybe we should give Sears a call. Uh-oh, no fucking phones!"

"Knock it off," Mead told him. "Where can we get one, Martin?"

Martin pointed to one of the hut's heaters. "From its control."

"What else?" Mead pressed.

"A coil," Martin answered. "Wrap a piece of wire around a pencil. That'll be our timer. For a capacitor we roll up some foil—from a cigarette pack—with a piece of paper. Increase or decrease the area of foil. We could use it as a tuner. Antenna should be easy. Scrounge a long piece of wire. Insulated or bare. Doesn't matter. Give it about ten feet of lead."

"And that's our radio."

"Uh-huh," Martin said, " 'cept for a pair of earphones."

"Where are we gonna get a pair of those?" Mead asked.

"There are nine hundred of us in here," Browne said. "At least somebody ought to have a pair."

"No," Martin said. "I've been asking around. Schmidt's goons got everything when we came in. So I've been looking at other options."

"And?" Browne pressed impatiently.

"One of the goons who drive the MREs in at chow time has a Walkman."

"Not for long he doesn't," Browne said. "We'll snatch it from the prick."

"No," Martin said, so unexpectedly that Eleen knew the private must have been thinking about it from his first days in the camp. "If we take the whole Walkman, it'll arouse suspicion. We only need the earphones. People lose them all the time. The jack wriggles free from the socket. Like reading glasses. People can't remember where they put them."

"All right," Mead said. "We'll need a diversion."

Eleen nodded at Browne. "How about it, Private Browne? You up to it?"

"You kidding, sir?"

"That's my man," said another private, name of Valdez, and gave Browne a high five.

Eleen didn't approve of the gesture. High fives conjured up

an image for him of blacks on the street jive-talking and not doing anything. The Mormon Church was accepting them now, and it was fine, but he believed you had to do it gradually.

CHAPTER THIRTY-ONE

The White House

THE NEW PRESIDENT and five assembled advisers dealt with those steps that had to be taken to quickly reassure the world community and the money markets that there was no sense of political or economic crisis in the United States—that the reins of power had been picked up. The armed forces remained on DEFCON Three, and the Federal Reserve had seen no reason to act, since American dollar holdings had seen no significant shift despite a sharp drop immediately following news of the assassination.

Investors, however—particularly in the Asian money markets, traditionally wary of internal upheavals in their own countries, most notably China and Hong Kong, Myanmar, Cambodia, and the Philippines—had withdrawn investments in U.S. dollars, drastically affecting money markets outside the U.S. They were not convinced by official U.S. assurances of "internal stability" in the U.S., their anxiety about the strength of the dollar fed by the knowledge that internal problems that became internal crises could divert a country's leadership from the critical questions and decisions concerning international trade. The new President's reassurances notwithstanding—he was still a *new*, essentially untried, President—much of the international reaction was determined by a perception of grave social instability in the United States, a perception of faltering control at the top, a perception that the President knew could quickly become reality if he didn't handle the situation deftly and quickly.

His advisers, primarily Delorme and Secretary of Treasury Nanton, told him that as part of his address to the nation scheduled later that evening at nine, eastern time, he should make it clear that the situations in the Northwest and Florida were under control by the appropriate authorities.

"Are they?" he asked, looking up at his advisers.

No one said anything, all eyes turning to the Attorney General.

"No," she replied, clearly exasperated. She gestured to the map of the U.S. on the stand. "In the Northwest we have definite suspects. A Nazi skinhead, suspected of the assassination of the President—" She paused for a moment. "—is presumed to be a member of the militia. And this Latrell, implicated in at least two murders, one of a black man in Oregon, is reportedly also a member of the Washington State militia, and he's still at large. He was supposed to have been killed in the fight between the militia and federal forces at Butcher's Ridge, but apparently this other skinhead, Hearn, another murderer who killed a Washington State highway patrolman, lied when he told General Freeman's people at Butcher's Ridge that Latrell had been killed. I wish I could report that things are going better in Florida, but they're not. The militias are extremely well armed."

The President turned to Delorme. "Where's General Shelbourne?" he asked.

"On his way over, Mr. President."

In his limo en route to the White House from the Pentagon, the Army's Joint Chief was also thinking of the militia, and of Douglas Freeman, who had been bugging General Read about the need to hit the militias hard even as Read was unpacking in Washington. "You know Douglas Freeman?" the general asked his aide.

"I don't know him," the aide replied, "but I've sure heard of him. Butcher's Ridge. Gung-ho type. His men used to call him 'George C. Scott.' "

"Huh," the general grunted. "They used to call him a son of a bitch too. He loved forced marches. Under fire!" The general leaned toward his aide as if he was giving him highly classified information. "He lost more men in training for the Gulf than he did in action. Doesn't send men in half-baked, I'll give him that. In the end, probably saved more lives. His favorite saying is from Frederick the Great: 'Audacity, audacity—always audacity!' You know what his standing order used to be?"

"No."

"Attack!" the general said. "Used to say withdrawal wasn't in his dictionary."

"Uh-huh."

"Also said that if you looked up 'sympathy' you'd find it halfway between 'shit' and 'syphilis.' "

The aide was struck by the general's use of the past tense when speaking of this Freeman. "May I ask what brought him to mind, General?"

"What? Oh, yes. Well, Freeman has this bee in his bonnet about the militias. In his inimitable style, he says we shouldn't, quote, 'fuck around with fuckers.' "

"So he doesn't like militias?" the aide commented dryly.

The general pondered his aide's question. At first the aide thought his boss hadn't heard him, but after a few seconds during which the only noise was the sound of Washington traffic, the general said, "Odd thing is, I think Freeman admires the militia—in a funny sort of way. In his career he had about as many run-ins with government officials as with Nordstrom's boys."

"Nordstrom?"

"New militia leader following Mant's death after the showdown on the Washington-Oregon border. Head of the whole shebang."

"Ah, yes, I've heard of him," the aide lied, adding as an afterthought, "Maybe Freeman was right. I mean, perhaps we should launch a preemptive strike, the amnesty for those militias who surrendered notwithstanding. Invite Freeman to—"

"No," the general said. "Christ, no, Douglas Freeman's retired. Besides, he's persona non grata around Washington. When some of us at the Pentagon advised a cautious approach to the Iraqi invasion of Kuwait, Freeman told President Bush that sooner or later, and I quote, 'We're gonna have to fight the fucker, so why not now?' "

The aide's bottom lip protruded as he envisioned Freeman's outburst. "Hmm, well, he was right, wasn't he?"

"Yes, yes," Shelbourne conceded, a little too irritably, so the aide knew his boss must have been among those generals who had advised caution against Saddam Insane. "It's his tone," the general told his aide. "Tone's everything in Washington, son. And he called our Arab allies 'fucking towelheads.' You can't get on like that. That's why the Joint Chiefs decided Freeman had to go. Early retirement."

"I understand," the aide said. "But he gave the militia their first whipping."

"Bull at a gate," the general added. "If you're going to get anywhere in this town, you have to be more subtle than that. Can't be a bull at a gate, 'less you want to be put out to pasture. I hear now that all he does is jog an' watch TV. No way to end a career."

"No, sir."

Everglades

Alpha and Bravo companies and those of Charlie-Delta, having started out from Echo Island to Red and Blue islands, respectively, were halfway across the water, the two tips of the V a thousand yards apart, when Lieutenant Sides in Alpha-Bravo heard the first pop, then a rapid series of pops as smoke containers arced through the early blue sky, streaking out toward both tips of the V. The effect on the National Guardsmen in the airboats was electric as they turned, not only alarmed by the profusion of smoke canisters, some of the latter glinting in the nascent sunlight, but confused as to what to do.

Major Gill broke radio silence. "Full speed to your respective

LZs. I say again, *full speed!*" Before he'd concluded his order, the bows of the eleven-airboat armada were suddenly thrust forward and up as the huge driving fans poured on the power, and to hell with the noise. There was no need for silence now.

Gill, Lieutenant Sides, and the others on the federal side were nonplussed. Had the militia gone wacko? Yes of course their thick smoke would obscure the militia's White Island, situated halfway between Red and Blue, but so what? It would also obscure the V of the Guardsmen from the militia's view.

"Maybe," Sides radioed to Gill, "they've got see-through smoke I.R.?" He meant smoke-penetrating infrared.

"Any of your I.R. penetrating it?"

"No, sir," Sides replied.

"Then they're not penetrating it either."

Sides felt stupid but recovered quickly. "Then why in hell are they laying down smoke?"

Amidst the whine of the V-shaped armada it was difficult for Sides, Gill, or anyone else to ascertain whether there was other traffic on the water, but Sides thought he could hear airboats coming from the direction of White Island. But what good would it do them? he asked himself again. The militia had the same limitations as the National Guard—you could only shoot at what you could see.

"Hey, Lieutenant!" someone in Ambleside's boat called out. "Some of that smoke's yellow."

"Gas!" Sides shouted, and within thirty seconds Sides and his other twenty-first-century warriors donned their chlorobutyl rubber S-10 respirators and gloves, as well as their NBCs— nuclear biological chemical warfare—camouflaged MkV protective suits, and upper arm hostile vapor detection patches. Sides was punching in a message to Gill on the wrist-mounted keyboard of his two-and-a-half-pound NIMPEC, or belt-worn Nightingale ministyle pencil Everglades PC, taking off his protective gloves, telling the driver to stop momentarily while he, like a warrior of old, wet his finger and held it up to tell him wind direction. Only then did he realize the futility of his effort, for in the air and water turbulence whipped up by the armada it was impossible for him to gauge the true direction of the wind. Sweating profusely in his gear, he, like every other man in the tiger-camouflaged fatigues, guessed that both arms of their V would, like the militia, have to wait until the smoke cleared to identify one another. But then why the smoke if neither federal arm of the V could fire in one another's direction anyway for fear of hitting one another? Didn't make sense. Sides glimpsed a darkish green smudge of shoreline—his target, Red Island. There was only a hundred yards to go when he felt, then heard, something he'd never forget, a tearing sound and a wind of such velocity it knocked him down, accompanied by a sound like a million hands slapping the air all about him.

"Jesus—" someone began, but didn't finish, the shallow water churning like a caldron, the screaming of men mortally wounded and a furious sound in his ears like that of a hailstorm, bloodied water now invaded by dozens of black shapes as alligators slid off hammocks, entering the fray, their vice-tight jaws opening, then just as suddenly shutting, as they began rolling their human prey over and over, slapping the bodies in bloody arcs of torn flesh from one side to the other, water twinkling in the sun as the smoke began to clear. Men panicked, ripping off their gas masks but snatched from behind, some at waist height, to be dragged under as they tried desperately to reach the tangle of water hyacinths, saw grass, and wild stunted pine that fronted Red Island. One second Sides saw a man, his left arm missing, camouflaged fatigues shredded, and turned to help him, only to see the man snatched back by one of the huge dark reptilians leaping with surprising agility to drag the soldier down, its greenish-black stomach engorged by the dead.

Sides heard more pops of smoke canisters, and about five seconds later saw one descending, its white chute almost blending with the smoke that had already formed a shroud about what historians would call "the battlefield" but which was in fact a watery slaughter yard, a swamp that had become the grave of the Tampa National Guard, most of whom were floating either whole or in pieces, trapped by the saw grass as if some giant had literally chopped them to pieces and flung the remains into the 'glades.

Sides hauled himself ashore. Exhausted by the effort, his ears still ringing with hellish screams and other agonized cries of the dying, it was a minute or two before he heard the noise of several smaller two-man airboats and thanked God for his deliverance, until he glimpsed what was happening through the smoke. It was a militia boat, and the sharp cracks he was now hearing were pistol shots as the militia—now there were more of the two-man boats—passed through the sea of dead and dying, finishing off any survivors not taken by the gators. A dozen or so of the remaining Guardsmen, despite their wounds, went stumbling and crashing through the saw grass toward the tangle of Red Island, only to be mown down with stuttering bursts of M-16s and to the tearing sounds of M-60s. Not one of them, unlike Sides, made it to the island.

But Sides knew that the island was only safe as long as he remained hidden. He was under no misapprehension about the militia's intention. If they were so bent on killing every last Guardsman they could find, they would search the island as soon as they'd finished off those in the water. Or was he mistaken? Perhaps, he told himself, some of the voices belonged to other survivors of the 53rd Battalion, which had been cut to pieces, its remnants—what had been its youth, its soldiers—strewn through what the Seminole Indians, the original inhabitants of this strange, watery world, had called the "river of grass."

With the smoke now clearing, the dawn's sun fully ablaze, beating down on the vast expanse of the 'glades, Ambleside saw birds flying above the high trees of the Big Cypress reserve east of the saw grass. He also saw something that astonished him—the shorn appearance of Red and Blue islands, as if somehow massive hedge shears had descended to top off the growth of stunted pine and other trees and bushes. Two things happened to Ambleside almost simultaneously. He immediately thought of some kind of beam that in one wide sweep would decapitate the undergrowth, creating the hedgelike appearance on the two plant-congested hammocks or islands, and here, on Red, he heard a rustle of undergrowth nearby, not more than ten feet away. He had lost his rifle in the whirlwind militia attack but still had his .45, which he now slid quietly from its holster, careful not to bump the binoculars suspended by a neck strap. The .45 wasn't one of the sexy new 9mm pistols, but Ambleside put his trust in the .45's reputation. The one thing you could be sure of if you hit the target was that the hydraulic shock of the impact would be a knockdown punch.

His gun hand was slick with sweat, but he feared that moving the .45 from one hand to another to wipe off the perspiration might give his position away. He was momentarily comforted by the thought that perhaps what he'd heard was one of his own. He tried to will his breathing to slow down, but his heart was banging inside his chest like a bass drum. Through a break in the thick foliage Ambleside could see the green northern tip of Blue Island, the watery saw grass expanse about it littered with dark specks. Bodies. But whose? Militia or federal, he couldn't tell with the naked eye and was too wary to make any movement with his binoculars, his heart beating even faster now. Then the noise stopped.

CHAPTER THIRTY-TWO

THE AMERICAN PUBLIC was told that all available federal military forces were ordered by the newly sworn-in President to "contain all militia base camps in the area."

It sounded good—decisive. But any private who could read a map of the Pacific Northwest, especially the eastern Washington–Idaho part, knew that this was like ordering a sieve to catch water. The base camps of the Northwest militias spread far and wide from the Idaho panhandle's Selkirk Mountains in the east to the Cascades, over 150 miles to the west, in Washington State. Still, as the White House staff knew, public perception often bears little resemblance to fact, and something had to be done immediately to regain public and indeed international confidence in the ability of the U.S. government to govern.

"What we need," White House aide Delorme opined, pondering the huge computer-generated map in the basement war room of the White House, "is someone to coordinate military operations up there." He was indicating the disparate forces from I Corps at Fort Lewis, Washington, the National Guard's 81st Infantry Brigade in Seattle, Tacoma's 66th Aviation Brigade, the 41st Infantry Brigade in Portland, Oregon, the National Guards' 116th Cavalry Brigade in Boise, Idaho, and the Guards' 163rd Armored Brigade in Bozeman, Montana. As impressive as the list looked on the map, the fact was that in the northwestern U.S. the distances were huge and there simply wasn't anything like the heavy concentration of force there was, for example, in the eastern United States.

"How about Freeman?" Attorney General Helen Wyeth put in.

"No," Delorme said. "He was outstanding at Butcher's Ridge, capturing Hearn and wiping out Mant's headquarters on the Washington-Oregon line, but he is an unmitigated public relations disaster. What he accomplishes militarily in the field he undoes politically in front of a microphone. After Butcher's Ridge he told Marte Price of CNN that one of the militia commanders called 'Lucky McBride' was an outstanding warrior and should be treated with 'honor.' "

"Where's he now?" the President asked.

"In a POW camp," Delorme said. "Camp Fairchild—where he belongs."

"No," the President said. "I meant Freeman."

"In Monterey, I believe, where *he* belongs."

"What do you think, Helen?" the President asked his Attorney General.

Helen Wyeth visibly exhaled. "Delorme's right. Politically he's a pain in the butt."

"General Shelbourne?"

"I honestly don't know, Mr. President. Problem is, he's difficult to stop. Once he starts, he doesn't engage in half measures."

"For instance?"

"In the Gulf he was racing for Baghdad, telling his troops that he was personally going to hang the son of a bitch— despite President Bush's order."

"What stopped him then?"

"Gas. We delayed his supply of gas. Otherwise he would have been in the city within twenty-four hours. As I recall, his exact words promised that he would 'turn Baghdad'—excuse the language, Helen—'into the largest parking lot in fucking Arabia.' On the way he gave a Republican Guard battalion five minutes to vacate their bunkers."

"And . . ."

"They wouldn't surrender. Freeman ordered his 'dozer-bladed tanks to fill in the bunkers—which they did."

"Jesus Christ!"

"Exactly."

It was then that ex-Brigadier General Levy, the President's National Security adviser who had not yet spoken, said firmly, "But we won."

The President nodded. "General Shelbourne, can we keep him incommunicado as far as the press is concerned?"

Shelbourne thought of cellular phones, the Net, land line, all the ways Freeman could communicate with the press if he wanted. "Mr. President, the only way is for you as commander-in-chief of all U.S. forces to expressly order him, and any of his staff, to have no contact with the media unless authorized personally by you."

"You think he'll go for that?"

"If it's a condition of him being given command, yes."

"Very well. Contact him. He'll be second-in-command in the Northwest, Continental Sixth Army. You'll oversee him— that way he hasn't got free rein. He'll be Norman Schwarzkopf to your Powell. If he accepts, tell him I want those military bases contained and/or incapable of insurrection while we hunt for the President's assassin, and that other scumbag, Latrell."

As Shelbourne called the Pentagon for a relay call to Freeman, the President was assailed by another fear of failure. If all the troops and high tech at his command couldn't run the late President's alleged assassin to ground or bring the burgeoning Florida militia to heel, it would not only be an acute embarrassment personally and for his administration, but would embolden everyone from illegal immigrants to drug cartels to take on the United States and win.

In the Everglades, Lieutenant Ambleside, determined not to lose patience, waited a half hour before he dared move toward the fern in which he'd spotted some movement. Cautiously, he crept forward in the cordite-stained air and found a fellow Guardsman who, with a massive hole in his chest, had bled to death.

Looking through his binoculars, Ambleside saw his worst fears confirmed. The dead bodies off Red were Guardsmen— hundreds of them. He could hear the voices of the militia's killing squads. Were they receding or was it wishful thinking? Then he heard a moaning sound and a strange, strangulated cry for help.

When Walter Shelbourne reached him, Douglas Freeman was on a Monterey fairway, trying to contain his temper following a particularly nasty slice. He slammed the wood back into the bag, roundly cursing the game that someone, perhaps one of his Scots forebears, had called a "a good walk ruined." So when he heard his cellular ringing, he answered gruffly.

"Well, Douglas," Shelbourne began in a deliberately casual tone, "you're going to have to be in a better mood than that if you're to have tactical command of the Continental Sixth." There was a long silence.

"This a firm offer?" Freeman inquired.

"Pending one condition, Douglas. And it's ironclad."

It was Freeman's turn to surprise the Army's C-in-C. "That I keep my yap shut?"

"How did you know that?"

"I'm psychic, Walter."

Shelbourne didn't know what to make of it. Freeman, like Patton before him, was a believer in reincarnation, an avid listener to the "Art Bell" radio show, and was one of the few generals who had admitted publicly that he believed in UFOs.

And he was the only general who, in what he referred to as his habitual "Scrabble playing method," stood back from a problem to get the whole picture rather than concentrating on one particular "word" or problem. The latter, in his opinion, was an unfortunate inheritance from the mind-numbing over-specialization of the last years of the twentieth century. His method, in contrast, enabled him to make connections between apparently unrelated events. Because of this he was the only general to suspect that the stunning success of the militia, thousands of miles away in the Florida Everglades, augured ill for federal forces *all over* the country, and to suspect that unless the secret of the Florida militia was unearthed, any federal venture in the Northwest or anywhere else would be doomed. Everyone else had been accounting for the federals' defeat in the Everglades as the "obvious result," as the *New York Times* put it, "of the extraordinarily difficult terrain. Even the most amateur military strategist," the *Times* went on, "knows that attackers normally require a three-to-one advantage in men, sometimes a ten-to-one superiority, if any headway is to be made. And in all but impenetrable swampland . . ."

But Freeman suspected there was much more to the militia's Florida victory than the difficulty of negotiating swampland whose highest point, he knew, was only eight feet above sea level. He had been dreaming about it constantly, waking up at night in a cold sweat from a nightmarish vision of an enormously ugly creature from the black lagoon, a horror left over from his childhood cinema days. But what was this nocturnal creature that had an entire battalion of Florida's National Guard in its thrall? It was because this mystery had so disturbed him that he urged Walter Shelbourne to send in two ten-man teams from his much larger handpicked SALERTs—Sea Air Land Emergency Response Teams. Known by Special Operations Command as ALERTs, these were made up of experts scattered throughout the Special Forces of the Army, Navy, Air Force, and Marine Corps.

Now, with the kind of chutzpah only Freeman could manage, he made it a condition of his acceptance of tactical command of the Continental Sixth that his two handpicked ten-man ALERT squads be rushed to the Everglades on a seek and destroy mission.

"Destroy what?" Shelbourne demanded. "The entire Florida militia?"

"To destroy whatever—" He almost said *creature*, but stopped short—there were those at the Pentagon who already thought he was nuts. "To destroy their command center."

"Very well," Shelbourne acquiesced, albeit tiredly. "I take it, Douglas, you still think the militia is up to something we don't know about?"

"I do."

"Some secret means of communication, perhaps. Some new electronic wonder."

"Possibly," Freeman said. "Something that could affect the disposition of all federal forces."

"All right. I'll call in your twenty ALERT." Shelbourne, like most military commanders who knew of the force, dropped the S. "You want to meet with them, Douglas?"

"No time, Walt. Besides, I handpicked every man Jack of them. They get an order, they know what to do. Just get Special Ops aircraft to get 'em there. They'll do the rest."

At least he hoped and prayed they would; otherwise they'd all be dead and he'd be none the wiser, with the rebellious Florida militia's secret available to their comrades in the rebellious Northwest.

* * *

The first thing Vance knew he had to do was create as much chaos as possible. Just as Allied POWs in Germany in World War I and especially in World War II caused hundreds, sometimes thousands, of enemy soldiers to be diverted from the front in order to hunt them down, Vance was determined to buy valuable time for his militia base camps. Accordingly, he sent coded radio messages all over the 135,000 square miles of the Northwest for POW camps everywhere to undertake maximum disruption of federal forces wherever and whenever possible.

CHAPTER THIRTY-THREE

Ops Center, Fort Lewis

FREEMAN'S FIRST ARMORED column from Washington's state-based I Corps, consisting of M-1A2s, Bradley Fighting Vehicles, Hummers, a supply truck tailing behind, and motorcycle scouts ahead, moved north from Fort Lewis on I-5 toward Sedro Woolley and the high mountain road that cut right through the inhospitable Cascade Range.

Freeman was remembering how, months back, the beginning of hostilities between the federal government and the militias had been marked by a particularly brutal ambush of tanks on both the eastern and western approaches near Sedro Woolley, on the 130-mile-long Cascade road. Though in the fall, it had been a day, he told the new I Corps commander, Brigadier Stan Black, not unlike the present. Snow had been falling, and in a show of force the late President, via C-in-C General Shelbourne, had ordered several troops of M-1 105mm and M-1A2

120mm tanks to block both ends of the road. They were hit by militia guerrillas and most of the tanks destroyed. On the eastern terminus a general, Limet, was killed as he arrived to inspect the situation. "Know what they told the press?" Freeman asked without taking his eyes off the computer screen showing the armored column's progress. "That is, what the Pentagon told them?" Freeman added.

"I don't recall, General," the brigadier replied.

"Told them," Freeman said, still watching the screen, "that the tanks had been on 'static patrol.' " Freeman shook his head, his still, blue eyes now shifting to the brigadier. "*Static patrol!* Now there's a goddamn weasel phrase if ever I've heard one, and I've heard plenty from the Pentagon and the United Nuts building in New York. *Static.* Meant the goddamn tanks, eleven of 'em—over a million apiece—were just sitting there. What'd they think the militia was going to do, take pictures?"

Stan Black shrugged. "I guess at first no one realized how vicious the militia would be."

"Vicious? They weren't vicious. They were damn good soldiers. Trained by the likes of that Lucky McBride—Gulf and Vietnam vets. Militia got to within a hundred yards of 'em, and our boys didn't see a thing till the militia opened up. At the eastern end our boys thought it was a company level attack. Wasn't, of course—only one squad. And they killed Sid Limet before he got out of his Hummer. Good soldiers, Stan—that's all."

"For the wrong side."

"Yes," Freeman admitted. "But brave as lions."

"Maybe, General. But they haven't been so brave down in Florida. Beating our boys in battle is one thing, but going around like SS, executing the wounded like that—that's un-American. Barbaric."

The computer was showing virtually no movement in the column.

"Get onto them, Stan," Freeman ordered, pointing at the screen. "Tell 'em any man slows his vehicle below thirty miles an hour, he'll be fined. Keep moving, goddammit!"

"There might be a reason for it," Black opined wryly.

"There's always a reason—indecisiveness, bad maintenance, confusion, cowardice, ninny-picking. I don't want excuses, I want movement. On the flanks as well as guarding the supply line, especially when the choppers are grounded by the snow."

"Maybe it's a traffic tie-up on I-5."

"That's no excuse. Should have outriders well ahead on megaphones: 'Get off the road or we'll run over you.' "

Black looked across at Freeman. "Are you serious?"

"Damn right I am. This isn't some goddamn parlor game we're in. The rule for victory is the same as for survival. Keep moving!"

Black was about to answer but Freeman, his voice reverberating in the ops room at Fort Lewis, looked around at the more than two dozen officers, NCOs, and a few motorcycle runners. "Now listen to me. Any one of those *civilian* vehicles on the road could be carrying a LAW, Predator, or some other kind of antitank missile. One hit, scratch one tank and its crew, and factor in a delay of the entire column. Sitting ducks. The answer, gentlemen, is movement! Movement! I repeat, any man, rank, or file, who delays my column will be fined one hundred dollars, and I'll kick his ass for good measure. And he'll be confined to barracks indefinitely. Do I make myself clear?"

There was a murmur of assent before the men returned gratefully to their banks of monitoring computers.

Freeman donned his overcoat, pulled his Fox leather gloves on tightly, then took his cap and a short, silver-tipped Rommel-like baton he'd had specially made, and told Black, "I'm leaving it in your hands, Stan. Be ready for anything!"

Black nodded. He looked glum.

Freeman came closer. "Don't worry, Stan. I've every confidence in you."

"Thank you, sir."

"And you might think I didn't hear what you said about that Florida business. I agree it's barbaric. Whether it's un-American—well, I think you'd better read about the burning of

Atlanta. That didn't just happen in the back lot of Universal, Stan. It happened in our *first* civil war. Civil war brings out the worst. You should know that. At the Point you topped your class in history. Ninety-seven percent. Civil wars are the most brutal. D'you know a family who doesn't fight?" Freeman pulled his gloves on more tightly. It seemed to give him particular pleasure. "I'll tell you something else, Stan. There's something damned peculiar about that Florida massacre. Did you see that lieutenant's report? Ambleside?"

"No, sir."

Freeman was surprised. "You should have. He was the only survivor. Casualty rate was unbelievably high. And, if they can do it down there in Florida, they can do it here. Or anywhere. It's why I've sent in my ALERT team." He paused a moment, then told Black, "Tell me the minute the column reaches Sedro Woolley."

"Uh-huh," Black responded, trying not to let his annoyance show. Everything with Freeman, he'd noted, was *my*: My column. *My* ALERT team. So all right, he was second-in-command, in charge of strategy for the NWTO, but damn it, he was such a prima donna. Trouble was, the son of a bitch was on the ball. Who else in I Corps—in the whole NWTO—in the Pentagon, for that matter—knew that he, Stan Black, had topped his class, way back when, in history? Ninety-seven percent. Was that what it was? Say what you like, Freeman, alias George C. Scott, alias Patton, alias Rommel, did his homework.

What else did he know? This Florida business, for example.

As he'd walked out the HQ hut door, Freeman called over a motorcycle rider, name patch Jennings, W. "Yes, sir?" said the private, clearly awed by talking with the old man.

"Jennings, I want you to know that you have one of the most important jobs in this army." Freeman jerked his thumb back in the direction of the HQ signals room from which he'd just come. "All that computer gizmology in there is a marvel to behold, Jennings. But if Nordstrom's militia puts a glitch in it or gets a virus through, all our goddamn megabytes'll bite the dust. Follow me?"

"I think so, sir."

"Good. And if that gizmology fails—" Here the general stabbed the soldier's chest. "—if that happens, you boys'll be our *only* means of communication. It might only close down for a quarter hour, but in that time the battle will depend on *you*. You read me?"

"Yes, sir, General."

"Good. Carry on." They swapped salutes.

As he walked to his waiting Hummer—his aide, Colonel Norton, and driver aboard—the general stopped and called back to Jennings, "How's that mutt of yours. Prince, isn't it?"

Jennings, open-mouthed, was stunned. Douglas Freeman climbed aboard the Hummer knowing, as did Field Marshall Earl Mountbatten before him, that the trouble he'd taken to read the personal file of one of his low-level soldiers, a signalman, would invest in the soldier a pride, an esprit de corps. The knowledge that his commanding general had taken the trouble to know about his family, his dog even, would impress the signalman, who might hold out for that vital extra minute that could turn the tide of a battle.

Within two hours the story had spread, taking on mythic proportions. "Yeah, and so the old man says to this Jenkins, 'How are your two boys, William and John? And your dog?' Names the fuckin' dog. Knows the fuckin' name of the dog. How d'you like that?"

"You're shittin' me."

"No! Old Doug knew the fucking dog's name as well. The *dog*, man."

And so the legend of Freeman, his attention to detail, grew: how he had once fired an officer on the spot during the time of the U.N. peacekeeping force on the Siberian-Chinese border for not knowing the difference between the width of railway tracks in Russia and China, a detail, he had pointed out, that could have led to major logistical problems in supplying his army. Or how knowing the freezing temperature of the oil used in Russian-made T-72s was higher than that of the oil used in

American-made tanks, which meant that the lower the temperature fell, the quicker the hydraulics of the Russian T-72s would seize up, the waxes in the oil separating. Knowing this, Freeman, almost driving his meteorological officer to distraction by requesting a temperature reading every *minute*, had given an order for his tanks to retreat from the T-72s, an order his men had never heard before. The rebel Siberians were equally perplexed and, smelling blood, they sped deep into American-held territory, the temperature falling as the day wore on. Then near Omsk, where it was usually coldest, the wind chill factor dropped the temperature to minus 79, and the T-72s began to rapidly seize up. It was then that Freeman ordered his tanks to stop their pell-mell retreat and counterattack. The Russians, hydraulics shot, could barely return fire, and they could not move. Freeman's Abrams tanks, moving now at speeds in excess of forty miles per hour, engines still purring, decimated the Russian armor and emerged victorious in the key battle of the U.N. intervention.

Brigadier General Black, who had joined his armored column, radioed Freeman in digital-burst code from the outskirts of Seattle that the armored column was making extremely good time on the I-5 and should reach Sedro Woolley within half an hour, upon which Freeman ordered the general to slow down to no more than twenty mph. Black was flabbergasted. "But General, you ordered us to keep on the move."

"Yes," Freeman replied, standing outside his Hummer, the snow still falling. "But I never said anything about breaking a speed record. Drive those tanks too hard and you'll end up with tits down." He meant the tanks would be down with mechanical failure. "The Abrams is the best tank in the world, but even it needs servicing." With that, Freeman put down the phone.

"What are you up to, General?" his aide, Colonel Norton, inquired.

"Nothing," Freeman replied quietly, almost in a whisper, adding with a cheeky grin, " 'Least nothing I want heard over the air."

"But it was scrambled in DBC."

Freeman, his Hummer flanked by MPs, nodded toward the driver, virtually invisible through the door window's bullet-proof glass but still within hearing distance, and walked over to the snowcapped shoulder of the road. There, the general relieved himself of a full bladder. Meanwhile he told Norton about the suspected defection of Colonel Leigh, an Armored Division commander. Leigh, it was believed, had been a sleeper until war broke out, and was then activated by the militia in a pitched battle in the Alvord Desert. So now he, Freeman, couldn't afford to trust anyone.

"You trust me," Norton said.

"And you're the only one I confide in, Norton. So if there's a leak, then I'd know it was you. And I'd blow your goddamn head off."

By now the militia's Northwest supporters had advised the militia that I Corps was heading north on the quickest route to eastern Washington and the militia base camps from Winthrop all the way to Spokane. At its present rate, the column would be entering the Cascades as darkness fell, led by Hummers armed with TOW antitank missiles and, most important, given the coming darkness, state-of-the-art mounted infrared scope arrays that would enable the column to turn night into day.

Vance was east of Spokane beneath a snow leopard camouflage net. He had been joined by Norman, who was flushed with excitement, on what he called a "superman high" from the assassination, from killing the most powerful man in the world and getting away with it. At first the other three Nazis with Vance were scared witless by Norman's unauthorized attack on "Federal One," but Vance, after the initial shock, had embraced the event like a man who'd suddenly won the lottery. The federal panic he was seeing following the assassination played right into his hands. His militia, badly demoralized from the trouncing they'd so recently suffered everywhere from the Washington-Oregon bridge to Packwood, in the southern Cascades, were suddenly galvanized into action.

A confident Norman nonchalantly suggested ambushing Freeman's column along the mountain road through the Cascades. "We could blow down half a mountain on the bastards."

"Yes," Vance agreed, "and bury the highway for us as well. No, Norman, this time they'll be ready, alert for ambush. If the weather clears tomorrow, they'll use armed helos to scout ahead. We're not talking here about half a dozen or so tanks sitting still. We're talking about an entire column, and if it gets through the Cascades, our base camps are in trouble."

"You don't think we can stop them?"

"I didn't say that. But hit and run won't do it this time. We'll have to marshal a good-sized force, half the Washington militia, at both ends of the road. First we'll let them enter the Cascades, and then plug both ends. Close the trap."

Norman nodded sagely. Even though he was no military strategist, and was more in awe of Vance than the other three realized, he felt that having "wasted" the President he'd earned the right to be consulted. Conscious of being a maker of history, he saw his role as not unlike that of the Führer, who had also served his apprenticeship in the trenches before rising like a phoenix from Germany's defeat marked by the ignominious Treaty of Versailles.

I Corps' armored column, still traveling north, approaching Burlington, seventy-four miles south of the Canadian-U.S. border, was about to turn east five miles to Sedro Woolley and the mountainous northern Cascades road when Freeman, watching his three-dimensional mobile computer display, countermanded his earlier order, telling General Black to stop, secure his position, and await further instructions. Black was annoyed. He had been faithfully carrying out Freeman's order to keep moving, indeed Freeman's obsession with moving, only to have his column abruptly halted near Sedro Woolley where, he remembered Freeman telling him, six M-1 tanks had once been captured and torched by militia guerrillas.

Black was taking no chances, immediately deploying MZ Bradley Fighting Vehicles armed with their main 25mm chain gun, a coaxial machine gun right of the main gun, seven TOW missiles on the left side of the turret, and six 5.56mm ports for infantry automatic weapons. The ports would allow the nine infantrymen inside to shoot from inside the Bradley, or if they were required outside, they could quickly exit either by using a rear hatch or by dropping the entire rear door.

Black also had the five-man crews of the twenty-five-ton M-3s, the cavalry fighting Bradleys, on high alert. There wasn't going to be any capture of tanks under his command, and he had everyone expecting a militia attack. A quarter hour later Freeman instructed Black to continue heading east. He was, however, not to go beyond Sedro Woolley that night, onto what Freeman called "Ambush Heaven," the winding mountainous route of Highway 20 through the towering northern Cascades. "Infrared notwithstanding, you get one tank jammed up on an S-curve, Stan, you're in deep doo-doo. Wait till the morning."

"Yes, sir," Black replied, replacing his scrambler phone. He complained to an aide, "I'm commander of this federal column, and I don't know what the hell's going on."

"Well, sir," the aide opined, "I don't think anyone knows what's going on."

The aide, whether he was sucking up to Black or not, had spoken the truth. High technology had ironically spawned a war that harkened back not to the typical wars of the twentieth century, of the Maginot Line, of Blitzkrieg. Rather, this conflict more resembled those of feudal times, in which there was a hodgepodge of battle areas, albeit large ones, rather than fronts. Now a town, railyard, or communications center was attacked individually, as targets had been attacked long ago, the shapes and perimeters of the battle areas constantly changing. The battles of the last century had depended in large part on diverse units maneuvered by central commands. Now, even a small unit's computer allowed it to plug into the intelligence network, which relied heavily on spy satellites and unmanned aerial vehicles for battlefield information. Smaller outlying units, knowing as much as divisional HQ, and knowing it at the same time, meant that instead of waiting for the slow, often lumbering movements of an entire division of eighteen thousand men, smaller self-contained units—like the ALERT, sent to the Florida Everglades by Freeman—could act upon their own recognizance without waiting for larger bureaucratic HQs to move. And guerrillas were no longer at an "information disadvantage" vis-à-vis larger groups. With handheld GPS units, lumbar-belt mode computers, and wrist-attached keyboards, an individual soldier could have as much battlefield information as a general. Or even more.

Despite this, or because of it, a decisive battle was yearned for by both Vance and Freeman, a blow so severe that the enemy's morale would be devastated, the will to fight lost. Such a battle was shaping up in eastern Washington State. Freeman's HUMINT, or human intelligence, and SIGINT, signal intelligence—limited because of bad weather—confirmed that large numbers of militia were moving north toward the Cascades in order, as one military traffic observer put it, "to plug the Cascade dike." That is, to prevent I Corps' armored division of 36,000 men from breaking out from the Cascades.

With something like awe for Freeman's deviousness, Norton hypothesized, "You never meant for General Black's column to break through into eastern Washington on the Cascade road. This is a sucker ploy, isn't it, General? You frighten Nordstrom into rushing everything he's got up north to protect his base camps, while you plan to hit him in the south instead."

"Ah, Norton," Freeman said in a celebratory tone of approval, "you should have been a strategist."

"I *was*," Norton reminded him. "Which is why you requested me—at least that's what you told me."

"Was it?"

"Yes, General."

"Yes I did, Dick, but I also chose you because you don't panic when it gets hectic."

"Is it likely to?"

"It is if I can't get Nordstrom's boys boxed up."

Norton was looking at the computer's map of Washington State and its eastern abutment, which was the mountains of

northern Idaho's panhandle. The only active forces in the entire
Northwest, as opposed to National Guard units, were I Corps,
with its two eight-thousand-man artillery brigades, the Ninth
Infantry Regiment's five thousand, Third Brigade's five thousand First Armored Division, and Special Forces—Airborne's—
twenty thousand men. It sounded like a lot, but this was the
only full-time professional army force for over 26,000 square
miles in four states of the Pacific Northwest, which included
some of the most mountainous, inhospitable country in America.
And they had been ordered to contain over nine thousand militia in Washington State alone, most of whom had recently seen
active service.

It was a race against time, Norton realized. Freeman, using
Black's armored column as bait, was successfully drawing
Nordstrom's militias northward to the eastern exit of the Cas-
cade Mountains. Still, Norton didn't like Freeman's prospects.
"General, it's going to take a while to get the bulk of the Fort
Lewis forces into play. By the time the southern arm of your
pincer movement moves east into the basin, Nordstrom, after
plugging the Cascades highway, will be halfway to Idaho."

"Don't worry about it, Norton," Freeman told him. "We'll
be knocking on their back door before they know it. And here's
how we'll do it. . . ."

After Freeman revealed his attack plan, Norton was incredulous. "But General," he said, "the weather's appalling. It's still
snowing, and that's never been done before."

"That's precisely why the opposition won't think of it. Too
daring."

Norton still looked worried.

"Dick," Freeman said, "I'll be on point. I won't ask my men
to do something I wouldn't." He paused. "Now are you with
me or not? Absolutely no recriminations if you withdraw. I
understand—you're a married man with children. It's just that
I can't have people with me whose heart isn't in it. I need full
commitment or it won't work."

"I'm with you," Norton said, but there was no joy in it—
only a sense of professional obligation and a cold fear that if

he didn't go through with it, he would lose a good measure of self-respect.

"You can go in one of the helos," Freeman told him.

"No, sir," Norton replied gamely. "I'll be on the point."

Instead of a look of satisfaction on his face, Freeman's expression was one of grim concern. Norton hoped he was reconsidering the dangerous plan.

CHAPTER THIRTY-FOUR

The Everglades

MA AND RILEY drove back to the Kozan house, Ma unable to accept the proposition that Kozan hadn't written down something about the militia. Why else would the militiaman he'd come across suddenly panic and fire on him?

"Should've looked around when we were there," Riley complained.

"Yeah, well, I didn't hear any objection from you when we left." When they got to the bungalow, a strip of torn yellow crime-scene tape left behind by the police was flapping from the veranda.

"So what are we looking for?" Riley pressed.

Ma surprised him with the specificity of his answer: "A camera. It's something I didn't recall at the time—when you waxed his wife. Guess we weren't thinking straight. Nowadays a lot of rangers pack cameras as well as sidearms. They have pictures of a park violation—a militia gun in an airboat, for example—and they've got him cold in court."

"I don't remember seeing a camera," Riley growled.

"My point, exactly," Ma said.

They knocked on the bungalow's front door. As they'd expected, there was no answer. Ma slipped out a credit card, forced the spring lock, and was inside. The linoleum leading from the kitchen area to the living room was dirty, probably from the sheriff's deputies tramping about, he thought. "I'll do the bedroom." Ma tossed a pair of surgical gloves to Riley. "You look in the living room." Riley took out a switchblade. "Hey," Ma cautioned, "I said *look*. Don't *trash* the place. If the cops come back, it'll pique their interest."

"It'll *what* their interest?"

"*Pique.* You know, arouse their interest."

Riley walked out toward the kitchen.

"The living room!" Ma called after him.

Riley kept walking.

Ma went through the bedroom dresser, then a closet. That was about it. The bungalow was even smaller in daylight than he remembered. A few minutes later Riley walked into the bedroom with a Canon 35mm camera. "On a shelf in the washroom," he explained. "Above a boot rack. Guess it was the last thing he'd pick up on his way out. First thing he put down when he came home." Ma was impressed; Riley was a grumpy bastard but he could use his head when he wanted to. Still, Ma wasn't going to let his partner get too full of himself. "You take out the film?"

Riley handed him the camera. "You do it."

"Sure."

The camera was empty.

"Well that's no fucking good," Ma said.

Riley opened his hand, the rewound film sitting there. He grinned. "Stupid cops missed it!"

Ma didn't smile at the joke. "Well now we've got to get it developed, and I don't mean here in Chokoloskee. We'll have the film run off up in Everglades City."

As they walked back to the car, Ma stopped and bent down, pretending to do up his shoelaces. When he got into the car, he kept one eye on the rearview mirror as he turned the ignition. "You know those stupid cops you were on about?"

"Yeah," Riley said.

"Don't look now but I think one of 'em is tailin' us."

"What's he drivin'—a gator?"

"Don't know, but the fucker's in the brush with what looks like a cell phone."

Riley eased out his Browning thirteen-shot 9mm. "Uniformed?"

"No, plainclothes."

"Then it might not be a cop."

"Don't give a shit who he is. He's seen us. Keep your eyes open."

"Nah, thought I might take a nap."

"Can't see him now," Ma said, driving off, "but he's got our number."

"He alone?" Riley asked.

"How the fuck do I know?"

"Go down the road a bit and stop."

At McChord Air Force Base, outside of Tacoma, an argument was in progress between General Douglas Freeman and McChord's base commander.

"Goddamn it, General!" Freeman berated the Air Force base commander. "This *is* a national emergency. We're within striking distance of Nordstrom's base camps and you're refusing to help."

"That's out of line, General, and you know it. You may be C-in-C NTO, but I have a responsibility to my men. In case you hadn't noticed, General, it's snowing. We haven't had an out-of-season snowstorm like this since May of 'ninety-seven, and I don't want to risk my airmen when in forty-eight hours or so the sun could be shining." He paused. "Besides—"

But Freeman interrupted. "General, we *can't* wait. If we could, I would. I don't want to put men in harm's way any more than you do, but once Nordstrom plugs the eastern end of the Cascades highway, he's going to be mobile again."

"Not if you send Stan Black's column through from Sedro Woolley."

"Are you serious? At night through Ambush Alley? Besides, it's a moot point. If Nordstrom's boys blow up that end of the highway—which I would if I were in their position—then no one can get out. Only reason the son of a bitch hasn't blown it yet is that there are still militia units coming out from the Cascades to join him. But once they're down, they're going to scoot east to the Rockies."

"Are you sure of that?" McChord's base commander pressed.

"Well," Freeman said, eyes narrowing, temper rising, "where would you rather fight if you were being hunted, General? On the flat country in the basin, or in the Idaho mountains where every nook and cranny is a defender's dream and you've got the Idaho militias to help? We must hit them *now*!"

The base commander was unmoved. "I'm not giving the order for my pilots to fly in this. Especially not with your dangerous scheme."

Freeman stiffened. "I haven't time for this bullshit, General. As C-in-C Northwestern Theater, I'm ordering you to proceed."

"I want this in writing and signed by you."

"Fine."

"And you'd better talk to the men. I want to give them the opportunity to—"

"I'll address them."

Freeman gave it to the assembled pilots short and straight. "Gentlemen, our federal forces, of which you are an integral part, have a window of opportunity—which will close in a few days—to deliver a decisive blow to the rebels. But if you're too scared to fly in whiteout conditions, we'll ask the Navy to do it." He waited a few seconds for the mumbling to subside. "Are we going—yes or no?"

"You coming with us, General?" came a lone, strong voice.

"In the first goddamn plane!"

They would do it—or try to do it.

Within three minutes a skinhead armorer walked into a public phone booth and rang his brother-in-law in Seattle. "They're gonna try a drop."

"Supplies?"

"And men."

"In this weather? He's crazy."

"That's what everybody says. But Freeman's got balls."

"Thanks, *Kamerad,* I'll pass it on."

"Do it quietly, man."

"I will."

"Why are we stopping?" Riley asked Ma. "You see a vehicle or what?"

"Didn't see anything," Ma answered. "But I don't think he would've walked out from town this far."

"Maybe he's riding a horse."

"What?" Ma said.

"It was a joke, for Christ's sake."

"You trying to be cool? 'Cause that's not cool, that's fucking stu—" He stopped, looking in the rearview mirror. "D'you hear it?"

"Nothing," Riley said.

"It's probably a pickup."

"So what if it is?"

"Well, we can't let him go," Ma said coolly. "He's seen us."

"How do you know?"

"What d'you think he was doing on the phone back there? Ordering ribs?"

Riley was getting fidgety. "So what d'we do?"

Ma swung the Plymouth Breeze around so it blocked the narrow levee road. The driver of the vehicle Ma had heard wouldn't spot the Breeze until he made the turn, when he'd have to slow.

By the time the vehicle, a red Dodge Dakota, rounded the curve and stopped in a cloud of gravel dust, Ma had walked back along the shoulder above the drainage ditch. He was behind the van, in case the driver decided to tear back in reverse. The driver, a stocky redneck with a scraggly beard and an Atlanta Braves cap, started to back up the van before he saw Ma in his rearview mirror. By then Riley was in front of the van. The driver's hand went for the door lock, but Riley beat him to it, holding a Hi-Vel .22 against the driver's ear. "Get out! Leave the keys in." Riley marched him over to the shoulder. "Why were you spying on us?"

"What? I wasn't—"

Riley whipped him across the face with the gun. The man lost his balance and fell down the slope into fetid green slime. "Don't shit me," Riley told him. "You lie to me again and I'm gonna do you, hear? Now why were you spying on us?"

"I—" the driver began. "We wanted to know who you're working for."

"Who's *we*?"

"Militia."

"You know who we are?"

"No. Just seen your car. Then you got out."

"You had Kozan's place staked out?"

"Last coupla days, yeah."

Ma strolled up. "What are you militia guys so worried about down here?"

"Federals."

"You think we're federals?" Ma asked.

The driver shrugged. "Dunno."

"Who'd you tell about us?"

"No one."

Ma stuck his head into the van. "You were on a cell phone."

"What? Ain't got no cell phone."

"I saw you on a fucking cell phone."

"No way. I was just standing back there in the trees taking a leak."

Ma stared at him, got into the van and searched it, but couldn't find a cell phone.

"You had it back there near the swamp," Ma charged.

"Yeah," the militiaman said, "that's what I do. I drive 'round the 'glades hidin' cell phones for the gators."

"Well then," Ma said, "I must've been mistaken."

"Guess so."

Without warning, Ma shot him. The man's left hand jerked out as if trying to catch something in the air before he splashed into the ditch, insects already on the blood spilling from his head.

"We'll take the pickup," Ma told Riley. "Come back for the Breeze later just in case there was a cell phone and he reported the Breeze to someone. Cell or no cell, we still know one thing for sure—militia's shitting themselves over what that Kozan might have found. If we find out, we can sell it to the feds. Let's get this film developed."

Riley shut the door and buckled up. It was one of those corrugated southern roads, shake your eyeballs out, he thought. "You sure it was a cell phone?" he asked.

"Yeah."

"Maybe it wasn't."

"I know what I saw, Riley. All right?"

As they rounded the big curve north of Chokoloskee, en route to Everglades City, they slowed behind a semi trailer riding the center line. Ma, glancing in the rearview mirror, saw a battered Hummer fifty yards back and closing. He bipped the horn and the semi slowed, pulled off to the side, but before they could pass, the semi's driver swung the cab hard left, stopping his rig in an inverse V. The Hummer, closing behind, stopped about twenty feet away and four heavily armed men with pump action shotguns and rifles quickly alighted, their weapons leveled at the van. Two other men—one wearing a Braves cap and holding a shotgun, the other with a Winchester .30— came around either side of the semi.

"Don't even think about it," the one in the Braves cap told Riley and Ma. "Get out of the car!"

Riley and Ma did as they were told, standing clear of the van, hands up. Three of the militiamen went through the van, found nothing that interested them, and asked Ma and Riley what they'd taken from the house. Any bullshit, he warned them, and they were dead.

"A roll of film," Ma said. "In my right pocket."

"Go get it, Marlon," said a short, chubby man who'd been driving the Hummer. Marlon, motioning Ma up against the car, found the film and tossed it to Chubby.

"What'll we do with 'em, Leroi?"

Riley and Ma were struck by the fact that none of them had asked about what had happened to the militiaman with the cell phone. Or maybe they didn't know what had happened and had a reason for not letting on? They must have heard the shot. "Put 'em in the truck," Leroi said, chewing tobacco and letting go a spurt of long black liquid into the saw grass on the road's shoulder without taking his eyes off his two prisoners. "We're gonna see what's on that film," he said. "We find nothin' but pretty pictures on that film, you're free to go."

"What're you looking for?" Ma asked.

"Now you're gettin' too nosy, feller." Leroi turned to his men, who were now glaring at Riley and Ma with ill disguised rage. "We hired these sumbitches to tell us what that ranger might know, now they're goin' in business for 'emselves."

"Hey," Ma said, "you got it all wrong."

"I got it all right," Leroi retorted, his red face bloated before he spat again, telling his posse, "Y'all go into the 'glades. Marlon and Teddy, you take the rig farther up to D Camp." A car pulled up behind the big semi, tooting its horn impatiently. "Hey!" its driver yelled. "Move ass!"

Leroi and Marlon, Leroi's 9mm back in his holster, walked around the offside of the semi. The driver of the RAV 4 was a youngster of about eighteen, with shades and T-shirt, another man in front and two scantily dressed girls in the back. They saw Marlon's shotgun and went real quiet.

"How y'all doin'?" Leroi asked, peering in the open window, taking in the honeys. "You girls better put somethin' on—likely get a chill." Leroi looked at the driver. "We got your number, boy, and we're militia. On militia business. Unnerstand?"

"Yeah," the driver said.

"Boy, you know it's bad manners to wear shades when you're introduced?"

"No—no, sir."

"Well it *is*. Ain't that so, Marlon?"

"That's right, boss."

"Where you goin'?" Leroi asked the driver, the other man rigid with fear.

"Naples."

"Uh-huh. You support the federals?"

"Hell no."

Leroi smiled. "Good boy. You should think 'bout joinin' the militia." Leroi paused. "You gonna think about that?"

"Yes, sir."

"Good. Now you ease on outta here and y'all have a good day. Y'hear?"

"Yes, sir."

As Leroi walked back with Marlon, he pouched another plug of Redman tobacco in his cheek. "Y'know, up north there in Washington State young men like that are flockin' to join our boys. Hell, better than unemployment."

"Ain't that the truth," Marlon said, walking off to the semi's cab, holding his Winchester by the barrel, the rifle's stock resting on his shoulder as though he was a big-time game hunter.

The car with the four youths passed by, very slowly, the driver forcing a smile in Leroi's direction. Leroi didn't see it and spat. " 'Course, Marlon, what you got to remember is it's a lot colder up there than down here in Florida. Easier for you young'uns to bum 'round in the South. What d'you need? T-shirt, pair o'shorts. You wear that up in the Northwest you'd freeze to death."

"Or drown," Teddy commented, still watching Ma and Riley.

"Yeah," Marlon ventured. "But it can get pretty cold down here in the panhandle."

"I'm not talkin' 'bout the *panhandle*, Marlon. I'm talkin' 'bout Miami side—all those goddamn krauts and spics. Well, I tell you one thing: we get control, t'ain't gonna be no bummin' 'round allowed anywhere in the South. An' that's fer damn sure."

"Amen," Marlon said.

"Now," Leroi said, "you bring those boys up to D Camp with Teddy. I'm gonna see what's on that iddy biddy film."

D Camp was the site of an old diesel still several miles into the maze of the 'glades. Marlon ordered the pair out of the truck on the side of the road near a fetid gator hole before asking Ma whether he liked Cajun chicken and grits. Ma said he liked both of them. Riley told Teddy he didn't like any kind of "hot shit" and he especially didn't like grits. They looked too much like baby's puke.

"Now ain't he a happy one?" Marlon said.

Teddy said hell, it didn't matter 'cause he wasn't going to offer them any vittles.

"Well neither was I," Marlon retorted, "just askin' 'em."

Teddy told the prisoners to give him their wallets.

Ma and Riley looked at one another uneasily.

"C'mon," Teddy told them. "Hand 'em over or I'll take you off at the knees." They handed over their wallets. "Now go down there an' stand by that gator hole."

Neither one moved.

"Yer gettin' me mad," Teddy told them, waving the twelve-gauge in the direction of the hole. "You git in the gator hole, you got a chance. You don't get in the gator hole, you're fly meat."

"Thought you said we only had to stand down there," Ma said, his lips drier than leather.

Marlon was chewing on a strip of beef jerky.

"Changed my mind," Teddy said. "Yer gittin' in the hole."

Riley rushed him, but Teddy had already pulled the trigger, blowing Riley off his feet. Ma turned and ran, and Teddy got him with the second shot.

"Don't matter a coon shit whether it's on the film," Teddy said, bending down to pick up the spent cartridges. "They seen *us*—that's enough."

"Matter of opinion, Teddy," Marlon enjoined.

"No it ain't," Teddy retorted. "Ain't this what it's all about—makin' our own rules?"

Marlon shrugged. Teddy had never been the full dollar. Lot of them in the militia, he figured, just like Teddy, and some in the federals like him too. One sure as hell didn't argue with 'em when they were half tanked, as Teddy generally was.

CHAPTER THIRTY-FIVE

Camp Fairchild

THERE WAS A crisis, the tunnelers running out of boards for the shoring that would hopefully prevent cave-ins to the project they called Archie, and the "dirtmen"—men who had to hide all the soil dug out of the tunnel—were running out of hiding places. They had been hiding dirt in the huts, in the space between the ceiling and roof, at least in those huts that still had enough timber in them to support the crawl space. Normally, a lot of dirt could have been gotten rid of by using the pull-release pockets that the dirtmen had sewn into their trousers, the dirtmen strolling the compound watching the noisy ball games and other activities that were covering the noise and any vibrations caused by the tunnel's diggers. The problem, however, had been the late fall of snow. Not since near the close of the last century, in May of 1997, had there been so much snow in the Pacific Northwest. With the topsoil frozen, it was impossible to distribute the dirt in the yard, hence the overload building up between the huts' roofs and ceilings.

It was hut 5B, Browne's hut, that had raised the first alarm. Several men were awakened one night by thin, hourglasslike falls of dirt. Hut 5B was immediately declared off limits by Eleen's escape committee. That night, Browne and others hurriedly cleaned up and halted the dirt falls before the guards' morning rounds.

There was an urgency to complete Archie because, huddled by the radio that Martin had made, the escape committee heard that Freeman had been made C-in-C of the Northwest Theater of Operations, with orders to seek and destroy all militia base camps and to capture Latrell and the Nazi who had assassinated the President. The news had swept through the camp like a blizzard, exciting the POWs. They felt that now that the hostilities had resumed, they should be out helping their comrades battle the federals. The men who felt the greatest need to break out were those, seldom if ever spoken about, who felt a deep and pervasive sense of shame at having surrendered, severely depressed by having caved in, as they saw it, to the enemy. This was most obvious among younger men who hadn't seen combat before the militia's surrender, men denied the chance to test and therefore know themselves. The depth of their guilt, a subject normally avoided by the POWs themselves, was a hard thing to live with. This was true even for young officers like Eleen who *had* seen more than their share of combat but who were still oppressed by their failings. Eleen still wondered whether his leaving Rubinski behind was more the result of cowardice than a necessary command decision.

Early the second morning after news of Freeman's seek and destroy mission had been announced, lookouts signaled one another, "Goons in the compound!" Dirtmen, including Browne, Mead, and Martin, immediately stopped work on Archie, dropped down from the crawl space trapdoor, ran to their bunks, and busied themselves with writing letters and playing chess and draughts.

Eleen was especially worried this morning because with the news of Freeman's federal offensive and the nearness of Archie to the wire, there was an almost palpable excitement among the prisoners in the normally dull and oppressive atmosphere of Camp Fairchild. Eleen, Mead, Browne, and Corporal Mulvane, back from solitary, had all remarked on the feeling. As Schmidt entered hut 5A, followed by Thug and four other guards, Eleen, not wanting to betray the slightest optimism, took a long, slow breath, holding it longer than usual, imagining he could see the air spreading deep into his lungs, calming him.

Schmidt stopped halfway into the hut, his gaze shifting from the triple-deck bunks on one side of the hut to the other. He was alert, listening intently, sniffing the air, reminding Eleen of a hound close to his quarry. Eleen wasn't the only person who sensed it. He saw Browne unconsciously frowning with apprehension.

"You have been washing," Schmidt said. It was such an unexpected remark, so far from what they were all afraid of, that Eleen relaxed.

"Yes, sir," Mulvane said in a cheeky tone. "We're clean boys, we are!"

Browne laughed.

"Shut your mouth, Mulvane!" Thug warned. "Or you'll be back in solitary."

"It was only a joke," Browne said. "Can't we—"

"Take him to the bloc," Schmidt ordered.

"What?" Browne said. "I—"

"Quiet, Browne!" It was Eleen, angered by Mulvane and now Browne's remark. Sometimes Browne's stupidity vied with his cocky gung-ho attitude. His comment had angered Schmidt to no good purpose. Now, Eleen knew, he would have to get a new man to help on Archie, an untrained man who would take time to break in.

Browne was marched off by two of the guards. No one in Eleen's hut said anything, but once he was outside trudging through the snow, the occupants of other huts nearby began shouting and whistling and clapping as if Browne had hit a home run. Browne raised a fist and was promptly smacked to the ground by one of the goons, who then became the object of open and loud derision from the prisoners.

In the hut, Eleen could hear the ruckus quite clearly as

Schmidt suddenly turned about and, with Thug, went into the washroom.

"Mother of God!" whispered one of the militiamen, a rebel from the Moses Lake detachment. "He's on to the trap door!"

"Come here, Eleen!" Thug shouted. "On the double."

Eleen, who instinctively wanted to answer, "*Lieutenant* Eleen to you," held his tongue and with a forced casualness walked toward the washroom. "Yes, Commandant?" He always used "Commandant" instead of "Major."

"Look at all these T-shirts and underwear. You can't move in here. Have your man dry these outside—in the fresh air." Eleen deliberately shifted his gaze upward, away from the floor.

"Washing'd freeze stiff as boards out there."

"It's too cluttered in here," Schmidt insisted. "Have it taken out. Immediately!"

Eleen ordered two militiamen to take down the wash. "Set the line up outside," he told them.

"That won't be necessary," Schmidt cut in, telling the militiamen, "Take it outside. We'll give you a ball of string. Thread it between the huts."

"We can use this wire line," Eleen said, perhaps a little too quickly.

"We'll give you string," Schmidt insisted. "I don't like you having wire. We had a man hang himself with wire in another camp."

Eleen wanted to object further but knew if he did it would be protesting too much. Instead, the only sign of his utter frustration at seeing Thug take down their only aerial for the radio was the clenching of his jaw. Was it true that someone in another POW camp had committed suicide? He remembered how at school in Salt Lake City once a boy had hung himself in a toilet from a cloth towel dispenser, and because of that, all cloth towel dispensers in the area had to be replaced by paper towels.

Or did Schmidt know about the radio?

* * *

The Chinook helo flew low through the peat-black darkness of a moonless Florida night. Aboard, the two ten-man ALERT commando teams were en route south to the Everglades. They had been dispatched from the Special Operations Center at Elgin Air Force Base in the panhandle. Their mission was to find out what the militia had in the 'glades that had wiped out Colonel Armani's National Guard battalion, and to call in Intruder bombers to destroy whatever it was before it could be moved to wreak havoc in the Northwest.

Team Victor was headed by Medal of Honor holder David Brentwood, and Team Romeo was headed by Aussie Lewis, close friends familiar with one another's modus operandi. They'd fought together before.

It had sounded straightforward enough at Elgin's SOC, but now, studying the map closely, they saw how formidable their mission was. They were faced with a search area of over a thousand square miles.

Even with their headsets on beneath floppy and mottled Southeast Asia hats, Brentwood and Aussie Lewis found it difficult to hear over the loud *wokka-wokka* of the CH-47's rotor blade. They shouted their insertion procedures. The interior lights of the Chinook were redded out so that when they exited the chopper there would be a minimum of adjustment time needed for their night vision goggles, starlight scopes, and their starlight camera. Insertion should be easy enough. It wasn't as if they were going into deep water. Even with the recent rains from the Gulf, the average water depth of the 'glades, barring the odd deep hole and pond, wasn't much more than two feet.

"So," Brentwood said, his voice vibrating with the shaking of the helo craft as he addressed his men, "chopper takes Victor in over this levee off this 'Red Island' and we go in. Drop two Air Fan inflatables first, then us." Brentwood then turned to the Australian-born Lewis. "Aussie, you and your nine insert off Blue Island. We see if there're any survivors of Armani's National Guard. Get what info we can about what hit them."

"Remember," Aussie said, "no matter how careful the 'glades' militia may have been, they must have left traces. They wasted nearly a whole bloody battalion. It's a dollar to doughnuts they've taken some of our guys to pump for information."

Often viewed by others in the armed services as a stand-offish bunch, made up of cocksure SEALs, Delta-cum-British Special Air Service, Special Ops types, the ALERTs were a close-knit group who despised Rambo types. They knew that a unit's real combat toughness came from highly trained individuals who acted as a team. Fields of fire, for example, had to be *felt* as well as merely seen, and this kind of knowledge— a compendium—ready for split-second decisions, came from only the most rigorous training in the world and from living as well as working together. Wives were number two after the team, the divorce rate over fifty percent.

The ALERT teams had to be proficient in everything, from bettering the British SAS requirement of running one and a half miles in twelve minutes with heavy boots to storming hostage/terrorist targets, which meant being able to tell the difference between terrorist and hostage, and taking out a terrorist in less than two seconds without harming anyone else. They had to be adept at high altitude/low opening jumps with wrist altimeters, and the use of night vision and combination bubbleless Draeger underwater rebreather gear at night. Training had a way of sorting out the men from the boys. There was the twelve-day survival test where ALERT candidates were dropped in rough country with nothing but what they stood up in. In addition to being involved in a survivalist course, trainees were simultaneously being hunted by a well-armed unit of "finders." If captured, men were subject to brutal interrogation. A failure of either nerve or the strength to stand up to the twin assault of harsh environment and "finders" was enough to wash most men out. Because the failure rate was almost ninety percent, Freeman, despite his preference for sending single men only into harm's way, had to concede that any married man who passed the course must be allowed in, to fill the small but elite force he wanted.

Save for the designation of team leader, rank was thrown out. First or last names were used, the utterance of which was normally—and especially if Aussie was along—accompanied by a string of profanities.

Now, the men, weighed down by full-load vests, backpacks, ammo bandoliers, assorted weapons—in all, a hundred pounds of equipment—moved to the rear ramp door of the Chinook. Each of them could feel the rush of wind carrying the nose-stuffing stink of aviation gas. There was also the smell of impending rain in the thick, dark thunderheads above the hammock-strewn vastness of the 'glades.

The big Chinook hovered just feet above the swamp, as the first of four inflatable Zodiacs was pushed down the ramp into the water.

"Go, Victor," David Brentwood said, his tone remarkably unhurried.

The nine men with him moved down the ramp into the knee-high water, quickly depositing their heaviest gear into the rubber boats. A Yamaha generator would power the outboard AirFan that sat atop the boat's stern by means of Nylex C mounts.

The big Chinook nosed forward a few feet before depositing Aussie's first Romeo team boat. Being the first man of his five-man Romeo Two boat, Aussie stepped off the ramp and disappeared beneath a surge of bubbles. He was gone for what to the men in Victor One and Two seemed a very long ten seconds before he broke surface, spluttering and cursing. "Fuck it! Fucking ten feet deep! Bastard pilot dropped us into a fucking hole!"

Despite the seriousness of their mission, both ALERT teams couldn't contain their amusement at Aussie's disappearing act, the noise of their comments drowned by the sustained roar of the Chinook's twin rotors. The time for silence, or as near as they could get to it, would be the moment the big Chinook left, despite the fact that its rotors no doubt had already alerted any militia in the area that a new force of federals had arrived in their territory.

At SOC Elgin Air Force Base, Brentwood, Aussie, and the other eighteen ALERT members of the two ten-man squads had gone over Armani's radioed and coded situation report. They were as puzzled as he had been by Gill's last report, only moments before he too fell, of what seemed to be a rushing wind that had further whipped up the already frenzied water. It sounded as if a storm was blowing in from the Caribbean across the inch-in-a-mile gradient of the Everglades. Whatever it had been, it didn't help Aussie Lewis or Brentwood in determining what extra gear should be taken. They had assigned to one man in each of the four rubber boats a Draeger rebreather, should any "underwater nonsense," in Brentwood's words, be called for.

It was one of these men, Bronx in Aussie's Romeo One, who now had to go into the deep water and retrieve Aussie's backpack, for even though Aussie had quickly pulled the CO_2's cartridge lanyard that had immediately inflated his Dolly Parton life vest, the weight of his extra gear threatened to drag him under. It took Bronx, devoid of his other heavy gear, only a minute and a half to retrieve the pack and surface with it, but the moment he surfaced, Aussie Lewis was good humoredly berating him. "Fark! Bronx! What's the matter with you, you fucking ninny? You were supposed to get the gear, not have a fucking swim around."

"Puss nuts!" Bronx replied.

"Oh lovely!" Aussie retorted, hauling Bronx aboard but addressing the other three in Romeo One. "Insubordinate son of a bitch is insulting his leader."

But then the ear-drumming shaking of the chopper that had drowned their banter was gone, vanishing into the blackness more quickly than it had arrived. Now, everything would be done by hand signal and touch. Not even the waterproofed-to-one-hundred-feet headset with only one earpiece, the left, and fiber-optic-sized mike could be used, unless it was critical in a life or death situation. They used paddles to take them in close to the hardwood hammocks, Romeo One and Two to Red, Victor One and Two to Blue, to look for any federal survivors. It was more than a humanitarian gesture. They needed sitreps from any surviving National Guardsmen who might be able to clue them as to the deadly force that had annihilated Armani's battalion.

They paddled quietly and in unison, eyes already feeling strain from the night vision goggles. Now and then they glimpsed the twin red coals of a male gator's eyes, sliding silently through lily pads and packerel weed. Bronx, a devout Catholic, thanked the Holy Virgin that he hadn't encountered one during his "swim around" for Aussie's pack.

As the four boats got closer in to Red and Blue islands, away from the main rain-swollen current, they saw the bodies, bloated masses of decaying entrails and limbs, dozens putrefying in the saw grass. Bronx now realized why the gators and, since they weren't that far from the sea, the big salt crocodiles hadn't come near their boats. The reptiles had had their fill on Armani's dead. For a moment Aussie thought of the sheer terror that must have enveloped the badly wounded and dying as the gators and crocodiles closed in for the kill. He expelled the horrible sight he'd once seen as a boy, before he'd come to the States, of a croc *leaping* out of a stream, dragging down a full-grown water buffalo. It would soon be dawn, and though, like his nineteen comrades, he was as much a warrior of the night as of the day, he longed for the light, to find the enemy and radio in the attack Apaches. They, like his men, knew just what to do with militia butchers.

CHAPTER THIRTY-SIX

McChord Air Force Base

THE PILOTS OF the big transports at McChord Air Force Base had reacted en masse to Freeman's threat to call on Navy pilots to ferry his Rapid Reaction Force through the snowstorm. They were to fly across the high, rugged Cascades, called by some the loneliest place in the lower forty-eight states.

Despite the Air Force's state-of-the-art computerized instrumentation, it would have been a challenging enough mission for fighter pilots, but for the "bus drivers" of the big planes upon which Freeman's offensive depended, it was particularly hazardous flying. Not only did they have to ferry their loads of men and matériel to Freeman's designated drop zone in central Washington, east of the Cascades' crags, but they would have to go low, in "touch and go" landings during which the chute-braked load pallets would slide down their ramps' rollers. It was a tricky operation in the best of weather, but in zero visibility, on instruments alone, the intuitive desire of the pilots to see where they were going had to be reconciled with their confidence in the machinery of their planes.

Fairchild Air Force Base just west of Spokane was the ideal logistical place for Freeman to base his Rapid Reaction Force, but it had been effectively closed by militia threats nationwide that any military aircraft would be shot down on sight. There was every reason to take the militia threat seriously, as all air-fields in "the cleaver," the shape formed by Washington State,

Oregon, Idaho, Montana, and North Dakota, had closed in the earlier showdown between the militia and federal forces after a Hercules troop transport out of Colorado Springs had been blown apart at twelve hundred feet by a militia Stinger surface-to-air missile. Witnesses, in reports similar to those of the mid-air explosion of TWA flight 800 off Long Island in 1996, had told CNN's Marte Price that they had seen the bodies of federal troops afire as they tumbled out of the hard blue Colorado sky to the red earth below.

A Lockheed C-5 Galaxy, over five stories high and more than eighty yards wide, is an awesome sight to behold, the cavernous interior or cargo hold almost fifty yards long by nineteen feet wide, and over 140 feet high. The plane is pushed through the air by four thunderously roaring General Electric turbofan engines with a combined thrust of 54,000 pounds at a speed of over five hundred miles per hour, carrying a maximum war payload of over 129 tons, consisting of thirty-six fully loaded pallets.

As if this wasn't impressive enough for Freeman's purpose, the Galaxy, in addition to its crew and relief crew of four pilots, four engineers, and four loadmasters in its forward upper deck, could carry over seventy troops in its upper deck rear compartment. Most important of all for Freeman's mission, the enormous plane, fully loaded, could land if necessary in less than the width of a football field.

What astonished Colonel Norton and the other officers in Freeman's Hummer mobile staff was the speed with which Freeman had moved, once given the mission by Washington, D.C. Behind this lay the secret of all of Freeman's successes. He knew that no matter how grand the sweep of a general's strategy—and his *was* grand—victory, like God, resided in the details. While his peers in both Washington and in the field were scrambling to see if his plans were logistically feasible, Freeman already knew they were because, whereas others ran to their computers, he knew the specific requirements of a massive strategic airlift.

Freeman still remembered the lessons of Patton, with eastern Europe lying ripe for liberation in front of his Third Army tanks, unable to move for the want of "a few lousy gallons of gas!" Like Patton, who had studied the Normandy roads while on holiday in France during the 1930s, Freeman had made it his business to know the location of every gas station in the sparsely populated area between Odessa and Spokane.

Entering this information into his computer, he had enough copies printed for every one of his spearhead force's fifty tracked fighting vehicles, of which six were state-of-the-art M-1A2 Abrams main battle tanks with 120mm cannon, twenty 25-ton 25mm cannon and TOW-missile-equipped Bradley Fighting Vehicles, twenty M-113A2 personnel carriers capable of carrying twelve fully equipped combat troops each, and four direct-fire M-551A1 Sheridan light tanks armed with a main 152mm gun with 7.62mm and .50 caliber machine guns. While most of Freeman's spearhead was capable of being dropped by air—including the largely aluminum 105mm howitzers and a score of two-and-a-quarter-ton battle-equipped Hummers, the M-1A2 main battle tanks, at seventy tons, were far too heavy to be either dropped from the air or pallet rolled.

"For those suckers," as Freeman told Norton, "you have to stop the Galaxy, then drive my brutes off it—and I sure as hell don't like it, but if we drop enough paratroopers to secure the LZ, then the Galaxies can unload everything."

"How many troops?" Norton inquired.

"Two companies should do it. We can drop them from Hercules."

Norton grimaced. "In this weather, General? I don't know if it's been done. With zero visibility? To say it's risky would be an understatement."

They'd been waiting in line to drive on up the ramp at McChord, Freeman always wanting to lead his troops by example if possible, when he abruptly turned on his aide. "What the hell's the matter with you, Norton? You going soft in the head? 'Course it's risky—driving the I-5 is risky. Anyway, they'll be dropping radio beacons first—then they'll jump."

"Even so, General, it's asking a lot."

Freeman was about to bark when he reminded himself Norton was playing devil's advocate, doing his job, the very reason he had requested Norton in the first place. "Look, Norton, I'm jumping with them," he said. Freeman paused as the loadmaster waved his Hummer driver to bring the vehicle up the ramp.

"I know, sir," Norton replied. "That's another thing I don't like—"

"I'm not ordering you to jump, Norton."

"That's not the reason I'm objecting, sir. What happens if you get hurt? You're the brains of this whole op."

"Norton, I've assigned the spearhead one task and one task only—to go like hell and secure Fairchild's perimeter and environs so it'll be Stinger free. Once that's secured, we can pour men and matériel in from McChord—fast. And with Fairchild as the hub, we can spoke out and hit the militia base camps. Christ, we'll be through 'em like greased lightning before they know what hit 'em. They're worried about being hit by us from the Northwest—by Stan Black's column through the northern Cascades—and that's where this Nordstrom son of a bitch is going to concentrate his forces."

Before the two hundred paratroopers behind Freeman boarded their C-130 "Herkys," the big four-engine turboprop planes that, despite their size, were two and a half times smaller than the Galaxy, Freeman overheard a sergeant trying to reassure a short, stocky paratrooper about jumping out in subzero weather and with, as the young soldier put it, "fuck-all visibility."

"Soldier!" Freeman called out, his battle smock covered by confettilike snow. "Come over here!"

The soldier, name patch "Jorgensen," saluted bravely. "Yes, sir."

"You afraid of a bit of snow?"

"No—ah, no, sir. But—"

"But what?"

"Poor visibility, sir, and possibility of—"

"Possibility of *what*?" Freeman cut in, answering his own

question. "*Collision?* That all you worried about? By God, you can thank your lucky stars you have parachutes."

The line of paras feeding into the belly of the Hercules slowed as men strained to overhear the general, who was fully aware of their attention.

"You know the first air drop, Jorgensen? The first drop in history?"

Jorgensen was stiff from fright. "No, sir."

"Russians—under Stalin," Freeman said. "Flew the plane at near stall speed just above the snow—'bout eighty miles an hour. Troops made their way out to the wing and jumped. No chutes."

"Jesus!" a para officer nearby said.

"Any of 'em survive, General?" someone shouted.

Freeman turned to the man who'd spoken in the line of paras. "Some of 'em," he replied. "Over thirty percent casualty rate, but enough of 'em were left to do the job." He turned back to young Jorgensen. "So you see, son—you've got a parachute. How lucky can you get?"

Jorgensen forced a weak smile. Freeman put his hand on the boy's shoulder. "I'll jump with you. Deal?"

"Yes, sir."

Suddenly, the hesitation in the line was gone, replaced by a jocular macho mood, each man kidding the next. "Just stay outta my way, French!"

"Stay outta *your* way? Listen, shit-for-brains, I'll be down and on 'em 'fore you jerk your fuckin' cord! And keep out of Corban's way. He farts and we'll end up in Idaho."

Corban, from the high desert in Nevada, and one of the tallest paras, grinned at the insult.

"Hey, Corban, don't take that crap from Frenchy. Sit on 'im."

"Please," French enjoined. "On my face!" Corban was still grinning. French affected disappointment. "Prick teaser!"

A sergeant passed down the line, checking the men's equipment, making sure all the barrel caps were on. The last thing you needed was to have the snow packing a barrel and turning to ice. He was also checking to see that all safety catches were on.

"They'll be fine," Freeman told Norton. "All we need is thirty minutes on the ground near Odessa, enough to assemble our spearhead in strength and go for Fairchild." He watched the huge ramps closing on each of the ten Galaxies that would be preceded by the Herks dropping the two hundred paras to secure the LZ, and Freeman felt proud. Where else in the world could a force with so much punch have been organized so quickly? "A can-do outfit!" he told Norton, who grunted, uncharacteristically grumpy.

"American know-how, right, Norton? Best in the world."

"Yes," Norton agreed.

Freeman looked down at Norton, who was unhappily buckling up. "If you'd prefer, Norton, you can stay here at Mc-Chord—fly in later once we've seen Fairchild and environs?"

"No, sir. I'll go now."

"Good man!" Freeman shouted, slapping his aide's back. "Norton, we'll be in Fairchild before Nordstrom's boys even know we're there."

"I hope so."

"Know so, Norton. You'll see."

As the first of the four Hercules took off, the men's senses were somewhat subdued by the noise of the four Allison turboprops. It wasn't until they'd reached thirty thousand feet, breaking out from towering white cumulus into the dazzling sunlight, that some of the paras felt relaxed enough to talk. That came to an abrupt halt as they heard the jumpmaster begin the time-honored litany of the jump. "Stand up!"

"Stand up!" came a concerted roar, with Private First Class French adding, "Please."

Freeman was pleased to hear the friendly banter. Morale was high.

As they hooked up on the line, shuffling awkwardly forward with full loads behind Freeman and Norton, the plane having descended to jump height, the Herk's huge rear ramp yawned open, revealing a world of swirling whiteness. The plane was now at 1,500 feet above the hidden Columbia Basin.

As each heavily loaded paratrooper stepped into the swirling whiteness, he immediately vanished from sight. The chute snapped open, he felt the jerk, and began his slower descent. The jumpers couldn't see one another in the snowfall. They could only pray that the pilots were qualified for Computer Airborne Release Point flying and had brought them in right over the Odessa LZ. Once they secured the zone, they would plant the transponders that would guide in all subsequent Rapid Reaction flights. But for now, there were no electronic beepers on the ground to help them. Each man, including Freeman, was unable to tell when or where he would touch down.

Freeman's feet disappeared into soft snow, then struck something. He fell hard to the right, his fall broken by the fresh powder, his chute dragging him several feet before he came to a stop against a snowdrift, a wire visible atop it—a fence. Quickly unclipping and hauling in his chute, he looked about, saw no one, and noticed that he'd landed in a depression. His chute in and roughly bundled, he was whipping off the barrel protector of his M-16 when he realized it was a drainage ditch. He'd landed just beyond the road. Buoyed by the realization, he immediately began looking for his paras. They emerged like ghosts from a fog. The pilots had done a superb job, instrument flying at its very best.

The militia was pleased too. Tipped off hours before by the militia sympathizer's call from McChord that Freeman's RRF spearhead was coming to eastern Washington, and having received a fax giving the exact coordinates, Vance had sent a militia mobile strike battalion to the federals' LZ. As yet, no firing by the militiamen was allowed, however, lest Freeman's force, hearing the racket, alert their planes circling above.

To prevent this, Vance had ordered his mobile strike battalion commander, Lieutenant Colonel Tier, to surround the federals' LZ and to hold fire until the planes either landed or unloaded their pallets. The only danger had been if Freeman's dropping troops had scattered beyond Freeman's designated LZ. Then the militia might find themselves infiltrated by federals: the trappers becoming the trapped. But ironically, due to the airlift pilots' accuracy, the two hundred federals under Freeman were now surrounded by an eight-hundred-man militia ring, less than a half mile from both sides of I-90.

One of Tier's men, Sergeant Eugene Hartz, a veteran of 'Nam and the U.N. Siberian "Police Action," but who, like so many other American vets, had become disillusioned by his government and gone over to the militias, recalled that the Russians had a saying that perfectly described the beautiful tactical advantage Tier's eight hundred now enjoyed over Freeman's two hundred. "It shouldn't be better."

"Maybe," one of Hartz's corporals opined, "the federals'll give up."

Colonel Tier looked across at the corporal, the latter's scraggly beard white with lumps of congested snow. "Give up? With Freeman in charge? Not a chance." Tier turned next to the sergeant. "Hartz, you have your vehicles ready. A car at each end of the LZ—two miles from one end of the LZ to the other."

Hartz replied, "We'll need it if they try to bring in the Galaxies. They'll need that much of the highway for their planes to take off."

"I don't think they will," Colonel Tier opined. "Galaxies'll be hauling all the big stuff—M-1s, Bradleys, et cetera. First in for my money'll be the Herks—ammunition and Hummers. And I doubt that they'll land—I mean come to a complete stop. It'll be touch, out pallet, and go."

"Sir," Sergeant Hartz said, "case o' cider it's a Galaxy in first."

"You're on," Tier said, winking at the bearded corporal and taking his hand off his AK-47 to jab toward Hartz. "Corporal, this man is about to lose a bet."

The corporal, though nervous, like all his fellow militiamen, grinned. Tier was pleased. Morale was high.

CHAPTER THIRTY-SEVEN

The Everglades

AUSSIE LEWIS SIGNALED "danger." The men of Romeo stopped paddling their Zodiacs and froze. There was only a faint trickle of water audible as it ran slowly through the mangle of mangrove roots that intertwined in tortuous profusion along the shore of Red Island. Spotting a Moor's hen passing by, Aussie waved them on, his finger still on the trigger of his folded-stock MK-I Remington ultraquiet machine-gun shotgun. With each of its waterproofed rounds loaded with nine .00 buckshot .33-caliber lead balls, it was a formidable gun. Because of its innovative piston-driven silent shotgun cartridges, there was no escaping gas, the cause of a shotgun's roar. All that would be heard if he pulled the trigger was the click of the firing pin. And he could fire all eight rounds in under two seconds. His backup handgun was an "underwater-capable" Smith & Wesson fourteen-round 9mm Mark-22 Hush Puppy, its plastic-gut noise suppressor good for twenty-two rounds before it had to be replaced.

"Don't shoot!" It came from the fern, and all ten men of Romeo One and Two had it covered.

"Throw your weapon out!" Aussie ordered. "Then stand up—slowly." The top of the fern quivered and the ten men of Romeo saw a hand, badly lacerated, reach over and drop a standard officer's issue .45. Lieutenant Ambleside stood up unsteadily, weak from shock and from not having eaten in over twelve hours.

"How many of you are there?" Lewis asked, careful not to speak any louder than necessary, even though White Island was off to their right.

"There's two of us," Ambleside answered. "We separated when we first heard you coming. He's gone south of here— about a hundred yards. He's wounded. Heard him crying for help and—"

"Why didn't you move back to the levee?" Bronx asked him.

The lieutenant didn't answer, but Aussie knew why. He'd been scared witless to show himself, and who wouldn't be, having seen everyone about you dead or dying? Aussie, anxious not to pursue the point and humiliate the man, changed the subject. "How'd you know we were feds?" The ALERTs didn't carry insignia, only the plastic-enclosed microchip dog tag around their wrist that contained name, rank, serial number, blood type, allergies, and religion.

"I didn't know," Ambleside confessed, his face reddening.

"Ah," Aussie said. " 'Course. Other guy knew, right?"

"Yes," Ambleside lied, grateful that this ALERT commando had stepped in to spare him further embarrassment. Lieutenant Ambleside, Tampa National Guard, had decided he couldn't take it anymore, that he'd seen too much death in the last twelve hours. He had sent the other federal survivor, the perennially terrified Rafael, away—farther down the island—because he, Sides, had decided to surrender—to *anybody*.

"We're looking for militia," Aussie Lewis explained. "I can't spare anyone to take you back to the levee. Best I can do," he added, picking up Ambleside's .45 and handing it back to him, "now that it's daylight, is spare a couple of Mars bars and a canteen, that's about it. But I doubt there's any militia between here and the levee by now." Lewis looked about to see if any of the federals' airboats were visible and might still be serviceable—maybe they'd just been swamped.

"See anything?" he asked the five men from Romeo Two who were out of their Zodiac, dragging it behind brush at the edge of the hammock, eyes peeled for militia.

Romeo Two had no sooner replied that everything seemed

quiet when the silence was broken by a vigorous slapping
sound recognizable to Floridians as the mating call of a male
gator. Ambleside's fear-filled eyes made it clear he didn't want
to strike out for the levee, but Lewis had no choice. Apart from
not being able to spare anyone from Romeo One or Two, he
wanted to push on quickly, try to pick up the militia trail while
it was still reasonably fresh. It was getting hot. Sticky. Aussie's hand shot out, smacking a mosquito dead, its engorged
body's fluid spattering his Gore-Tex fatigues. He spotted a
half-submerged boat about ten yards farther down in the saw
grass and walked down to have a look. "Jesus!" He turned to
Bronx and signaled him over, Aussie wondering if Brentwood
and his boys in Victor One and Two, well off to his right, had
found the same devastation off Blue Island. "Have a look at
this!" he told Bronx, who stood there shaking his head.

The near side of the half-submerged boat was so perforated,
Bronx said it looked like Swiss cheese. "I dunno, Aussie.
Looks to me like someone cut the friggin' side out with a blow-
torch or something."

"Then why so many perforations?"

"Damned if I know."

Both men walked back to Romeo One and Two and told
Ambleside what he already knew—there were no serviceable
boats. Ambleside and his buddy, if they found him farther down
the shoreline, would have to hoof it back to the levee.

"Can't you call in a chopper?" Ambleside pleaded anxiously.

" 'Fraid not, mate," Aussie told him. "We're on strict radio
silence. And we can't use purple smoke. Militia'd know exactly where we are."

"They must know you're here," Ambleside said, all shame
gone now, the hostile edge of a whiner to his voice. "I mean,
we could hear that Chinook and—"

"Get a grip!" Aussie told him, explaining, "Sure they know
we're here in the area. But knowing that and pinpointing our
position for 'em are two different things, right?" Ambleside
was shaking. "All right," Aussie said, "we'll give you a purple
flare, but don't use it—" He glanced at his watch face on the

underside of his wrist. "—till 1000 hours. That'll give us a good four hours. Fair enough?"

Ambleside nodded, and one of Romeo Two's ALERTs handed him the flare. As Ambleside snatched it he looked at Lewis.

"I appreciate this," he said. "I—"

"Hey, no sweat," Lewis said. "Now let's pick up this mate of yours down yonder."

They found Rafael wedged into a protective tangle of mangrove roots as if he'd tried to barricade himself in. Headless, his severed neck swarmed with a gray cloud of mosquitoes, and now, not far from them, they heard more slapping sounds. Aussie felt bad for Ambleside, but there was nothing he could do but leave him. The man had been struck dumb by the sight of Rafael, but now as Aussie shook his hand and wished him well, Ambleside blurted, "A warm wind."

"What d'you mean, warm wind?" Bronx asked.

"He means the sun's heating up, birdbrain," Aussie said in an attempt to lighten the somber mood.

"It was very hot," Ambleside said, his tone sounding strangely detached from his body. "There was this wind."

"You take care," Aussie told Ambleside. "Y'hear?"

Ambleside tried, but his fear of not making it back to the levee by himself overcame any commitment he'd made to the ALERT team. All his National Guardsmen but one had been unmercifully killed by the militia. And now Rafael was dead, from another kind of savagery. Alone, he told himself, he'd never make it back to the levee. He fired the flare.

Both Brentwood's Victor One and Two, having found nothing but dead Guardsmen on Blue Island, saw the flare smoke just as they pushed their boats off on Romeo's right flank toward the Big Cypress.

Then Romeo saw it. Not a word was said, however, for no matter how angry they were, and Aussie was infuriated, all twenty men were now in full search and destroy mode. You kept your cool, kept quiet, and moved on, looking for expended cartridge casings, discarded pop-can-like pull-rip aluminum cover strips from ammunition boxes, gum wrappers floating or caught in the saw grass or by the cluster of swamp lily stems. Or perhaps a streak of black "tabaccy" spit from some good ol' boy in the militia who'd been this way after the ambush that had killed so many federals that Colonel Armani's career in the Guard was now effectively ended.

But how was Armani to blame? David Brentwood wondered. The colonel had sent out two well-armed forces to either side of the then militia-occupied White Island. That one militia force on White had been able to virtually annihilate two federal forces on either side of it was an extraordinary feat of arms, particularly—and this was what really stuck in Aussie's craw—when the militia was firing into smoke. Perhaps it had something to do with a laser aim beam that, unlike most lasers, could penetrate smoke without being degraded to the point of being useless. Aussie put it out of his mind because he and his men, like those in Davy Brentwood's Victor One and Two, knew that the ever-expanding column of purple smoke rising above the bright rain-washed green of the glades and Big Cypress ahead must surely have been seen by a militia lookout, or else they were asleep on the job.

Romeo and Victor, on full combat alert, two hundred yards apart and approaching Big Cypress, now diverged, Romeo following one channel into the cypress swamp, Victor taking a channel five hundred yards away on Romeo's right flank. The saw grass in both channels had obviously been trampled by a large number of men.

Both ALERT teams hid their boats well away from the mouths of the two channels, Romeo's two boats behind a rush of sway lilies, Victor's two boats a little farther in Big Cypress, the cypress stands too close together to allow any use of the Zodiacs. From now on it would be a foot slog through the channels that were almost overgrown with water lily and pickerel weed.

Here the boundary between the low-lying glades and the tall stand of cypress was abrupt. One moment the men stood on a

watery plain of saw grass surrounding the thick hardwood vegetation of a hammock, and a few steps later, they were in a watery forest of tall, rough-skinned cypress, the air pungent with
the stink of skunk cabbage.

Romeo and Victor had plotted the exact position, within five
feet, of their hidden boats via their GPS when they heard the
telltale *wokka-wokka* of a CH-47 coming low over the glades
and heading, they guessed, toward the lazy spiral of purple that
had begun to dissipate. Then they saw the chopper, probably
dispatched from the levee, making a wide detour south, then
east of Red, White, and Blue.

One second Romeo and Victor were watching the banana
shape of the Chinook, the next there was a tremendous *boomp*
sound, the chopper exploding, hundreds of pieces of metallic
debris raining down a mile or so east of Romeo and Victor. But
the thing that most astonished every man, except for the man
on the point of both ten-man teams, where attention would not
wander skyward, was the complete disintegration of the helo's
twin props. Aussie for one had seen choppers go down, including several CH-47s, but you always saw either the prop or at
least recognizable sections of it. But in this explosion it was as
if it had been all but vaporized—splintered beyond recognition.

No one spoke in either team, eyes searching the cypress
forest with an X-ray intensity, the long trains of gray Spanish
moss everywhere hanging forlornly. The only movement, toward
which all weapons were pointed, turned out to be nothing more
than a water turkey, its blue-ringed eyes standing out in a shaft of
sunlight that permeated the forest's canopy, giving the ALERTs
a fine view of the bird in the process of swallowing a fish headfirst. If only the militia's hiding place would be so easily revealed.

It grew much hotter, the gentle, cooling breeze that had come
with the dawn now turning warm and unpleasant. Aussie and
Brentwood, using the location of their hidden boats as a reference point, had "guesstimated" that the chopper had been
downed about a mile and a quarter east of them, probably in an
area where Big Cypress turned into more open watery saw grass

country, or at least where the militia force must have had an unimpeded view of the Chinook.

Romeo and Victor followed their respective water channels. But no matter how thick the vegetation, they would deviate from the water channels if necessary in order to stay within two hundred yards of each other. This was because if either group ran into trouble, the other would be able to quickly assist.

Aussie cursed himself for giving Ambleside the flare, but he wouldn't obsess upon it. The helicopter pilot's death had been an accident of war.

They moved through the undergrowth beneath the cypresses, long fingers of Spanish moss wrapping about them, bugs crawling into their hair, ears, eyes, and nose, eager for any orifice available. The ALERTs' insect repellent worked only up to a point. It took extraordinary discipline—the kind of self-restraint that ALERTs had trained for—not to slap, scratch, and rant against nature's invasion. But no matter how much they tried, special-soled Vibram boots notwithstanding, the two teams couldn't proceed as quietly as a counterinsurgency mission demanded, for every step in the shallow water made a noise. Aussie would have preferred wading in chest-high water, where the noise would be less. Ahead of him, Aussie could now see Bronx emerging from a clutch of scraggly pine, the New Yorker miraculously free of bug attack while everybody else was being swarmed. Bugs didn't like Bronx, and that's all there was to it. Must be some kind of chemical, Aussie reckoned, that made Bronx's—

Aussie heard a sound like someone spitting, then a thump. Palmer stumbled, falling into water now turning red.

"Break!" Aussie shouted. They were in a firefight. Aussie grabbed Palmer's pack straps and pulled him behind a tree. The first shot that hit Palmer had obviously come from a weapon with a noise suppressor, but the ensuing shots were from a silenced sniper's rifle. The crashing sound of rifles and the rapid staccato of AK-47s and other automatic weapons echoed among the stands of cypress.

"Two o'clock!" Bronx yelled as he fired and dove behind an ugly pine stump. Aussie, seeing a militiaman's shoulder no more than twenty feet away, fired four shots in less than a second, the second shot obliterating the shoulder and causing a momentary lapse in the militia ambush, the militiamen having gone for cover as Aussie's .00 buckshot spread out, shredding leaf, bark, and fern. It was too thick with pine, cypress, and undergrowth to use grenades—they were likely to bounce back at you. Aussie, reloading from his vest load pocket, glanced at Palmer. Just as he thought: Palmer was dead. His face had been smashed beyond recognition by what must have been a soft-nosed dumdum. Aussie calculated the angle of the fatal shot. It had to be close, given the heavy timber; otherwise a bullet would never have gotten through. The AK-47s opened up again, bark and wood chips flying every which way.

"Must be about ten o'clock high!" Bronx yelled, letting fly with a burst from his Heckler & Koch 9mm parabellum submachine gun. Aussie, crouching, his back to the tree, called, "Together, Bronx—now!" Each man knew the maneuver by heart: Aussie stuck out his Remington's heat-shielded barrel, and immediately withdrew it as the sniper's shot tore past the tree, by which time Bronx had gotten a fix on it and fired a full burst with his HK. There was no scream, no sound punctuating the continued bursts of AK-47 and M-16 fire, indicating the sniper had been hit, but Bronx glimpsed a branch shaking, the militiaman's body caught for a moment in the fork formed by the tree's trunk and its branch, then shifting, the sniper's hands flailing, trying to grab the branch but falling twenty feet to make a loud splash.

The AK-47s kept up, strap ferns shivering beneath the hot wash from the guns' barrels, Aussie figuring it must be a patrol with about the same number of men as he had, confident that his eight ALERTs, with what he believed was their superior training, would win out now that they were rallying after the initial surprise. Bronx, one eye on the tree cover, making sure that no more snipers were at large, kept firing high. Aussie's Romeo had established fields, or rather, given the heavy density of the cypress trees, cones of fire, that formed a 360-degree perimeter around them.

There was a decrease in the intensity of the firefight following its chaotic start, the hot, humid air filled with the reek of cordite and the groaning of a militiaman, probably an M-60 feeder. Normally favoring a continuous attack in such situations, Aussie held back. Not because he was afraid—indeed, the adrenaline rush of close order combat had sustained him so well he was ready for anything—but he held back because he knew Brentwood's team would already be on its way. Besides, Aussie had been ordered by Freeman to "seek and destroy" whatever it was that had annihilated Armani's battalion, and he had to restrain himself, his inclination always to fully engage the enemy at hand, knowing how, through determination and skill, a small but powerful force can gain the psychological high ground and overwhelm an enemy superior in numbers.

Off to his right there were more Kalashnikov bursts, again thudding into wood, slapping the air. Now, again on Aussie's right, there was the sound of an airboat, a big one, and farther west, behind him, the sounds of two or three smaller airboats.

Scrunched up as he was behind the cypress, there was no way he could reach down and extract his map from his right thigh pocket without presenting himself as a target. In his mind's eye he went over as much detail on the map as he could remember: the cypress stand Romeo was on, projected out into the glades like the left hand of a U. The other half, way off to his right, was made up of a similar stand of cypress, the two arms of the U separated by a saw grass/water expanse a mile wide. The noise of the smaller boats could be those of Victor One and Two, the larger boat maybe coming out from the levee to pick up Ambleside.

That didn't make sense. Why would Armani risk a large airboat when he'd seen what had happened when his entire battalion had ventured forth? Or perhaps Armani had been replaced by a more tenacious commander. Maybe Armani was looking to redeem himself by sending out help, figuring the militia had withdrawn deep into the Big Cypress after the slaughter of his National Guardsmen?

Well, hell, Aussie thought, there wasn't any point in maintaining radio silence now that the militia knew exactly where they were. He might as well get Mickey La Rue, his R.O., to call in a helo or two, not to help Romeo directly, because he and his men were too close to the militia for any pilot to differentiate friend from foe, but to help indirectly on the off chance the big boats or the two smaller ones he could hear were militia. Then the helos, providing they flew nap of the earth and not high as the Chinook had, presenting themselves as targets for any alert militia Stinger operator, could relieve pressure on both Romeo and Victor.

"Lash!" he yelled out—the nickname for La Rue—and fired off two rounds from his shotgun to keep heads down.

"Yeah?" came La Rue's voice.

"Indian!" Aussie yelled, Romeo's code for a helo air strike by Apaches, armed with longbow air-to-surface rockets. "That ought to stir the bastards up!"

More AK-47s opened up, or, Aussie wondered, were they the same ones firing longer bursts to cover a possible retreat? He hoped so, his expertly trained ear already having differentiated the sound of one weapon from another. That was an added bonus, using his UQ Remington. Bastards didn't hear a thing, just the deadly whistle of .00 buckshot ripping through fern and leaf, every one hitting the dirt or water.

Bronx took the opportunity to unleash a burst from his HK, and another ALERT fired his M-16, an upgraded A-2 version using the lighter 5.56 NATO rounds. There was an agonized scream, sounding as if it came from the militia side. Aussie hoped so.

CHAPTER THIRTY-EIGHT

Near Odessa, Washington

THOUGH MOST OF Freeman's paratroopers hadn't made contact with one another, they were feeling confident, largely because there had been no ground fire as they'd descended south of I-90. Of course, the zero visibility wouldn't allow anyone to get a bead on paratroopers, if there were any on the ground, but no matter how bad conditions might be, you always stood a better chance on the ground than you did descending, coming down amidst another two hundred men whom you couldn't see and whom you might hit if you started blasting away while still in harness. If someone started shooting at you on the ground, you could shoot back.

"R.O.?" Freeman shouted, calling his radio operator, who'd made the jump immediately behind Norton.

Freeman saw a grayish figure coming out of the white, and swung his shotgun loaded with flechette rounds.

"It's Murphy," the R.O. told him, quickly putting his hands up to reassure Freeman.

"Good to see you, Murph. Radio okay?"

"A-one, sir."

"Good. Stay close to me, son. Soon as we get our men in and radiate them out—secure a perimeter—then we can get a Herk in and unload our Hummers. Too damn far to walk to Fairchild."

"Yes, sir," said Murphy, who within seconds was in direct if somewhat crackly communication with the flying boxcars circling above, each Herk ready to air-land four Hummers. By now Freeman's paras were all down, and with only four injuries. Two men had landed on the icy I-90 with sprained ankles. One man's chute, blown by the wind, dragged him up a snowdrift formed by one of the fences on either side of the road, jamming him into the barbed wire. The final casualty was a trooper who came down with one leg going on either side of the snow-hidden wire, a painful experience that, while it tore out the crotch of his pants, didn't threaten to turn him into a soprano.

These were remarkably light casualties for a two-hundred-man drop, due both to the men's superb training and physical conditioning and the snow, which, while no more than a few inches deep in most places, had stacked up against the fences and in the drainage ditch. One glance at the highway's surface and Freeman could tell that no one had been over it recently, a fact he attributed to the assistance he'd asked for from the Washington Highway Patrol, whose cars, he guessed, must now be at both ends of the road, a mile to the northeast and a mile southwest from where he, Norton, and Murphy were standing. Buoyed by a successful jump, the paratroopers were quickly forming themselves into squads and platoons, moving out in a circle to points fifty yards from both fences in amidst snow-covered sagebrush. The profusion of the bushes resembled a garden of giant white ice cream scoops, their usual tangy, spicy smell overwhelmed by the clean, fresh smell of the blizzard, the biggest in this area since the crazy frigid weather that had swept down from Alberta in the spring of '97.

"Fifty yards—far enough!" Freeman radioed his platoon and squad commanders. He couldn't see them beyond ten feet. "Dig in until we unload the Hummers."

Jorgensen, the anxious para whom Freeman had spoken to as they'd boarded the lead Herky, pulled the barrel protector off and griped, "Dig in! Fuckin' ground's frozen solid. Snowin', fer Christ's sake."

"Quit your squawkin', Jorge," one of his comrades said. "You landed okay, and no militia in sight. Fuckin' picnic. We get some skis, we can have winter games."

"Bullshit," Jorgensen responded, his profanity the rough expression of his newfound confidence. "It's too fucking flat."

"Rolling country," his comrade corrected. "It's undulating. Anyway, you *could* cross-country ski."

"Bullshit!" Jorgensen was more than confident, experiencing the adrenaline rush that follows unexpected success. This would be a story to tell his grown-up grandchildren: "Yeah, we jumped out blind. Colder'n a fish's tit, and visibility—forget it—couldn't see a thing, not a damn thing."

Back behind him, he heard a vehicle, then moments later saw its blinking red, white, and blue lights. A police car, and behind it a van of some kind, red light flashing. Though still falling, the snow had eased up a bit, powder giving way to bigger, wetter flakes. Visibility was easing, not very much, but enough for Jorgensen and his SAW comrade to see it was an ambulance pulling up behind the police car.

Freeman, Norton, and the R.O., with a three-man cell of M-16 equipped paras, walked up to the state patrol car, and began talking to the two cops.

"Good to see you boys," Freeman said, shaking their hands. "I see you've kept this road clear for us."

"Yes, sir," one of the cops replied. "But we got a report that this General Nordstrom, whoever he is, has ordered a column of militia types this way, and we figure the bulk of 'em are only about an hour away. If you ask me, I wouldn't be surprised if some advance units are hereabouts already. We haven't seen any, mind, but that doesn't mean much in this weather. Could be anywhere along here."

"I don't think so," Freeman said. "Feels secure." The ambulance driver, a woman, came up and nodded at the group.

"Hope you're not expecting customers?" Freeman joked.

"No, General, but Highway Patrol here said I might come along, seeing your boys were jumping in this pea soup." Straining to read the woman's name tag, Freeman put out his hand. "I appreciate that. Emery, is it?"

"Yes, sir, Georgina Emery."

"Well, Georgina, all I can give you is a couple of bum ankles, and those have probably been wrapped by our medics already."

She grinned. "I can do without the work."

"Well," Freeman said, smiling, "I'll try not to bother you." He turned to his R.O. "Murphy, tell those Galaxies and Herks to come in for air-land in five minutes." He turned back to the Highway Patrol. "I suggest you boys get off the road. Those planes are big bastards."

"Don't worry, General. We got a pull-off—farm road intersection a hundred yards back. Tell your sky jockeys we'll keep our lights on, cruiser one side, ambulance the other."

"I will. Thanks, boys."

"You betcha!"

While the ambulance and highway patrol car pulled off left and right, parked so their taillights could help guide in the planes, the intensity of the snowfall continued to abate, with Freeman's computerized Weather Data Link forecasting an easing up in general in the front that had swept down from Canada.

The Galaxy gave Norton a heart-speeding fright. It did not become visible gradually, but emerged all of a sudden from the snowfall, its enormous dark green shape appearing black, its nose and clutch of twenty-eight landing wheels visible first, then its massive body, almost as long as a football field, and wider than one. Its wingspan was over two hundred yards wide, the howl of its engines deafening, the thunder of its approach so powerful that Norton could feel its pulsating in his bones. Snow on the fence wires on either side of the highway fell off due to the vibration.

The moment the huge craft touched down, Freeman glimpsed a red flash from the ambulance's interior, its rear door open, but before he had time to react, the sleek 2.76mm-inch-diameter Stinger missile was streaking toward the Galaxy, the missile barely having time for its eight control vanes to deploy, the am-

bulance-cum-militiamen hearing the high-pitched tone signi-
fying the 6.6-pound high explosive head was in "lock-on."

The sound of the brilliant orange and ruby-red explosion at
the junction of the Galaxy's left wing and fuselage reverber-
ated along the road, and the noise of the secondary explosions
as the 357-ton plane erupted in flames was heard ten miles
away as a dull thump. Crimson flames leapt over two hundred
feet into the air, the heat wash searing Norton's face as he
instinctively dove into the snow. The burning wreck was un-
approachable by Freeman and his men, though they tried. In
addition to the heat, they were prevented by the M-60 machine-
gun fire coming from the ambulance, now speeding off. It
was a chaotic scene. The enormous plane burned fiercely, men
scrambled for cover, some screaming from burns, desperate radio traffic shooting through the air in panic. It had all the elements of a nightmare. Jorgensen wondered if they should pull
back to help on the road, but there was nothing they could do.
There was an ugly series of secondary explosions spewing the
doomed Galaxy's burning avgas, followed by the eruption of
ammunition, including TOW missiles, on the doomed Hummers inside. The road was now stripped of snow, its bare, burning blacktop revealed like a long, ugly, inflamed scar against
the whiteness.

Incredibly, the back ramp was down, and two Hummers
roared out of the rear of the plane, which was now skewed
toward the snowmelt of the drainage ditch. One of the Hummers went nose down in the ditch, the second Hummer slamming into it, then reversing a foot or two and careening around
the first, readying to negotiate the ditch's incline. A vomit of
fiery fuel exiting the rear ramp, however, engulfed and inciner-
ated the men in seconds.

"Keep down!" Freeman was yelling into Murphy's mike.
There was no point in his men trying a futile rescue. He could
hear 5.6mm fire and incoming mortar from beyond his perimeter. He would need every able man he could get just to hold it
until he could be reinforced. He cursed himself for not having checked the fake cops' and ambulance drivers' ID. But

then, of course, they would have had ID. It occurred to him they might well have been militiamen who weren't in disguise—militiamen and women whose normal peacetime jobs were in the Highway Patrol and ambulance service. It was a crazy conflict.

Freeman smelled burnt flesh along with the suffocating fumes of spent fuel from the seventeen-million-dollar plane and its invaluable cargo of six Bradleys, nine Hummers, and eighty-four men.

CHAPTER THIRTY-NINE

The Everglades

ON THE WATERY plain of saw grass between the two arms of the cypress U, David Brentwood's air-propelled Zodiacs, Victor One and Two, sped toward Romeo, guided by the sounds of the firefight. Victor's two Zodiacs, heading east, fifty yards apart, were approaching a quarter-mile-long tear-shaped hammock dead ahead of them, several deep gator holes visible along the way. The two Zodiacs diverged, Victor One negotiating the channel at the hammock's northern end, Victor Two, with Brentwood aboard, taking the southern channel. Because of the tear shape of the hammock, the result of eons of time during which the north-south flow of the water over the 'glades' limestone base had made the northern ends of the bright green islands narrower than the southern ends, Victor One was past the northern tip, while Victor Two was only halfway along the wider southern tip. This meant that the five men aboard Victor

One were the first to glimpse the big thirty-foot-long militia aluminum airboat just beyond the island's northern shore.

"Victor One to Victor Two. Thirty foot bogey one hundred—"

It was the last transmit ever heard from Victor One, for by the time Victor Two, hearing a sound like hail, emerged from the cover of the wider southern end of the island, Victor One was no more.

David Brentwood screamed at his tillerman to come hard about, back behind the shelter of the southern end of the island. Once there, Brentwood immediately requested a helo missile attack on the militia boat he hadn't yet seen but knew the approximate position of from Victor One's final transmit.

No sooner had Brentwood requested the air strike than he and his four ALERTs spotted thick, white smoke rising from the far northern end of the island, from the area where Victor One had been wiped out. The smoke was billowing across the U-shaped watery saw grass plain, effectively hiding the U from pilots as well as drifting into the Big Cypress arms of the U.

Once Brentwood saw that the militia were "smoking" the U, he realized they must have guessed that either Aussie's "Indian" or his own last radio transmit had been a request for an air strike. All right, he decided, make the best of a bad situation. By using the militia's own anti-air-strike smoke cover, he could slip across the U to help Aussie and the other nine men in Romeo. Brentwood had barely given orders for Victor Two to gun its engine to cross the U when he heard the distant air-chopping sound of one—no, three—Apaches. He cut his engine, on the off chance that his Zodiac might be glimpsed through a gap in the smoke and draw the helos' fire, it being easy in this situation to mistake friend for foe.

Up in the lead Apache's high seat, his gunner immediately in front and below him, the pilot could see nothing but smoke swirling about him. He was flying, like Freeman's transport pilots, solely by instruments, the radar scope indicating two blurred targets, one at either end of the island, one much smaller

than the other, the larger moving slowly down the western side
of the hammock toward the southern tip. The gunner was all
ready to go, but the pilot said no, their infrared sight wasn't
getting through, which meant the smoke was particle infused,
which would scramble the helos' infrared as well as radar signals. The Apaches, armed with six state-of-the-art 114F Hell-
fire missiles, pods of Hydra rockets, and 30mm chain gun,
banked, swinging about their radars' long, fuzzy image of the
hammock. With all three choppers going in low, the lead pilot
thought it might be possible to blast a hole—disperse enough
smoke to get a visual as well as indistinct radar fix.

The big militia boat had a fix on them and fired. The five
ALERTs in Victor Two, including Brentwood, heard a tremendous rush, thousands of egrets rising from the 'glades, a sound
like hail, and immediately after that another, softer but nevertheless clearly audible rush of air followed by three loud explosions. Within thirty seconds burning debris rained down
from the smoky air, in pieces so small it was as if some prehis-
toric monster had clasped the burning page of some huge book,
crushed it, and let the flaming remains fall into the swamp, several toppling onto Victor Two.

"Scratch fifty million bucks!" one of Victor's crew said.

"Shut your mouth!" Brentwood hissed in an uncharacteristic burst of temper. He'd said it for two reasons: because the
man's comment might be heard by the militia in the sudden
ear-ringing silence that had replaced the hopeful sound of the
approaching Apaches, and because Brentwood didn't approve
of the catastrophic shootdown of six airmen being referred to
in terms of dollars. He signaled "paddles," and he and his four
men began a strong nearly silent series of long, hard strokes in
order to clear the smoke-filled area in which they could hear
but not see the militia boat closing.

What had astonished Brentwood and his four ALERTs in
Victor Two was that all three choppers had been downed simultaneously in what must have been one of, if not *the* most
spectacular antiaircraft engagements in the history of modern

warfare. But for the moment he and his men needed all their concentration and fortitude to relieve the pressure on the men of Romeo.

Bronx, alert for trip wires and having taken the dead Palmer's position and ammo, now moved cautiously and silently on point, passing through sword ferns that looked like broad daggers wreathed in thinning smoke. One of the fern's fronds was smeared in blood. He smelled it before he saw it. An ALERT's carefully trained sense of smell was one of his most vital attributes, the reason he never wore any deodorant, aftershave, or cologne of any kind. More than one American had lost his life because a Viet Cong had detected the scent of even a slightly perfumed body. Only an unscented antibacterial agent was used—to kill the equally potent telltale smell of body odor.

In a normal military unit, a close buddy's death would often stall an advance or at least slow it down temporarily while the evacuation of a badly wounded individual was undertaken. Not so for the ALERTs. As the nation's preeminent commandoes, they were trained to run "counterintuitively"—to press ahead with any seek and destroy mission. Those few seconds when an enemy anticipates you will slow down because of the casualties he's inflicted on you, and so attempts to use that time to realign his attack, are precisely when you ought to apply increased pressure. It was like Formula One champions who know that whenever there's a bad accident on the track, many drivers, particularly novices, intuitively take their foot off the accelerator for a fraction of a second. The pro pushes it to the metal.

Brentwood and his four neared Romeo's men. The latter had broken left and right to take up firing positions to cover alternate 180-degree flank sweeps. They were still moving behind Bronx on the point. Aussie was behind him, keeping Bronx, who was free to swing 180 degrees in front of him, in view. The potential for blue on blue remained high, given the persistence of the smoke in the Big Cypress. Aussie heard a slithering noise, like that of a gator slipping into deeper water than that of the squad. First Bronx, then Aussie, passed the militia-man whom Aussie had hit with a round from his UQ Remington. He was dead. Neither Aussie nor Bronx touched him. An FBI agent up in Washington State during the militia showdown had rolled a dead militiaman over to check for ID and was killed by the booby-trap grenade whose lever had been held down under the militiaman's weight.

As Aussie indicated the position of the dead militiaman by hand signal for the man coming after him, something about the dead man, or rather his equipment, caught Aussie's eye. On the man's top left vest load strap there was a "Smalltalk," an "in-squad" high-tech attachable sixteen-frequency radio. It was about the same height and width of a cigarette pack but much thinner, with a quarter-inch fixed antenna and three AA batteries that gave it a twelve-hour operational range, and weighed less than eleven ounces.

The radio, Aussie knew, was capable of being set with any one of over sixty spread-codes whose whispered messages from one squad member to another's feather-light, one-earpiece head-set could be heard up to half a mile. It meant that the militia had access to, and were using, state-of-the-art electronics. So what in hell were they using to kill three helos simultaneously in the blink of an eye?

Bronx, sweat coursing down his face, paused, knelt down, and was trying to deduce which way the militia had retreated when he heard, or rather sensed, movement off to his left, about twenty feet away. He froze, safety off. To advance was one thing, to let impatience have you make the wrong move was another. He'd wait.

CHAPTER FORTY

AFTER THE DESTRUCTION of the Galaxy and its cargo, Freeman knew that, like MacArthur, he had to do something— something spectacular. But he had no armor, no Hummers, no artillery. No wheels. He drew his Smith & Wesson 9mm—the ambulance beyond effective shotgun use—and pumped all his remaining twelve rounds of parabellum at the departing vehicles. His R.O., Murphy, yelled Freeman's orders into the radio to aim for the drivers, not the vehicles' engines. Neither he nor Freeman could hear either the noise of the retreating Highway Patrol and ambulance or his shots, these sounds drowned by the feral roar of the dying Galaxy. Only five men—a medical corpsman, three Hummer drivers, and a loadmaster who knew the ninety-second rule for exiting before toxic fumes, the greatest killer, reached them—had escaped the Galaxy. The sprinklers in the rear of the cargo area had come on, incapable of saving the aircraft but allowing three of the drivers to get three of the Hummers out, driving them away from the intense heat, down the road into the cooling fence-crested snowdrifts, the vehicles' TOW missiles intact, a rear wheel of one of the Hummers on fire until a snowdrift smothered it.

The ambulance had gone three hundred yards before its driver and co-driver, the latter firing an AK-47, saw the windshield crack and turn to a milky white web, both the woman driver and her gunner dead a millisecond later, killed by a long burst of M-60 fire.

The police car escaped the M-60 fire and was doing sixty

miles an hour on the flat, snow-lined road, when a trooper from
Private Jorgensen's squad, running onto the road, lifted his LAW
antitank weapon, sighted, and fired. His run to the road with
heavy gear had made him short of breath and the LAW round
went wild. Exploding to the right of the road, it killed two fellow paras manning the perimeter, the Highway Patrol car meanwhile careening out of control on the icy surface, then rolling
and overturning in the ditch, its engine, despite Freeman's order, struck by a hail of M-16 rounds.

As Freeman's troops reached the upturned vehicle, the patrolman emerged, having been badly scratched by flying glass, his
bleeding hands held up in surrender. A paratrooper shot him
point-blank. Resisting arrest. Farther back, the two militia bodies
were unceremoniously dragged from the ambulance and dumped
into the ditch.

Freeman immediately radioed his planes to airdrop what
hardware they could in the LZ. The seventy-ton M-1 main
battle tank was ruled out. Like the Bradleys, it could be carried
by the big Galaxies and EROL'd—engine running off-loaded—
on a strip but not air-dropped. The best he could hope for in
the way of heavy firepower was a few sixteen-ton M-551A1
Sheridans with 152mm guns, which, like the Bradleys, could
be dropped from the air and had a range of almost two miles.
And hopefully he could receive the air-droppable, aluminum-
framed 105 howitzers with a good punch range of seven miles.
But undoubtedly his best bet if he was to secure the LZ was to
put his three TOW missile-equipped Hummers to work. The
weather was clearing somewhat, but not enough to permit any
close air support for the paras.

It was then that what would become known to those involved
as the "Odessa Incident" occurred, an occurrence that would
also be talked about in military circles. Freeman called for Jorgensen's squad, which had earlier moved back closer to the road
to help stop the ambulance and Highway Patrol, to lay smoke as
an LZ marker for the transports making pattern in the pea soup
high above. Jorgensen, his earlier confidence gone, shaken up

like many others by the militia's ambush of the Galaxy, did as he was told, pulling the ring on the smoke round and, confirming the color for the squad's radio operator, saying, "Purple."

"Shut up!" his squad leader snapped. "What's the matter with you?" It was fundamental. You never told what color smoke you were using. You simply said, "I'm marking with smoke," in case the enemy, listening in on your frequency, heard what color you were using and released the same color, thus creating a fifty-fifty chance of your aircraft delivering your supplies to them. And that's precisely what happened, Freeman's transporters dropping two Sheridans and four Hummers, chutes on all six vehicles deployed, before the error was realized.

Freeman was in a rage, but Norton, doing his job, told the general bluntly that the important thing was what to do about it. Freeman took a deep breath, knowing, as he put it to Norton, he'd been "well rebuked," and immediately ordered his paras aboard the three Hummers and in the captured ambulance to attack.

No sooner had he given the order than he, Norton, and others near the road heard an angry buzzing noise to the northeast, which reminded him of Vietnam, of clouds of insects in the jungle. The buzzing approaching them on the I-90 was still in the distance but definitely getting closer.

"Goddamn it, Norton! What is it?" Freeman asked.

Camp Fairchild

In hut 5A, with Archie now under the wire despite some seepage, and the breakout set for the following evening, a concerned Browne asked Eleen if he could see him out in the compound for a minute.

"What is it?" Eleen asked anxiously as they stepped out on the dirty, snow-covered ground. "More water?"

Browne, hands in his pockets, affecting a nonchalance he didn't feel, looked over at the guard tower a hundred yards away. "Captain, I think we have a snitch in 5A."

Eleen felt his stomach knotting. "Why?"

Several other POWs came striding out to the compound, bragging about how they were going to kick ass in the ball game against 5B. Browne waited till they passed.

"Why?" Eleen repeated. They began walking away from the hut, parallel with the trip wire.

"That clothesline bullshit," said Browne, who was usually careful not to curse in front of the devout Mormon, but was too worried this morning to care. "Commandant saying he didn't like the clutter."

Eleen, head down, jaw set grimly, hands behind his back, nodded. "I've been wondering about that too," he conceded.

"Yeah, well, I'm damned sure he didn't *guess* that the clothesline was our radio aerial. Someone told him."

"How do you know?" Eleen pressed, his stomach tighter than a drum. "You hear something in the blockhouse?"

"Never heard squat in the blockhouse. All you hear there are the fucking rats. But it gave me a chance to think about it. Focus on it. If that bastard Schmidt knows about a radio, it's ten to one he knows about Archie. And—" Browne kept talking, but not about the tunnel. There were two guards, one of them Thug, coming their way. "—5B's pitcher," he told Eleen as they passed, "isn't worth a damn.

"Point is, Captain," he continued once the guards were well away, "I don't want to be the fly in the ointment but there's no way I want to be trapped in that friggin' tunnel with guards waiting for me at one end and a German shepherd biting my ass from the other. I hate fucking dogs—pardon my French, but I do. They scare me sh—witless."

Eleen rubbed his forehead as if to forestall a migraine, something he was prone to under extreme stress. Though combat itself with all its stress wouldn't trigger it, this kind of pressure—him wondering whether to proceed now with the breakout—created precisely the type of angst that could bring on the aura, followed by a throbbing pain so deep, so violent, that it was one of the few times—he asked God to forgive him this—that he understood why some people committed suicide.

Having confessed a weakness for the dogs, Browne felt acutely embarrassed. "I'm sorry, sir, I just—"

"I understand," Eleen said quietly, walking slower now, meanwhile massaging a pressure point at the base of his skull. "The problem is, what to do?" He looked at Browne. "I mean we can't be sure, can we? That he knows, I mean. He took the wire clothesline, but if he knew we had a radio, why didn't he ransack the hut? Rip it apart if need be?" Browne was about to reply, but Eleen was still following his own line of thought. "Schmidt's got that totalitarian personality. Wants to control everything and everyone, right down to the smallest detail. If he didn't search for the radio, it means he doesn't know about it. And if he had been told about the radio by an informer, then the informer would have told him about the tunnel." Eleen was nodding to himself, his self-confidence returning. "No, Browne, I don't think he knows, or else—"

"Maybe not," Browne cut in, still worried, "but the thought of being trapped in that tunnel—it's not like digging, it's different, it—"

"Panics you?" Eleen said, not in an accusing tone, but with understanding. Had he, Eleen, panicked in the Huey when they'd pulled away from—

"Look," Eleen said, cutting off the familiar thought while placing his hand on Browne's shoulder, "if you don't want to go, you don't have to." He paused. "You could get a couple of guys and try your ladder idea if you're ga—" He'd almost said, "Game for it," but instead said, "—if you'd like to."

"If I've still got the guts for it, you mean?" Browne said resentfully.

"No, I didn't mean that. I—" Eleen wanted to tell him that he really did understand, that he wasn't the first POW to have a panic attack. He, Eleen, wasn't Patton. He wasn't going to slap him, call him a coward.

"I won't try it the same night," Browne promised. "The ladder—just in case. I don't want to screw anything up."

"Good."

*   *   *

The Hummers and Sheridans had come down closer to the
militia than to Freeman's federal force, but because of the
changing weather—the warming had produced a thick mist rising from the snow, which had now begun to melt—neither the
militia nor the federal force could find the vehicles. Freeman
immediately dispatched the three Hummers with troops and
TOWs aboard to find the air droppables before the militia. He
also dispatched the ambulance, with its TOW in the back, northeast along the I-90. Corban, the butt of the paras' fart jokes, was
on the perimeter a few hundred yards north of the burning
Galaxy, the latter's fuselage gone, its ribs revealed like the skele-
ton of some great dinosaur glowing red from the flames, some
of the ribs now collapsing, like Freeman's planned strike north.
The peculiar buzzing sound heard a quarter hour earlier had
risen in pitch like a swarm of gnats, then abruptly stopped, the
paras who formed the rough oval-shaped perimeter around the
LZ unable to see under the blanket of mist. Visibility no more
than thirty feet one moment could suddenly increase to fifty
yards or so, then just as rapidly thicken again to produce near
zero visibility.

By now the media had found out about Freeman's hoped-for
"curved ball" from the south to the militia base camps in the
north, and the fact that he'd been stopped dead in his tracks at
the LZ on I-90. The *New York Times* was mildly critical of
what its armchair quarterbacks called "insufficient force" and
"hasty action." The tabloids, some of which seemed to be en-
dorsing the militia, were more blunt, with headlines ranging
from FEDS FAIL to FREEMAN'S FOLLY. Several radio operators
among Freeman's men had picked up snippets of radio news
and heard damning indictments of Freeman's "fiasco" on I-90.
However, Marte Price, reporting to Linden Soles at CNN Atlanta, said, "No one seems to realize the extraordinary organization required to move paratroopers with heavy matériel into
battle on such short notice. The weather, Linden, a snowstorm

moving down from the Canadian Rockies into Washington, Idaho, and Montana, has created all kinds of problems. It's changing rapidly now, but apparently all the weather reports at the beginning of Freeman's mission indicated that visibility was zero and it was snowing heavily. It took extraordinary courage on the part of military airlift pilots."

Soles cut in. "Yes, I suppose, Marte, we have to remember that and the fact that the Hercules—"

"It was a Galaxy, Linden. They're several times bigger than a Hercules."

"Yes, that the Galaxy didn't crash but was brought down, or rather, destroyed by enemy fire on the ground."

"That's right, Linden. I don't think that the general public has any idea of how complex it is to mount and field a rapid reaction force virtually overnight."

"I'd like to mount *her*," the man next to Corban said. Corban turned to him and then heard a high, shrill, Stukalike whistle. "Incoming!" he yelled, flattening himself in the snow. The explosion of the 81mm round shook the earth, showering Corban with dirt-streaked snow, a clod hitting his helmet with such force that it knocked it off. His buddy lay dead, his head splintered with shrapnel; the radio, amazingly enough, was still on the civilian band, news of the NASDAQ Index heard clearly until Corban, still stunned, switched it off, the mortar barrage creeping into the perimeter.

Over fifty miles north-northwest of Freeman's force, Vance, taking advantage of the appalling weather and realizing General Black's armored column was not foolhardy enough to charge blindly into the northern Cascade highway—that the column was in fact a feint—had recalled his men from the north Cascades, ordering the "convoy" toward the Idaho redoubts seventy-five miles to the east.

Speculation at the Pentagon was wild as to whether Nordstrom's militias' main, northern, force would join the smaller southern force that had blown up the Galaxy and was now holding Freeman at bay, bracketing his paratroopers with heavy mortar fire, or whether the militia's main force would run for the Idaho redoubts while they had the chance.

There were senior commanders at the Pentagon who almost felt sorry for Freeman. He had been ambushed, the militia waiting for the Galaxy. For once it seemed George C. Scott had bitten off more than he could chew. The problem was an age-old military one, that of speed and distance. If Freeman was to make a right hook northeast of where he was on the Odessa-Sprague line in order to stop Nordstrom's militia from reaching Idaho, where the militia would have the support of the Montana militia, he had to break out from I-90 and help secure the landing zone in order to funnel in more heavy transports. They would provide him with the men and matériel needed to make the dash to Fairchild field. Once the latter was secured, he could pour in all the men and armor he wanted to bar the militia's escape into its Idaho fortress. The overwhelming unknown was how many militiamen were on his immediate front— perhaps no more than he had. *"L'audace!"* he told Norton. *"L'audace, toujours l'audace!"*

Wonderful, Norton thought, but what with? Three armed Hummers and an armed militia ambulance?

The buzzing noise became louder now, carried forward on a breeze that was at once helping the warm air melt the thin covering of snow and also blowing away the mist. On the northern horizon about a thousand yards away, Freeman could see a line of five whitish dots, blurred images, made so because the militiamen, coming at him in at least five different columns rather than abreast, were wearing white coveralls and white helmet wraps, which tended to merge with the snow.

Freeman immediately ordered the Hummers and ambulance to split up, two of the four vehicles to head northeast, the second two northwest, and to hit the oncoming columns of snowmobiles on their flanks. It was a split-second decision by Freeman, who calculated that if the columns of what he estimated must be at least fifty snowmobiles—nine behind each of the column's five front riders—were hit on the flanks, they might immediately form a long, straight line east to west coming at him abreast to minimize casualties from the federals' Hummers and ambulance. This east-to-west line would then enable his two hundred federal paras to have what they called a "line of ducks" which two or three M-60 machine guns could handle.

"Hold your fire!" Freeman ordered. "Five hundred yards."

Then everything happened at once. The five columns coming at him broke and he could see there were at least a hundred snowmobiles, the driver of each, as Freeman tried to keep the image steady in his binoculars, apparently armed with what looked like AK-47s, the pinion rider behind each driver armed with everything from AK-47s, AK-74s, and M-16s, to SAWs.

"The man!" Freeman ordered, gripping the radio's mike. "Go for the man, not the vehicle." It was the kind of order regular infantry might not bother with, happy to have the bigger target of the machine. But Freeman knew his paras were all crack shots; they had to be in this elite unit. Still, Norton was puzzled by Freeman's insistence on targeting the men. Certainly that was the intention of any engagement, but surely any way you stopped them would do.

The snowmobiles split into twenty groups of five, ten of these groups, fifty snowmobiles in all, coming due south straight at Freeman's front, the other ten groups of five snowmobiles each breaking to hit Freeman's perimeter on his east and west flanks, which meant that the four vehicles he had, two east, two west, were on a direct collision course with twenty-five snowmobiles racing in on each flank.

The TOW missile is designed for antitank warfare, but if its operator could guide it into the midst of the snowmobiles, it would be catastrophic for the militia riders. Just how catastrophic was about to be realized when the first Hummer's TOW operator selected a firing position in a depression between two hillocks of sage, his TOW barely visible to the oncoming militia.

The operator lined up the crosshairs on the target and pressed the firing button, the fifty-seven-pound missile, its sustainer motor kicking in after forty yards, pushing its speed to nine hundred feet per second, its warhead now armed as it streaked toward a fast-moving group of four snowmobiles, one having flipped over a hidden sagebrush, unzipping the shallow snow cover to reveal a gravelly red earth below. The TOW operator was a good one, and he had the self-discipline to stand his ground, using the joystick to guide the missile via its trailing wire as dexterously as any teenage ace in a computer arcade.

The operator had no way of knowing how many of the militia snowmobiles had seen the TOW's back-blast, but while one group of five snowmobiles had scattered as he'd fired, the group off to its rear was tighter. It was this section that the soldier kept in his sights, knowing that the missile's stand-off probe would explode the warhead fifteen inches away from the target in the event it was armor plated, penetrating the latter up to 900mm.

It hit the leading snowmobile in a blinding flash, its gas tank exploding, shrapnel and concussion knocking off the other riders and wrecking their machines, two of these also exploding. Riders were thrown high, one of them on fire and screaming. Meanwhile, the remaining twenty snowmobiles on the Hummer's flank were coming straight at him. By the time he reloaded, the Hummer was taking multiple hits, the Hummer's crew stopping another four snowmobiles, one of which somersaulted, smashing into the ground so violently it flew apart, its impact tearing up the reddish earth through the few inches of snow.

Freeman, having just ordered his men to go for the men and not the machines—though he knew this was impossible for his TOW operators—was being told that intelligence from the National Guard in Spokane, which had effectively cut off Interstate 90 east of the city to prevent a militia retreat into Idaho, now believed that Nordstrom's base camps had amalgamated and were driving due south to crush his paratroopers.

"Dammit! It's not supposed to work this way, Norton. Our

presence here was supposed to channel them northeast. Nord-strom's not supposed to come at me."

"Apparently," Norton said wryly, "he's read Frederick the Great."

"Huh!" Freeman growled unappreciatively. "He probably thinks if he comes at me now he's got a free ride before I get reinforced." Freeman looked at his laptop's generated map of the area. "I'll give Nordstrom one thing. Bastard's got balls."

At closer range now, the heavy .50 caliber machine guns on each of the federals' Hummers were taking a deadly toll on the militiamen's snowmobiles. Their riders were literally disinte-grating when hit by fire from the .50s and assorted M-16s and M-60s.

But the next sitrep from Spokane brought more bad news, or rather, confirmation that the snowmobiles Freeman's men were engaging were the spearhead of a main force estimated at brigade strength—at least four thousand militia. "More goddamn snow-mobiles!" Freeman said. "If only the weather would clear more quickly. Norton, get me the met officer at Fairchild. Route it through Fort Lewis if you have to."

"Yes, sir. How about the planes? I think they're getting pretty tired of just flying around making pattern. Besides, they'll be low on fuel—can't loiter for much longer."

"You tell those sky jockeys to *keep* making pattern. But if they want to try landing," Freeman said, indicating the great burned-out hulk of the Galaxy, "it's okay by me."

The pilots replied that they were quite happy to make pattern until their fuel gauges told them to return to base.

CHAPTER FORTY-ONE

CAMP FAIRCHILD WAS locked in by the weather. Fog rolled in so thickly that the Air Force base's runways and planes a mile away were frequently obscured from view. For one moment one of the guards in the tower nearest the main east gate even lost sight of a prisoner. It was Browne walking perilously close to the trip wire. A voice, loud and sounding unpleasantly metallic, announced, "Man by the trip wire—move away!"

Browne stopped, turned, and yelled, "Fuck you!"

"Man by the wire, stay where you are. Don't move!"

Within a minute two guards, one of them Thug, were hustling Browne at gunpoint away from the wire to the blockhouse thirty yards away. The other prisoners whistled and catcalled the guards, the POWs more brazen than usual because in the fog only the vague shapes of the men, and not their faces, could be seen.

Thug opened a cell door and shoved Browne in. "You'll never learn, will you, Browne?"

In the next cell the Nazi, Hearn, waited until Thug and the other guards had exited the blockhouse and were well out of hearing range before he tried to communicate with whoever had been brought in. He hadn't heard what Thug had said or the prisoner's name, but knew there was some kind of altercation. A short time later Hearn heard muffled boots again in the corridor, the prisoner's door flung open, and then Schmidt's voice.

The commandant didn't waste time on niceties. "Well," he said to Browne. "When's their ETD?"

Hearn knew what that meant: estimated time of departure.

"Tomorrow night," Browne said. "The tunnel's already under the wire."

"You're sure?"

"I wouldn't be here if I wasn't. It's tomorrow night."

"What about you?"

"I told 'em I'd be too claustrophobic down there."

"Who did you tell?"

"Eleen."

"You think he believes you?"

"Yeah, he believed me. I set him up with the radio aerial business. After that there's no way he wouldn't believe me."

"I knew you had initiative," Schmidt said in a congratulatory tone.

"Not until you blackmailed me."

Schmidt ignored Browne's defensive tone. "I'll keep my word. Your wife and child'll be released from custody. But you tell your wife that if you two don't sever all your ties with the militia, the state child agency'll take your kids away again."

"Was—" Browne began. "Is it true—she was raped?"

There was a pause, and Hearn heard Schmidt say, "She was removed from the general women's POW quarters to the family compound. She's safe."

"Was she *raped*?"

"We'll keep you here for a day or two after the breakout attempt, then we'll release you."

"Was she raped?"

Hearn heard the muffled thud of Browne's cell door closing. The Nazi, his hands stiff from the cold, began massaging his thighs. Like the rest of his body, they were stiff from the beating administered by Schmidt's henchmen demanding a detailed description of what Nordstrom looked like.

On the I-90, Freeman's two hundred men had driven off the militia's snowmobile attack. With a heavily armed federal Hummer blasting away on each flank, the militia had made what

Freeman inaccurately but understandably boasted was the quickest goddamn U-turn in history.

"I suspect they'll be back," Norton said.

"Yes, yes," Freeman conceded irritably. "But we'll have a chance to dig in *deep*. And I'll tell you this—once we've dug in, the last thing those jokers'll expect is for us to switch from defense to attack *before* we get all our supplies flown in as this weather clears further."

Before Norton could inject any caution about the weather possibly not clearing, or anything else, Freeman had grabbed his R.O.'s phone and ordered the Hummers to "hustle back here." He instructed ten men on the perimeter to assemble as much ammo as possible from the dead snowmobilers and the twenty or so wounded who'd been left behind by the fleeing militia, whose rules of engagement forbade any operational units from risking capture or destruction by staying behind to pick up wounded. It was a hard rule, but they were a hard bunch.

Of the twenty-two wounded militiamen, seven were critical, and Freeman's six corpsmen, who had come in with Freeman's spearhead, were attending to them as well as they could. Unlike the federal troops, however, who wore a standard personnel status monitor belt under their T-shirts, the militiamen had to be dealt with in the old-fashioned way. Instead of getting instantaneous readouts, as in the case of the wounded federals, of mean arterial blood pressure, heart rate, temperature, and hypothermia danger index, from the PSM belt, including a visual display on the medic's handheld PSM computer of the patient's blood type, allergies, and inoculation history, all the information militiamen had for the medic was contained on plastic dog tags. It wasn't much to go on in the golden hour during which wounded soldiers stood the best chance of survival.

Freeman, leaving Norton in charge of the LZ, had joined the eight men in the two Hummers for a reconnaissance foray north, where, as he told Norton, he hoped to observe "what's coming down the pike."

Norton was at least thankful for Freeman's order about digging in deeper than the normal slit trench. The general was obsessed with *"L'audace,"* but he wasn't a fool, and knew that if he confirmed the initial intelligence reports of four to five thousand militia en route to attack and annihilate him before he could mount a reinforced drive to Fairchild AFB, then he would have no alternative but to dig in and slug it out until Fairchild could give close air support, weather permitting.

As Freeman's Hummer sped through the open, thin snow-covered country north of the perimeter, following the tracks of the snowmobiles, the men on the perimeter, not knowing when a militia counterattack might materialize, quickly unpacked their eight-pound "Badgers," or XM300 fighting position excavators. These commercial off-the-shelf kits were designed to reduce the time and energy required for DID—dig in defense. The Badger's tough auger, a foldable 8mm-diameter post hole digger, was twisted into the ground to a depth of about forty-five inches. This was repeated again forty-five inches from the first hole. Normally this shouldn't have taken more than five minutes, but because the first few inches were partially frozen, it was eight minutes before Jorgensen and his buddy, Melrose, had completed the task, and another few minutes to mix two explosives, which were not dangerous by themselves, but when mixed together made for a potentially unstable mix. Jorgensen and Melrose moved back about eighty yards, as did all the other paras who in pairs had carried out the same procedure after blasting caps had been placed in the holes.

Norton asked for quick radio confirmation that everyone on the perimeter had moved back and was clear, then gave the order to blast. A *choomp!* could be heard for miles, together with a glass-cracking sound, ice needles shattering in the blast. It was only a little while before the paratrooper pairs, using their entrenching tools on the softened earth, had excavated small, rectangular trenches approximately seven feet long, three feet wide, and five feet deep. The floor from its midpoint sloped away at each end into a grenade sump into which a militia grenade would roll, should it clear the protective walls of tightly packed excavated earth in front of each trench.

When the tail-end Charlies of the retreating militia scout snowmobiles looked behind them and, through the mist, saw what might be two federal Hummers, they radioed ahead to the forward echelons of Nordstrom's main force, asking whether there was any news yet of Nordstrom's northwestern force obtaining the awesome weaponry enjoyed by the Florida militia.

In the Everglades it was already nightfall and raining. As David Brentwood and the other four men of Victor Two joined up with the nine remaining members of Aussie Lewis's Romeo squad, the decision was made jointly by Brentwood and Aussie to post four guards equipped with night vision goggles, while the remaining men rested, the change in watch coming in at 0400 hours.

Initially, Aussie had been for pushing on, but Brentwood's view that with the rain and rising water obliterating many of the signs of the militia's passage into the Big Cypress, it would be just as well to wait till dawn. Aussie was impatient for combat, the thing he loved best along with making love, but saw the wisdom of Brentwood's more contemplative decision. Being brave, fit, and willing was one thing, but to be too hasty would imperil the entire fourteen-man squad, now divided into two teams of seven Romeo and seven Victor.

They settled down in the underbrush, hearing the water trickling by and the rain drumming on the dark canopy of cypress, mahogany, and paradise trees overhead. Aussie checked his weapons and Draeger bubbleless underwater breathing apparatus. The others also took the opportunity to "feel check" everything. What they didn't want was some damn gator looking for a predawn snack, and the guards were constantly checking the sodden underbrush for any sign of white on green, showing the presence of a foreign body in their rain-drenched bivouac. No one spoke unless absolutely necessary, and then in a whisper with his mouth "à la Tyson"—as the instructors had taught them—virtually on the next man's ear.

The constant patter of the rain covered most of the night noises, but the bellow of gators could still be heard. One of

Aussie's guards, Billy Rosco, originally from Los Angeles, was starting to feel sleepy, the sound of the rain at once comforting and cooling compared to the heat of the day. He wriggled his toes to increase blood flow and tried to think of all the things he had learned about the swamps—red eyes a male gator, green for the female, and how many a time he'd marveled at how the swallowtail kites high above the tall pines would swoop, take, and eat prey in midair. And how after the rain you could expect a plague of mosquitoes. His musings kept his mind off his buddies who had died that day. Rosco was trained to shove thoughts of death from his mind, to concentrate solely on the job at hand. Still, the rapidity of the militia's slaughter of Victor One had thrown them all. He saw two tiny, warm dots on the green background of the night vision goggles—the eyes of a striped tree spider. He thought the rain had eased, or was he simply getting used to it? He wriggled his toes again, forced himself to stay alert, and thought about the swamp again. For all he'd been told, no one had ever explained to him where birds die. There were tens of thousands of birds over the Everglades, so many egrets, for example, that at times they covered the island like a white sheet. And there were thousands of birds in the cities too, from L.A. to Tampa, but rarely did you see even one dead bird. Where did they all go?

In the early predawn light Aussie Lewis, who'd relieved Rosco for the dog watch, watched the tortured shape of a young pine strangled by an Australian melaleuca tree emerging from the dark mist. Beyond it he saw blood-spattered undergrowth and two lizards coupling by the ant-infested remains of what looked like a human hand. Through the underbrush he glimpsed a stretch of water speared by dozens of narrow-stemmed melaleuca plants, their tops bluish purple from herbicide sprayed on them by park rangers in their constant war against the foreign vegetation strangling everything in the 'glades.

The sight of herbicide, however, wasn't the only evidence of man's passage through the swamp, for despite the rain having temporarily flattened much of the vegetation, there remained clear enough signs: crushed saw grass as well as spots of blood on bark protected from last night's rain by the hammock's thick canopy growth.

Once they'd eaten and were ready to push off, Brentwood's Victor took the right, southern flank of the waterway, Aussie's Romeo taking the left, or northern flank. The two groups advanced about fifty yards apart—the width of the waterway.

Hugging the rough, ghostly white melaleuca-lined shoreline, they were able to make better time in the two-foot-deep water despite its hazards of an uneven bottom and the ever-present threat of gators. Mosquitoes by the thousands attacked the commandos, covering the torsos, arms, and legs of all fourteen of them like gray overcoats, the men's faces eyeless behind the green head nets that hung down from their floppy green jungle hats, the nets pulled in by large rubber bands, which the ALERTs found more efficient than the gap-plagued, regular issue drawstring.

The buzzing of the mosquitoes became so persistent and loud that Aussie Lewis, leading Romeo along the left shoreline, was concerned that this sound alone might give them away. And Rosco, tail-end Charlie in Brentwood's Victor, discovered, to his intense discomfort, that there was a hole in the net over his neck that now felt like it had been punctured by dozens of hot needles. The unscented bug spray he'd slapped on before they'd left seemed ineffective, and the result was a swelling so severe he thought he was in danger of going into anaphylactic shock. That would certainly screw up the mission.

CHAPTER FORTY-TWO

Washington State

THE SUN, A blurred opaqueness in an opaque sky, was setting. The snowfall had ended, but left enough bad weather in its wake to cloud the sun and hurry the darkness as Freeman, closing in on the retreating snowmobiles, saw through his binoculars the advance elements of Nordstrom's main force. He'd seen a lot in his time, and had once told his aide, "Norton, I'm never surprised by what human beings are capable of."

"For good or evil, General?"

"For both."

But now even he was surprised. "Jesus!" he exclaimed, then passed the binoculars to the paratrooper manning his Hummer's machine gun.

"Son of a bitch, sir!"

"What's going on?" the driver asked.

"Heavy traffic," Freeman said.

After the machine gunner handed him the binoculars, the driver felt his heart race. There was heavy traffic all right, the longest line of vehicles—they looked like pickups—that he'd ever seen, army convoys included. The assorted pickups, however, many of them Ford extra-canopy Rangers, looked strange. "Covered in bumps," as one of Freeman's eight-man scouting party commented.

In the rapidly fading light, Freeman couldn't distinguish the vehicles as clearly as he would have liked. Even the Hummer's infrared scope was good only up to 150 yards as darkness fell.

Freeman estimated the convoy was composed of at least a hundred vehicles, all bristling with men holding weapons from AK-47s, M-16s, M-60s, and canopy-mounted .50s. Here and there, Freeman guessed about every ten vehicles, there was a pickup sprouting what looked suspiciously like Stinger ground-to-air missiles. The downed Galaxy had already demonstrated the militia possessed these. The "bumps," however, looking like blocks of dull-colored crocodile skin, puzzled him. He told the driver to head back to the LZ, and radioed ahead with what he told Norton was an "ultra urgent" message to McChord Air Force Base, and also told Norton to have his two hundred paras pair off and redistribute the excavated earth from the already dug foxholes.

It was still dark, the moon hidden by thick stratus. Half of Freeman's force of two hundred were now in a state of high alert, one man in each two-man trench on guard, the other sleeping or trying to.

No matter how well the paras had been trained, the expectation of imminent combat strained nerves. Opinion was divided. Some believed that despite the high risk of fratricide, Nordstrom would launch a head-on night attack. Others were convinced that Nordstrom, not wanting to risk unnecessary casualties, and wanting to show the world he could crush the federal force, would, with military history and common sense behind him, wait till dawn. By then he would have had time to totally encircle the federals' oval-shaped LZ perimeter.

Norton argued that the weather was the main component in the hypothetical equation because Nordstrom must know that clear weather would favor the federals because of close air support. Therefore, Nordstrom would rush their force to overwhelm it before a dawn that might bring clear skies and an air strike from Fairchild, should the Spokane National Guard be able to establish a missile-free zone about Fairchild. In short, the situation was not a matter of clear alternatives. Rather, there was a mishmash of possibilities and variables.

Freeman told Norton that all he could hope for was another

half hour, by which time he trusted his coded "ultra urgent" request to McChord would be answered. The general had no sooner finished speaking than he and everyone else on the northern side of the perimeter heard a series of pops. Night became day as parachute flares blossomed like suns, descending slowly, revealing the stark scars of earth that marked the federal trenches. Immediately, fire erupted, red streaks of tracer arcing lazily from what looked to the paratroopers in their foxholes like a line of Tinkertoy vehicles, militia pickups, their guns blazing at the dirt piles of what the militia thought were foxholes. In fact these were the "redistributed" piles of earth and snow that Freeman had ordered be put in place when he was returning from his reconnaissance patrol.

"They're falling for it!" Jorgensen yelled at his foxhole buddy Melrose before shoving another magazine into his M-16.

But Freeman knew that while his fake trenches trick would deplete a substantial amount of the enemy's ammunition and buy them some time, hopefully time enough for his requested airdrop from McChord, it wouldn't fool Nordstrom's militia for long.

"Where are those goddamn planes I requested?"

Norton glanced at his watch and heard the slapping sounds of rounds streaking above the ditch in which one of the Hummers and ambulance were parked. "Should be here in twenty minutes, General."

"*Should* be? *Have* to be, you mean." Standing up, his head just above the parapet of the ditch, the general looked through the I.F. goggles. "That son of a bitch only has a third of his vehicles out there—if that."

"Jesus, get down!"

"Sergeant!" Freeman bellowed, totally ignoring Norton.

"Sir?"

"When I give the word, take this Hummer out on our right flank. Take four men with you, one on the TOW, two on machine guns. Go like hell and take out as many of those fucking pickups as you can. Extra TOW rounds."

"Yes, sir."

"Tell me when you're ready."

"Yes, sir." The sergeant disappeared.

"General!" Norton shouted. "Get your goddamn head down. I don't want to be in command of this unit."

"Norton, get on the blower and tell our Hummer on our left flank to do the same. Give him ten minutes prep time."

"Not until you get your head—"

"Yes, yes, all right." He knelt down on one knee to consult his map under his red-glow penlight. "That rebel bastard is trying to put a noose around us, Norton. Estimate he's divided his vehicles into quarters—one each side of our perimeter." With that, he grabbed his own phone and on the platoon frequency instructed all two hundred or so of his men—he couldn't know how many were already dead or wounded—to be ready on his word to launch a sustained enfilade of M-16, M-60, SAW, and LAW antitank missile fire toward the militia's vehicles a quarter mile off.

"What the fuck does he think we're doin'?" Melrose asked.

"He means in unison!" Jorgensen shouted, too frantically busy to be frightened.

"I know what he fucking means."

"Then pick your man," Jorgensen told him.

"*Pick* 'im. I can't fuckin' *see* 'em. I've lost a fucking contact."

"Oh, shit."

Even Jorgensen's curse seemed more authoritative, more self-confident, now. He was as surprised at the change in himself as Melrose. His training now took over and he chose not the vehicle that was the front runner well left of him, but one of those in his *own* field of fire, each section looking after its own sector. No point in expending your ammo in another section's cone of fire. They heard aircraft overhead.

"You fucking beauty!" a para in the next foxhole cried ten yards away.

A green flare was fired by a para inside the perimeter to mark a drop zone for the aircraft overhead. The noise of the aircraft, a relatively quiet hum, like that of a well-tuned sports car, had disappeared, but then just as quickly was heard again as it swung back. Still, they couldn't see it until, swooping in at a hundred feet, the fast, ultraquiet Boeing helo—no tail-assisted rotor—opened fire with its M-60. The fleeting hump of its side gunner was silhouetted by the flash of his machine gun, which poured down a steady stream of red tracer. The gunner took out six paras in three trenches before anyone realized that the super quiet aircraft was militia. Then four more swept in low abreast, taking out another twelve trenches, killing fifteen paras outright, critically wounding six, and disabling another three.

At this rate Freeman knew his two hundred would be reduced to zero in a matter of minutes. The five NOTARS, however, made a mistake in their third sweep. With their element of surprise gone, and not wanting to attract a barrage of antiaircraft, small arms fire at such low altitude, they decided not to pop aircraft decoy flares, which would have hopefully suckered away any heat-seeking missiles. It gave the paras a brief window of opportunity, during which they fired four Stingers, two of them connecting in two big, almost simultaneous, orange ball explosions, a third NOTAR hit with assorted bursts of M-60 and SAW fire. Who could claim the fourth kill was a matter for argument, but all that mattered now was that it too was destroyed.

This left only one of the Boeing-made machines in which the antitorque to the rotor was not provided by a tail rotor but by a radically designed alterable vent sleeve in the tail shaft. The two-man craft, beautifully maneuverable because of the computer-controlled vent sleeve, was so quiet that it was on you before you knew it.

On Freeman's left flank, one of his Hummers fired its TOW, and seconds later a pickup exploded in flame, bodies flung like rag dolls from its back, their World War II helmets flying high from the concussion of the hit.

A second bumpy-sided pickup was aflame, but, unlike the one before, it kept going, careening madly across the snow, bodies toppling and hanging from it as it suddenly swerved into a tight turn and rolled, the dying, burning men's screams drowned in the din of militia LAW, antitank missile, TOW, and small arms fire that quickly became a sustained roar as Nordstrom's flank forces advanced to be met by deadly accurate fire from the well-dug-in paras. The latter's most pressing danger was not so much the fire from the militia's vehicles but an impending shortage of ammunition, even though they had stripped the dead militia snowmobilers of their ammo and arms.

It wasn't until about ten minutes into the battle that Freeman's paras understood for sure what the pickups' bumps were— reactive appliqué armor, that is, armor made famous by the Israeli armored divisions who had stuck the slabs of steel-Kevlar-ceramic sandwiches on their tanks to prevent the Syrians' Russian-made T-72 TOWS from penetrating. It wasn't preventing the sheer force of a federal's TOW missile from knocking the armored pickups "ass-over-tit," as Jorgensen put it, but it was acting like a bulletproof vest on the trucks, so far as the paras' small-arms fire was concerned.

Now the militias heard the roar of other aircraft, and Nordstrom's armed pickups were pulled back for fear it was federal bomber aircraft arriving, something Nordstrom thought the federals wouldn't try in poor weather because of the acute danger of blue on blue. He was right. They were federal aircraft, but not bombers, the latter being held at Fairchild for possible release pending clear weather *and* the President's personal order. The White House was still reluctant to use B-52s against their own kind. Instead, the planes were the Herkys from McChord that had had to return to refuel, and because of Freeman's message from his Hummer, to reload with other equipment that was air-droppable and not heavy enough to require the dangerous kind of landing the Galaxy had attempted.

Freeman himself popped a second green flare to signal the federal drop zone, the militia withdrawing for fear of federal bombs. The loadmasters aboard the Hercules ordered the pallets dropped into the blackness. Black drogue chutes deployed as the pallets floated to earth.

"I.F. scopes!" Freeman bellowed into the radio, sending each man in each ten-man section scrambling, lifting his infrared scope skyward, there being a real danger of some loads dropping onto foxholes.

"Bravo down!" a para shouted, and the next minute there was a loud thump, then another, loud curses and a noise like wheat pouring from a silo. It was the sound of snow and piled trench earth pouring down atop the occupants of five foxholes who'd had to duck down so low to avoid being crushed that their boots were in the trench's grenade sump. They were sealed in.

"Get this fucking thing offa me!" was the gist of the trapped paras, a few warriors like Melrose becoming decidedly claustrophobic. "Fucking tomb! Get this mother offa me!"

"Hang on!"

"*You* fuckin' hang on. I can't breathe!"

They could hear men working quickly, the scraping sound of boots as the paras topside worked feverishly not only to free their buddies, but to unload the new heaven-sent cargo before the militia woke up to the fact that there were no bombs.

Jorgensen, whose newfound sense of confidence was retreating under the closed-in feeling, was relieved at last to hear throaty engines starting up and being driven off the pallets, then the pallets themselves being towed off by the vehicles.

"Come on!" Freeman shouted. "Get 'em off!"

Jorgensen felt another fall of snow and pebbles as, once the pallet above him was towed away, snow debris fell on him and Melrose, cold as sin down behind his collar.

CHAPTER FORTY-THREE

The Everglades

IT WAS SO hot, the rivulets of sweat coursed down Rosco's back like a river. His green camouflage shirt stuck to him like Saran Wrap, and the itchiness of the mosquito bites ached to be scratched. The remainder of Romeo and Victor pressed forward.

Ahead, the bayou between the southern and northern flanks was a fifty-yard-wide waterway, swollen by the night's torrential downpour to a thigh-deep stream of debris, again from the rain. A roost of zebra butterflies clung to a bayhead on Victor's southern side, some of the butterflies flicking excitedly out to midstream and back. On Romeo's flank a turtle could be seen attacking a lily flower by first bending the flower's stem with its body weight, bringing the flower down to water level.

Ahead lay an outgrowth of strangler fig roots. The stream was narrowed by the mangle of roots to about twenty feet across, and both Romeo and Victor could see signs of bruised plants, sap bleeding, where something of considerable size, most likely the big militia airboat that had taken out Victor One, had passed through, scratch marks on the root mangle visible a foot above the waterline. It was then that both Brentwood, leading Victor, and Rosco on Romeo's point, sensed something amiss.

Perhaps it was the ALERTs' training, requiring that they mentally record every odor they encounter, the brain constantly inquiring, "Does it belong here?" A foreign smell could ID an enemy far more quickly than a visual fix. The odor, albeit faint on the westbound breeze, was the smell of cordite that lingered after a firefight, which only the best-trained noses could detect hours later. That they could detect it at all told Aussie Lewis and David Brentwood that wherever it was coming from up ahead had to be covered, otherwise the previous night's downpour would have washed it away. The sun was shining, the sky above the expanse of the glades a vast cerulean-blue devoid of cloud.

Intuitively, Rosco slowed, signaling the other six in Romeo to do likewise. Across the stream to his right the seven men of Victor had come to a complete halt. Rosco motioned Bronx to come forward and take over the point. It was the responsible thing to do. Rosco's mosquito bites had now swollen to form clusters of huge lumps about his neck, and his breathing had become labored. Aussie had always stressed: "Don't try to be a bloody hero. If you feel knackered, get off the point immediately. Everyone in the squad's depending on you."

The changeover, as Bronx moved forward to take Rosco's place, was a delay that saved Rosco's life and those of the other six men in Romeo, for in those seconds that Romeo stood still, Brentwood on the other side of the stream glimpsed the brutal-looking prow of a big airboat jutting out beneath a huge jungle camouflage net that blended with the hammock's undergrowth. He signaled "Down" and immediately submerged, the other six men of Victor following suit, but not before the hot wind came, followed by a feral roar. The tops of all vegetation on Victor's side of the narrowed stream had disappeared as if severed in one swipe by a gargantuan machete.

Only Brentwood survived, being the only one who'd completely submerged. Breaststroking back underwater, his free left arm struck one of the bodies of his already dead comrades. Their corpses sank, weighed down by their equipment. The water around Brentwood was sizzling like a frying pan, and hot slugs rained down from the surface, falling on his Draeger pack.

With half his breath gone, Brentwood rolled and turned to the north, back toward Romeo, not yet seen by the militia. When he felt the mangle of fig tap roots, he surfaced, gulping for air, a hand from one of Aussie's men hauling him in closer to the protection of the vegetative camouflage. Now they could hear shouting about a hundred yards away under the camouflage net and men running down what seemed like planks, boots thumping on the aluminum of the big boat which, Brentwood glimpsed, had two enormous air propellers instead of one for its power source. Still unable to speak after the superhuman effort it had taken to swim across with all his gear, his nostrils filled with the stench of cordite, Brentwood handed something to Aussie. It was a 5.6mm bullet. Finally Brentwood found his voice, whispering hoarsely, "Fell into my . . . my vest load while I was under." The bullet still felt warm.

Aussie, craning his neck past his Draeger rebreather pack, looked over at the sheared vegetation of the southern side. "Bullets can't do that!" he told Brentwood. "You'd need a—"

"Enemy coming!" Rosco signaled, his itch momentarily overcome by the sheer terror induced by the horrendous noise and sauna-hot wind that had enveloped them as Brentwood dived. Then Romeo heard more voices, the militia obviously believing the six dead men of Victor had constituted the full complement of commandos.

"He dived over there, Rory. Down by that iddy biddy sword fern."

"Not to worry, Leroi. Gonna plug him same as I did that ranger."

"We gonna use the box, Leroi?" another militiaman shouted.

"Hell, no. Don't need all that fo' one federal. We'll get him like Rory says. Bring out them hounds—and cover the box. Metal gets so damned hot in this sun, burn ya cotton-pickin' hand off."

"Will do, boss."

"And Rory?"

"Yep?"

"You take a few boys down yo' side o' this crick—case sum-a-bitch pops up over there."

"How 'bout them red sticks?"

"Hell, yes," the militia boss answered, the one they were calling Leroi. "Might as well have some fun."

Washington State

It was still dark as the last of the air-dropped pallets landed in Freeman's LZ, the advanced light strike vehicles, known as SVs, driven off their pallets the moment the chutes were discarded. With a three-man crew—driver, LAW, M-60 machine gunner, and a 40mm grenade-round dispenser in the back where the machine gunner could pop up through the circular mount hole in the roof—this four-wheel-drive fighting vehicle was designed to be roll safe. Aluminum had been used structurally wherever possible to reduce the weight, allowing the SV's 2.5 five-cylinder 115-horsepower diesel to reach eighty miles per hour if needed, as fast as or faster than a fully loaded four-wheel-drive pickup or Jeep in this rolling plain terrain.

Now ten of them, plus six drum rolls of "springback" razor concertina wire, were on the ground, three of them already fifty yards or so outside the perimeter, seven inside. On their own initiative, in accordance with Freeman's training methods, twelve of his paratroopers, in three teams of four, made a dash for the three vehicles outside the perimeter as another ten paras laid down covering fire.

As one team reached its SV, the vehicle was suddenly lifted into the air, exploding in a fierce white flash that turned blood-red and tangerine. A second later the vehicle's side-stored auxiliary fuel bladder ruptured, flame engulfing two of the four paras, shrapnel killing a third man, the remaining para looking like a vaudeville clown, combat uniform in tatters, hair singed, face blackened and bleeding, dropping to the sand and rolling in it to extinguish residual flames. Another para had run out to help as Freeman ordered mortar-smoke cover for all the SVs. The burned man's condition was so bad, however, his right arm gone, blood jetting from his throat, that he died as he was being dragged back to the perimeter by his buddy.

In the "heavy" particle-grained smoke, impenetrable to any

infrared scopes or goggles Nordstrom's troops might have, the other two light strike vehicles were quickly manned by three paras in each, Jorgensen and Melrose in one of them. The other seven SVs, which had been within the perimeter, were already deployed by Freeman, two on each flank inside the perimeter, two joining the two already outside, the four abreast, of necessity out of sight of each other in the thick smoke, racing toward at least twenty militia pickups somewhere ahead.

It was, as Freeman's paras were fond of saying, TAT—tight ass time—each man's sphincter contracted by the inescapable pressure of fear and anticipation. Any minute, any second, a shape could emerge and there would be a millisecond to decide friend or foe, small arms behind and in front of them subsiding for fear by both sides that they'd hit their respective war wagons. Which meant most of the action was now taking place on the flanks, where Nordstrom's vehicles, without their own troops behind them, had an advantage as they drove toward the dug-in paras who, like their comrades on the front, were holding fire for fear of hitting either of their Hummers, TOW ambulance, or SVs in the perimeter.

Freeman was on the radio only seconds after the smoke curtain had been laid. "V for Victor!" he shouted for all nine SV drivers to hear, an instruction that the paras knew meant breaking away in a V shape, each vehicle taking one side of the V, heading for the end points of the oncoming force, the latter numbering almost a hundred, about twenty-five militia vehicles allocated to all four sides of the federal perimeter. In this way the SVs on each side would escape the full force of a frontal attack in hopes of picking off the vehicles at each end of the oncoming militia line.

To the north it was successful, Jorgensen's Mark 19 automatic grenade launcher gun making its rapid choking noise, spitting out forty belted rounds. Immediately, the SV vehicle took a barrage of small arms fire, its armor, like the armored pickup, withstanding the rounds until three grenades flew into the militia's pickup. One grenade was quickly retrieved and heaved out by an alert militiaman, but the other two, lost in the dark and in a panic of scuffling feet, exploded. It was a blood-bath, one militiaman, his finger locked on his AK-47's trigger, involuntarily letting go a long burst that killed two of the six other already badly injured militiamen.

Jorgensen swerved hard left, felt a thud behind him, his M-60 machine gun beside him still firing at the pickup's cabin until both driver and co-driver were dead. Back in thick smoke at the western end of the pickup line, Jorgensen's machine gunner glanced behind to see what had hit them. Nothing had, at least nothing other than small arms fire that had struck their grenade gunner, the latter bleeding profusely, his body slumping during the hard turn. Melrose on the M-60 reached back, feeling for the man's carotid pulse. "He's dead," he told Jorgensen, whose infrared goggles now found a hole of visibility in the dissipating smoke. "Bogey ten o'clock!" he yelled. Melrose glimpsed the shape and fired, hearing his burst hitting the target. After six rounds the gun jammed. "Fuck!" He tried to clear, couldn't—the buffer spring broken. Punching his lap/chest/crotch harness release, he squeezed into the back, shouldered the dead grenade gunner aside, and took over the M-19. There was a loud curse as the two vehicles whipped by one another, Jorgensen realizing the short burst from his SV and now jammed M-60 had tattooed the side of another SV. A blue on blue—fortunately, without casualties.

Then he glimpsed a white blossom on the I.F.'s green background, the back-blast of an antitank missile. He heard it hit the SV they'd just passed, the vehicle somersaulting, its ammo cooking off, one of its paras crying in agony, the stench of burning oil filling the air. A hail of AK-47 fire punctured the tires of another strike vehicle—the tires self-sealers, but not after long, consecutive bursts of automatic fire at close range. The driver shoved it into overdrive and had it running on rims, but it proved too slippery despite the fact that the snow was only a few inches deep. Once the vehicle slowed, a militia Arpac missile, the same type used by Norman to kill the President and First Lady, took out the SV.

Now Jorgensen on the northern front figured there was only

his SV and the captured militia ambulance up front, loaded with six TOW rounds in its stretcher compartment. In fact, on the northern front only his SV had survived, the ambulance riddled by mobile AK-47 fire before its paras could get off a round.

Freeman ordered Jorgensen and whatever other SVs were left to return in the disappearing smoke to the perimeter, where Jorgensen found that all but one of the six SVs that had gone out on the flanks and rear had been taken out. It meant that Freeman now had only two SVs intact, over a third of his force killed or wounded, and the realization that all his *"L'audace"* had bought was the prevention of a mass frontal assault on his ever-shrinking perimeter.

On the plus side, his audacity in unexpectedly having his highly mobile SVs going on the attack against the slower moving militia force, despite his paratroopers being outnumbered by at least thirty to one, had discombobulated Nordstrom's offensive and bought Freeman's paras valuable time, for now federal land forces were on the way and more paras were loading at McChord. Still, Freeman knew these would be useless if his surviving paras could not hold the LZ open long enough.

The Everglades

Brentwood, Aussie, and the other six ALERTs in Romeo had to think fast. The wide, blunt prow of the big airboat was nosing farther out from the camouflage net into an hourglass-shaped stretch of waterway that fed into the main stream. Aussie, Brentwood, Bronx, Rosco, and the other four commandos realized they stood no chance in a firefight with the big boat whose "box," whatever it was, had completely denuded the hammock's vegetation in under a second. If they were to win, it would have to be an oblique attack—quick and deadly. Aussie had an idea, and with no time for explanation, he told Brentwood to take off his Draeger and surrender. Now, the result of all the years of training became apparent, not simply because the men—Rosco's acute allergic attack from the mos-

quitoes notwithstanding—were in Olympic physical condition, but because they were a consummate team. They were
willing, trained, *expected,* to give of themselves if the mission
or the team was at risk. Wordlessly, Brentwood unclipped the
Draeger rebreather and handed it to Rosco, Aussie slipping in
the mouthpiece of his own Draeger.

"Hold your fire!" Brentwood called out as he waded out in
the black water, made so by the silt runoff of the previous
night, his hands held high. "Don't shoot!"

The sound of an AK-47 burst charged through the undergrowth. "Rory! Goddammit, stop shootin'," the one they called
Leroi yelled. "I got 'im covered. He's comin' out from the narrow neck!"

"Might be more of 'em," Rory called out to the boss. "Can I
use the red sticks?"

"Maybe, but first I'd like to talk to this feller."

By now Aussie, having swapped his shotgun for another
ALERT's Heckler & Koch, and Rosco, using Brentwood's
Draeger, were submerged, wrists connected in the pitch-dark
water by a four-foot length of fishing line. Even with the morning sun beating down on it, only the top inch or so of the air-
water interface was visible as a dark band of cola-brown water,
present one second, gone the next. Bronx and the other four
ALERTs had retreated back down the mangle, crawling into
undergrowth by the hammock's shore, praying that the damn
"box" or whatever the hell it was wasn't going to be fired in
their direction.

CHAPTER FORTY-FOUR

Washington State

SO AS NOT to arouse any suspicions among the militia POWs, Schmidt made no changes in the number of guards he normally posted at Camp Fairchild. Instead he arranged for two platoons of federal troops from the Spokane National Guard to be trucked under cover of darkness to his administration building, one of the series of Quonset huts a quarter mile beyond the camp's main east gate. These additional troops would augment the thirty officially off-duty military policemen he'd armed and had ready to encircle Archie's exit, which, as Browne had estimated, was now well beyond the main wire. The breakout of more than one hundred militia, as Browne had informed him, was set for near midnight, when the vibration created by the usual changeover of guards all around the camp would cover the initial funneling of POWs from hut 5A into the tunnel. After that, any residual vibration that might trip a sensor close to 5A would be covered by a POW party, fueled by camp-made potato hooch, being thrown in huts 4A and 4B.

What was torturing Browne, alone in his cell, was whether Schmidt would take the escapees captive.

In Schmidt's office, Hearn was being interrogated again about Nordstrom. What did the militia leader look like? Hearn refused to cooperate. The man the prisoners called Thug put his hairy, beefy hands around the prisoner's neck, choking him. Gasping frantically for air and trying in vain in his weakened condition to pry Thug's hands free, Hearn lost consciousness, his body going slack. He was held upright, head lolling to one side, only because of the tautness of the ropes that bound him to the chair. A few minutes later, when he regained consciousness, he tried to speak, but couldn't.

"Give him some water," Schmidt commanded, and Thug's flunky, a man whom Hearn had heard addressed as O'Keefe, brought over a small, cone-shaped paper cup from the water cooler.

"You were going to say?" Schmidt pressed.

"No—" Hearn began with difficulty. "You wouldn't—"

He swallowed hard, and it obviously hurt him, but now, after days of Hearn's isolation and deprivation in the blockhouse, Schmidt finally sensed a breakthrough. "I wouldn't *what*?" he asked Hearn, trying not to sound eager.

"Wouldn't believe me." Hearn gulped greedily for air. "You'd think I was just making it up to—to stop this bastard beating the shit out of me."

Schmidt stared at his prisoner for a long time. "Try me."

"How do you—I need more water."

Schmidt nodded, and O'Keefe obediently ran across with another cup.

"Why do you think," Hearn began, "the militia was waiting for you feds at Astoria?" He was referring to the slaughter of the 82nd Airborne in and around the Columbia River mouth. "And your General Limet getting wasted up near Pateros? You think—" He signaled, paused, and sipped more water. "—you think the militia just happened to be there? In the middle of the fucking wilderness? Eh?" The "eh" was a tone higher, spat out with defiance despite the pain he was in, as if to say, "You jerk!"

There was a long silence. Schmidt may have been a sadist, but he wasn't stupid. "You're suggesting Nordstrom's one of us?"

"I'm not suggesting anything of the sort. I'm *telling* you."

There was another long silence before Schmidt would concede Hearn might have a point. "Who?"

"No fucking way." Thug moved closer. "This fucking goon touches me again, you'll never know—and that's a promise!"

Thug said, "Put a couple of alligator clips on your balls, Hearn, pass a current through, you'll eat my shit before I'm finished with you."

Hearn smiled crookedly despite the pain from his throat, now radiating high up into his temples, piercing and throbbing at the same time. "Yeah, I bet I would," he conceded, shifting his gaze toward Schmidt. "But your boss here—up on his dais—needs to know about Nordstrom *now* to make himself the big man in Washington before we push Freeman's outfit right out of the state."

Schmidt tried not to show surprise, but his eyes betrayed him and so he decided he might as well ask after all. "How do you know about Freeman?"

Hearn nodded in Thug's direction but kept looking at Schmidt. "This shit-for-brains gets bored in the blockhouse. Keeps his radio on KHQ—Spokane."

Schmidt's eyes didn't move from Hearn as he asked Thug, "Is this true?"

Thug hesitated. Schmidt, though no doubt having made a mental note of Thug's hesitation, still had his eyes on Hearn, repeating his original question. "*Who* is it?" Schmidt sat forward. "If you don't tell me, you'll be shot while attempting to escape."

Thug, eager to redeem himself with Schmidt, stepped forward and twisted Hearn's ear, jerking his head back. Hearn's face contorted in pain.

"Raython," he said, his voice barely audible. "Brigadier General Raython. C.O. of Fairchild." Hearn waited for a second before he delivered the coup de grace. "You know, the guy who's boning your wife."

Schmidt's face drained of color, his clasped hands turning white. He walked down from the dais and over to Hearn as if about to hit him, then hesitated, drew his pistol and smashed Hearn in the mouth—so hard that the Nazi's chair backflipped, his mouth bleeding profusely, three teeth missing.

Schmidt was breathing hard, as if he'd just worked out. He

pointed down at the Nazi. "You'll write out what you told me, and by God you'll—you'll sign it. Now."

Hearn tried to speak but was unintelligible as he attempted, unsuccessfully, to spit out a loose tooth.

"You'll write it out and you'll sign it," Schmidt repeated. "You hear me?" Hearn didn't answer. Schmidt kicked him in the testicles. "You hear me?"

Hearn's groaning filled the room, blood still pouring from his mouth. Hearn nodded affirmatively.

"Good," Schmidt proclaimed, suddenly switching his attention to Thug. "I'll deal with you later."

In a marked display of chutzpah, Hearn asked again for cigarettes.

"Give him one," Schmidt instructed O'Keefe. "And one only."

"Yes, sir."

Freeman was under no illusion that the militia had withdrawn. They were merely reconstituting themselves for what both he and Norton expected would be an all-out attack when the light of dawn and the better weather allowed Fairchild to launch a bombing run against Nordstrom's numerically superior forces. He looked around at the dozens of wounded and dead paratroopers and immediately called Ginger Olafson, one of the platoon commanders. Freeman told him to go out in a Hummer.

"Ours *are* out, General."

"Damn! We get any of those snowmobiles intact?"

"Yes, sir," Olafson said. "Three are in working order."

"All right. Take one of them—white flag. I want you to take a message to the militia." He hesitated. "You know how to ride one of those things?"

"Had one as a boy, General," Olafson replied. "Rode it all the time, though this snow's melting pretty fast. They won't go well if we hit gravel."

"Do your best."

"Yes, sir." Dawn was fast approaching, the sky changing from black to a deep, metallic gray.

"All right, Olafson. Now here's what I want you to do . . ."

It had occurred to Schmidt that Hearn, the murderer, might simply be making up the story about Raython. But if so, he thought, Hearn had taken a lot of unnecessary punishment for it.

Schmidt was in a quandary. In the federal military's pecking order, Brigadier General Raython was in the stratosphere, and he himself was well below. What's more, the fact that he was the cuckold in the affair would immediately make any move he made against Raython suspect. Yet if he did nothing, and if Raython was a Benedict Arnold, then the consequences for the federal forces could be disastrous. In addition, subsequent investigations by his own military police, or a congressional hearing, would prove him derelict in his duty if he failed to arrest Raython. He would be drummed out of the military police, the best job he'd ever had. Besides, underneath, he relished the idea of knocking Raython off his perch, to even the score. As for his wife, Schmidt knew what to do with her. He wouldn't touch her, wouldn't give her the slightest reason to charge him with assault so she could whine and get alimony. Instead, he'd destroy her lover. But the question of adultery could be kept out of it, Schmidt told himself, lest it embarrass him. The charge of conspiracy against the federal government was more than enough reason for him to take Raython into custody. MAJOR ARRESTS MILITIA LEADER would catapult the name Schmidt to national fame.

It would be claimed later that General Raython's staff got the tipoff from a hacker on the Internet. Others said it was one of the MP drivers calling a buddy. However he found out about Schmidt's impending arrest party, Raython acted quickly, ordering the base sealed off and "to let no one, repeat, *no one,* past the gate without my personally delivered permission. Deadly force authorized."

"Holy shit!" said one of the guards on Fairchild's main gate. "I haven't fired this fucking rifle in months."

"Well," the sergeant said wryly, "this could be your lucky day. Scuttlebutt is there's a bunch o' militia posing as MPs comin' to arrest Raython."

"You're shitting me?"

"That's what they say."

"Holy shit!"

What made the whole business even more eerie for the four guards on duty at the gate was that they could see the shapes of three Hummers outside Camp Fairchild, a quarter mile south, emerging ghostlike from the mist.

Freeman's messenger on the snowmobile, a large, white flag streaming from its high rear antenna, had a simple request for the forward elements of Nordstrom's army. It was a demand from General Freeman to surrender immediately to him or face annihilation.

The incredulous forward militia commanders relayed Freeman's demand to Colonel Vance, who told them he would in turn relay it to General Nordstrom. Within twenty minutes Vance, citing "General Nordstrom's headquarters" as his source, told General Freeman's emissary that it was General Freeman who needed to surrender to the militia or face annihilation.

When the federal emissary returned to Freeman, he could not refrain from asking the general whether he had really expected Nordstrom to surrender.

Freeman did not look up from his map but merely replied, "It bought us half an hour."

CHAPTER FORTY-FIVE

Everglades

"SIT Y'SELF DOWN," Leroi, a medium-size, thickset man with eyes that seemed half shut, told Brentwood amicably. "You're the first federal we've taken in the 'glades."

"Congratulations," Brentwood said. "I won't be the first you've killed." He could still see the bodies of Victor, cut to pieces, floating in the swamp water, raw meat for the gators.

"Now," the boss said, "who said anything 'bout killin' anybody?"

"'Least not right away," Rory said, four men behind him tying the boat closer in to a weather-beaten wharf made of sun-bleached hardwood, a scum from last night's high water eddying about the big twin-air-prop boat.

"Rory," Leroi said, "why don't you give your tongue a rest. 'Sides, this feller's got a clear choice. If he cooperates, we mightn't have to kill 'im." Brentwood was thinking hard—it was essential he try to distract them while Aussie and Rosco went about their business.

"What's that?" Brentwood asked, indicating the big black rectangular box amidships.

The boss smiled. "We call her Betsy. That right, Rory?"

"Yes, *sir.* Betsy knows what to do with federals."

It was as clear to Brentwood as the blue sky that they were going to try to extract information before shooting him. Still, despite the danger he was in, his natural curiosity, whetted by an ALERT's professional fascination with new weaponry, needed to be satisfied. "Laser?" he asked.

"Laser?" Leroi repeated. "Hell, no. This here's a prototype." With that, he removed a cover from the front of the black, rectangular box, the latter on a vertical and horizontal rotating plate so the box could traverse 360 degrees on the azimuth or horizontal plane, and vertically move through 180 degrees. Behind it there was a portable Yamaha generator. When the front of the box was removed, it revealed protuberances that Brentwood could see were the tips of gun barrels arranged in two rectangles, one set embedded in the top half of the box, the second rectangle of the same size on the bottom half, making for thirty-six barrels in all.

"Electrically driven!" boasted Rory Mason, Kozan's killer, who, Brentwood saw, had only one tooth. "Barrels are preloaded, y'see. Computer runs the firing." The latter fact surprised Brentwood as much as the drab, utilitarian design—a big, black box like a sea trunk. Brentwood had assumed from the militiamen's redneck manner and poor grammar that this gang would somehow be incapable of handling computerized equipment.

Brentwood's second mistake was to assume, as Aussie had, that upon his surrender and after the slaughter of Victor, the militiamen would give up their search of the area. However, a patrol of at least seven heavily armed militiamen with "red sticks"—dynamite—now left to comb the bank opposite the one where Victor had been gunned down. Brentwood could only hope Romeo's five ALERTs, apart from Aussie and Rosco, had hidden themselves so close to the earth that their faces were in the mud.

The other thing that dawned on Brentwood was that even with the patrol of seven militiamen, the total enemy count was around fourteen. From the terrible slaughter this weapon had exacted upon the Tampa National Guard and the ALERTs, he, like the others, had assumed a much larger number of militia would be present, which made him even more curious about the weapon. He knew there was no way the militia would release him, even in a one-for-one militia/federal exchange, now that he had seen their weapon—unless Aussie and Rosco could bring it off. Still, he asked, "What's its rate of fire?"

"Prototype came out in nineteen hundred an' ninety-six," Leroi said proudly. "Made by a company down under. Metal Storm."

"You don't say," Brentwood said.

"We do say," Rory jumped in.

"Shut up, Rory," Leroi said, still watching Brentwood. "You ready for this, boy?" he asked. "Them Mark 5 thirty-six barrels fire *one point one million* rounds a minute." He paused for effect. " 'Case your 'rithmetic is a little rusty, that's over sixteen thousand rounds a *second*, boy. A second fills the air with so much hot lead you think you're standing outside a blast furnace. Biggest problem we got is keeping enough ammo. You see those choppers we shot down? Metal Storm evaporated the sumbitch."

Brentwood was trying to act nonchalant, but inside he could feel his gut knot up. He'd heard whispers about this Australian gun in the late 1990s, but that was all. If ever the militia at large, across the country, got hold of this kind of weapon . . .

He *did* remember the choppers going down and the massive kill rate inflicted upon Colonel Armani's National Guard. *Kill rate?* It had wiped them out in seconds. And the tremendous blast of heat when he'd lost Victor Two. Still, damned if he would give the militia the satisfaction of knowing he was truly awed by the weapon. Its possibilities for the federal forces were equally awesome.

"Not bad," he said easily.

"Not *bad*. You hear him, Rory? Not *bad*. Son, with this little baby we can rule the roost. Hell, there ain't no moving parts. Barrels are preloaded. Hell!"

"Rule the roost!" Rory said.

Swimming submerged in the pitch-black water, weighed down by their Heckler & Koch submachine guns and Draeger rebreathers, Aussie and Rosco knew they had reached the big boat when Rosco's elbow touched it, but having submerged before the boat was tied in closer, they had no way of knowing whether it was tethered to the shore or held by anchor. If the latter, then the current could well have slewed the boat around from its original position so that now the bow could be where the stern had been. The fishing line still tethering them several feet apart, Aussie tapped and squeezed Rosco's wrist, their "Search vessel bottom" signal. Feeling their way, they eased themselves under the boat's flat bottom. Again strictly by feel, Aussie placed a palm-sized, half-spherical-shaped magnet midships, which would provide them with a reference point in their dark world. The water was made even murkier by the action of their fins. No matter how gently they were used, the ALERTs' swimming stirred up even more silt from the gooey, peat-based swamp bottom.

They felt around for the stern. It was important that they place the C-4 plastique charge there, where damage to the two big air props would immobilize the boat more than a charge placed midships, where a charge might blow a sizable hole in the aluminum boat, but a hole could be mended. Without the two big air propellers, however, the boat couldn't move. Both men knew that the tricky bit would be to give Brentwood time to get away before the charge they now set would blow. First they would have to get ashore or at least close to it, well away from the explosion, so they could give him the signal and immediately provide covering fire to provide those vital seconds in which to somehow escape the blast.

As he set the timer, again by feel, unable to see an inch in front of his face, Aussie coolly remembered how earlier one of the militia had referred to the commander as the boss, who had answered, "Shut up, Rory!"

"Rule one in combat, gentlemen," the ALERT instructors had pointed out. "Never call one another by name. It's fucking dangerous. Many a Jap sniper got his Aussie or Yank by listening for names. Ditto in Korea. Ditto 'Nam."

"How 'bout the Gulf War, Sarge?" a young soldier asked. "Didn't get fucking close enough."

Once Aussie and Rosco had placed the C-4 plastique underneath the stern, they swam, still tethered together by the length of fishing line, then moved away from the boat toward the hammock directly behind the big boat. There, surfacing quietly beneath the deep shadow cast by the camouflage net, overhanging vegetation, and a mangle of tap roots, they could see the two big eight-foot-diameter air props in their protective cage like two enormous electric fans. The boat was moored to the narrow rickety-looking hardwood jetty at the hammock's edge.

They could see only a part of the waterway downstream where it narrowed, the boat blocking most of the view. And though they could see the one called Rory and got a glimpse of the boss, Leroi, and the big, black, boxlike rectangular weapon, they were unable to see Brentwood. He must be on the port side of the big boat, hidden from their view by the box. Beyond the jetty, the remaining five men of Romeo were lying low so as not to be seen by the militia search party. It was then that Rosco spotted one of the search party returning. He'd seen the man for only a fraction of a second. He tapped Aussie's wrist and pointed to his right at about two o'clock, three o'clock if you were on the boat, whispering, "Militia." Without hesitation Aussie shouted toward the big boat thirty feet in front of them. "Rory—federals three o'clock!" They could hear feet running on the aluminum boat, the boss yelling, "Swing 'er, Rory! Swing 'er!"

The black box moved quickly right and fired. The noise was like nothing Aussie or Rosco had ever heard, like a million pieces of linoleum being ripped simultaneously, the heat all but unbearable, with the result that the militia search party was wiped out. "Mincemeat," as Aussie would riposte.

Rosco now tossed two smoke grenades onto the boat, and it was up to Brentwood to use his initiative to get off the boat, to realize that if his comrades were that close, the boat must now be mined.

One minute later the charge under the boat's stern blew in an enormous, purplish, ear-ringing explosion that killed Leroi and Kozan's murderer outright, its concussion throwing green sheets of slime aloft and creating a huge tsunamilike wave that washed over the nearby jungle and the five ALERTs, the boat itself leaping into the air, ripping out its tether lines as if they were string. A gash six feet across and four high sank the boat in the deep hole immediately. For this, Aussie, Rosco, and Brentwood would find themselves in trouble with the Pentagon because they failed to save the prototype Metal Storm gun.

It wasn't that they didn't try. David Brentwood, who'd jumped ship moments before the explosion, had helped Rosco and Aussie to quickly improvise a grappling hook with what had been the boat's tether lines to attach to the sinking black gun box. But like the wreckage of the Valujet back in '96, the boat, including the bodies aboard it, was rapidly sucked down into the black peat and silt. Metal Storm, despite the Herculean efforts of the five remaining ALERTs, sank without a trace.

As Aussie dropped a purple smoke for helo pickup, he half expected the chopper to be blown out of the air by another black gun, but as the late boss, Leroi, had boasted to Brentwood, the Metal Storm was the only Australian supergun the militia had. *For now.*

As the eight ALERTs, including Rosco, Brentwood, Bronx, and Aussie, were extracted by "dangle rope," Aussie heard Brentwood yelling something to him, but he couldn't hear exactly what because of the chopper's noise.

"What'd you say?" he asked Brentwood as they touched down on the levee, crouching beneath the roar of the Huey.

"I said thank God they had only one of those guns."

CHAPTER FORTY-SIX

Camp Fairchild

ELEEN WAS GOING over the final details. God is in the details, he thought. All the POWs' money and driver's licenses had been confiscated by the federals along with social security cards. In some cases the guards had also taken away the "allergic reaction" medical cards from POWs for no other reason than a POW's less than enthusiastic surrender. Organ donor cards, however, were not taken because if some fatal accident should befall a POW while playing ball in the inclement weather, or if they were shot "while attempting to escape," the POW would provide a ready source of spare parts for surgeons in the MASH units operating on severely wounded federal soldiers.

Precisely when he didn't want it to, Eleen's latent self-doubt about having left Rubinski behind at Packwood began to haunt him again. It was because he was anxious about the impending breakout. It was a free-floating anxiety ready to attach itself to anything, any detail that might have been overlooked. He was sorry, as was Sergeant Mead and others, about Browne, who would have to be left behind in solitary, but they couldn't postpone the escape timetable for one man. Besides, he thought, Browne ought to have known better than to deliberately bait the goons. Hearn too would have to be left behind, though Eleen didn't have regrets about him. Though Eleen's Mormon scriptures taught him there was some good even in the most evil man, it was hard to forgive a man like Hearn. A self-confessed Nazi, he had murdered people, and so in his opinion deserved imprisonment even if people like General Nordstrom tried to use him as another militia hero, à la Randy Weaver. Weaver had fought in self-defense, protecting his family. Hearn had killed for the pleasure of it. So far as Eleen was concerned, Hearn deserved Hell.

Eleen asked Mead if everything was set.

"Yes, sir," Mead told him for the third time that hour.

"Air supply? It's going to be crowded down there."

"The bellows are fine, sir. I've got a backup if the squeeze box ruptures. Don't worry. There'll be enough air."

Eleen was frowning. "I'm worried about the money situation—or I should say, the lack of it. Once out, our boys won't be able to pay for a meal, a bus—anything."

"Sir, I don't think there's a militiaman in this camp who doesn't know how to hot wire a vehicle—or knock off a grocery store."

Eleen winced. Yes, he knew it would have to be done for survival in the sparsely populated wilds of eastern Washington, but he was a soldier, and the thought of his men having to stoop to the practices of a common thief, no matter what the reason, bothered his conscience. Still, he saw no other way. As in any other army, it was every militiaman's duty to escape, to create as much trouble as possible for the enemy. If he could get at least a hundred men out, it would tie up thousands of federal troops trying to hunt them down. And in the TV propaganda world, the federal humiliation alone would be worth it. The President of the most powerful country in the world had been assuring the world he was in control. A massive POW escape on top of what the POWs were sure would be Nordstrom's victory against Freeman on the Odessa-Sprague front would be wonderful P.R.

"Clothing?" Eleen inquired.

"Nobody's gonna die of exposure, sir."

"It's unusually cold," Eleen countered. "World's weather's gone to pot." He was thinking of Korea, of his grandfather and the other Marines retreating in the awful cold from the Chosin Reservoir.

"Sir," Mead reassured him, "nobody's gonna die of hypothermia. Most of our boys are from this state. They know their way around. And per your instructions, those who are from out of state have been paired with a guy from in state."

Eleen allowed himself a nod of satisfaction. But you never knew, could never be sure. What if Schmidt or one of his goons stumbled upon Archie in the next few hours?

"Don't sweat it, sir. Soon as it's dark we move, before the goons' vision is acclimated to the loss of light. Tomorrow morning, sir, when he comes out for roll call, Schmidt's gonna have a fuck—gonna have a heart attack!"

The moment he'd finished his blockhouse "confession," Hearn, still recovering from the beating, signed the document. He signed without his usual flourish, but he did draw, albeit shakily, a swastika below. Desultorily he pushed the document forward on the rickety bridge table, and without a word O'Keefe snatched it up as if there was a chance Hearn would suddenly rescind the confession. O'Keefe was about to leave the cell when Hearn called out through bloodied teeth, "Hey, how 'bout that cigarette?"

O'Keefe pulled a packet of Camels from his top pocket, didn't offer Hearn the pack. Instead, as per Schmidt's instructions, he very deliberately extracted one cigarette and tossed it onto the bridge table.

"How 'bout a light?"

O'Keefe patted his pocket for a packet of matches, tore a match off, and readied to strike it.

"Leave it here," Hearn said.

"Can't leave a prisoner with a match."

"Shit, you think I'm gonna set fire to myself?"

"Wish you would," O'Keefe said. He struck the match and held it in front of Hearn. "Now or never, Hearn."

Hearn took the light, O'Keefe shook out the match and left, slamming the cell door.

Hearn's hands were still unsteady. Although the bridge table was light, Hearn still had difficulty because of pain from the beating when he moved the table over next to the wall. But that was the easy part. Getting up on the table was excruciating, and it was only after several attempts that he made it. Now he could glimpse out the small, barred six-inch-square window. Hearn thought that it would almost have been better to have no window, the latter offering no hope of escape, its patch of gray light on this foggy day more of a torment to a prisoner than if the cell had been completely dark.

Through this high window he could see several of the barracks, dark shadows wreathed in fog, but he knew that Camp Fairchild's main east gate directly behind the blockhouse was being watched at all times by POW lookouts to warn the camp of approaching goons. He knew the lookouts would be particularly alert in view of the escape at midnight, barely twelve hours away. Hearn's every breath was painful. He was convinced Thug or Schmidt had broken one of his ribs. Nevertheless he willed himself to be as steady as possible, holding the cigarette in his mouth in the middle of the small window. He sucked hard on the cigarette.

Several lookouts saw the pinpoint of red light. "Hey, who's that?"

"Must be Browne or that guy Hearn."

"He must have cigarettes," one lookout commented to another. "How the hell would he get that in solitary?"

"Schmidt must be getting soft. Must have given him a chair or somethin' to be that high up."

"Maybe Browne's grown."

Eleen was told about it and immediately guessed what the other POWs had been slower to pick up. "He might be trying to signal. Mead?"

"Sir?"

"Get a spotter who reads Morse. Check it out, just in case. Quickly!"

The more the lookouts watched, the more they saw that Eleen was right. The red dot of the cigarette was appearing and reappearing at what seemed timed intervals.

Hearn was worried. The cigarette had now burned away half its length.

Finally, a Morse spotter, an ex–Coast Guard militiaman, arrived at 5A and watched the dots and dashes of the red cigarette end. The message as he relayed it to Eleen and other expectant listeners crammed into 5A was short and devastating: Archie blown.

"Damn!" Eleen said. "Damn damn damn!" It was as if God had gone over to the enemy.

A massive wave of depression swept through the camp. Browne had been proven right, after all, to have been worried about the possibility of an informer in their midst. He'd told Eleen that Schmidt was up to something when he'd moved into the compound with his goons and confiscated the radio-aerial-cum-washing-line.

Eleen went to the makeshift chapel in the annex of 6B and prayed, first for forgiveness for having allowed himself to think that the Almighty was on the enemy's side, and second for guidance in what he should do. Deep in thought, he recalled his granddad and the Marines at Chosin: they hadn't given up. If Schmidt knew about Archie, he'd be careful not to show his hand until the time of the actual escape, and the fact that he hadn't closed Archie meant that come midnight he wanted to shoot as many POWs as possible.

Eleen's answer, he believed, came from the Lord. It was breathtakingly audacious—and dangerous, the kind of thing Eleen knew that the federals would expect of their flashy General Freeman but not of the militia. He called for an immediate meeting of the escape committee.

"We're going to use this bad weather to our advantage," he informed them. "The fog."

They waited.

"We're going to escape *today*—beat Schmidt to the punch by at least twelve hours. Fog'll give good cover."

"Jesus!" one of the escape committee said. "That's dangerous."

"So is life," Eleen replied evenly. "Any man wants out—
doesn't want to risk it—I'll understand."

Four men looked as if they'd decline, then changed their
minds. They'd go.

"Right!" Eleen said, exhibiting a newfound confidence that,
real or not, he knew he had to instill in his men. "Mead, get
Johnny Frost in 6C to put on one hell of a ball game immediately after noon."

"How about the fog, sir? Mightn't be able to see past first
base."

"Then arrange something else," Eleen said sharply. "Just so
long as there's enough noise to distract the goons."

"Roger that," Mead said.

Roger that? Sometimes Mead sounded like a dyed-in-the-
wool federal.

Eleen was thanking God for the fact that Schmidt had apparently left the camp with a party of goons on some special
hush-hush mission to Fairchild Air Force Base. Perhaps, with the
weather promising to clear later that day, he confided to Mead,
the federals were going to send planes up to bomb Nordstrom's
force before the land force coming from Fort Lewis could re-
inforce Freeman on the Odessa-Sprague front.

"I don't know what they're up to," Mead answered sharply,
too sharply even for Eleen, who was one militia officer who
didn't stand on ceremony but expected civility.

"Sorry sir," Mead apologized before Eleen could upbraid
him. "But I figure as long as Schmidt's out of the camp, it's
good news for us. Doesn't matter why."

"Yes," Eleen answered. "You're right." Everyone was on
edge. "How many have we got down Archie now?"

"Last count, twenty-three."

"Slow?"

"Not really. Bit of a squash down there with all their cold
weather gear and whatever extra rations they've managed to
scrounge from the meal trucks. And we had to replace Browne
on the bellows. Takes a little while to get the right push-pull

rhythm. If you don't, you drive the other guy nuts. Plus every time the fog thins out, the tunnel master'll have to hold them at the exit."

"Are any out yet?"

"No. First guy in line is from 5B."

"Do I know him?" Eleen asked, and immediately regretted it. Better not to know him if anything went wrong.

"Avery," Mead said before Eleen could stop him. "Machine gunner from the Moses Lake chapter."

"How many do you think will go join Nordstrom?"

Mead shrugged. "No way of telling. Lot of 'em want to strike back. Feel pretty ashamed of being here. Something I guess the public doesn't understand."

"I understand," Eleen said, and had a flashback of Rubinski. "I hope Nordstrom beats the crap out of Freeman."

Mead hid his surprise. *Beats the crap* wasn't this Mormon's style.

"It's going to be a horse race," Mead replied, "whether Nordstrom can overrun 'em before that crowd from Fort Lewis reaches Freeman."

While they'd been talking, the fog had rolled in, and now not even the perimeter of the air base could be seen. Mead glanced at his watch. "Avery should be knocking out the crust now." By this he meant the thin and final layer of grassy earth at the tunnel's exit that would have to be caved in by Avery's trowel.

"Sorry, sir," the base's guard sergeant told Schmidt and his posse. "We can't let you through. Base commander's orders."

"I'm here under orders of the Joint Chiefs!" Schmidt thundered.

"Major, sir—with respect—I don't care if you're Jesus Christ. You can't come on the base."

Schmidt was about to give an order to his MPs but heard the six base guards chambering rounds in their M-16s. "I'll be back!" Schmidt assured the sergeant.

The sergeant said nothing, his eyes still meeting Schmidt's, his thumb on the safety.

As Schmidt's MPs returned to their Hummers, he made a show of impatiently stabbing numbers on his cell phone as if he was immediately reporting to higher authority. "Damn batteries!" he muttered. In fact there was nothing wrong with the batteries. He was trying not to lose more face than he already had. He needed time to think.

"Where to, sir?" his driver asked.

"The camp—where else?"

When the lookout in 5B glimpsed Schmidt's convoy of three Hummers, bristling with weapons, coming back through the fog toward the camp's main east gate, he panicked, and what should have been a "Goons approaching camp" warning was quickly elevated to "Goons *in* the camp" and was passed on to Archie's lookout. A man about to enter the tunnel was hauled back, the trapdoor closed, wash stand atop it, several men already in place standing over it, attentively washing underwear and shirts. Immediately below the trap door the bellows stopped and the first string of grease candles at the ten-foot intervals in the tunnel was extinguished. Amongst the borderline claustrophobics—those prisoners of war who could bear the confined space only so long as they kept moving toward an exit, the latter now also closed—panic broke out and spread like an instantaneous contagion, and with it rumor: "The goons have found Archie!" "Goons at the exit!" "Goons at the bellows!" Goons were reported "bayoneting" the POWs who had just gotten out. Someone started yelling, "Let me out! Let me out!"

"Shut up!"

"Let me out! Let—"

"Shut the fuck up! Goons'll hear you."

"Fucking goons are here already—let the fucker yell."

"Let me out of here! I can't breathe—I can't breathe!"

Somebody punched him. He kicked back, smashing the nose of the man behind him. *"Let me out!"*

"Shut up, you rat!"

Five men back, a POW started with fright. "There's fucking rats! I can't stand—"

"Open the fucking trapdoor." "Who's on bellows?" "No one, you dork. Goddamn goons've pulled 'em out."

"Light the candles, for Christ's sake! Calm down, for Christ's sake. CALM DOWN!"

"Don't use the Lord's name in—"

"Fuck you!"

"Get out, man!" They were shouting at the man crouching by the exit—Avery. He hesitated. The man behind pushed him. "Go on, get out!" There wasn't enough room to pass by him. Finally, the man gingerly stood up on the ledge of earth formed below the exit and, looking about, seeing nothing but fog, hesitated again. This time the man behind punched him in the butt, hissing, "Go, you bastard!"

By the time Schmidt's Hummer had stopped by the gate, discharging the MPs at the guard hut, another forty-six men were out—for a total of seventy—before the fog thinned. Several of the most claustrophobic men in the tunnel were on the edge, or already in the pit, of nervous collapse because of the delay. It took several minutes for the men at the bellows to restore something like calm, passing down two precious flashlights and word that the goons had not unearthed the tunnel.

Afterward, a man in a gray Army jogging suit—no one in the camp had seen him before—approached the vicinity of the tunnel's exit. It was PFC Lapinski, a federal soldier, who decided that this would be his first day of a diet/exercise plan, lest he be fined by the Army at his annual physical for being overweight. As the jogger emerged from the fog, the lookout, "Gene" Autry, the man who'd bet his buddy Marty that Eleen would crack under pressure at Archie's exit, saw the jogger approaching, but before he could hide, the jogger saw him and the exit hole. Autry, drawing his knife, ran at Lapinski, who began yelling and running back parallel to the high barbed-wire fence of the camp, toward the nearest guard tower, fifty yards away and hidden by the fog. Unfazed, or at least not showing any signs of panic, Archie's exit boss calmly kept urging men to keep going, patting each one fatherly as they took the step up into the welcome damp air of freedom. "Go boy! Go!" he repeated as another nineteen emerged from the dark tunnel into the fog.

Eleen was the last of the sixty-six POWs waiting in 5A when the siren began wailing and a lot of shouting could be heard beyond the wire, the sound of several Hummers and three-ton trucks bouncing and gunning their engines amid the sagebushes. With the federals' nerves taut and expectant, the bushes looked like men crouching in the fog, some of them becoming the target of sporadic, nervous machine-gun and rifle fire.

There was confusion on both sides, and in the melee of fog, shouting, and mistakes, a Hummer was lost to a group of escaped militia. Armed and donning the helmets of the guards they'd taken prisoner, the escapees performed one of the most unselfish acts of the breakout when, instead of driving off, they drove to the nearest guard tower and, using one of the captured guards as a shield, sent two of their fellow POWs up the ladder to disarm and take over the tower. With a federal hostage in this tower and another federal from the tower now held hostage on the hood of their Hummer, a militiaman announced over the P.A. system that the main gate was about to be opened. By now Autry, unable to catch the jogger, had been cut down by one of Schmidt's returning MPs.

Schmidt was certain that somehow Brigadier General Raython had instigated and engineered the breakout earlier than expected to foil his attempt to arrest him, catching him and his guards, who'd just returned from the air base, off guard. Given the timing, there was no other possible explanation.

When Schmidt saw not one, but two, POW-occupied Hummers coming through the fog with some of his men held hostage on the vehicles, he was livid. He snatched his cell phone from its holster and instructed the main gate's guards to open fire on the Hummers.

"Sir, they've got our boys as hostages," one of the guards replied.

"I said open fire!"

They wouldn't. The front Hummer had one of the claustrophobes as driver. He was intent on redeeming himself for his panic in the tunnel and didn't wait for the gate to be opened. Instead, he rammed it, smashing it off its hinges as throngs of militia from all parts of the huge camp poured toward the gate, cheering.

If Eleen hadn't grabbed the mike of the bullhorn thrown down inside the wire from the captured tower, the massive breakout above the tunnel might well have degenerated into a riot of destruction, of pent-up emotions run amok. But seeing his opportunity, he seized the moment to galvanize the over five hundred escaping POWs into a fighting force, rather than a mob. A few minutes later the five hundred, with a vanguard of arms and Hummers taken from the hostage-induced surrender of more federal guards—and now with more federal hostages, including Schmidt—advanced at speed through the fog toward the heart of the air base, a few miles away.

Upon being told that "a battalion-sized force—probably more than a thousand" militia POWs—were on the rampage and approaching, Brigadier General Raython put the base on DEFCON Five, the highest defense condition, and ordered all plane "cells"—clusters of three bombers each—put into defense groups of up to six, and even nine, planes, rather than leaving them on the tarmac like a row of ducks. It was Raython's intention to concentrate the firepower of his base security guards around the group of planes rather than spread them thinly along the tarmacs, able to guard a plane with only two men apiece. It was, however, a potentially dangerous "Pearl Harbor" mistake, for while it did concentrate Raython's limited firepower around the groups of planes, if just one lucky militia round ignited one aircraft, all those parked so close together might be lost.

The militia's ETA at the air base, said base security, was in five minutes time. Brigadier General Raython told his men to ignore federal looking MPs, as they were, albeit unwittingly, traitors. The appearance of hostages would be just that—hostages—a careful ploy by a deranged colonel, who thought General Raython was Nordstrom, to take over the base.

Because of its weight, twenty-five tons, only one TOW-equipped Bradley Fighting Vehicle, an MK-3 cavalry-carrying vehicle, was dropped to Freeman's force. Its crew was ordered by Freeman to stand ready to run interference and to be on the same radio frequency as six of his paratroopers.

Jorgensen and Melrose, in the most forward foxholes, now reported another line of armored militia vehicles advancing in the cold, cloudy dawn. Snowflakes began to fall.

"Shit!" Jorgensen complained. "Goddamn met officers. They don't know dick. No close air support for us now."

"Hooray!" Melrose countered. "No CAS for them either."

"They haven't got any planes anyway."

"Don't care, man. It's still better for us. I'd rather be dug in than moving."

"We'll see."

On the Odessa-Sprague front the reassembled militia lines at 2300 yards were still beyond the maximum effective range of most of Freeman's small arms, and for a moment it looked as if the militia had stopped. It was an illusion—the militia's vehicles and troops merely spreading out to deny Freeman's dug-in force concentrated targets. The militia's armored pickups were leading, their heavy .50-caliber machine guns spitting fire beneath the slowly clearing overcast, though there was the smell of rain in the air, a strangely purifying smell given the carnage of bodies and machines that already littered the battlefield from Nordstrom's first attempt.

The area immediately around Freeman's force, smelling of battle, was even messier, strewn with the remains of hastily ripped ammunition and grenade boxes, discarded mortar-round tubes, and scattered chutes that paras had had no time to bury and that were now blowing ghostlike across the melting snow. Destroyed Hummers continued to burn, sending thick, black plumes of smoke curling high into the cold air. Amid all this were the dead, some identifiable, some not, heads and dog tags and limbs missing, the snow dirtied by cordite and stained with blood. Each man knew that Nordstrom's troops had now made their first run and gauged just how few of them there were. And they knew that in this militia attack, Nordstrom would throw everything he had at them, including the "reserves," a euphemism for the more fanatical elements of the militia. Nordstrom would either have to quickly triumph in order to hold his enemies hostage against the Fort Lewis force, or he would have to withdraw in haste, given the fact that the land force from Fort Lewis would soon arrive.

Nordstrom's force outnumbered them by more than forty to one. Freeman estimated that despite the occasional incident along the way, the major battle would be joined in less than five minutes. Then Freeman saw six of the pickups racing out in front of the others, their speed throwing up a mixture of dirt and snow as they fired their .50s from the ring mounts atop their canopies to keep the paratroopers' heads down. They drove in S patterns, popping flares and smoke.

"What the hell?" Jorgensen began. "It's not dark!"

"It's to dummy off heat-seekers."

"M-19s!" a sergeant shouted, and in half a dozen trenches paras checked to see that their M-19s were loaded with grenades from their weapons' underslung barrels.

"Hold your fire."

The paras had expected the pickups to emerge in the next few seconds from the smoke cloud that covered their front. Finally they came through, but without drivers or gunners.

"My God," Norton said, but Freeman beat him to the punch. "Radio controlled." In retrospect, it was an unwarranted assumption by the federals to assume that they were the only ones equipped with technology's magic tricks. After all, many of the militia had been in the U.S. armed forces once upon a time. The paras weren't ready for six radio-controlled pickups full of explosives racing toward them at over seventy miles an hour. "Sparks!" Freeman yelled. "Can you jam their frequencies?"

"Negative, sir."

"Shit!"

"Tires!" a sergeant shouted. It was an unnecessary order, for the men were already firing their valuable ammunition supplies at the tires, as well as the engines. One pickup's front tires blew, there was a rapid uncoiling of rubber, and the vehicle flipped. Gasoline was awash, darkening the snow, the truck's other three tires still spinning.

"We need more ammo, sir!" a sergeant yelled. "Badly!"

Freeman was already in contact with the transports overhead, which reported that they'd have no more ammunition until more transports arrived. They only had MRE field rations, water, and gasoline blivets, or bladders, which had been meant to fuel the now destroyed Hummers.

"Jesus Christ!" Freeman exploded. "Arnheim!" he shouted at Norton.

His voice was barely audible in the cacophony of grenade explosions, rapid small arms fire, and the steady *thoomp!* of 60mm mortar rounds being fired, and then the explosions. All the while the slapping sound of militia bullets streaked over their HQ trench by the abandoned and quietly burning Hummer. Norton had known exactly what Freeman meant when, as a measure of his frustration, the general had called out, "Arnhem!" That had been a savagely fought British paratroop offensive against the Nazis in World War II. The Royale Air Force had dropped a huge canister of ammunition to the desperate Brits. A para ran out under heavy German fire—to the cheers of his comrades—to retrieve the canister, before he was shot dead. The top of the canister came off, the new para's beret blown about the battlefield. The British had lost.

"Norton?"

"General."

"Get the head air jockey on the blower and tell him . . ."

Norton had to lean close to the general to hear his plan, the din of battle increasing as more pickups were reported emerging from the smoke, coming on behind the first—driverless or not, no one was sure. Either way, they knew that Nordstrom's men would soon be upon them, swarming behind their mobile screen.

"Left flank!" a para yelled, "ten o'clock."

Jorgensen swung his M-16 around, facing west-northwest, the steam from his barrel rising up to mingle with the militia's smoke cover, which was slowly clearing in the still air.

Eleen barely saw the strands of razor wire along the base's periphery, his Hummer bouncing at fifty miles an hour over a fold of earth. Intuitively, the driver slowed.

"Go through it!" Eleen ordered, and the next instant there was a frantic scratching noise as the Hummer bashed through to the tarmac of the air base, a coil of wire dragging behind it like a thornbush, sparks dancing wildly. The Hummer's tires, though pierced, kept going. The .50 caliber atop the vehicle spat out a deadly one-in-four stream of red tracer. But while tracer tells the shooter where his bullets are going, it also reveals his position to those at the target—in this case, a group of air base defenders behind a barricade of three Hummers. A burst from the barricade hit Eleen's driver, the vehicle skidding, flipping over, and sliding on an oil patch slickened by the damp fog.

Back in the POW camp, only a handful of prisoners remained, too ill or incapacitated to be moved. Two POWs had voluntarily stayed behind to look after them. Now they ran to the blockhouse with two M-16s taken from the dead tower guards. Pretending they had a much larger force at their disposal, they hammered on the door and gave Thug and O'Keefe two minutes to give themselves up. The two guards quickly complied. Thug figured that if things got nasty, he could save his skin by telling the militia who had betrayed their tunnel to Schmidt, and that the Nazi, Hearn, had broken under interrogation to reveal that Nordstrom was none other than Brigadier General Raython.

When they emerged, nervous, hands held high, there was a concerted cry from the remaining POWs to shoot Thug, because of his brutality toward them. In fact, the condition of several of the incapacitated POWs could be attributed to him. One man, Sammy Wong, had had his leg broken in two places by Thug, and a cattle prod had been applied to his testicles during an interrogation.

Marty, lookout Gene Autry's buddy, who did not yet know of Autry's death, cautioned the gathering crowd against holding a kangaroo court, telling them, "He'll have to go before a militia court-martial."

"Fuck the courts—" one man began, but he didn't finish, his mouth agape as a tall, sallow-looking POW stepped out of the crowd and plunged an aluminum shiv into Thug's chest, blood spurting from the guard's pierced heart. In vain, Thug, eyes huge with terror and surprise, gripped the shiv and tried to pull it out. No one helped him as he fell back, crunching the dirty snow, the smell of excrement in the air as he lost all control of excretory functions. "Browne—" he gasped, "told us— Archie—" and then he was dead, eyes still huge, staring at the gray sky.

The other captor turned to Browne. "That true?"

"Yes," Hearn said.

"No," Browne said. "That's a lie." But his face was ashen with guilt.

Another POW, a sergeant, angrily turned to Hearn. "You sure?"

Hearn nodded. "I signaled your lookouts with a cigarette. 'Archie blown.' "

The POW sergeant pulled the trigger and Browne was knocked back, dead before he even hit the ground.

There was steam and the smell of urine rising from the snow where O'Keefe stood. He was pleading for his life.

"I didn't . . . didn't do anything."

"Yeah," one of the sick POWs, a man with a cane, said. "Just following orders, right?"

"Yes," O'Keefe said. "Yes!" His body was rigid with fear.

"Don't listen to this bastard!" Hearn intoned. "He beat the shit out of Browne and others I saw interrogated."

Then a gift for Hearn came from heaven as one of the disabled POWs chimed in, "Yeah, he's the one who did me!" It was later found that the man—who had poor eyesight to begin with—had had his glasses smashed during an interrogation. He ID'd the wrong man—it wasn't O'Keefe who'd beaten him. But mob justice—emotion, not reason—was in charge.

O'Keefe bolted, and several POWs dragged him back, shoving him hard up against the blockhouse wall and giving his accuser an M-16. He was so close to O'Keefe that even with his poor eyesight, he couldn't miss. The burst thudded into O'Keefe's chest.

At the air base, Eleen was trapped upside down in the Hummer. The gunner, in severe pain from a ricochet that had opened his right arm, was working his way through the rear left side window, lowering himself to the tarmac. Smelling gasoline, he pulled and jerked the jammed seat belt harness, trying to free Eleen, not realizing that it was this delay that probably saved his and Eleen's lives. The federal defenders, once they'd seen the militia-occupied Hummer flip over, turned their attention to the other half-dozen or so military Hummers from the camp. These were now speeding down the runway in two lines of three, each with its .50 caliber machine gun in the ring turret and M-16 or M-60 from the passenger's window blasting away at the bunched-up planes on their side of the tarmac.

One of the Hummers was hit in the gas tank by federal M-16 fire and exploded, its militia driver and two gunners gunned down as they exited the vehicle.

It was inevitable that one of the parked planes that could be used against Nordstrom's force once the weather cleared would be hit—in this instance one of the huge B-52s. At first its fuselage soaked up the tracer fire like some gigantic black sponge. Finally, its wing was raked with red tracer fire from one of the Hummers and it erupted in flame, its burning avgas raining down upon the other aircraft in the group.

None of the men fighting on the tarmac had ever seen a train of explosions like it. Plane after plane exploded in flames that leapt hundreds of feet into the air, evaporating the fog, the waves of heat suffocating militia and federal forces alike, though most of the victims were federals in near proximity, as great gulps of oxygen were consumed by the conflagration. Soon two other groups, one of six planes, one of four—B-52s and several F-18s—blew.

Eleen, freed by his gunner and assisted by several POWs, was helping to right the Hummer when he saw a small clump of B-52s, three, possibly four—he couldn't be sure—parked at the far end of the runway, not yet in flame. He drove the Hummer toward them, his megaphone rattling in the back, the Hummer clanking, its fan blade gone but nevertheless managing a speed of seventy miles per hour. Reaching the end of the tarmac, he screamed at the militia to cease firing.

"What for?" a militiaman shouted, clearly angered by the order.

"Anyone fires on those planes, I'll kick his ass!"

Mead was among the men. "Ass?" he said, knowing Eleen's Mormon strictures against profanity. "He's fucking serious! Do as he says."

"Mead?"

"Sir?" Mead anticipated a dressing down. Instead Eleen told him, "Pile as many runners aboard this Hummer as possible. A megaphone if possible."

A megaphone was impossible to find despite the militia ransacking the main buildings of the base.

"Holy sh—" someone began. The sky flickered orange, the bang so loud Mead could hear nothing else for a moment. An ammunition shed two hundred yards farther down, near the four remaining Hummers, had started "cooking off" because of the intense heat of the nearby fires. Two of the Hummers were blown right off the runway into the razor wire where Schmidt, in a futile attempt, was trying to rally a dozen or so dispirited camp guards to stand their ground. One of the two remaining Hummers charged them. The driver, crouching low, missed Schmidt, but then caught him in the razor wire trailing behind it like a crazy metallic bridal train. He was torn to shreds.

Mead and the others were having a tough time silencing their fellow militiamen near the three as yet intact B-52s at the end of the runway. But after a few more errant bursts, the militiamen stopped firing while six runners were dropped off at other groups of militiamen who had successfully overrun the base. Even the pilots' ready room had been captured intact, with twenty-six stunned federal air crew unable to escape. Outside, each runner, on Eleen's orders, was going through the militia ranks. "Any pilots here? Pilots? Pilots?"

Out of almost three hundred militiamen on the base, there were only fourteen men who had been pilots. Ten of these were small plane drivers. That left only four who had flown "big birds," as Mead reported to Eleen. Eleen and Mead led the four to Fairchild's ready room, where the twenty-six federal air crew, a small number of Fairchild's total pilot complement, were being held prisoner.

"How many federals have we captured?" Eleen asked Mead.

"On the air base? Not many. Most of 'em have been killed in—"

"How many?" Eleen cut in. He had no time to lose.

"I dunno, sir. Maybe fifty."

"Have them brought here to the ready room. And Mead?"

"Sir?"

"National Guard from Spokane will probably be arriving soon. Have our man at the gate take twenty federal prisoners there."

"Hostages, sir?"

"Yes."

The remainder of the federal prisoners—over forty—were brought to the ready room. Eleen kept it short, sweet, and deadly. He chose ten air crew at random, including the only two women B-52 pilots at Fairchild. He then ordered all B-52 air crew to step forward and told them and their pilots to do as he said, otherwise he would shoot a hostage for anyone who refused.

"First," Eleen said, "I want the three B-52s now being guarded by my men at the eastern end of the runway to have their nuclear weapons replaced by conventional thousand pounders. If it isn't done within thirty minutes, I'll shoot a hostage for every minute over. We take off in half an hour. Questions?"

There was a stunned silence until one of the women told him, "You'll never get away with it."

"Watch me!"

Mead stepped forward and whispered, "Sir, it'll take a while to get to bombing height. Those birds drop their eggs from—"

"I know," Eleen said. "But we'll go in low. Give that wonder boy Freeman a big surprise."

Mead now saw something he'd never seen in Eleen before: a killer's eyes. He was *enjoying* this.

CHAPTER FORTY-SEVEN

FREEMAN'S FORCE WAS down to 103. They had expended all their LAWS. They had stopped the remote control pickups, but now the militia itself advanced, the numbers overwhelming. Where in hell were the Fort Lewis reinforcements? Freeman wondered.

The men with M-19s, the basic M-16 design with grenade tubes attached, heard Freeman's order to "fix bayonets!"—an order that in the twenty-first century they had never expected to hear. *When* and not *if* the militia infantry got through, it would be hand-to-hand. Claymore antipersonnel mines with their eight hundred steel balls would cut down the first wave, but Freeman guessed that Nordstrom had given an order to the militia not to

falter—not to waste time regrouping but to keep going. Freeman told Norton that if there was anything they knew for sure
about the militia, it was that they were "brave sons of bitches."
They had a cause.

"So do we," Norton countered briskly. "Survival!"

"You tell those sky jockeys what to do?"

"I did."

"Pray, Norton, pray."

"I already have."

There was a ferocious exchange of gunfire between three
militiamen and federals near the wire. A phosphorus grenade
was tossed, two paratroopers killed instantly, one dead militiaman. The other two of this group of three militia were caught
up in the wire. One had his uniform shredded by the razor
strands, a swastika tattoo peeping above his collar. Another
burst, and both men were dead.

Fairchild

The huge B-52s "crabbed it," the air crew's term for the unusual way in which the big bombers veered to one side during
takeoff. Eleen, in the lead plane of the three-bomber cell, knew
he was just minutes away from the Odessa-Sprague front,
where his bombs could pulverize Freeman's force. He had air
crew hostages aboard, two of them, sitting cramped in the small
space to the rear of the pilot, near the engineer. He'd given orders that everyone had to carry a parachute, which made it uncomfortable in the cramped space.

Eleen saw the computer's altitude numbers increasing and
told the pilot to go in beneath the stratus at a thousand feet.

"That's awfully low!"

"Do what I say!" Eleen shouted back and, snatching the helmet off a surprised co-pilot, which put him in the radio loop, he
spoke through the helmet's microphone. "If you have any *unexpected* difficulty with the bomb release, we throw one of you
two out. Understand?"

The two pilots exchanged looks like two schoolboys whose secret plan had just been found out.

Eleen glared at them. "Any other trouble with the aircraft, and the hostages go out without their chutes. Got it?"

The captain nodded.

"You got it?" Eleen asked the co-pilot, the militiaman's captured 9mm pistol jabbing the younger man in the back.

"Yeah, I got it."

"Good." Eleen turned toward the two hostages, a backup engineer and radar/radio operator. They obviously didn't view him as a fellow American caught up in a terrible civil war, but as a ruthless enemy.

The pilot saw a salient ahead with which he was long familiar from innumerable training runs out of Fairchild, an outcrop on the salient being chosen as the initial aiming point. "I.P. in sight," he said.

The co-pilot adjusted the flight path. They hit an air pocket, the plane dropping a hundred feet, everyone's stomach down near their boots, Eleen thrown back so abruptly that his coveralls caught on a headphone hook and tore right through to the Kevlar vest. One of the hostages laughed, despite his fear.

As the pickups hit the trip wires of the claymores on Freeman's perimeter, thousands of whistling steel balls filled the air. They took out every windshield and canopy machine gunner in sight, for there was no time to duck unless you'd kept your head down all along, in which case you were of no use anyway.

Within seconds the militia infantry poured out of the truck beds, racing toward the federals' foxholes and trenches. They now pulled the trip wires for the second line of claymores set at a lower angle than the first, situated immediately in front of their dugouts.

It would later be referred to as "Hamburger Hill," though there was only a gentle rise involved. The "hamburger," however, was apt, for here over a hundred militiamen were either killed or severely wounded by the claymores' withering fire and by an enfilade of small arms fire. Freeman lost seventeen men. Eleven were wounded, despite their well-dug-in defensive positions along the perimeter.

Now, the relatively few armored-machine-gun-toting pickups experienced a problem that would become a central concern of Nordstrom and his field commanders. Some of the pickups somehow, miraculously, hadn't been stopped by either the claymore barrage or the highly concentrated small arms fire. However, they were virtually useless once they were on top of the federals' trenches and foxholes since the heavy machine guns atop each pickup's canopy could not depress at a sufficiently acute angle to fire *into* the foxholes or trenches. The federal soldiers, however, couldn't miss.

Through the white obscuring smoke fired by the militia and the palls of black oil smoke rising from the knocked-out pickups, Freeman saw that another wave of militia was coming at him. It was a scene reminiscent of the Gulf War's enormous slaughter of people and vehicles on the Basra Road. Dead bodies littered the foreground of the rise, many in various states of amputation, others hanging grotesquely from the sides of the burning pickups. The sickly sweet smell of cooked corpses mixed with the fumes of burning gasoline and paint. It was so pungent you could hardly breathe. And Nordstrom's infantry still came.

"This is it, Norton!" Freeman shouted. "We still got that sky jockey on the line?"

"Yes, sir."

"Tell him to do it—he'll only get one pass."

"Yes, sir."

The steady drone of the thwarted air transports above became a sudden thunder as a Hercules appeared below the stratus five miles east of Freeman's drastically reduced perimeter.

"Tell him to move it!" Freeman shouted.

"General, you want him to come in awfully low!"

"Tell him to move it."

"General says to move it!"

There was a surge of static. "Fuck the general. We're nearly on the friggin' deck!"

It was true—they were no more than a hundred feet above the white blur of the ground.

"Jesus!" Melrose said, the noise of battle so loud, so belly-thumping, that it was frightening even to the veterans of Freeman's force.

At a distance of three miles the Hercules, its awesome sound like rolling thunder, dropped to fifty feet above the ground, the white landscape flashing past beneath its belly like a continuous, earth-spattered white sheet.

At one mile the wire began to sing, dirt leaking from trembling sandbags, falling into the trenches as if some great subterranean beast awoke from its winter slumber. Now ten feet above the fleeing earth, a long, black snakelike object dropped from the plane's cavernous rear, flattening on contact with the ground into a long strip resembling a series of huge, flattened inner tubes, known among the loadmasters as turd tubes. It was a series of blivets, rubberized fuel bladders normally used for in-flight refueling. Within a minute the Hercules, taking fire from the militia, was climbing, the last of the continuous-string bladders streaming out over the rollers, strung across Freeman's front like a line of giant deflating sausages.

"She's hit!" Norton shouted as flames licked the plane's starboard side, only the frantic tips of the flames above the main fuselage seen by Freeman's men. Then the huge Hercules slowed and began falling backward on Freeman's left flank, its tail hitting the ground and crumpling in flames that now consumed the aircraft. Several of Freeman's men ran toward the wreck through a hole in the wire, but the heat was so intense they couldn't breach the flames. An airman engulfed in fire came running out of the rear door ramp. Two paratroopers rolled him in the snow, dropping their ponchos on him to suffocate the flame. Though he was badly burned on the upper back, his hair gone, they saved him and carried him across to their trench, hollering for a medic.

God forgive him, Freeman thought, but he was half glad the Herk had crashed. It effectively cut off a shallow depression on his far side that the militia could have used as a trench. Now it was littered with white-hot wreckage.

Nordstrom's radio operator had intercepted busy communications traffic, which he described as "rush hour density," several miles to the south-southwest of the federal force. He assumed it was a large force coming to Freeman's aid on the I-90. With this information, the militia knew they had only one last chance before having to retreat and disperse. In an old but apt cliché from their commander, they were told it was "now or never." They attacked again.

Behind them to the northeast came the three B-52s from Fairchild, unable to find the militia's frequency but with Eleen determined to be their anonymous savior.

"Popping flares," the pilot informed Eleen. "Otherwise the militias'll missile us!"

Eleen nodded his assent and flares began streaming from the aircraft in a series of beautiful orange blossoms floating like dandelion seeds through the metallic sky. The pilot was right. Missiles, probably Stingers, could be seen streaking from the militia below, which looked like so many ants swarming forward.

When his six forward scouts, hiding amidst the enemy's fire-gutted pickups, reported to Freeman that the enemy were only three hundred yards from the wire, he ordered them back. By the time they returned from the pickups through the narrow gap in the wire to their foxholes, the militia wave was only fifty yards from the wire.

Freeman quickly checked to see if the two M-60 machine gunners he'd chosen for the task were in position on the flanks, then ordered them to fire. They raked the string of blivets with tracer fire. The blivets convulsed, then burst, spewing a river of burning fuel over their entire length, in effect creating a moat of fire in front of the militia now at the wire, some cutting it. The inferno met up with the burning Hercules, and the militia, while not stopped completely, were discombobulated, entire platoons unable to move forward.

Meanwhile, coming in low behind them, at about six hundred feet, were the three B-52s, Eleen intent on bombing the federals. He realized, now, that the two forces were so close together—handfuls of militia passing through a hole in the wire, some paratroopers taken prisoner—that any bombing would wipe out the forward elements of the militia, which would only help the federals.

"Turn around—" he began, but didn't finish, a barrage of small arms fire from both the militia and the federal positions ripping into the bellies of the three bombers overhead, the flares the planes were popping useless against everything but missiles.

Eleen's pilot was fighting the controls. "We're going down!" he shouted.

They were six miles south of the battle, but he couldn't hold any longer, the other two B-52s already having turned back. The floor hatch opened.

"Jump!" the pilot ordered.

"Jump!" Eleen ordered the hostages, letting them go first.

At the air base, confusion reigned. Federal security guards fled. Some were taken hostage by the militia for safe passage into the mountainous redoubt of the Idaho panhandle. Still others escaped west toward the equally rugged mountains of the Cascades, the hostages to be released only after the militiamen felt safe.

As the B-52's five air crew, his three militiamen comrades, and the two hostages floated to earth through intermittent wisps of stratus, Eleen could see a long line of vehicles stretching for miles below, like so many toy khaki trucks. Hummers. Bradley Fighting Vehicles, and M-1 tanks moved fast toward Freeman's beleaguered force only a half hour away.

Eleen knew that for the militia it was over. For now. Nordstrom would be in retreat, his discretion the better part of valor, for it was either stay, annihilate Freeman, and lose a battalion or more of men, or withdraw as quickly as possible to reach the Idaho and Washington mountain redoubts, using the handful of Freeman's soldiers taken as prisoners as hostages to guarantee safe passage.

Only fifty feet from the ground now, Eleen could see a troop of three Bradleys breaking away from the Fort Lewis column, racing across the snow-mottled ground to no doubt gather up those who had jumped from the B-52. Eleen felt the back of his air crew coveralls for the federal-issue 9mm he'd taken from one of Schmidt's MPs. No way they would take him alive again.

Suddenly his entire body was pushed sideways, the stratus above him glowing red, then the *boomp!* of one of the other two B-52s blowing apart. But he'd seen no missile trail, or had it been radar directed AA fire from the federal column below? He'd never know. As he hit the ground, hard, his right shoulder taking the brunt, he barely had time to punch the chute release when the Bradley about ten yards away stopped. Its hatch flew open, the turret gun whirred and was on him. A plan flashed into his mind. "Hey!" he called out to the federal soldier who, with wide, built-in-phone Kevlar helmet, was watching him. "I'm one of the air crew."

"Oh yeah?"

"Yes."

"You armed?"

"No, sir."

"You come over here. Keep your hands up."

"No problem," Eleen said, and walked toward the man, smiling. "That guy," Eleen said, nodding at a point behind the man as he neared the front of the Bradley. Had it been an M-2 Bradley, the nine-man infantry-carrying version, he would have been out of luck because the infantry would have piled out by now. But he'd recognized the vehicle immediately as a Bradley Cavalry FV—no infantry. The big, helmeted man holding a pistol on him, the only one out of the vehicle, instinctively glanced behind him, and Eleen dived, 9mm drawn, and pulled the trigger. Nothing. It jammed. The federal had already turned back and fired, hitting Eleen's Kevlar vest dead center, knocking him "ass over tit," as the man would later gleefully repeat. For a second, sprawled in the dirty snow, Eleen couldn't breathe. It was the hydraulic shock of the shot fired at point-blank range.

"On your face, asshole!" the federal ordered, then kicked away Eleen's pistol and trussed him upright. That was how they took him prisoner, along with the other two militiamen who'd bailed out. As they drove their captives in the convoy, which hadn't slowed down, and in fact was pushing maximum speeds to reach Freeman's position, Eleen asked his captor why he'd suspected that militia, as well as federals, had been aboard the B-52.

"Spokane radio station told us militia had stolen three B-52s," the man replied. "So when you jumped, buddy, we thought we'd be nice and pick you up so you can be put where you belong."

"Where's that?"

"Guess. You're gonna be very busy helping your buddies fill in a big tunnel some stupid shits dug at Camp Fairchild. Freeman's boys also downed your third plane. Not your day, is it?"

Eleen said nothing for a while, then told his captors, "This cord is too tight."

"Hey, asshole, don't piss me off. You've upset me already, tryin' to shoot me, you prick."

"That gun jamming," opined the driver, a black man so short he'd barely made the Army's height requirement. "Know what that means, militiaman?"

Eleen refused to answer.

"Means that God's on our side, that's what it means."

Eleen thought about it. He believed that the man was wrong. The gun jamming was clearly the hand of God at work. God had saved him, Jeremiah Eleen, for a purpose: to continue fighting the kind of tyranny his forefathers had fled from when they had come west to the Great Salt Lake. God had clearly not finished with him yet.

* * *

Freeman's men fired their last claymores. Low on ammunition, they were now out of their trenches, battle joined in the bloodiest hand-to-hand fighting since Butcher's Ridge. Melrose had shot his last round when he was bayoneted to death by a militiaman in a sheepskin-lined flier's jacket of World War II vintage.

"Latrell!" another militiaman called out. "Watch your back!" It was too late. Jorgensen, exiting the trench, plunged his knife deep into the tall, lanky militiaman's kidney and ripped. Latrell fell backward, knocking Jorgensen back into the trench. There, winded and utterly exhausted by his last effort in the battle, hidden from view by Latrell's dead body atop him, Jorgensen was unable to move, spending the remainder of the final assault on Hamburger Hill out of action.

Freeman, firing an M-16 from the hip, was blown off his feet by the concussion of a militia grenade. He struck his head on the burned-out hulk of the Hummer and for a moment thought Norton was an attacker, but the general's M-16 lay several feet away in mud formed by the heat of the burning blivets, which had cut off the militia attackers from their now-retreating force.

Though Freeman's men had suffered appalling losses—over 140 dead—and had had to retreat to their final defense position, the cut-off militia were ground down so badly on Hamburger Hill that by the time the forward Bradley Scouts arrived from the Fort Lewis armored column, there was, ironically, no need for them.

EPILOGUE

THE MEDIA WERE merciless, especially the newspapers, which, while celebrating Freeman's victory, his brilliant delaying action—in particular his inspired use of the blivets for a purpose they were never intended—lambasted the government for its failure to decisively defeat the militia. The Dow Jones had dropped a precipitous 214 points in one day. The NASDAQ nosedived. A *New York Times* editorial said:

> The mass escape from Camp Fairchild alone has torpedoed investor confidence all over the world. The scenes on CNN of thousands of federal troops having to be diverted in order to hunt down hundreds of escaped and armed militiamen who are holding hostages are hardly the images of a government in control.
>
> Everyone has some sympathy for the new President, thrown into office by such horrific circumstances, but he *is* the President and it is his job to gather about him men and women who can pilot the troubled ship of state into calmer waters.
>
> He must first clear the decks, as it were, of those who share responsibility for the failure to anticipate the audacious militia attack against Fairchild Air Force Base, one of America's key links in our northern air defense. We urge the President to pursue the militia with deliberate speed and urgency.

The President threw the paper down in anger onto his desk. "I can't move against them so long as they hold Americans hostage!

The American public won't stand for that. *I* wouldn't stand for that. And if I won't stand for it, how in God's name can I expect the public to?" He glared about the room. "Suggestions?"

Everyone was stymied. "If only we could shift the focus," General Shelbourne said. "Capture Nordstrom—or that Hearn."

The President looked up, stunned. "Hearn? I thought he was locked up."

"He was in Camp Fairchild. He's out."

"Good God!" the President retorted. "The Nazi—he's escaped!"

"Yes, sir, with about three hundred other militia."

The President shook his head. "You mean to tell me . . ." He stopped. Stay cool, he told himself. "Is there any good news? I thought Freeman won."

"He did, Mr. President, but here in Washington, we didn't." Shelbourne hesitated, unsure of whether to go on, but it was his job to be the bearer of bad as well as good news.

"You were about to say, General?"

"Ah well, Mr. President, we've also been unable to run the presidential assassin to ground."

The President cradled his head in his hands. Stay cool, he thought. He wanted to finish a job, wrap it up, have done with it, but he knew this was a childish view of the world. It was no longer the neat, ordered world of his parents in the Midwest. It was a chaotic world, and only children fed by a stream of television and movie pap believed every crisis had a neat and happy end. He even knew adults who believed in a nice, clean end to things. But life wasn't like that. Here he was, President of the most powerful country in the history of the world, and a Nazi murderer and a presidential assassin were still on the loose. It was humiliating, personally and nationally.

"We have to get those two bastards," he proclaimed. "That'd give us a shot in the arm, internationally as well as domestically."

"How?" someone dared to ask.

"We'll constitute a special federal force, dedicated *exclusively* to catching and/or killing both of them. Freeman can lead it."

"He mightn't want to," the Secretary of the Treasury put in.

"Oh, he'll want to. I'm beginning to know General Freeman. I'll make him an offer he can't refuse."

There was a ripple of laughter despite the seriousness of the subject.

"What's that, Mr. President?" Shelbourne inquired.

"I'm going to hold a victory parade in his honor—in New York. Give him some kind of medal. TV networks'll love it. And it'll give the people a lift. And does anyone here think General Doug Freeman—'the Mouth'—" Laughter. "—will say no to a medal?"

There was more laughter now. But General Shelbourne was stone-faced, standing his ground, defending a fellow officer. He shamed the others as he looked about the room. "Douglas Freeman is an honorable man," he said. "He is a devoted servant of this republic. Yes, he is bombastic at times. He is vain. He is ambitious, like many of us in this room, ladies and gentlemen. A medal to men like Douglas Freeman and to men like me is no boyish illusion, it is a badge of honor. When we were here wringing our hands about what to do about the militia, he was on the sharp end with men who, like him, were prepared to die for this country, and did. A medal is not the currency of Wall Street, but it is *our* currency. And those of you who were mystified by Mike Bordia's suicide in 'ninety-seven, because he was charged with not having earned one of the medals he wore, will never understand that code. I do. You *should*. When you give Doug Freeman that medal, it's something real. It means something."

There was a thunderous silence in the Oval Office. The President looked up at Shelbourne. "I am well-rebuked. General Shelbourne, order General Freeman to Washington. We have work for him."

"Yes, sir, but first he'll have to bury his dead."

"I understand."

At General Raython's funeral in Omaha, Nebraska, his hometown, Lefkin's Funeral Parlor was redolent with the scent of flowers, especially roses. Several stands of them had to be removed and placed in the hallway so extra seating could be arranged for the overflow crowd of friends, relatives, and dignitaries, as well as two FBI agents.

The FBI agents lingered after the service and, moving respectfully with other mourners, some of them latecomers, noted the names of those who had sent flowers and the names of the florists from which they'd come. Within two hours after the agents departed, the FBI's central computer investigation of aliases had ascertained that eighty percent of those who'd sent flowers in memory of John Eliot Raython were known to the Bureau as either militia activists or sympathizers.

It was "delicious," Delorme said, for it seemed to him, and the President, that this surely meant that the militia that had now hightailed it into Idaho and the Cascades had suffered a major if not fatal blow. They had shot and killed one of their own leaders.

For the good of the armed forces, of course, Raython's militia identity would not be released to the public. All they needed to know was that Nordstrom was dead.

As far as all federal servicemen and women were concerned, General Raython had been a loyal and brave soldier who died defending his base against a militia mob. He, like General Freeman, the President announced in his TV address, would be awarded a decoration for his service and loyalty to the republic "which he defended with his last drop of blood. Indeed," the President continued, "it might well be that General Raython's stand at Fairchild Air Force Base and the stand made by others like him in Florida and elsewhere in Washington State, have finally convinced the militia that further resistance against the federal government is futile."

Neither Bill Trey nor Linda Seth wanted to talk to Marte Price. They liked her, but her CNN special, "Who's in Charge? The Republic in Crisis," couldn't help but make the ATF and FBI look bad. But what could they have done to prevent the assassination? the agents wondered. It was a good question, but neither agency was interested in allowing either Trey or Seth on national television to discuss what the federal authorities knew about the militias and, embarrassingly, what they didn't know.

Right now all that both agents wanted was to be alone, with each other. It was not a romance—not yet—but a bond of friendship formed amidst the danger that had brought them together, as it had so many others.

By a stroke of luck, on the night following the massive militia withdrawal from eastern Washington State into the safety of northern Idaho's mountain redoubts and west into the Cascades, a militia officer traveling in one of the lead vehicles, which overturned and was waylaid by a blowout, was captured by a patrol of Idaho National Guard. One of the vehicle's passengers was an injured militia officer with a severely broken leg, a Colonel Richard C. Vance, who, when questioned by federal military personnel in Ravensnest Hospital, confirmed that General Nordstrom had indeed been General Raython. When asked whether he thought that since the militia had lost their leader they would now quit, the colonel nodded. He added that they were effectively leaderless, and so would be unable to ever recover.